PENGU
THE PO!

Saad Ashraf was born in 1937 in Peshawar and did his schooling from
St. Anthony High School. He graduated from Government College,
Lahore, and then went on to Engineering College, Lahore. After retiring
from government service, he now lives in Islamabad with his wife who
is an educationist.

He is the author of *Fifty Autumn Leaves*, a book of poems. This is his
first novel.

The Postmaster

A Novel

SAAD ASHRAF

For
Micheal
with best wishes,
Islamabad   Saad A...
                             15/5/06

PENGUIN BOOKS

PENGUIN BOOKS
Published by the Penguin Group
Penguin Books India Pvt Ltd, 11 Community Centre, Panchsheel Park,
New Delhi 110 017, India
Penguin Group (USA) Inc., 375 Hudson Street, New York, New York
10014, USA
Penguin Group (Canada), 10 Alcorn Avenue, Toronto, Ontario,
Canada M4V 3B2 (a division of Pearson Penguin Canada Inc.)
Penguin Books Ltd, 80 Strand, London WC2R 0RL, England
Penguin Ireland, 25 St Stephen's Green, Dublin 2, Ireland
(a division of Penguin Books Ltd)
Penguin Group (Australia), 250 Camberwell Road, Camberwell, Victoria
3124, Australia (a division of Pearson Australia Group Pty Ltd)
Penguin Group (NZ), cnr Airborne and Rosedale Road, Albany, Auckland
1310, New Zealand (a division of Pearson New Zealand Ltd)
Penguin Group (South Africa) (Pty) Ltd, 24 Sturdee Avenue, Rosebank,
Johannesburg 2196, South Africa

Penguin Books Ltd, Registered Offices: 80 Strand, London WC2R 0RL, England

First published by Penguin Books India 2004
Copyright © Saad Ashraf 2004

10 9 8 7 6 5 4 3 2 1

This is a work of fiction. Names, characters, places and incidents are either the
product of the author's imagination or are used fictitiously, and any resemblance
to actual persons, living or dead, events or locales is entirely coincidental.

Typeset in Sabon by S.R. Enterprises, New Delhi
Printed at Chaman Offset Printer, New Delhi

This novel is dedicated to the people of India and Pakistan whose hearts beat in unison on both sides of the border that divides the subcontinent. Their fate has prevented them from having free physical, spiritual, mental and moral interaction with one another for more than half a century.

acknowledgement

The author wishes to acknowledge the encouragement given by his old friend Minoo Bhandara and his sister Bapsi Sidhwa, without which this book might never have been published.

one

Ghulam Nabi was a faithful servant of the British government in the Indian Posts and Telegraphs Department in the Punjab. To him, a government job offered stability and prospects of advancement and, more than that, the respect and awe of his countrymen, including the people of his community. Very soon after getting into service, Ghulam Nabi discovered that his elders got up to greet him and his visitors stood in front of him with folded hands. The attitude of his family changed and they now addressed him as Ghulam Nabi sahib instead of his pet name Gama. Almost imperceptibly, Ghulam Nabi adopted the demeanour of an officer, though he was a mere clerk. His attitude towards relatives, friends, and acquaintances underwent a change and he now wanted his uneducated, rustic, and devout wife to address him as 'sahib'. Even when they made love—in the dark of the night, under the open skies, in the summer, with millions of stars as silent witnesses—the inadvertent use of his pet name would turn off his libido. At such times he felt like being rough with her but refrained from doing so because his Anglo-Indian postmaster had told him that the main difference between the white people and the Indians was that the latter did not treat their womenfolk properly; which was why the English people had come to rule over India.

After a tenure in his native Punjab, Ghulam Nabi was transferred to Delhi in 1880. He put up with an old family friend, Hakim Dilbar Khan, in the part of Old Delhi near the Royal Mosque which was inhabited mostly by the illegitimate progeny of the Mughal court after the events of 1857. Ghulam Nabi had left his family behind in the Punjab with the promise that he would call them to Delhi once he settled down and found a house and servants.

Hakim Dilbar Khan came from an old family of hakims who had for generations specialized in dispensing potions famous for their aphrodisiac qualities. The potions were made by grinding precious stones and then dissolving them in a secret concoction which neither affected the intestines nor produced flatulence in the stomach. The secret of the mixture was handed over from one generation to the next. A four-week course was guaranteed to give the greatest pleasure to the male and ensure the total submission of the female.

The aftermath of the events of 1857 had however affected Hakim Dilbar Khan's fortunes, although he was just a child when the Indian mutiny had broken out. Once things had settled down and the British had taken over, his family had been thrown out of the squalid corner of the Red Fort where they had a house. Hakim Dilbar Khan's father found himself on the streets of Delhi, without a regular livelihood and a wife and three children to support. Some relatives who lived in Old Delhi had taken pity on him and his family and had provided succour. With the Union Jack flying over the Red Fort and Muslim fortunes at a low ebb following the banishment of the last Mughal emperor to Rangoon, there were few buyers for Hakim Dilbar's magic potions. But that was some decades ago; with the passage of time, the relationship between the Muslims and the British had somewhat repaired. Some of Delhi's notables had rehabilitated themselves in the eyes of the British, thanks to Sir Syed Ahmad Khan. The market for aphrodisiacs had also taken a turn for the better. Not only did Delhi's rehabilitated nawabs resume using Hakim Dilbar's prescriptions, but the nouveau riche who had emerged by collaborating with the British had also started buying these potions.

Hakim Dilbar's clientele included an infamous Englishman, Mr Cyril Douglas, who was the assistant to the lieutenant

Saad Ashraf

governor of Delhi. He had a reputation of being oversexed, and the rumour that Douglas and the lieutenant governor had a homosexual relationship was quite widespread in Delhi. Anonymous letters, lodging complaints, had been written to the Governor General in Calcutta, but nothing came of it and both the lieutenant governor and Douglas remained in Delhi, working in the same office. Hakim Dilbar's aphrodisiacs earned him the patronage of Douglas and through him an introduction to the lieutenant governor, who soon became a valued client himself.

One day when Hakim Dilbar was sitting in his clinic behind the low desk on which he wrote his prescriptions, Ghulam Nabi walked in and sat on the stool in front of him.

'What can I do for you, sahib? Is your malady that of the heart or the body?' asked Hakim Dilbar jokingly.

'Of both, but primarily that of the heart,' remarked Ghulam Nabi.

'Why don't you do something about it?'

'What can I do? I neither have a house nor servants, nor has my travelling allowance been paid by the government to enable me to call my family here. It will take a couple of hundred rupees to bring them over and get them settled here and there is nobody to hear the voice of a poor government servant like myself,' said Ghulam Nabi.

'What then can one do for a poor government servant like you?'

'Nothing, except help me get my family here.'

Hakim Dilbar Khan knew that he didn't have the money that would enable his friend to fetch his family. He paused and thought for a moment.

'Why not take another wife and have another family? Delhi abounds in Mughal princesses who have nobody to support them. The women of Delhi are not only beautiful but also highly cultured and as good as the ones from any other part of India. They make dutiful wives and produce sons. Your religion permits you to take another wife,' said the Hakim.

After Ghulam Nabi had sufficiently recovered his wits on hearing this, he started analysing the pros and cons of the Hakim's suggestion. His Punjabi wife was backward, spoke loudly, had large hips and big breasts that were soft and supple and reminded him of flour which had been kneaded with too much water. She wore a dhoti, slurped when she ate and, in the past few years, their marriage seemed to have broken down with her spending more and more time on the prayer mat than with him. Coupled with this were certain glad tidings at work. Mr Williams, the English postmaster in Delhi, had been very happy with Ghulam Nabi's work; particularly with his report on a clerk who, having made an error in adding up, had been accused of misappropriation. This had helped Mr Williams to present himself as a model of meticulous efficiency before Mr Collins, the deputy postmaster general, who had praised his watchful eye. Mr Collins had promised to support a promotion for Mr Williams whenever a vacancy arose and Mr Williams in turn had made a similar promise to Ghulam Nabi for his promotion as deputy superintendent. Ghulam Nabi thought that his wife would hardly fit in with his elevated position if it materialized.

'I will think about it, but which Mughal princess would marry me anyway?' was all that Ghulam Nabi said in reply.

Hakim Dilbar did not let matters rest at that. He cited the availability of an eligible groom to his client Mirza Beg, an upper-middle-class Mughal fallen on hard times, who had mentioned in passing to the Hakim that he wanted to fulfil his worldly commitments by marrying off his only daughter, Noorani Begum, and then retire to Mecca to devote his time atoning for his sins. When Mirza heard about the availability of a groom for his daughter, his joy knew no bounds and he spontaneously accepted Ghulam Nabi as his son-in-law. It was true that there was a considerable difference in the ages of the bride and the groom, but the advantages that this marriage would offer were manifold. Ghulam Nabi enjoyed the prestige of being in government service, which could help in the Mirza's rehabilitation with the British, now that the events of 1857 were receding into the background. Maybe his son-in-law's influence could help in the restoration of some of his ancestral property. As the one mediating the marriage, it would also put Hakim Dilbar under some obligation, and his connections with Mr Douglas and the lieutenant governor could be put to good use.

Ghulam Nabi married Noorani Begum on 25 March 1885, at a simple ceremony held in Hakim Dilbar's pharmacy. The betrothal, attended only by men, was performed by the maulvi from the nearby mosque. The Hakim and his patient Mohammed Khan, a sturdy Pathan undergoing treatment for venereal disease for the past few months, signed on the marriage register as witnesses. After the maulvi recited the Quranic verses pronouncing Ghulam Nabi and Noorani Begum man and wife, Mirza Beg embraced his son-in-law, and holding both his hands in his shook them vigorously. Tears welled up in his eyes as his daughter's innocent face swam before him. He knew that if he had a choice he would have given his daughter away to someone who was younger and definitely better looking. Hakim Dilbar loaned the guest bedroom atop his clinic to Ghulam Nabi for the wedding night. His daughters worked hard the whole day, decorating the room for the occasion. They hung multicoloured strands of flowers by the bedposts and sprinkled rose water on the dark-red, satin bed cover and the pillow. An oil lamp in the corner of the room and the pervading fragrance were expected to create the romantic aura essential to arouse the senses. Late in the evening, Noorani Begum, a medium-statured woman with wheatish complexion, was led in a procession to the room by a number of her close female relatives. She was clad in the traditional red wedding dress of heavy brocade, her face hidden by an embroidered veil drawn low on her face. They seated her on the bed and delivered words of counsel in meaningful whispers, interspersed with intermittent giggling, on how best to handle the advances of a stranger who had been given the divine sanction of fornicating with her. Having done that for over an hour they withdrew from the room, leaving her all alone to face the vagaries of her fate.

A little after dark, Noorani Begum got up in her heavy attire and lighted the lamp in the room. She was tired, and fearful of what awaited her, and all kinds of thoughts passed through her mind. She could hear her heart pounding, while she waited for a man she had never seen and who would come and indulge in an act of which she had only heard from others. She had never been alone with any man other than her father. To steady her nerves, she recited a few verses from the Quran which her mother had made her memorize as a child. Her mother had died while she was still young, leaving her all alone in the world to be reared by her father and her aunts. Whenever Noorani Begum was unnerved she would recite these verses to herself and then wait for her inner voice to advise her on what she should do next; she was sure that any decision she made would have had her mother's approval had she been alive.

There was a knock on the door. Noorani Begum opened the latch and saw a middle-aged man with a slight stoop, clad in a white Mughal frock and a turban, step into the room. He greeted her and she mumbled a few words in reply.

'I am Ghulam Nabi, your husband,' he said.

She engulfed herself deeper into the folds of her dress to protect herself.

'It is terribly hot for the month of March probably because it didn't rain at the end of winter,' he continued.

Noorani Begum sat quietly on the bed, fiddling nervously with her dress, not knowing what to do. Ghulam Nabi continued with his monologue. He talked of the family he had left behind in the Punjab, and how lonely he felt living all alone in Delhi, and how lucky he considered himself to have found a beautiful and cultured wife like Noorani Begum.

Ghulam Nabi had been counselled by Hakim Dilbar.

'There's a great difference between the women of your native Punjab and those of Delhi. If you want to make your way into the heart of a woman from Delhi, you'll have to proceed patiently before reaching the stage of consummation. The women here like to be showered with compliments on their looks, intelligence, dress, and family background, and a wife wants to be told how lucky you are to be marrying her. They are quick to make out fake compliments too.'

Ghulam Nabi was following Hakim Dilbar's advice in totality.

An hour later he had managed to sit next to Noorani Begum on the bed, hold her hennaed hands, and get her to talk. The fragrance of jasmine pervaded the room, and the flickering light and the smell of fresh roses from her body aroused him.

Both Ghulam Nabi and Noorani Begum realized that they seemed to have a natural compatibility with one another and found that the rigours of the wedding night for two strangers had been put aside. Every now and then Noorani Begum would punctuate her conversation with couplets from Mir, Ghalib, and Sauda, with Ghulam Nabi listening on as an ardent admirer.

One thing led to another and Ghulam Nabi found Noorani Begum responding to his caresses. He found her highly passionate and full of physical desire. Her young body, craving for a man, came alive to his touch. Soon, they were reaching a crescendo from which descent is possible only through a physical union. He untied the cord which secured her embroidered skirt, removed her undergarments, laid her on the bed, and got on top of her.

'I'll be your ardent slave till the day of judgement,' he rasped in a voice choked with lust.

Then, in a finale in which both sides shrieked with intense pleasure, their marriage was consummated. As they lay on the bed in the aftermath, they both realized that physically too they seemed to have been made for one another by the creator.

two

Soon after the marriage, Ghulam Nabi and Noorani Begum took up residence in an old neighbourhood of Delhi popularly known as White Haveli. It was a complex of buildings located a mile away from the Royal Mosque. It was said to have housed the Mughal supervisors who were in charge of the construction of the mosque. The emperor had gifted the complex to them and their progeny as a sign of his satisfaction with their work.

Their marriage was turning out the way Ghulam Nabi had hoped for. Noorani Begum was a good cook and could make delicious rice puddings with saffron, unlike his first wife who was only adept at cooking vegetables and lentils. Noorani Begum knew how to keep Ghulam Nabi happy at home and in bed so that he could concentrate on his work and in pleasing Mr Williams, the postmaster. She once went in a doli through the weaving lanes of Old Delhi to the General Post Office (GPO) near Kashmiri Gate to call on Mem Williams. Very cleverly, she had taken ten silver rupees bearing Queen Victoria's profile wrapped in a red satin kerchief, which she pressed in Mem Williams's hand as soon as she was alone with her. Mem Williams appreciated this as she had been born in India and was used to its ways. She had smilingly accepted the gift and thanked Noorani Begum in her English-accented Hindustani. Soon thereafter, Ghulam Nabi had been promoted to the post of deputy superintendent.

But a year later, Mr Williams, postmaster, Delhi, and Ghulam Nabi's benefactor, was promoted and transferred to Madras. Ghulam Nabi's future would now depend upon the new postmaster.

Rumours making their way into the Delhi circle pointed to Mr Appleby, postmaster, Allahabad, filling this post. Reputations preceded the incumbent and the babus at the post office said that Mr Appleby was a person of strict countenance who could take exception to small things. All this because his grandfather, who was a pure white man, had married an Indian woman, for which reason Englishmen looked upon Mr Appleby with suspicion. In turn, Mr Appleby took out all his frustration on his subordinates in various ways, scolding them in front of their subordinates and using invectives in his conversation. Even worse was his tactic of cultivating a few favourites who were totally subservient to him and then using them as informants to keep a check on the people in his office.

Soon, a newcomer made his appearance at the GPO. He was Ghanshamdas, the head clerk from the Allahabad post office who had been transferred to Delhi. He had worked directly under Mr Appleby and was one of his principal informers. He had been transferred to Delhi to size up the people the new postmaster would be working with as a prelude to his arrival. Ghanshamdas was a quiet, bespectacled person about forty years of age who had already put in twenty years' service with the Indian postal department. He kept much to himself, observing the babus at work. Whenever somebody asked about Mr Appleby he would say, 'How can I know anything about an English sahib, though I work in the same office?' He did pick up the information though that Deputy Superintendent Ghulam Nabi had been spinning imaginary tales of the goodness of Mr Appleby which Ghanshamdas knew from personal knowledge were not true. After a week at the GPO, Delhi, Ghanshamdas left for Allahabad as quietly as he had come, ostensibly to bring his family to Delhi.

The great day finally came and Mr Appleby arrived in Delhi by train. As he emerged from his first-class compartment he was welcomed by the acting postmaster, Mr Griffiths, who was a stop-gap arrangement till Mr Appleby took over. Mr Appleby was a thin man, over six-feet tall. He wore a white toupee and spectacles made of wire and carried a tense expression on his face. The only time he smiled faintly was when he met Mr Griffith. When he came to shake hands with Ghulam Nabi, he muttered a few words, of which Ghulam Nabi could make out nothing, but presumed that he was being asked his name. Breathless and nervous, he said inaudibly, 'Ghulam Nabi, deputy superintendent, sir.' Mr Appleby looked at him closely, lips pursed and eyes fluttering with impatience, and said, 'So you are Ghulam Nabi.'

There was little sleep for Ghulam Nabi that night, and all kinds of thoughts raced through his mind. Despite entreaties by Noorani Begum that this could just be a casual remark, Ghulam Nabi felt that perhaps Ghanshamdas had filled the ears of the sahib with some unkind words about him.

Ghulam Nabi's first meeting with the sahib came a fortnight later when he was summoned by the sahib. He knocked softly at the postmaster's door and when a voice from inside stated an authoritative 'Come in' he turned the shining brass handle and tiptoed inside. Mr Appleby was busy with some papers and without raising his eyes addressed Ghulam Nabi, who stood in front of him with folded hands.

'Deputy Ghulam Nabi, there have been complaints about the late delivery of post in the Alipore area in the last two weeks. I would like to have a complete report on this as soon as possible. Keep an eye on your postmen. I don't want anyone fooling around here. Is this clear?'

'Yes. Yes sir,' was all Ghulam Nabi could mumble on his way out of his boss's office.

When Ghulam Nabi had recovered from his first encounter with the sahib, he decided to take on the task that his postmaster had entrusted to him. He made a list of all the postmen who had made deliveries in the last two weeks in the Alipore area, and quickly found that there were four: Chopra, Ali Bux, Ragbir Singh, and the Indian Christian, Stephen, who delivered post in the morning and afternoon shifts on alternative days. Next, he took out the register in which all the post to be delivered in the Alipore area was entered with the addresses and date of receipt of the post. The system was foolproof as far as the receipt was concerned, but there was no record of delivery. Too much trust had been placed in the postmen that it would be done expeditiously. Ghulam Nabi spent the next few days keeping a tab on all the post for delivery to Alipore. On these he marked a small identification in pencil, from which the date of its collection for delivery by the postmen could be deciphered. Ghulam Nabi was amazed to find that Chopra was delivering the post two or three days after its receipt. He discovered this by going to the addressee's house and threatening the servants of the sahibs with dire consequences if they did not fish out the discarded envelopes from the waste-paper baskets. With these findings, Ghulam Nabi sought an audience with Mr Appleby.

'Yes Deputy Ghulam Nabi, you wanted to see me?' said Postmaster Appleby.

'This postman Chopra is a very big rascal, keeping dak at his house for two or three days and not delivering the same day. Sahib, what is the meaning of this?' Ghulam Nabi explained in his Punjabi-accented English.

Mr Appleby's jaw dropped an inch or two on hearing this. It was possible that Chopra, though honest, was simply a lazy scrounger, a category to which he thought most Indians belonged. Or there could be something bigger and more sinister than met the eye. In any case the matter needed investigation.

'Deputy Ghulam Nabi, thank you for this information. I will look into this matter personally. A word of caution: don't let anyone know what you have discovered,' warned the postmaster.

As soon as Ghulam Nabi left the room, Mr Appleby was on the telegraph to the superintendent of police, Delhi, Captain Ignis, about the urgent need for them to meet in the afternoon in the Officers Club near the old residency.

Captain Ignis, formerly of Hodson's Horse, had been absorbed in the police on account of his reputation as a ruthless disciplinarian and his avowed aim of 'civilizing these bloody niggers' before he died, and given charge of Delhi, to get rid of the few badmashes who had escaped the Englishman's whip or the hangman's noose.

When Appleby explained the mystery of the late delivery of the post in Alipore area, and what Ghulam Nabi had found, Captain Ignis became deeply interested. It provided a break from routine police work which could be easily handled by his subordinates. In fact, Captain Ignis's specialization in third-degree methods had earned him the fear of the most hardened criminals of Delhi. He was the inventor of the famous 'mirchi danda', a short cane about eight inches long and half an inch in diameter which was kept immersed in a mixture of oil and green chillies and was used only with his express permission and under his personal supervision when all other methods of extracting a confession from a criminal failed. The story about the initial test of this device of torture had become something of a folklore in these parts. It was reported that Captain Ignis had been direct in asking the victim to confess, but the victim had refused and had shouted, 'You white monkey! You mother fucker angrez!' Captain Ignis had then coolly asked him to be tied to a charpai with his rear end naked and, with the care of a surgeon performing a delicate operation, inserted the device appropriately. The effect was instantaneous and, after a few minutes, the culprit not only admitted to the crime for which he had been hauled up on this occasion but a few others of which the police had been totally unaware. Soon, the fame of Captain Ignis's invention spread in Delhi's criminal world and it was said that families that had lived off crime for several generations either left Delhi or decided to call it a day and chose another source of livelihood.

Captain Ignis decided to head the investigation himself and deputed his spies around the hovel where Chopra lived. After a few days of surveillance, a raid was carried out on the hovel in the evening hours just as the sun was setting behind the river Yamuna and the red sky had mingled with the dark smoke from the funeral pyres. A police party dressed as women arrived at the hovel in dolis. While a few plainclothesmen stood guard outside, two or three went in and quickly seized Chopra and another man who turned out to be Ghanshamdas, the head clerk of the GPO and principal henchman and chief informant of Postmaster Appleby.

Saad Ashraf

It was a cold and bleak December night when the handcuffed culprits were produced before Captain Ignis in a small ante-room in the red-brick building housing the office of the superintendent of police, in Daryaganj, a locality which lies midway between the Fort and the wall that encircles the city. Captain Ignis sat in his chair, smoking his pipe. He wore a blue blazer and long grey flannel trousers, into which he had changed after eating his dinner of Mulligatawny soup and roasted beef.

'So you are the badmashes who have been fiddling with the post in my city. I want to know why,' he said, addressing the two.

'I am innocent. Head Clerk Ghanshamdas told me to give him the mail for a day and returned the envelopes to me for delivery the next day. I am a poor man who has eaten the salt of Queen Victoria. I beg your forgiveness. I am loyal to the sarkar! He is the culprit,' said Chopra, pointing his finger at the head clerk. Captain Ignis listened to Chopra, lying prostrate at his feet, while Ghanshamdas, the head clerk, stood silently in the corner with his head bowed.

'And what has the honourable head clerk to say for himself, eh?' sneered Captain Ignis.

Ghanshamdas stood still and silent.

'I am speaking to you, Head Clerk! Give me the courtesy of a reply or be ready for the consequences.'

Ghanshamdas stood with his head bowed and remained silent.

Captain Ignis sized up the situation. It was possible that Chopra had been roped in by Ghanshamdas for some sinister, unknown purpose, which required to be investigated without delay.

'Mr Head Clerk, I will leave this room and give you some time to think. On my return I would like a full confession from you.'

Captain Ignis took out his pocket watch and noted the time. With the suspects not revealing anything, his patience was running out. He left the room and went to his office. He opened the upper drawer of his writing table, took out his pipe and filled it from a pouch of local dried tobacco which the Indians smoked in their hookah. Having lit it, he drew on the pipe and puffed up his cheeks to get the pipe going. Captain Ignis was in deep thought. He opened the second drawer of the table and took out an eighteen-inch-long metal cylinder and a pair of surgical gloves. He shook the metal cylinder a number of times in the air and placed it on the table. After stamping out the pipe on a plate he left the room. When he returned to the ante-room, Ghanshamdas was standing in the same position in which he had left him and Chopra still lay prostrate on the floor. Captain Ignis motioned to one of his men and whispered something into his ear. Chopra was led out of the room and a little later two men brought an Indian charpai, a bundle of rope and some cloth. The charpai was placed in one corner of the room and the doors were locked from inside.

'Well, Mr Head Clerk, are you ready to tell us all?' Captain Ignis asked firmly. There was no reply from Ghanshamdas but the atmosphere in the room became tense. At a signal from Captain Ignis, his men seized Ghanshamdas, took off his dhoti and tied him to the bed, with his bare bottom facing the ceiling. A piece of cloth was put around his mouth so as to muffle his voice. Captain Ignis went to work quickly. He put on his surgical gloves, got hold of the metal cylinder he had brought with him, gave it a few vigorous jerks, and unscrewed the cap. He then took out a short wooden rod and with utmost precision, using the fingers of the other hand as a guide, conducted the operation. Ten seconds later, Ghanshamdas's shrieks were heard even through the wad of cloth around his mouth. In another minute he was coughing violently.

'Are you now prepared to tell us everything?' Captain Ignis shouted into Ghanshamdas's ears.

A muffled sound was all that one could hear.

'I think the blighter is still not willing to talk. We will have to deliver another dose,' said Captain Ignis to one of his men within hearing distance of Ghanshamdas. The captain's white-gloved hands went to work again with another one of his contraptions. This time Ghanshamdas's body shook from convulsions and his muffled screams became more pronounced. Captain Ignis pretended not to hear anything. From his experience he knew that an

Saad Ashraf

additional dose of the mirchi danda was the best insurance against any obstinacy on the part of an offender.

'Have mercy on me! My body is aflame and I am prepared to tell you all,' screamed Ghanshamdas. The captain beckoned his men to untie Ghanshamdas and bring him to his office after thirty minutes—the time it normally took to recover from the after-effects of the mirchi danda.

When Ghanshamdas was brought to Captain Ignis's office there were tears flowing down his eyes. He was made to sit facing Captain Ignis and a sheaf of papers and a pen were placed in front of him.

'Here's pen and paper to write your confession. The British in India are people of principles. We could never rule India if we were not just in our dealings. Take your time, because whatever you write will be taken into account at your trial. I will return after an hour to collect whatever you have written,' said Captain Ignis before leaving the room.

The captain decided to take a walk around his office building to while away the hour and recover from the effects which such an interrogation had on him too. He walked out of the building, on the road that led to the Red Fort along the old Mughal canal that flowed through its middle. The cold, fresh December air hit his face. The dust of the day had settled and countless glimmering stars lit the clear black sky. The road was deserted except for a few stragglers—covered in blankets with only their eyes visible—who slunk into the dark on seeing a white sahib coming their way. In the distance one could hear the sound of hooves as a horse-driven carriage made its way to its destination. As he walked, the captain felt a certain happiness and pride at the thought that he had made this city safe for anyone to venture out alone at any time of the day or night without the fear of being accosted or robbed. He kept walking on the dimly lit road till he reached the shrine of a hermit who had made Delhi his abode several centuries ago. The shrine was bathed in light in contrast to the surroundings. A bazaar had come up around it and, despite the late hour, shops buzzed with activity, full of noisy natives and merchants soliciting customers for their wares—flowers, food, perfume, and incense. Captain Ignis knew that Indians loved a tamasha whenever possible.

He took out his pocket watch and observed that it had taken him exactly half an hour to reach this spot, so he turned around promptly to return to keep the appointment with Ghanshamdas. When the captain returned to his office he found Ghanshamdas sitting on a wooden bench in the room. He was in a state of stupor, but a couple of written sheets were lying on the table. Captain Ignis picked up the sheets and started reading loudly to himself.

Excellency!
By your treatment of a poor servant of Queen Victoria you may have been able to break my body but nothing can break my spirit. I am an Indian and for us our motherland comes first and everything else, even life, is of secondary importance. Above all, we are truthful and simple people. So I will tell you the truth. I did take the post from Chopra's home with the purpose of opening and reading what was written in the letters. As you will observe, only the dak of military officers was taken. It is because of them that you rule over Mother India. I planned to kill those who bore ill will against us Indians. I am aware that there are Englishmen who are kind to us such as Appleby sahib who treats me like a son but such individuals are few and far between. How could I know what they thought of us if I didn't read their letters? This was the least I could do for my country. Postman Chopra is totally innocent. He objected to my asking him for the post, but I am the head clerk and superior to him in rank. So how could he have refused an order? Nobody else has anything to do with this. I am writing this down because I know that the English people do not believe what they are told, so if you like, you can continue investigating this matter and waste as much of your time on it as you want.
I remain, sir,
Your most obedient servant,
Ghanshamdas
Head Clerk, Delhi Post Office.

Saad Ashraf

Because of this written confession by Ghanshamdas and subsequent trials by the courts at Delhi, he was sentenced to transportation for life in the Andaman Islands, and Mr Appleby was asked to proceed on early retirement on the grounds of socializing too much with the natives. Ghulam Nabi, the deputy superintendent, was promoted to the rank of a fully-fledged superintendent—the first Indian to hold that post at the GPO in Delhi.

Ghulam Nabi ascribed much of his success to Noorani Begum's wise counsel. Every evening she used to sit with him and go over the events of the day in his office. The secret identification marks made on the letters which had finally led to Ghanshamdas's downfall and Mr Appleby's early retirement was her idea. The promotion to the coveted post of superintendent came at a time when their son was born. They named him Ghulam Rasool, the slave of the prophet.

The years rolled by uneventfully, with Ghulam Nabi enjoying the prestige and power of a government babu at the fag end of the nineteenth century. He had the usual crowd of sycophants from among the babus of the post office, people who would nod their heads the way he did, and who would listen endlessly to his monologue on his achievements and services to the British Raj. There were a few messages that Ghulam Nabi relentlessly conveyed to his listeners:

Be loyal to the British because loyalty pays.

Shy away from arguments on matters of religion and politics.

Always greet a white man or white lady with a low bow no matter what the position and address him or her as 'sir' or 'lady memsahib'.

The British are the most intelligent race of the world.

And may the sun never set on the British Empire.

In his heart Ghulam Nabi was quite concerned about the creation of the Indian National Congress and was sure that the British had an ace up their sleeve as they were its creators. 'Look at their genius, creating awareness about rights in the people they rule,' he said to Noorani Begum. 'Nobody but the British would do this kind of thing. The Indians are lucky to have the British ruling them!'

Ghulam Nabi was greatly enamoured by the technological prowess of the British. He felt that if it wasn't for them it would still be taking his countrymen two weeks to get to Delhi from Lahore—that is, if they weren't held up or killed by highwaymen during the journey—instead of the two days it took to travel in comfort and safety on a train. He could not understand why some of his countrymen still thought well of those days when law and order existed only inside the royal fort.

In the summer of the year 1900, with the advent of the new century, and the forty-fifth year of his life, Ghulam Nabi applied and obtained six weeks' leave from his boss and decided to take his family to Kashmir for a holiday. As a superintendent in the Indian postal department, he was entitled to travel first-class by train, in compartments entitled for the use of Europeans and Anglo-Indians. However, to avoid any complications, Ghulam Nabi booked himself a full second-class compartment to Rawalpindi from where he planned to proceed to Srinagar by road. During the journey, he passed through Lahore, a city close to his native place. He hadn't seen the family he had left behind in the Punjab for several years and wondered what his children— they would have grown up by now—from his first wife looked like. However, Noorani Begum's companionship and her continued presence in whatever he did and the children that she had borne him—there had been two more after Rasool, both daughters—had made him forget that he had another family. His marriage with Noorani Begum had worked out well and his inadequacies were overcome by her strengths. As far as he was concerned, she had no weaknesses except that she was an Indian and a woman living in nineteenth-century British India.

three

2 January 1901 was a cold and bleak day in Delhi. The stagnant pools of water on the roadside were covered with thin, transparent layers of frost. The coal, wood, and dung which its inhabitants burned in their houses and hovels to keep warm had enveloped the city in a dark, black smog. Some of its residents wrapped themselves in blankets and went to work early, shortly after the muezzin called from the mosques for the morning prayers and the sounds of sweet hymns and the clang of cymbals started emanating from the temples. They were the ones who delivered the morning newspapers or poultry and meat, or freshly baked European bread to the residences of the sahibs who lived outside the famous Kashmiri Gate through which the British had launched their final attack to dislodge the last Mughal emperor in 1857. These delivery men walked, bent under the weight of their sacks of newspapers and bread, in the shadow of the wall that ran on either side of the gate, pockmarked almost half a century earlier with cannon fire from both sides. Finally, when the sun started playing hide and seek with the clouds in the sky, the community of clerks who worked in the government offices around Kashmiri Gate made their appearance. These babus were easily discernible by the uniformity of their dress—white tunic, dhoti, black waistcoat, and cap for the Hindus; straight pyjamas, shirt, waistcoat or long coat, and fez for the Muslims. There were a small number too, labelled as 'toadies' by some of their countrymen who tried to copy the sahibs by wearing their dress— a western-style shirt, with or without a tie, and slacks and a coat.

Among such a crowd near the Royal Mosque, Ghulam Nabi waited for a horse-driven carriage which he hired every day for his exclusive use—a privilege he felt entitled to as superintendent of the GPO. Ghulam Nabi wore a white shirt with a black tie, grey slacks, a dark-brown coat with a white handkerchief in the top pocket, and an old felt hat with a parrot feather fastened into its ribbon which an Englishman had gifted to him while leaving India. He signalled to an empty carriage to turn around and stop in front of him. He climbed into the back seat with his head facing skywards and whispered into the ear of the driver, 'General Post Office, Kashmiri Gate, and no other passengers.' The carriage was soon on its way.

After about half an hour, the carriage stopped near the large yellow building of the GPO beyond the railway bridge. Ghulam Nabi disembarked. He headed for the inside of the building towards his office but found an unusual melancholic air about the babus who had gathered in small groups and seemed engrossed in intense but muted discussion. This appeared to him to be an abnormal state of affairs because the early morning hours were usually the busiest and the noisiest time at the post office as the clerks directed the work of the sorters to segregate the morning mail and thereafter made parties of postmen to deliver the mail to the sub post offices. As soon as Ghulam Nabi was seated in his office there was a knock on his door as his assistant Mirza Ali Beg walked in with a depressed countenance.

'Sahib, have you heard the latest news? Queen Victoria passed away today according to a telegram received from London.'

Ghulam Nabi felt a big lump in his throat. His heart beat quickly and erratically and it appeared to him that he was going to faint. He clasped the arm of his chair firmly.

'There must be some mistake or somebody must be trying to create mischief,' he rasped nervously.

'There is no mistake, sahib. I have myself seen the telegram from London,' said Mirza Ali Beg, his discomposure at being the harbinger of bad news apparent. It was a catch-22 situation, given that his boss was overawed with everything British, including Queen Victoria. He knew that if he did not break the news, the superintendent might get angry at not being informed by his assistant of the most important news of the day, and if he broke the news there was bound to be an unpleasant reaction.

'Go, get me the master copy of the telegram immediately,' ordered Ghulam Nabi. He had never been weighed down with so much grief—not even when his own mother had died in the Punjab. He felt unwell, as if overwhelmed by a great weight on his chest, and was unable to think coherently. He left his chair and started pacing around the floor of his office. There was another knock on his door and Mirza Ali Beg walked in with the master copy of the telegram.

Convinced of the authenticity of the tragic news, Ghulam Nabi wondered how India would be governed now that such a benign ruler had gone to meet her maker. He told his assistant that he was feeling unwell and wanted to go home. Mirza Ali Beg got him a carriage and told the driver to take the sahib home at a fast trot. When he got down from the carriage, outside White Haveli, Ghulam Nabi felt wobbly on his feet and had a tingling pain in his left arm. He was sweating profusely in spite of the cold. He managed to climb the stairs of his house with the greatest of difficulty. When Noorani Begum saw him, she let out a shriek, alarmed at his visibly pale and drained countenance.

'What has happened to my husband!' she cried.

'Water, water!' was all that Ghulam Nabi could utter.

He lay on his bed, blanched and covered with beads of cold sweat on his forehead. He motioned to Noorani Begum to come near him and put his mouth close to her ear. With hardly half an inch separating them, he whispered, 'Noorani Begum, the mother of India, Queen Victoria, has passed away in London. What will happen now?'

Ghulam Nabi's wife understood him like the back of her hand, and knew what sort of a reply would please him.

'The English people are the brightest in the world. They must have worked out something beforehand regarding what to do once the great queen passes away. Now don't worry yourself unnecessarily and get some sleep. You will be all right after a couple of days' rest.'

Ghulam Nabi lay in a state of stupor for some days after which he found his strength returning sufficiently for him to saunter to the bathroom with the aid of a walking stick. He took the opportunity offered by this enforced rest to play with his son, Ghulam Rasool, about whom he held a high opinion. Although only seven years old, his son had sparkling eyes that shone with intelligence.

'What will my son be when he grows up?' Ghulam Nabi would ask his son.

'I will grow up and be an officer serving Britannia like my father,' Ghulam Rasool would reply. Ghulam Nabi would chuckle with glee at his son's remark.

'See, what an intelligent boy Rasool is. He will surely become someone big when he grows up and make us famous,' the proud father would say to Noorani Begum.

A month later, Ghulam Nabi had recovered enough to think of going back to office, though Noorani Begum tried her best to dissuade him from doing so. As a wife, she knew that Ghulam Nabi was not in the same state of health as before.

On her advice and those of others, Ghulam Nabi agreed to consult the German doctor, Menkle, who had recently set up a clinic in Daryaganj. On the day of the appointment, Ghulam Nabi felt nervous at the thought of being at such close quarters with a white man. However, Ghulam Nabi was pleasantly surprised when Dr Menkle addressed all manner of questions regarding his state of health in broken Hindustani and thereafter asked him to take off his pyjamas and lie on a table. Dr Menkle started probing him with an instrument, two of whose ends he stuck in his ears while the other he kept pressing on various parts of Ghulam Nabi's chest. At intervals, he would utter a satisfied and loud exclamation or mutter something in his own language. When the examination was over, Dr Menkle briefed Ghulam Nabi on his malady.

'I don't think you will live for more than six months if you do not take care of yourself, which means less work, less worries, and more exercise. It may be better for you if you can take early retirement and live in Nainital with your family. Here is a bottle containing some pills which you must place under your tongue whenever you feel pain or heaviness in the chest or a tingling sensation in your arm. These pills may help to save your life.'

Ghulam Nabi kept the bottle with him, feeling quite depressed about Dr Menkle's diagnosis. He looked at the bottle containing the tiny white pills and wondered what they could do which the golden pate prescribed by Hakim Dilbar, of which he ate a spoonful every morning, could not. Ghulam Nabi was not sure how by just moving a small instrument over his chest, Dr Menkle could say with such conviction that he would survive only six months. Dr Menkle's medical advice gradually receded from Ghulam Nabi's mind but he kept the bottle of the tiny white pills on his person all the same.

four

It was a hot day in June 1901. The sun was up, shining with unusual ferocity for seven in the morning, when Ghulam Nabi left White Haveli for his office. He walked the first half a mile to reach the steps of the Royal Mosque from where he hired his exclusive carriage. It was nearly six months since he had fallen ill but Hakim Dilbar's golden concoction had almost brought him back to his previous level of fitness. He had never felt the need to either go back for a consultation with Dr Menkle or to use the little white pills the doctor had prescribed. He felt happy and active in spite of the dust, the flies, the overpowering stench, and the infernal heat of Delhi, but for some unknown reason he still felt weak in the legs. Maybe it was because of his indulgence last night. Noorani Begum had got two small bags of fresh jasmine flowers from a famous flower seller in Delhi and had strewn them on his bed so that the room smelt nice—a subtle indication that she was in the mood to make love. Ghulam Nabi and Noorani Begum had then talked into the late hours of the night about how lucky they both had been in their marriage and their children. They talked of the promise that the future held for them. Ghulam Nabi was certain that within the next two or three years he would be bestowed a prestigious honour by the British sarkar. Their daughters would grow up into beautiful and educated Muslim women and marry young men from renowned families. His son would be educated in good schools and thereafter go to join Sir Syed's famous college at Aligarh. Ghulam Nabi was an ardent admirer of Sir Syed Ahmad Khan and believed that he was the saviour of the Muslims in India for whom the only way ahead lay in obeying the British, learning the English language, understanding their methods of governance, and equipping themselves with knowledge of western science. Ghulam Nabi and Noorani Begum decided that once their children were grown up and settled, they would build a small house on a tract of land on the outskirts of Delhi and do some farming, leading an idyllic existence.

The piercing cries of two brawling cats on the street below finally brought the husband and wife out of their reverie. Ghulam Nabi removed his pocket watch and observed that it was almost eleven in the night. Two hours had passed in this tryst with fantasy during which it seemed as if time had stood still. Ghulam Nabi clasped Noorani Begum affectionately in his arms and placed his head on top of her bosom. He was primed for lovemaking.

'It's too late for those things now. You have to go to office at seven in the morning,' remarked Noorani Begum.

Ghulam Nabi wouldn't let go.

Ghulam Nabi and Noorani Begum were soon united in passionate lovemaking, and disentangled well after half an hour. Ghulam Nabi lay breathless and panting, gasping for air, his pyjamas down to his knees. A year ago he could make love two or three times in a night and now he was dizzy with breathlessness only after half an hour of an encounter. Something was definitely wrong. He thought of mentioning this to Hakim Dilbar when he saw him next. Maybe the hakim would prescribe another one of his father's ancient potions which could rekindle the spirit of youth. It was past midnight now, and once Ghulam Nabi had recouped and had some water from the earthen pitcher, he put the soft cotton pillow under his arms and was soon fast asleep.

When Ghulam Nabi arrived at the GPO nearly fifteen to twenty minutes before it officially opened, the first to call on him was Mirza Ali Beg who put him in good humour by relating interesting anecdotes and passing on the latest office gossip. Ghulam Nabi knew that much of what Mirza Ali Beg related was the product of his fertile imagination, but he listened intently just in case there was something of consequence. Mirza Ali Beg's departure was followed by meetings with other babus who came with their reports on the number of ordinary and registered letters and parcels received at the post office, together with details of the staff available to distribute this mail, taking into account those on duty and those who were absent. Ghulam Nabi made a note of habitual latecomers with patent excuses such as 'the wife wasn't well' or that the 'second cousin had started vomiting and is suspected to be suffering from cholera'. An application dropped by a neighbour, announcing the sudden demise of an aunt, could possibly be an excuse for enjoying a day off. Ghulam Nabi kept the individual and the excuse made by him in mind and checked on its veracity through his network before firming up his opinion of the individual. Ghulam Nabi spent time assigning the available staff for distributing the mail in different suburbs of the city, with the most efficient and reliable postmen for the Alipore area which was inhabited by high-ranking British civil and military officers. Lifting his eyes from one of the registers on which he was working, he noticed that the clock on the wall opposite his desk had just struck eleven. It was time to take a round of the office just to make sure that everything was in order.

To check whether the public was being properly attended to, Ghulam Nabi went out of the building to visit the area where people stood in queues to buy stamps and envelopes or to despatch registered letters or parcels. The babus had a natural tendency to gossip and procrastinate but on seeing Superintendent Ghulam Nabi they perked up instantly. After this tour, he peeked through the door of the postmaster's office, left ajar, and found that Mr Durand was standing opposite the large window overlooking the road, puffing a cigarette. He decided to knock on the brown door to inform his boss that everything was shipshape in his domain.

'Sahib, I just came to present my salaams and to tell you that the office has never worked better than it is doing now. It is all

Saad Ashraf

because of your vast experience and knowledge as an administrator,' said Ghulam Nabi. He knew from experience that sycophancy was the major weakness of every boss.

Mr Durand put on a sly smile, visibly happy.

'We must get ready for the inspection by Sir Griffith, the director general, next month. Everything must be polished and cleaned. The brass railings in the service hall should glitter and one should be able to see one's face in the floor. I think you should put your chappies to work straightaway. I'd like to see things for myself ten days before the date of the inspection is fixed. You have work to do, Ghulam Nabi, and I'd like to see you start without further delay,' Mr Durand stated.

'Yes sir, your orders will be carried out immediately. May I have your permission to leave sahib, so I can take matters in hand,' said Ghulam Nabi.

Mr Durand nodded and Ghulam Nabi moved towards the door. Once outside, he started walking briskly towards his office. Suddenly, he found it difficult to lift his legs as they seemed heavy as lead. He felt a pain in his chest and left arm. Ghulam Nabi quickened his pace. Entering his room, he slumped on a reclining chair which the British sarkar provided to their officers for three-quarters of an hour of relaxation after tiffin at half past one in the afternoon. The pain in his chest and left arm was becoming unbearable with each passing moment. A thousand invisible hands were trying to throttle him and he involuntarily moved his hands to free himself from their stranglehold. He lunged for Dr Menkle's bottle of pills in his left pocket, but his grasp weakened even as he clasped the bottle. He turned pale, his eyes bulged out of their sockets, and a sinister gurgling sound came from his throat as he gasped for air.

A quarter of an hour later, Mirza Ali Beg came to the superintendent's office to apprise his boss of the progress of mail distribution in the Alipore area according to his standing instructions. He was surprised to find Ghulam Nabi's chair empty. When he craned his neck a little further he found the superintendent asleep in the reclining chair. This was unusual because Ghulam Nabi never slept in the office. Mirza Ali Beg dared to walk closer to his boss whose left eye was three-quarters open. 'Sahib,' he said softly, but loud enough to be heard. There was no response. Mirza Ali Beg tapped Ghulam Nabi on the shoulder, and watched him slump to the floor. Seized with panic, and not knowing what to do, Mirza Ali Beg rushed out of the office into the hall and drew the attention of the babus.

'Come here! Something has happened to the sahib,' he shouted. A number of babus rushed inside Ghulam Nabi's office. Soon, there was a large crowd inside, jostling and shouting. Somebody produced a glass of water and another sprinkled it on Ghulam Nabi's face. When this didn't work, someone put the glass to his mouth but that didn't elicit any response either. The onlookers were in a state of shock and helplessness. A peon was despatched to fetch Dr Sen, the Bengali doctor, who had a clinic nearby. Having trained as a compounder in one of the first hospitals that the British had set up in Calcutta, Dr Sen had been quick to realize the potential that lay in opting for private practice in a city like Delhi. When Dr Sen reached Ghulam Nabi's office, he took out a stethoscope and started probing Ghulam Nabi's chest for any sounds, simultaneously clasping his left wrist to feel the pulse. He tried dilating his pupils for a sign of life but found none. It was sad but true that his patient had passed away without giving him a chance to practise the skills he had acquired from the English doctors in Calcutta. Dr Sen folded up his instrument and, putting it back in the old, tattered leather bag, said, 'I am *shorry*! He has *pashed* away ... please *advishe* his next of kin.' This was a patented statement which Dr Watson, one of those with whom Dr Sen had been apprenticed at the hospital in Calcutta, had made him memorize for announcing whenever a death occurred. In spite of Dr Watson's recurring efforts he could not make Compounder Sen utter these tragic words without his Bengali accent. At the GPO the babus were left with their revered superintendent's dead body in his office and without a clue as to how they should proceed. Mirza Ali Beg took the initiative and said, 'I am going to inform the

Saad Ashraf

postmaster sahib.' He departed for the postmaster's office and knocked at his door. On hearing the response to his knock, he entered.

'Who are you and what do you want?' enquired Postmaster Durand, raising his eyebrows.

Mirza Ali Beg tried to answer in his brand of Hindustani English, but having failed to do so, switched over to the local language. 'Sir, I am Mirza Ali Beg, the superintendent sahib's assistant.' After this the Mirza's tongue got tied in knots due to nervousness as he couldn't find the words to break the news.

'Continue man! Speak up! Surely you can't stand here all day long. Tell me what you want to say,' Mr Durand said impatiently.

'Sarkar, Superintendent Ghulam Nabi is dead,' Mirza Ali Beg announced with an expression which indicated that he was just about to break down with grief.

'Are you serious man, how can this be? He was in this office not more than an hour ago, and I had told him to get ready for the director general's inspection due next month. Are you sure? Where is he now and have you had him examined by a doctor?'

'We called Dr Sen who has pronounced him dead. There is nothing more that can be done. His body is lying in the office.'

Postmaster Durand had recovered somewhat from the initial shock although he was still in a state of disbelief. 'We must get the superintendent's body removed immediately. I will supervise the overall arrangements myself. Please lead me to his office,' he said.

Mr Durand was truly moved by the sudden death of a man he had just talked to in flesh and blood, an hour earlier, but more than that he was worried about being without his principal assistant who had a long experience of handling inspections. It would take time to find a suitable substitute.

With his head hung downwards, and a semblance of grief showing on his face, Postmaster Durand followed Mirza Ali Beg to Ghulam Nabi's office and saw the superintendent sitting in the armchair as if asleep. His hands were folded in front of him in his lap. His jaw was sagging and he was slipping towards the left side of the chair. Mr Durand recited the Christian prayer for the dead under his breath. His grandmother, an old toothless woman, had taught him the prayer as a child. He remembered that his grandmother, Sita Bai (later named Victoria in honour of the great Queen), a dark woman, was a convert to Christianity who spoke of herself as a companion to Mrs Rupert, the memsahib of the house in which she worked as an ayah in Lucknow. Victoria prided herself on having stood by Mrs Rupert and her husband Captain Rupert during the siege of Lucknow in 1857. Granny Victoria had related tales of her many imagined Indian and English admirers who had sought her hand in marriage on account of the beauty of her face and body. But she rarely spoke, if ever, about her husband, the old, Madrasi, half-white watchman, Peter. As time passed and she grew older, Granny Victoria talked all the time about people who were dead or were about to die, until she herself passed away one day after having a series of violent fits. Mr Durand remembered reciting the prayer for the dead on her burial in the Christian graveyard. His mother, Angelina, a woman of stunning beauty, had met his white trooper father Durand, of the Gardner's Horse, at a dance in the Troopers mess. Thereafter, Durand senior, who lived in the nearby British cantonment, had become a constant visitor to his mother's house, culminating in his premature birth six months after their marriage in the small chapel behind their house. Three years ago his mother too had died of old age. He was deeply grieved and remembered reciting the prayer for the dead on her death too.

Postmaster Durand quickly took charge of the situation. He assigned individual babus to specific tasks after enquiring about their names. 'Brij Mohan, you will obtain a buggy on which you will place the superintendent's body to carry it to his house. Yusuf, Latif, Qamar, and Yasin will be in the buggy with the body and will be responsible for bathing the body and arranging for a coffin. Zamir and Mohammed will go to the graveyard closest to Ghulam Nabi's house and arrange for a grave and

Saad Ashraf

inform those at the house when that is done.' Finally, he addressed Mirza Ali Beg. 'Ali Beg, you will leave immediately for Ghulam Nabi's house and inform his widow of this tragic incident.' Having assigned everybody their chores, Postmaster Durand went back to his office. Using the telegraph key installed on a small table in the corner of his office, he sent off a telegram to his boss, Mr Clark, the deputy postmaster general.

From: DURAND, POSTMASTER, DELHI GPO
To: MR CLARK, DEPUTY POSTMASTER GENERAL

REGRET TO ADVISE THAT SUPERINTENDENT GHULAM NABI OF THE INDIAN POSTS AND TELEGRAPHS DEPARTMENT PASSED AWAY TODAY AT 1200 HOURS APPROX. IN OFFICE DUE TO UNKNOWN CAUSES. AN IMMEDIATE REPLACEMENT IS REQUESTED IN VIEW OF THE IMPENDING INSPECTION BY THE DIRECTOR GENERAL. REGARDS.

five

In accordance with the instructions given by Postmaster Durand, Mirza Ali Beg immediately hailed a tonga for Ghulam Nabi's house in White Haveli. He was still trying to catch up with the events of the last two hours and the delicate issue of breaking the news to Ghulam Nabi's purdah-observing wife—a woman he had never seen and never met and with whom he could only communicate from behind a door—weighed heavily on his mind and brought a lump to his throat. He first thought of taking his wife along with him and tutoring her to break the news, but soon discarded the idea as impracticable. He practised many combinations of the way he would bring up the matter before Ghulam Nabi's widow but found none that satisfied him. By now, the tonga had reached White Haveli and eventually came to a halt near the narrow lane in which stood Ghulam Nabi's house. Mirza Ali Beg disembarked, paid off the driver, and walked towards the house. He entered the house through the main door, climbed ten-odd stairs, and found himself knocking on a freshly painted green door fitted with a thick iron ring fixed for this purpose.

'Who is it?'

Mirza Ali Beg coughed—a quaint custom to make the ladies of a Muslim household aware of the presence of a male outside.

'It is Mirza Ali Beg, the superintendent sahib's assistant.'

There was an uneasy silence.

'The superintendent sahib has gone to office and is not at home,' said a female voice from inside.

'I know. I have just come from the office and I have a very important message to deliver to his wife, so could you please ask her to come to the door.'

'Yes, this is his wife Noorani Begum,' said the voice.

'Begum, I have some unbearably sad news to break to you. It is all Allah's will. We all live by his grace and life is in his hands. If he wants he can make us live for a hundred years and if he wants he can call us back the next moment ...'

Behind the door, Noorani Begum had already become apprehensive at the sermon being delivered by somebody from her husband's office, somebody she had never seen and whose name she had heard once or twice from her husband.

'Is superintendent sahib all right?'

Mirza Ali Beg realized that this was his moment to break the tragic news.

'I am afraid that ... w-we tried to do our best for him, but it couldn't be helped. People from the office will be bringing him here soon. We are making all arrangements. I can help you inform the relatives.'

A queasy, deathly silence reigned.

Though she felt like she had been struck with a thunderbolt, Noorani Begum's upbringing did not allow her to exhibit her anguish and shock before an unknown male even from behind the door. Ghulam Nabi could not have died. It was only last night that they had made love and dreamed the most fanciful dreams for the future. Noorani Begum imagined that the most that could have happened was that he was unwell and would be bedridden as in the recent past. How could he have just left her like that, without notice, with three young children to rear? Noorani Begum sat down behind the door, totally broken, clutching her head in both her hands, weeping. Her heart beat faster and faster till it seemed like it would explode. She felt faint. She yelled to her elder daughter to get her some water to drink. There would be a stream of her relatives to console her and wail and cry over the tragedy that had afflicted her. They would mention her misfortune, not knowing the happiness she had enjoyed for more than a decade of marriage. Her world had slipped from under her feet and she could do nothing about it. She recalled the cool waters and the snowy mountains of Kashmir when they had visited the valley less than a year ago, her unbounded joy and happiness, and how she had prayed to Allah that this blissful state should never end. Her mother had always said that misfortunes came in droves and the quality of an individual lay in how one faced adversity. For the first time in her life Noorani Begum felt her wits deserting her and forlorn hopes overriding reality. Her husband could still be alive in spite of the news conveyed to her by the Mirza. This could all be a big mistake and he might be in a state of prolonged unconsciousness, nothing more. She closed her eyes and prayed hard: Allah, may all this be a bad dream and when I wake up, may things be as they were yesterday ... Allah could not be so cruel as to rob her of her man and their little children of their father.

Noorani Begum was still in the state of unbelieving daze a couple of hours later, unmindful of the shrieking and sobbing women around her, even unmindful of her traumatized, innocent children with fear-filled eyes. The wailing got louder and louder as the time for taking Ghulam Nabi's body to the graveyard approached. She caught a last glimpse of his face before the men came to take his body out. She hoped that even at this last moment Ghulam Nabi would get up from his sleep and surprise her. Supported by some of the women, she moved across the large courtyard to the covered area in front of the two rooms of the house, and collapsed in a faint, oblivious of the din, and the grief and misfortune that had overtaken her.

Babu Ghulam Nabi, superintendent, General Post Office, Delhi, left this world for his heavenly abode on 24 June 1901, at the age of forty-six. As he had not reached the age of superannuation in government service, he was not entitled to receive a pension though he was to receive some money from the Indian Post Office Benevolent Fund on completion of the formalities. The only other income available to Noorani Begum for the years ahead was the rental she received for the ground floor of her house in the White

Saad Ashraf

Haveli from her tenant Nawab Aziz Rehman. In the matter of a day, Noorani Begum and her family had fallen on hard times to face the cruel realities of life.

For a couple of days after Ghulam Nabi's demise, his widow lay lifeless in bed as grief overpowered her. To those who saw her, she appeared to be in a perpetual daze laced with a touch of insanity. She sighed and shed silent tears for most of the time yet there were occasions when she would recollect the past and smile to herself. One of her major regrets was that she was not with Ghulam Nabi to share his thoughts and pain during his last moments and to seek his counsel as to how she was expected to meet the adversities of life alone.

Two of her aunts had taken over her household temporarily, till such time that she could get back on her feet. They looked after the children, cooked, cleaned and washed, and took turns to be with Noorani Begum and attend to the constant stream of female visitors who came to condole with her. They knew from their own experience how hard it was for a Muslim widow with stringent means to find acceptability in the social fabric of Delhi and that time was the only healer in such tragedies. They also knew that if Noorani Begum resolved to fight back, the battle for her family's survival could be won.

A few weeks later, Mirza Ali Beg knocked at the door of her house to speak to her. Though Noorani Begum was in no mood to talk, her aunts persuaded her to pull herself together and listen to what the Mirza had to say.

'Begum, I have come to tell you that at the Delhi GPO we are doing the best we can to see that all dues of the superintendent sahib are settled at the earliest. The matter has already been taken up in Delhi as well as with Calcutta. We hope that some money from the benevolent fund would become available to you within a month's time. The staff at the office has contributed some money to tide over immediate financial problems. I am leaving a bag containing a hundred rupees outside your door which I hope you will accept on our behalf. Another thing I want to tell you is that Mem Durand, the postmaster's wife, will call on you tomorrow afternoon at three. She would like to condole with you on behalf of Postmaster Durand and other European staff of the Delhi circle.'

Noorani Begum knew that she was in dire financial straits, and though she appreciated this gesture by the babus in her husband's office, she felt that accepting the money would injure her pride. She recalled what her grandfather had often repeated during his days of penury—that one could be poor but noble and that one's pride in the face of odds was all that mattered in life.

'I thank you and the colleagues of my husband for this kind gesture, but I am sorry that I cannot accept this money. Please try to get my husband's dues settled as soon as possible. As far as the postmaster's memsahib is concerned, I shall consider it my privilege to welcome her to my house tomorrow,' said Noorani Begum from behind the door, with a finality which left little room for an argument.

Under normal circumstances, a visit by Mem Durand to the house of an Indian would be an occasion about which one could be proud and boastful. The females from the neighbourhood would vie with one another to be invited to a home where an Englishwoman was visiting. But Noorani Begum was seized by depression out of which she had to make a determined effort to salvage herself if she was to accord a proper welcome to the mem.

'We must get ready to receive the mem in a befitting manner and make her visit a memorable one. Please take out my black embroidered dress from the trunk under my bed. I'd like to wear that. I have read somewhere that English widows wear a black dress when they are in mourning. I'll do likewise. I'd like you to take the China crockery bearing the scenes of British victories in Lucknow and Kanpur out from the box lying in my almirah and make arrangements for tea to be served with English cracker biscuits which would surely please her,' Noorani Begum said to her aunts who were both very pleased to see her fighting her way back to normality.

Saad Ashraf

Mem Durand knocked at Noorani Begum's door the next day promptly at three in the afternoon. She wore a dark-blue cotton dress which fell up to her ankles, and a matching hat with white flowers of cloth woven into it. She was a middle-aged woman of medium height, about two inches taller than Noorani Begum, with a milky-white face delicately powdered. The most noticeable features of her anatomy, which attracted Noorani Begum's immediate attention, were her melon-sized breasts—big, taut, and inviting. One look at her and Noorani Begum could easily tell that men of any caste, creed or colour would naturally be attracted towards Mem Durand.

An exchange of courtesies, at which Noorani Begum was adept by virtue of her grooming and background, followed. Once Mem Durand was comfortably seated in one of the ornamental chairs borrowed by Noorani Begum from her tenant downstairs, she started addressing her in slow, broken Hindustani.

'Begum, we were all very sorry to hear of your husband passing away but this was the Lord's will. Durand sahib was in a state of shock and lost his appetite for several days. Superintendent Ghulam Nabi was respected not only by his Hindustani colleagues but more so by his English superiors. I would like to give this letter of condolence to you on behalf of the postmaster sahib and his English colleagues. Keep this letter with you carefully and present it before English officers whenever there is a need and you will find that everyone will try to be of help to you.' Mem Durand opened the purse she was carrying, fiddled with its insides, and took out a black envelope which she gave to Noorani Begum. Noorani Begum opened the envelope and pretended to read the letter—no word of which she could understand—written in floral, longhand English on embossed Government-of-India stationery. The letter read:

Postmaster Durand met with the European staff of the Delhi postal circle at the Delhi Club, Alipore East, at 6 p.m. for drinks on 29 June 1901. The officers who met and whose signatures appear below expressed their heartfelt sympathies at the sad and sudden demise of Mr Ghulam Nabi, superintendent, General

Post Office, Delhi, on 24 June 1901. Mr Ghulam Nabi was the senior-most native officer in the Delhi circle whose loyalty and services to the Indian postal department remain undisputed and were amply demonstrated. This letter of condolence is being delivered to his widow for her future use whenever required and the reader is requested to provide all possible assistance and succour to her on its presentation.

'Memsahib, I am deeply indebted to you for your feelings and have no words to thank you. It is my privilege that a personage like yourself, having beauty, intelligence, and wisdom should grace my humble abode. Whatever I have lost cannot come back and whatever we have is because of the kindness of my husband's English superiors such as the postmaster sahib and the British Raj which my husband admired. I am very grateful to you for this letter and have no words to express my gratitude,' Noorani Begum said with tears in her eyes.

Mem Durand was not only impressed by the hospitality and conduct of this native woman but her ego too was considerably boosted by the praises showered on her by the grieving widow. Noorani Begum poured tea for the mem in teacups which the mem admired as she munched on the English cracker biscuits with relish. After another quarter of an hour, in which Noorani Begum showered further compliments on Mem Durand's beauty, brains, and breeding, their meeting ended on the promise that they would meet again in the future. Noorani Begum knew that her sycophancy had worked on the mem to some extent, but she also knew that the mem had probably mentioned a future meeting more out of courtesy than in earnestness.

Saad Ashraf

six

The first few months after Ghulam Nabi's death were traumatic for Noorani Begum, but in due course she found that she was able to think more clearly. She realized that the first thing she had to do was to get on her feet financially and this was possible only if she could get her dues from the department. Towards that end she found herself earnestly pursuing the matter for an early settlement of the money owed to her. Being a purdah-observing woman she had no experience of dealing with a government department and her efforts were made through intermediaries such as Mirza Ali Beg. The files were moving, though at a snail's pace, between the General Post Office, the Delhi Circle Office, and Calcutta, and she was finding it more difficult by the day to support her family. Whatever money she had on her had been spent in a couple of months and she had to resort to obtaining her daily needs on credit with the promise to pay back as soon as possible. For her other expenses she had to raise loans from the neighbourhood, which did not hurt her pride as in the past she had helped her neighbours in their time of need. She was able to raise some money from Nawab Aziz Rehman, her tenant, to be adjusted against future rentals. In the course of her experiences however, she became conscious that when it came to real help, many friends and relatives, some of whom she had helped in their hour of distress, deserted her.

On a cold February morning of 1902 Mirza Ali Beg came calling on Noorani Begum.

'Begum, there is some good and bad news for you,' said the Mirza, standing outside the door. 'The good news is that Calcutta has approved a payment of two thousand rupees from the benevolent fund to the successors of the superintendent sahib. We received a telegram this morning that the amount should be paid to his successors forthwith from the post office treasury.'

Noorani Begum sighed in relief. This money along with the rent she received would see her through at least the next five years by which time her son would be a little older.

'And now the bad news ... the lieutenant governor's office has received an application from a woman called Jannat Bibi in Punjab who claims to have been married to Superintendent Ghulam Nabi and to having children from him. I have got a copy of the letter from a friend who works in that office. Here it is,' said the Mirza, handing over the letter from behind the door. 'Jannat Bibi has appealed to the lieutenant governor of Delhi that she should get her share from the payments made by the government and the property left behind by the superintendent sahib as she was also his legally wedded wife. Furthermore, she has claimed the custody of your children on the grounds that you will not be in a position to support them. You will have to consult a lawyer to find out how this threat can be met.'

On hearing this, Noorani Begum sat down on the floor in desperation and thought of the fate that Allah had ordained for her. Ghulam Nabi had left her with major liabilities, three children, and no money. And now she stood a chance of losing everything, including her children, to some woman in faraway Punjab. She had often told Ghulam Nabi to make a settlement in his lifetime with the family he had left behind there, but he had always avoided talking about this matter, not wanting to be reminded of his life in Punjab. She would now have to pay for his tardiness.

A week later, a messenger came to Noorani Begum's house to deliver a summons from the court of the lieutenant governor of Delhi. A hearing had been fixed for 25 August 1902 which gave her a little over a month to locate a lawyer to represent her.

Saad Ashraf

Noorani Begum didn't lose much time in getting in touch, through her neighbours, with Azmatullah, an advocate at the courts in Delhi who was a distant relative of hers. She was soon talking to him across her door to brief him for the first hearing and show him the summons she had received.

'Noorani Begum, we shall have to fight this case and I must say at the outset that we have a fifty per cent chance of winning. Though nobody can deny that Jannat Bibi was the wife of your husband, we will have to prove that since he married you nearly two decades ago, he never contacted his first wife in the Punjab and was not interested in remaining married to her. You may also have to say in court that as far as you know he had verbally divorced Jannat Bibi. It will strengthen our case,' said Advocate Azmatullah.

Noorani Begum knew that this was not true but decided to act according to her lawyer's advice.

Azmatullah was taken aback when Noorani Begum said that she wanted to be present at every hearing. A purdah-observing Muslim woman appearing in a court was unheard of in Delhi.

'Don't you have faith in my abilities to defend you and win your case? What would be achieved by your presence? No Muslim woman of noble background ever goes to a court, and I am saying this not only as a lawyer who has been practising for two decades but also as your cousin. This kind of thing just does not happen here and I think you should drop the idea,' Azmatullah said in a frantic bid to dissuade her.

'I have faith in your abilities and I am prepared to pay you your fee, but I cannot let matters relating to the custody of my children be decided without my presence. Whether you like it or not I am going to be present at all the hearings of this case,' insisted Noorani Begum.

Azmatullah had to relent, although he felt that Noorani Begum's presence in the court would cramp his style of advocacy. Noorani Begum attended the first and subsequent hearings of her case in the court of the lieutenant governor of Delhi where the case was heard by a young English assistant commissioner,

Mr Donaldson. The fifth and last hearing of the case was held on 16 October 1902. The proceedings seemed to be evenly matched. While Jannat Bibi had established her credentials as Ghulam Nabi's first wife through her Hindu lawyer Kishenchand, Noorani Begum had been able to create a doubt in the mind of the assistant commissioner. Advocate Azmatullah had argued convincingly to ask the court as to what kind of a marriage existed between Ghulam Nabi and Jannat Bibi in which her husband did not maintain any contact with her in all the years of his marriage to his second wife and nowhere did her name appear as a successor in any property held by the deceased. This obviously proved that there was no relationship between them because Ghulam Nabi had verbally divorced Jannat Bibi as permitted in the Islamic religion. Jannat Bibi's lawyer was handicapped by the unavailability of documents and the physical absence of the petitioner who could not brief him adequately. On the other hand, Noorani Begum talked with Azmatullah both before and after each hearing, making suggestions on the line of argument that could produce results. Azmatullah was amazed at her incisive intelligence and clarity of thought, and became both aware and fearful of her ruthlessness in achieving her objectives. When the last hearing was over she discussed the case with him.

'Bhaisahab, what happens now?'

'The assistant commissioner sahib will write out his judgment on this case and send the papers to the lieutenant governor sahib. He can accept the judgment or modify it or completely reverse it if he likes. The lieutenant governor is the final authority and the losing party can appeal against the ruling in the viceroy's court in Calcutta. For all practical purposes the lieutenant governor's judgment should be considered final, as nobody goes into appeal on the judgment because of the expense involved in pursuing the case in Calcutta,' explained Azmatullah.

'Bhaisahab, is it possible for you to let me know when these papers reach the lieutenant governor so I can try and meet him?' enquired Noorani Begum.

Saad Ashraf

Azmatullah gave his cousin a quizzical look. 'I can get the information through a friend who works in that office but I don't know how you could meet the lieutenant governor who is the highest government functionary in Delhi and therefore accessible to very few people. It is just like being able to go and see the viceroy of India which, as you know, is impossible for even a well-to-do Indian,' he said.

'I will try and see the governor sahib if you let me know when my case goes to him. Surely you can do this much for a relative and a client,' requested Noorani Begum.

Azmatullah was convinced that Noorani Begum had become mentally unbalanced. First, it was her fixation for a personal appearance in court where she would sit clad in a burqa, an embarrassment for her family and community in Delhi, and now she believed that she could establish a personal connection with the lieutenant governor. Azmatullah felt that he had done his best in arguing her case in court. Now it was Allah's will and Noorani Begum's fate that mattered as far as the judgment was concerned.

'I will speak to my friend in the governor's office and let you know when the file is sent up,' said Azmatullah, departing from his client's house.

seven

Several weeks rolled by without any further development on this front till on 16 December 1902, an exceptionally cold morning, a knock on Noorani Begum's door announced the arrival of Advocate Azmatullah.

'Noorani Begum, I have been in touch with my friend in the lieutenant governor's office and he told me that the file with the judgment written by the assistant commissioner was submitted yesterday to the lieutenant governor. From what my friend said it appears that the judgment wasn't in our favour and we may have to go into an appeal in the viceroy's court at Calcutta. I just came to tell you that the time for efforts is over and that for prayers has arrived. I will let you know if I learn anything else,' said Azmatullah. He departed, leaving Noorani Begum with her woes.

She came back to her charpai, took out a small piece of betel leaf for herself, and carefully spread all the condiments on it. She put the leaf in her mouth and started formulating her plan for survival. She decided that the only way out for her was to somehow meet the lieutenant governor and to convince him of the great wrong that the government would be inflicting on the family of a loyal servant of the British by depriving her of half of her husband's dues and handing over her children to another woman who at best would be a cruel stepmother. If she could persuade the lieutenant governor, she would win. If she couldn't, she was losing the case anyway.

She tried to get some information about Sir Wilbur Bright, the lieutenant governor of Delhi, and managed to learn that he spoke fluent Hindustani and was said to be distantly related to Queen Victoria. Two days later, Noorani Begum donned an embroidered, red Mughal dress, and put on a pearl necklace and gold earrings given to her at the time of marriage and two rings studded with rubies which Ghulam Nabi had presented to her. She painted her lips and passed a silver slide with collyrium through her eyes. She stained her eyelids with kohl, brushed her hair back over her head, and tied her long hair in a tight pigtail whose end was clasped in a red-coloured band that hung on the left side of her shoulder. Noorani Begum stood before the rectangular yard-long Mughal mirror on the wall of her room to examine herself from different angles, her head raised in pride. She felt sure that in spite of being thirty-three years of age she could arouse any man who might see her.

Noorani Begum took out the black envelope containing the condolence letter which Mem Durand had given her, and tucked it carefully in her frock. She put on her burqa, ordered an exclusive tonga, and started for the lieutenant governor's office located beyond the Old Delhi fort, a mile outside the stone gate where the English had executed the mutineers of 1857. Three quarters of an hour later, the tonga slowed down outside the lieutenant governor's office, a semi-circular, yellow-coloured building with tall, thick pillars which lent the building an awesome majesty. There were policemen all around and as soon as the tonga came to a standstill one of them rushed forward and enquired about the passenger from the driver.

It was Noorani Begum herself who answered. 'I am Noorani Begum, wife of Ghulam Nabi, the late superintendent of General Post Office, Delhi. I have come to meet the lieutenant governor sahib bahadur.'

The guard put on a puzzled look and marched towards the office of the head clerk in the governor's office.

'There is a woman here who calls herself Noorani Begum and claims to be the wife of some superintendent. She wants to see the sahib bahadur,' the guard said to the head clerk, Lal Din.

Lal Din had been seconded from the army to serve in the civil as a reward for his grandfather's services in the Indian mutiny when he had saved the life of a British officer near Mehrauli, on the outskirts of Delhi.

'The woman must be mad. How can anyone come to see the sahib bahadur unless the sahib wishes to see that person himself, and a woman on top of it all? Astounding what the world is coming to!' the head clerk remarked angrily.

Meanwhile, Noorani Begum's patience was wearing down as minutes ticked by, so she quickly handed over a few coins to the driver, got down from the tonga, and walked to the office of the head clerk. The appearance of a woman in a burqa somewhat flustered Lal Din. No Muslim woman had ever appeared in his office in the six years that he had worked there.

'I am Noorani Begum, wife of the late Ghulam Nabi who was the superintendent at the General Post Office, Delhi. I have come to meet the sahib bahadur,' said the voice from behind the burqa.

'Behenji, this is the lieutenant governor's office, not the post office where anybody can walk in and buy stamps. The governor is the biggest burra sahib in the whole of the Delhi province and you just expect to walk in and see him? The sahib bahadur only sees people he wishes to see and not the other way round. I am afraid you will not be able to see him though I would like to be of help to you,' said Lal Din.

'Since you say you would like to help me, can you have this envelope delivered to the lieutenant governor while I wait,' said Noorani Begum, drawing the black envelope out of her frock.

Lal Din took the envelope and left his office to take it to his boss, a young British probationer, Ferguson, fresh out of England.

'A Muslim woman in a burqa wants to see the governor sahib bahadur. She gave this envelope to deliver to His Excellency. What do I tell her, Sahib Bahadur?' Lal Din asked in his imperfect English.

Ferguson was new to India and its people and had yet to acquire the hang-ups which created the disdain in the English mind about Indians. He had been born twenty years after the Indian mutiny to a rural Middlesex family that knew very little about India and its people; their prime concern in life being the quantity and quality of potatoes produced on their land. Ferguson could not fully grasp the meaning of a woman in a burqa wanting to see His Excellency and, in this confusion, took the envelope along with other papers that His Excellency wanted to discuss with him to his office.

His Excellency Sir Wilbur Bright, the lieutenant governor, sat on his revolving chair behind a massive mahogany table facing a portrait of King Edward VII in his Victorian office with a high ceiling. The fireplace, with its polished copper canopy, was alight with a fire of moderate intensity. It was replenished with fresh coal every half hour by a native. Sir Wilbur had just finished working on some papers and was reading the daily *Delhi Gazette* which provided social and other news in and around Delhi. There was a mention of a ball attended by him two nights ago in Alipore and news of the posting and transfers of military officers to Meerut and Agra cantonments. There was a column on the fresh arrivals from Britannia who had landed in Bombay and those that had arrived by Mail train at Delhi.

Sir Wilbur was a white Anglo-Indian whose forefathers had served British India for almost a century and a quarter. He knew India and its people like the back of his hand. He spoke Hindustani as proficiently as English and was a notable poet in that language.

Ferguson's knock interrupted his reading. Ferguson entered and, standing next to the governor, passed papers to him for signatures, briefing him on the contents of each matter. When the paperwork was done, Ferguson placed the black envelope before him.

'And what may I say is this?' exclaimed Sir Wilbur.

'Your Excellency, there is a Muslim woman in a burqa wanting to see you.'

'A Muslim woman in a burqa? To see me? How very interesting and unusual. Muslim women generally do not venture out of their homes and rarely interact with outsiders. Is she with a man or is she alone?'

'Alone as far as I know, Your Excellency.'

'Very odd, that a Muslim woman should come all alone. Show her to my office.'

Ferguson walked back to his office and summoned Lal Din to present the woman. The head clerk ushered Noorani Begum into Ferguson's office, where she was asked to sit on a bench.

'The governor sahib bahadur will see you. Please tell me who you are and why you want to see the sahib bahadur,' said Ferguson, with Lal Din acting as an interpreter.

'I am Noorani Begum, wife of the late Ghulam Nabi, superintendent of the General Post Office, Delhi, who passed away in June last year. The matter I want to see the sahib bahadur about is private in nature and therefore I cannot talk about it to anyone else.'

Ferguson got up from his seat and escorted Noorani Begum to the governor's office.

After a short exchange of conversation with Noorani Begum, Sir Wilbur asked Ferguson for privacy.

'Well, what brings you here, a Muslim woman, all alone to the governor's office?'

'I told you who I am, Your Excellency, and the letter in the envelope says more.'

Sir Wilbur lazily raised the flap of the envelope, took out the piece of paper, and started reading it.

'Well, what can the government do for you? We have always tried to help our loyal servants and their families as far as we can,' he said, raising his eyebrows.

'Sahib Bahadur, I am the second wife and widow of Superintendent Ghulam Nabi. As permitted by Muslim law, he had verbally divorced his first wife, Jannat Bibi, who lives in the Punjab. In nearly two decades of our marriage, my husband never wrote a letter or travelled to the Punjab to see her, nor did his first wife ever raise the question of support or maintenance for herself or her children during this period. After my husband's

Saad Ashraf

death, Jannat Bibi has emerged from nowhere to file a case in your court to claim my late husband's dues as well as the custody of my three little children, whom she has never seen or met, on the grounds that I will not be able to support them. I am here to ask for justice and your help in my case.'

By the time Noorani Begum finished her speech, the lieutenant governor was enamoured with his visitor. He sat quietly in his chair, listening to her advocacy of her viewpoint, not realizing that she had stopped speaking.

'You have heard my case, Sahib Bahadur. I hope you will give due consideration to what I have said,' interjected Noorani Begum.

'Yes, I will see what can be done within the ambit of law. I will keep what you have said in mind. If you need to come again to see me for anything, don't hesitate to do so. I shall give instructions to my staff so that you can meet me whenever you want,' said Sir Wilbur, handing the envelope back to Noorani Begum. He got up and Noorani Begum took the cue that it was time for her to leave. As soon as she left, Sir Wilbur Bright pressed the silver mechanical bell which rested on his table and asked his peon to summon Ferguson.

'Ferguson, is there a file here regarding Jannat Bibi or Noorani Begum? If so, please see that it is submitted to me immediately. Ah yes, this lady in the burqa is Noorani Begum ... make sure that she can see me without any inconvenience whenever she comes here.'

Ferguson returned to his office and found that the case of Jannat Bibi versus Noorani Begum had been submitted to the governor only two days ago. It should be lying on the rack behind the governor's table, he reasoned. Ferguson went back to the governor's office when the latter was away for lunch, took the file out of the pile, attached a priority label on it, and placed it on the governor's table.

A few months later, a voice loudly beckoned Noorani Begum from outside her house.

'Noorani Begum! Noorani Begum, this is Kamaldas, the court messenger. There is a court order for you. Please come to the door.'

Noorani Begum, busy cooking lunch in her smoke-filled kitchen, surmised that this court order must be the judgment in her case. She threw away the iron pipe with which she was unsuccessfully trying to get a fire going in the fireplace and headed for the door.

'Begum, this envelope contains some good news for you, get it read and see for yourself,' Kamaldas informed from the other side of the door.

Noorani Begum opened the sealed envelope using her kitchen knife and found two handwritten sheets in English bearing the mark of a large stamp on each page. She had no way of knowing whether the order was in her favour or against her and this made her quite apprehensive. She calmed herself down, drank some water from the pitcher, and decided to send for Azmatullah.

Within the hour, a soft knock and a stifled cough announced the arrival of Azmatullah at her door. Noorani Begum hastened, holding the two white sheets of paper in her hand.

'Bhaisahab, the court messenger brought these two pages this morning. Please explain their meaning to me,' she said.

Azmatullah put on his wire-framed spectacles and started reading the pages, rendering a simultaneous translation for Noorani Begum.

As he read on, his voice became fainter and fainter as one surprise followed another. While the Assistant Commissioner Mr Donaldson's judgment had given some credence to the appeal made by Ghulam Nabi's first wife in the Punjab, the lieutenant governor had reversed the judgment with finality in favour of Noorani Begum on the grounds that it could not be proved whether or not Ghulam Nabi had pronounced verbal divorce on his first wife as was permissible among Muslims. With the benefit of doubt in favour of Noorani Begum, he ordered that the monies owed by the Indian Posts and Telegraphs Department be paid to her immediately under advice to his court and that she be allowed to live peacefully without let or hindrance, with her children wherever and however she may want.

Saad Ashraf

Azmatullah was flabbergasted that a judgment written by an English officer, on a matter concerning the natives, was reversed by his superior. Something like this had never occurred before in the courts of Delhi. The judgment would raise many eyebrows among the English and Indian communities. Azmatullah had heard Noorani Begum mention that she would go and see the lieutenant governor, and he wondered whether she had somehow found access to the leading personage of Delhi and managed to influence him. Azmatullah's perplexed train of thought was interrupted by Noorani Begum.

'Bhaisahab, does this mean that I have won the case and shall have access to my money. Isn't this a day of rejoicing for both you and me? After all, you worked very hard on this case. Do you think that this matter will drag on any more? Can Jannat Bibi still make an appeal to Calcutta?'

'Begum, those who cannot fight the case in Delhi cannot fight the case in Calcutta. I cannot recall a court case in my twenty years of experience where the judgment of an English assistant commissioner has been reversed by his English superior. Indeed, it is a day of rejoicing. You should distribute sweetmeats in the neighbourhood and give alms to the poor. I don't think there will be any problems in getting your dues delivered to your doorstep by the department. I still cannot believe that this has happened. I think Allah came to your rescue,' remarked Azmatullah.

'Of course, Bhaisahab, Allah is the provider of the helpless and the orphans and he answered my prayers, but surely your hard work and advocacy counted too,' said Noorani Begum.

Azmatullah descended the stairs of Noorani Begum's house, shaking his head, not too convinced that it was his brilliance or ability that had won the case.

eight

Azmatullah was correct in his assessment of the effects of the judgment. The department settled Noorani Begum's dues of two thousand rupees in silver coins exhibiting the profile of the late Queen Victoria. After the mandatory period of three months for an appeal with Calcutta had lapsed, the money was delivered to Noorani Begum on the morning of 28 March 1903, in four leather pouches bearing the seals and emblem of the Government of India. It took her half a day to count the coins and put them back in the pouches, which she then put in a large, empty jar—once used to store pickles—kept in the attic facing her bed, from where she could keep an eye on the money. She put a heavy padlock on the latch of the attic and passed the key through the string of the amulet she wore around her neck. Thereafter, she prostrated herself on the prayer mat and wept, thanking Allah for having ensured her family's respectable survival for the next five years.

Noorani Begum knew that she had won the case because of the kindness of one man—the lieutenant governor of Delhi, Sir Wilbur Bright, to whom she was beholden and whom she felt obliged to go and thank in person. She wanted to present a token of some kind to the governor to express her gratitude. From what she had heard, Englishmen in power could be temperamental, taking offence on petty matters not worth bothering about and yet showing extreme magnanimity on grave issues. In her first and only meeting with Sir Wilbur she had tried her best to gauge him from his mannerisms and body language by observing him through the slits in her burqa. She however felt that she did not have enough knowledge of the man to figure out his reaction to a symbolic gesture of thanksgiving. Noorani Begum remembered a gold armlet engraved with Allah's name that belonged to Ghulam Nabi, which she had carefully put away along with his other belongings into his black steel trunk. She decided this would make a suitable, though modest, gift for Sir Wilbur.

The following Friday morning, an auspicious day, Noorani Begum dressed herself in her finery, making sure that she put on the two ruby rings on the fingers of her left hand. She recalled Sir Wilbur observing them closely the last time she visited his office. She boarded a tonga from White Haveli for the lieutenant governor's office. Noorani Begum had carefully wrapped the armlet in red tissue paper and put it in the purse that she carried.

Three quarters of an hour later she reached the lieutenant governor's office. This time she felt more confident than on the previous occasion, and was escorted to Ferguson's office without any ado. She felt more comfortable asking Ferguson for an audience with the lieutenant governor and observed that everybody seemed to be going out of their way in arranging her meeting with Sir Wilbur who was said to be busy in a conference. After a short while, Noorani Begum was ushered into his presence.

'Your Excellency may recall that I, Noorani Begum, met you a few months ago concerning the case filed against me by my late husband's first wife, who wanted a share in the dues to be paid to me by the department as well as the custody of my children. I received your judgment in my favour as well as the money that was due to me and have come to thank you for your kindness which neither I nor my children will ever forget. Your sense of justice has saved my family and I have no means to show my gratitude,' said Noorani Begum.

A short silence followed.

'Of course I recall your visit, Begum ... a Muslim woman had never visited me before ... but you need not have taken the trouble to come because I only did my duty. Your case was decided entirely on merit.'

'Your Excellency, I don't want to take any more of your valuable time. I have brought a small gift for you to express my gratitude and I am sure you will accept it.'

Before the lieutenant governor could say a word, Noorani Begum removed the armlet and placed it on his table.

'Begum, you know that as government functionaries we are not allowed to accept any gifts. In fact, some of us, not well acquainted with the traditions and ways of Hindustan, may get offended by such presents. I was born in Hindustan and I love this country and its people. I do not wish to offend you, but not a word of this to anyone. You know how news can travel in this big country,' said Sir Wilbur.

'Your Excellency, you must trust me. No woman worth her salt would ever let down a benefactor such as yourself, which is what you have been for me and my family,' said Noorani Begum.

Sir Wilbur sat quietly in his swivel chair, observing Noorani Begum minutely while she spoke. He was as much enamoured by this Muslim woman's intelligence, confidence, and forthrightness as by her fair, well-kept hands with identical ruby rings on two of her fingers which emerged now and then from the burqa to emphasize a point. The lieutenant governor was a great connoisseur of native women, having been initiated at the early age of twelve when his Bengali ayah of twenty had seduced him. That was decades ago, when his father, a doctor, had been posted in Calcutta. Sir Wilbur was now fifty-two years old. He had married a young Englishwoman who had landed in Bombay to hunt for a husband ten years ago. The marriage did not last long due to incompatibility and after much bickering he had divorced Marjorie.

Noorani Begum's melodious voice, and creamy hands and fingers were prodding him as each moment passed, and he wondered that if her hands could set his mind afire, what would her face and body camouflaged by the folds of cloth be able to do to his passions.

'Begum, what a beautiful gift—a gold armlet inscribed with God's name. Surely this gift is too precious to be accepted,' remarked Sir Wilbur.

'Your Excellency, Allah's name will protect you from all dangers and keep you safe from the evil intentions of others. I brought this especially for you, keeping my benefactor's high office in mind.'

Suddenly, Sir Wilbur wanted to be close to this mysterious woman. He wanted to discover her and in turn be discovered.

'Perhaps the Begum would take the trouble of tying this armlet herself on me,' said Sir Wilbur, excitedly rolling up his sleeve.

Noorani Begum was in a fix. Being alone with a man in a room was one thing but tying an armlet on his bare arm another. She had called the lieutenant governor her ultimate benefactor so many times in the last half an hour that there was no way she could refuse his request. She advanced towards the other side of the table where he sat on his swivel chair, took hold of the armlet, and with her two hands emerging out of the burqa, she tied the armlet around his right arm. Suddenly, she found Sir Wilbur's right arm around her waist. Noorani Begum tried disentangling herself but his grip tightened and she heard him breathing heavily. She somehow freed herself and managed to get to the other side of the table. Her heart was pounding as if it would blow itself out of her chest. She was unnerved and felt like a trapped cat. She had never had an encounter of this kind before. The only male who had ever put his arm around her waist was her late husband.

'Noorani Begum, I am sorry I lost myself. My desire and passion overtook me. I have everything in life—wealth, position, and power and yet I have nothing. There is nobody to share my life. Some years ago I was married but it didn't work out. Sitting on this chair I can't even have friends. Indeed I am the poorest man in this world, a man who has everything yet nothing. Please forgive me for what I did,' said a tearful Sir Wilbur in a quivering voice.

Noorani Begum observed from the slits of her burqa that Sir Wilbur's face had contorted with remorse. It was obvious that

The Postmaster   {55}

he was overcome with the guilt of having made a pass at a woman who had come to thank him. If she had her way she would have gone up to him and put his arms around him as he sat on the swivel chair, and consoled him by telling him that while she could not be his wife, she could be the best friend he would ever have and that from this moment on he was no longer alone in the world since both of them were together and that was what mattered. She would have put his head on her lap and wiped the tears from those blue eyes and told him that she would never desert him and that he could bare his heart to her without fear. She would have pacified him that with her by his side he was the richest man in the world because only the fortunate were blessed with such friendship, a gift of Allah which could never be measured or bought. She wanted to say this and much more but realized the terrible constraints society forced on her. She had been brought up as a conservative Indian Muslim within the four walls of her home. She had never been exposed to the outside world—and what went on in it—in which there was no place for a woman like her. Similarly, there was no place for men in her life other than her husband or the closest of relatives. Her ambitions or desires to do something outside the home were motivated purely by the need for survival. Her loyalties lay with her deceased husband and her children, for how could she go back on Ghulam Nabi, who had proclaimed on her wedding night that he would be found by her side as long as he lived and who while alive had worked to her benefit and that of the family. It was his untimely death that had made her venture out to approach Sir Wilbur Bright and had placed her in this predicament where she sat pitying this man of authority so broken in spirit. Yet her heart went out to him. She consoled herself that this was not love, which was forbidden outside of marriage, but the most superior kind of friendship.

'I was married till my husband departed this world,' said Noorani Begum softly, consoling Sir Wilbur. 'I know that desire and passion can besiege a man's mind and make him act like an animal, putting aside the virtues ingrained in him by religion,

Saad Ashraf

education or civilized upbringing. Among us, such things are permitted between a husband and wife only. The only thing we can do is to ask for forgiveness from the Almighty and continue to be friends. I can listen to the cries of your heart and you can listen to mine.'

Saying this, Noorani Begum left the lieutenant governor's office. The entire meeting had taken a little under an hour.

nine

Having finally received her dues from the Indian Posts and Telegraph Department, Noorani Begum sat down to plan a strategy for herself and her children so that they could have a fair chance of survival and success. She sat with her children for dinner and in spite of their tender ages impressed on them not only the precarious financial situation they were in but how they could get out of it if they all stood together. Her plan held hope for everyone. Since her resources were limited, her strategy centred around getting her son, Ghulam Rasool, to stand on his feet. If somehow he could be given the best possible western education for the next twelve years, and if he could graduate and get a government job, the future of the entire family would be secure. Once the family acquired some prestige, the girls would get good proposals for marriage. She outlined the principles to be followed by her family for the foreseeable future: hard work, family unity, western education, determination to succeed, and a non-controversial low-profile existence.

To augment her income, she took to stitching clothes at home and bought a sewing machine which had been recently introduced in Delhi. Long into the night, when the chores of the day were done and her children were asleep, Noorani Begum laboured at her machine, stitching shirts, trousers, jumpers, and other apparel for women in the neighbourhood and those referred to her by her satisfied clientele.

To keep her expenses in control she got rid of all domestic help she had when Ghulam Nabi was alive. Ghulam Rasool went to the market to buy provisions for a month, carrying as many bags on his young shoulders as they could bear.

Ghulam Rasool did not let his family down. On returning from school, he would sit down with his books and slate and study in the light of the lantern while Noorani Begum's sewing machine whirred. When electricity came to Delhi, Ghulam Rasool took his books and writing materials out on the street after dark and sat under the street lights, studying until the early hours of the morning when the lights were switched off. His hard work, diligence, and quest for knowledge became proverbial in White Haveli.

Ghulam Rasool appeared for the matriculation examination of the Delhi Board in March 1912. When the results were announced in May of that year, he was one of the three Muslims who had passed in the first division—no mean feat for an orphan struggling against adversity who spent most nights studying under the dim, yellow street lights of Old Delhi.

When the news of Ghulam Rasool's success reached Noorani Begum, her joy knew no bounds—her gamble for survival was paying off. Ghulam Rasool himself came and touched his mother's feet, kissed her hands, and cried, 'Ammi, all this is the result of your hard work and prayers. Otherwise, I know I am not capable of passing in the first division.'

Ghulam Rasool's sisters crowded around him, exuding happiness at their brother's success. Neighbours and relatives came with gifts of sweets, fruits, and flowers to see this marvel of a boy who had passed the tenth class with flying colours. Some of them even brought their little boys along, hoping that they would one day grow up and emulate Ghulam Rasool.

On the heels of this joy followed the dilemma of selecting the college to which Ghulam Rasool should seek admission for his intermediate. There was the famous Islamia College, a Muslim institution built on the remnants of the Delhi College of the pre-mutiny days, which the Muslim youth of Delhi who excelled in academics invariably joined. Islamia College boasted of world-famous scholars of Arabic, Persian, and theology—subjects for which Ghulam Rasool had a natural aptitude—on its faculty.

Then there was the relatively newer Missionary College, established on the outskirts of the city beyond the Kashmiri Gate on the site of a razed palace of a Mughal nawab who had erringly sided with the last Mughal emperor. The land for the college building was given to the Mission by virtue of a government grant on the express understanding that they would implement Lord Macaulay's policy of turning out English-speaking brown sahibs through whom the British could rule India forever. Missionary College thus had an edge over Islamia College in terms of the anglophiles produced and their acceptability for employment with the government. The college, however, had been the target of one Mullah Rabbani of the famous Pearl Mosque built by Aurangzeb.

In a fiery address one Friday, the mullah had proclaimed, 'And now they have set up a college to convert the Muslims of Delhi into Christians. They have set up Missionary College near the Kashmiri Gate where Christian padres disguised as teachers are converting young Indians of other religions, in particular Mussalmans, to Christianity by teaching them western mathematics, science, and astronomy. No young Muslim should join this institution ... otherwise they themselves and their parents will surely burn in hell with others like Sir Syed Ahmad Khan.'

It was only after Mullah Rabbani was summoned by Inspector Braganza to the Daryaganj Police Station and confronted with a transcript of his speech and told that discretion is the better part of valour that he desisted from bringing up any mention of Missionary College in his future Friday sermons. The mullah's visit to the police station did not remain a secret for long and divided the Muslims of Delhi into two distinct camps, with the progressives supporting Missionary College in a distinct minority. This controversy confused Ghulam Rasool's young mind. With nobody to turn to for objective advice and with the last date for putting in applications drawing near, he felt that one person who deserved to be consulted was Noorani Begum who through her sacrifices of over a decade had brought him to this stage of life.

Saad Ashraf

One August afternoon of 1912 with the Delhi sky overcast with monsoon clouds and tired kites flying around in the steamy air, Ghulam Rasool sat on the brick floor, at his mother's feet.

'Ammi, through your prayers and Allah's blessings I managed to pass the matriculation. Now I have to make a very important decision within a very short time. I have to choose between the two colleges in Delhi—Islamia College, the institution which Muslim youth usually join, or Missionary College, a creation of the British. Which college do you think I should join?'

Glowing with affection, Noorani Begum looked at her son, a faint smile on her face. She pulled out the silver betel-leaf box from under her bed, removed two damp leaves from its upper tray, and started applying lime and catechu on them with the small spatula. She sprinkled some areca nut on the leaves, stuffed the whole into her mouth, and started chewing and thinking. All of a sudden she felt very lonely, the absence of a man at her side making itself felt. Here was her son asking for a vital piece of advice which she felt she was inadequately equipped to give.

'I think you should join Missionary College. The English are very clever people. Their science and knowledge makes them rule the seven seas ... they have even learnt to fly like birds and have invented horseless carriages. They will surely rule over Hindustan for a long time to come. The future will lie with those who know English and have knowledge of western science. You must learn to speak read, write, and behave like an Englishman. Do not pay heed to what people say about Missionary College being an infidel institution. Such people speak the same way about the college in Aligarh and Sir Syed Ahmad Khan ... see what good work that college is doing in educating Muslim youth. In my opinion there's no choice except Missionary College,' advised Noorani Begum.

Ghulam Rasool applied for admission to the intermediate class of Missionary College commencing in September 1912 and received a letter to appear for an interview before a panel of the faculty. He was overjoyed at being called for the interview but nervous as he had never had any significant interaction with white people and the admission to the college depended entirely on the interview. When he broke the news about the interview to Noorani Begum, she suggested that Ghulam Rasool go and see Azmatullah for some tips on how he should conduct himself at the interview. The next day, Ghulam Rasool was with the advocate in his office near the Royal Mosque.

'The English are a very finicky people,' said Azmatullah, when Ghulam Rasool explained the purpose of his visit. 'Therefore, you have to be very careful about what you do and say. The most important thing is to keep your hands in control. We Indians tend to be fidgety, shaking our legs, picking our noses, or handling our private parts before others. Avoid these mannerisms like the plague because the English detest them. Keep your hands in your lap if you are sitting and behind your back while standing. If you do not understand something, say, "Pardon, sir." Try to use the word "please" as frequently as possible, and whenever you find the interviewer getting even slightly agitated, just say, "I am sorry, sir." Speak softly and slowly so that only the person you are addressing can hear you. Never stare into the eyes of an Englishman; look at the person only when you are being addressed or when you are giving an answer. Be forthright, as the English are intelligent people who don't like being fooled.'

Azmatullah had Ghulam Rasool rehearse a mock interview with him, in which he asked him all kinds of questions relating to his studies and his personal life. At the end of an hour and a half of practice, Azmatullah concluded that if nothing untoward happened, Ghulam Rasool stood a good chance of being admitted to Missionary College.

On the day of the interview, Noorani Begum woke up early and said special prayers for her son's success. She went over her rosary two hundred times, seeking Allah's mercies for her son. She woke up Ghulam Rasool who dressed himself up in coat, trousers, and tie. He had purchased these three days ago from a dealer in second-hand apparel behind the Royal Mosque and got them altered to his size by a tailor who did work for British regimental officers. He drank his glass of milk and devoured

Saad Ashraf

half a loaf of bread left over from the previous night's dinner, before starting out for Missionary College.

When Ghulam Rasool got down from the tonga after what seemed to be an endless ride, he was overawed by the sheer size and majesty of the college building. He walked down the long driveway that led to the red-bricked main block in which the principal's office was located. It was here that the interview would take place. Three large, white marble domes with golden spires similar to the Royal Mosque towered over the lush green grounds on both sides. They stood like three sentinels dressed in white, guarding the honour and sanctity of the institution. Ghulam Rasool made his way to the principal's office where he found a large crowd of aspirants—fifty or more young Indians of all colours, shapes, and sizes—awaiting their turn to be called for the interview which was to begin soon and which was to be conducted over several days.

Missionary College had acquired an enviable reputation under the ruthless administration of its principal, Professor Thompson, who would brook no nonsense from any quarter, be it the faculty, the student body or an outsider. The principal believed that it was not possible to impart the benefits of western education to the masses of India and only temperamentally suitable young Indians who genuinely idolized the English way of life could benefit from their association with his college. Any aspirant who gave the slightest indication of not fulfilling the criteria was considered unfit for admission and the interview brought to a close without loss of time. To qualify for admission, a candidate had to get a favourable vote from each of the three members of the panel. On an average, only one Indian out of twenty who appeared for the interview was lucky to get admitted to the college.

Ghulam Rasool was still trying to familiarize himself with his surroundings when he saw a babu clad in white, moving around, ticking the names of those who were to appear for the interview.

'You must be Ghulam Rasool, the Muslim boy—there are only three from your community in today's interview. The peon will call out your name. Please follow him to the ante-room in front of the principal's office,' said the babu.

After he left, the name of the first candidate was called out. A quarter of an hour later, the candidate emerged out of the principal's office with a perplexed and worried look on his face. Two others displayed no better expressions, with one candidate, a lanky Sikh, emerging with sodden cheeks. When his turn came, Ghulam Rasool followed the short-statured dark figure of the peon to the ante-room. He knocked on the door. The peon opened the door and pushed Ghulam Rasool in. He found himself inside a large room whose walls were panelled with wood. Three white men sat on a long table covered with a thick and coarse, green woollen cloth. The man in the centre gestured to Ghulam Rasool to take his place on a single chair facing the panel.

'I am Professor Thompson, the principal, and these are my two colleagues—Professor Joseph Moses of the philosophy department and Professor Pringle of the mathematics department,' said the white man in the middle. Ghulam Rasool surmised that the interview was all set to begin.

'Mr Ghulam Rasool, we are impressed by your academic achievement of getting a first division in the matriculation examination, and we got a good report on you from your school, but tell us something about your background and how you managed to achieve this,' Professor Thompson continued.

Ghulam Rasool remembered all the tips that Azmatullah had given and kept his hands folded in his lap.

'Sir, please, I come of a poor but noble family. My father, Ghulam Nabi, was the superintendent of the General Post Office who died over a decade ago, serving his country and his king. Thereafter, my family underwent hard times and I had to study under the street lights of the neighbourhood. I have had to borrow books from public libraries and from my teachers in order to equip myself with knowledge. It was the devotion of my teachers and their guidance and my mother's prayers that have been responsible for whatever little I have achieved academically,' said Ghulam Rasool.

'Mr Ghulam Rasool, are you a religious person? Do you believe that persons who do not share your faith are infidels? Please let me know what you think of the equality of human beings,' asked Professor Joseph Moses.

This, Ghulam Rasool knew, was a tricky question, the answer to which could become source of controversy. For a moment he was tempted to make up an answer which would please the panel but then he remembered Azmatullah's advice of being forthright.

'Please sir, if saying one's prayers is the basis of being classified as religious, I would fall in that category. But I feel that there is a distinct difference between being religious and being a religious zealot. I do not think of anybody as an infidel, because one's faith is a personal matter to which one is born. I think all people are created equal and should be treated as such by society. If this is not so, it is because of human prejudices.'

The serious, expressionless face of Professor Moses showed a discernible sign of satisfaction on hearing Ghulam Rasool's reply.

'Mr Ghulam Rasool, what are your views on British rule in India?' questioned Professor Pringle, the third member of the panel.

Ghulam Rasool knew that if he overly praised the English he would appear to be a sycophant.

'I think that the British have given a lot to India. They have given this country modern technology like the railways, the telegraph, and metalled roads, and made life safe for its people. But a lot more needs to be done to promote amity between the various communities that live in India,' replied Ghulam Rasool.

Professor Pringle, an avowed racist who washed his hands with soap every time he shook hands with a local, felt that as long as Indians like Ghulam Rasool were around, the British would have no problems ruling over them.

Ghulam Rasool was granted admission to the academic session of the intermediate class at Missionary College which commenced on 1 September 1912. He took mathematics, philosophy, and Arabic as his main subjects of study.

ten

Another Muslim who had been admitted to Missionary College along with Ghulam Rasool was Syed Ahmad, the scion of the famous imam family of Delhi. The imams had migrated from Central Asia during the Mughal period to become the keepers of the Royal Mosque that the Mughal emperor was building in Delhi. Since then the family had extended its influence and size through intermarriage with those who were in favour with the Mughal royalty. The imams had deftly treaded the complicated maze of the royal political chessboard for over two centuries and managed to survive as caretakers of the great mosque regardless of who emerged as the emperor of India. This was no mean feat considering that the death of every Mughal emperor was followed by wars of succession and bloodshed and the ouster of the nobility which was in favour with the deceased emperor. The imams did this by keeping their channels open with all warring parties and proclaiming their allegiance to the new ruler once he had emerged and consolidated support. They had mastered this art of survival to the extent that during the mutiny of 1857 they were in touch with the Mughal emperor in the fort through intermediaries right till the very end when he escaped by boat to take refuge in his forefather's tomb. When the British had entered Delhi later that year and were rounding up people on the flimsiest excuse to be hung from hastily erected gallows outside the Kashmiri Gate or blown from the mouths of their cannons parked in the open prayer area of the mosque, Hassan, an informer of the British had approached Colonel

Huddersfield who was then commanding the Fifth Native Infantry in the mosque area.

'Kernel Saab, this imam very bad man, very much against white sahibs. If you will make cannonball of him, good example for others, they be afraid you make cannonball of them,' he had said in his broken English.

Colonel Huddersfield had called one of his men, Surbjit Singh, and told him to take a detachment and trace and produce the imam in the least possible time. The imam was produced, summary charges read out and translated, and he was asked to say whatever he wanted in his defence. The charges were grave indeed and included showing disloyalty to the English, collaborating with the Mughals, and holding views prejudicial to the British interests in India.

'Sir, please send your men to the north-west corner of the mosque where a stairway leads to the basement under the main prayer hall and ask them to bring whoever they find there and you will know where my loyalties lie,' the imam had said.

Half an hour later, Colonel Huddersfield's men were seen escorting two dozen English men, women, and children, no doubt bedraggled but otherwise in good health. As soon as they saw the imam, the men came forward and tearfully embraced him and fell on his feet while the women cried aloud and kissed his hand and called him their saviour. Embarrassed, the colonel felt more like a defeated soldier than victor of Delhi and had stood with his head slung over his chest while Hassan, the informer, looked so stupid that he muttered a silent prayer to Allah to open the earth under him so that it could devour him. Colonel Huddersfield had apologized to the imam in front of his countrymen and women and said how sorry he was to have put him to such inconvenience. He said he was prepared to make amends by hanging Hassan or by blowing him from the mouth of the biggest cannon he had if the imam so desired. When the imam had refused this offer, the colonel appointed him his special aide with powers of remitting all sentences of imprisonment or death without any questions asked. As the imam had hardly any enemies, all cases referred to him got reductions in their period of imprisonment or clemency in their death sentences, which made him very popular with the people. The imam had quickly sized up the situation and, seizing the initiative, had assumed the role of the principal negotiator between the Muslims and the victorious English. As his influence with the English widened, so did his power and authority over people of his community.

Syed Ahmad was the great-grandson of this imam. Though he had not passed his matriculation in the required grades, he was admitted to Missionary College on the single seat placed at the disposal of the lieutenant governor of Delhi to nominate whomsoever he preferred. Except for adequate academic credentials, Ahmad had everything else. He was rich, generous, and handsome, and everybody's favourite including that of Principal Thompson.

Both Rasool and Ahmad attended lectures in philosophy delivered by Professor Joseph Moses. While Ghulam Rasool concentrated in class and tried to make up for any deficiencies through extra reading in the library or through borrowed books to be read under the street lights of White Haveli, the pearls of wisdom dispensed of in the lecture rooms of Missionary College by Professor Moses hardly made a dent on Ahmad's intellect. Whenever Ahmad was asked a question by the professor about the fundamentals of philosophy, he stood up and looked around sheepishly. Eventually, Professor Moses called Ahmad to his office and suggested that he try and get Ghulam Rasool to coach him.

Ahmad broached the matter with Ghulam Rasool and promised to pay him thirty rupees a month in cash or a higher amount in kind if he could unravel the mysteries of the discourses given by Professor Moses. While undoubtedly happy with the offer, as it would pay for at least a part of his college expenditure, Ghulam Rasool felt that he needed some clarifications.

'What do you mean when you say that you could pay in kind? Will you give me flour, rice, and vegetables from your farm for my mother's kitchen?' asked Ghulam Rasool.

'I promise you that once you see the way I settle the tuition charges in kind, you'll never regret having opted for this manner

Saad Ashraf

of settlement. Just coach me for a month and find out for yourself,' said Ahmad.

Ghulam Rasool started giving tuitions to Ahmad twice a week and discovered that unlike the impression he conveyed, Ahmad was not dull. He had a prodigious memory and when he wanted he could remember whatever he heard or read even once. With a little encouragement from Ghulam Rasool, he started reading the works of ancient and contemporary philosophers both from the East and the West, such as Rumi, Saadi, Kant, and Hegel.

At the end of the first month, Ahmad presented fifteen silver rupees wrapped in a silk handkerchief to his teacher.

Ghulam Rasool was quick to remind his pupil, 'And what about the balance amount we agreed upon?'

'Be ready tomorrow evening at five ... we shall go out together and settle the balance. If you don't like what I give you in kind you can claim it in cash,' said Ahmad.

Next day, promptly at five in the evening, as the crimson winter sun was in the process of dipping below Delhi's horizon, Ahmad, clad in a cream-coloured silk pyjama suit, a black waistcoat, and a silk scarf around his neck, made his appearance at Ghulam Rasool's door.

'Well, well, this indeed is a surprise. I could hardly recognize you in all your finery. Philosophy has surely worked wonders on you but you seem to have chosen the ways of the world rather than that of Rumi. Are you certain that you are not planning to take me to somebody's wedding?' said Ghulam Rasool, as both of them headed in the direction of the Royal Mosque.

From the big mosque they turned left and then right to Nooruddin's restaurant where Ahmad ordered two plates of special gravy, heavily spiced. Having spent an hour at dinner and gossip they left the restaurant and began to walk in the direction of Chawri Bazaar, the famous red-light area of Delhi. Although Ghulam Rasool had passed through this bazaar many times, he had never done so at this hour when it opened for business. From his very childhood he recalled Noorani Begum telling him that the followers of Satan took over Chawri Bazaar in the evening and managed to possess the souls of the passersby, making them do evil things after dark. Ghulam Rasool had strictly followed his mother's advice all these years. But now, as the beat of the tabla kept time with the mellow sound of the harmonium and the sarangi, and the jingle of bells on the feet of the dancing girls filled the bazaar with music so overpowering, Ghulam Rasool's young mind knew of no other way except to follow Ahmad like a pet dog.

'Just keep following me and do what I do and you'll be okay. There is much protocol to be followed which I have taken years to learn,' remarked Ahmad with an air of confidence.

'I thought you were born in a family of imams, the keepers of the Royal Mosque of Delhi. When did you learn all this?' asked Ghulam Rasool, as they climbed a wooden staircase.

'During the spare time I get from the philosophy lessons you give me, my dear friend. By the way, this is the house of Roshan Ara, the most beautiful and accomplished dancer of Chawri Bazaar. She is the mistress of Seth Banke Das, the famous Marwari banker of Bombay who pays her two thousand rupees a month for her services and sacrifices a goat every day so that no evil eye falls on her beauty. The seth can spare very little time from his business and comes to visit her once a month when she is not available to anyone else,' said Ahmad, knocking softly at a green door on the second floor.

As the door opened, Ahmad pushed his way inside, followed by Ghulam Rasool. They entered a roomful of people sitting on a snow-white sheet that covered the floor, helping themselves to paan that was being passed around by the aged matron of the house. A young, strikingly beautiful, fair-complexioned girl with large, brown eyes, wearing a red Mughal dress, long golden earrings and a studded necklace, was twirling to the music. She was dancing the Kathak, performing intricate movements with her hands while the bells on her feet chimed with the beat of the tabla and the accompanying music. Every time a bar of music ended, there was a loud 'dha' from the tabla and the dancer would come to a standstill, holding a pose in time with the music. The crowd would leap to its feet in acclaim, and coins would be thrown at her feet. The fragrance of perfume pervaded the air in the room, as Ahmad and Ghulam

Rasool took their places on the floor. While Ahmad pressed a fistful of silver coins into Ghulam Rasool's hands, the dancer came near and sat on the floor close to him. Ghulam Rasool could smell her scented breath and feel her warm, taut, young breasts brush his chest. She looked invitingly into his eyes. No woman had ever looked into his eyes like that nor made him feel the warmth of her body from such close quarters before. Ghulam Rasool was entranced. Oh, how he wished he could hold her in his arms and kiss those slightly parted lips. She was singing a couplet of an unknown poet:

I have given you my heart, what else can I give you
I have nothing more left to give you except my life

The dancer held Ghulam Rasool's hands in hers and opened the one which clasped the silver coins. Taking one coin, she closed his palm over the rest, smiled seductively, and danced her way in another direction to loud 'wah wahs' from the gathering. The effect of her song, her movements, and her body was ethereal and mystifying. Roshan Ara seemed to be enamoured with young Ghulam Rasool, teasing him with another part of the song, using her seductive looks to entice him:

I will lay my eyelids for you to walk on
If you promise to give me your eternal love

This time, Ghulam Rasool opened his fist and let her help herself to all the coins she wanted. When she moved away, Ghulam Rasool sat transfixed, staring straight ahead, empty-handed. There were loud requests from the crowd, calling for a repetition of this verse. Ahmad nudged Ghulam Rasool to bring him back to the world of reality.

'Enjoying yourself, Mian? Wouldn't you say that this dialogue of love in a harlot's house moves one more than any philosophical theory ever propounded. What better use can there be of one's wealth than the enjoyment of the five senses that Allah has endowed to his human beings,' exclaimed Ahmad.

The performance continued for another two hours and the crowd thinned. Roshan Ara, the star performer of the evening, took time out from dancing and singing and sat next to the matron, showering smiles on her remaining admirers and raising her palm to the middle of her forehead in acknowledgement of the praises of her art. This signalled the end of this house's entertainment for the evening.

'It is time for us to leave now, Professor Ghulam Rasool ... the management has decided to close for the day,' Ahmad said in a voice louder than usual.

Ghulam Rasool was still in a reverie, staring at Roshan Ara who was busy admiring herself in a pocket mirror she had taken out from her blue satin purse.

'Allah, help me! There couldn't be a more perfect creation of his on this earth,' Ghulam Rasool exclaimed, within hearing distance of Roshan Ara.

Roshan Ara smiled and bowed her head low, raising her palm twice to her forehead in the direction of Ghulam Rasool in a prompt and special acknowledgement.

'Come again and honour this house,' she said, smiling, her palms raised in a parting gesture.

'Well, Professor, would you still prefer half of your tuition fees in cash? Mind you, this is just the first chapter in the arts of pleasure. There is much more to come,' Ahmad said to Ghulam Rasool as they descended the stairway of Roshan Ara's house, on their way home.

'From next month you will pay for my coaching in cash at the rate of thirty rupees a month in advance, otherwise there will be no more tuition. I won't insist on your paying half my charge for this month because it was I who agreed to compensation in kind by consenting to visit Chawri Bazaar with you,' said Ghulam Rasool, approaching the intersection of the two lanes which led to their respective houses. This cold and unemotional response from somebody who he thought had become an intimate friend embarrassed Ahmad. It was obvious to him that in his relationship with Ghulam Rasool he had yet to cross the narrow chasm that divided friendship from intimacy.

Saad Ashraf

eleven

For Ghulam Rasool, the four years at Missionary College, studying for a bachelor's degree, passed quickly. He immersed himself in reaping the maximum benefit out of its intellectual and academic environment. The excellence of its faculty members, who had authored several books and had studied at the best universities of the world, rubbed itself off on Ghulam Rasool. Slowly but surely his fear of the white man was disappearing. His professors were polite, soft-spoken, and friendly though they possessed a discernible reserve. Ghulam Rasool found Professor Joseph Moses most amenable. Professor Moses was born of an English father and a German mother. He had spent his childhood in Bavaria and his youth in the beautiful city of Heidelberg about which he talked often, sighing sadly with a faraway look in his deep blue eyes. He was a bachelor and was in charge of the college library where he spent most of his time after the college closed for the day. Ghulam Rasool studied in the library till the late hours of the night. Sometimes when it was too late, he would decide to spend the night there and draw the reading tables together to sleep on them. Professor Moses and Ghulam Rasool held long discussions on philosophical topics which sometimes continued till the early hours of the morning. Master and pupil became friends and developed a deep intellectual equation with one another.

Ahmad, on the other hand, did not fare well academically and had repeatedly failed in the intermediate examination for the past three years. He was however unmoved by this, strongly believing that every moment of one's existence should be enjoyed to the hilt as one came into this world but once. He had started visiting Chawri Bazaar more frequently to find out whether it had more beautiful girls to offer than Roshan Ara. He was surprised at what he discovered. Roshan Ara was merely at the middle of the scale of beauties in the bazaar. In fact, the most beautiful girl he had come across was one Yasmeen from Kashmir. She had the eyes of a doe, jet-black hair that fell to her knees, and a creamy white complexion before which the full moon would blush, but it was her mellow nature that combined with her physical attractiveness to ensnare him. She was honest, sincere, and loving, and from the moment their eyes first met there was a natural, physical, mental, and spiritual communion between the two. Whenever they had a rare chance of meeting alone, there were proclamations of love and promises of lifelong devotion to one another despite their personal situations.

'Would you like to meet Yasmeen who dances like a firefly, sings like a nightingale, and, above all, has fallen in love with me? I will arrange for a private session of song and dance for both of us at my expense. Roshan Ara is nothing in comparison to Yasmeen,' Ahmad said to Ghulam Rasool one evening.

'Ahmad, these are all women of the bazaar with no morals whatsoever. I am surprised that despite your religious upbringing you continue to visit Chawri Bazaar, rather than spending your time on studies and the worship of Allah and his prophet. How can you be so naïve as to believe that a girl like Yasmeen who sits in the bazaar has fallen in love with you? She must be making protestations of this kind to scores of men she meets every evening. Why don't you just stop going to such places and instead do things that will bring honour to your family,' counselled Ghulam Rasool.

'Mian, I am merely suggesting you have a look at one of God's loveliest creations and see how well she has learnt to sing and dance from her teachers. Please tell me why you think it is not possible for a girl from the bazaar to have the character of someone from a respectable background—simply because it was

Saad Ashraf

her fate to have been born or brought there, like it is my fate to be an imam's son who likes visiting the red-light area?' countered Ahmad.

Ghulam Rasool could see that it was pointless arguing with Ahmad. He simply did not take life seriously and would always find reasons to justify his visits to the bazaar and extol the virtues of fallen women.

In the meantime, while Ghulam Rasool awaited the announcement of the results of the bachelor's examination, Principal Thompson had offered him a short-term job for which he was paid hundred rupees every month. He was to work in the library, catalogue books and receive and issue them to those who came there during the long break. This kept him busy from nine in the morning to four in the afternoon, and he reached home an hour later on an old bicycle which Principal Thompson had contemplated consigning to the junkyard, but which he presented to Ghulam Rasool instead.

Ahmad, who had appeared for the fourth time in the intermediate examination that year, too anxiously awaited the results for more than one reason. His father, the imam, had told him that if he failed this time he would have to say goodbye to college and join the family profession by calling the faithful to prayers five times a day from the northern minaret of the Royal Mosque.

Eventually, the results were announced and Ghulam Rasool passed in the second division—the only one from Missionary College to get this grade. Principal Thompson was satisfied but would have been happier if Ghulam Rasool had done better. The residents of White Haveli, young and old, Hindu and Muslim, got together to fete Ghulam Rasool. He was profusely garlanded by the neighbours till only his eyes showed above the mound of wet, golden and dark marigold flowers, then mounted on a white charger and taken around the streets of Old Delhi and shown off as their proud possession.

Ahmad's result followed a week later. As was expected, his name appeared nowhere in the gazette and anxious enquiries made from the board which conducted the examination confirmed that there was no mistake. Ahmad was unnerved for the first time in his life and his devil-may-care attitude deserted him. It seemed to him that he was standing on the edge of a precipice with no way out from what now seemed his fate— becoming the muezzin of one of the largest mosques in northern India, beckoning the faithful to prayers from its towering minarets.

A few days after the results were announced, the imam, a bearded, fair-complexioned man of stocky build, called Ahmad to his quarters in the mosque and asked him when he could be expected to join the family vocation. Ahmad pleaded for a month's respite to settle his affairs at the college. The imam said, 'A month you have asked for and a month you will get and no more. You will take over the duties of a muezzin from the fifteenth of September on the northern minaret, starting with the morning prayers at five a.m. I am sure that you will do better than your forefathers with the benefit of an education that they did not have.'

On a hot August evening of 1916, when the sun had set but the stone and mortar of the old buildings of Delhi were still shedding their heat into the narrow streets, there was a knock at Ghulam Rasool's door. He wondered who it could be at this hour. He opened the door to find Ahmad in all his finery but without his usual smile.

'Ahmad! What a surprise! Is everything all right? Come in, come in, and have a glass of rose sherbet.'

'This is no time to come in. I have to talk to you and take you somewhere.'

'Well, what is the urgency that you don't even have the time for a glass of the rose sherbet made by Ammi,' said Ghulam Rasool, with mock disappointment. 'By the way, where have you been all this time, eh?'

'Mian, I want you to do me a favour. Please don't ask any questions and follow me.'

'Follow you to hell without asking any questions? I am sorry but that's not my style,' Ghulam Rasool said curtly.

Saad Ashraf

'Mian, do you remember that some years ago when both you and I had time on our hands, one day in the heat of July we went to the banks of the river with a basket of mangoes and you said that I could test your friendship in times of need. Well, that time has come now,' implored Ahmad.

'I don't remember having made any such promise but in any case I am available as a friend for anything which is not immoral.'

'You have to promise me, Mian, that whatever happens this evening goes with you to the grave as a lifelong secret between two good friends.'

'I promise.'

'Then follow me,' said Ahmad, starting off on a brisk trot, with Ghulam Rasool close on his heels.

After meandering through the alleys of the old quarters behind his friend, Ghulam Rasool found himself in the heart of Chawri Bazaar, climbing a wooden stairway. It was early evening and business in the red-light area had still not commenced though one could hear the unexpected beat of a tabla or the wail of a musical instrument being tuned. Now and then these sounds intermingled with the sudden jingle of bells that a dancing girl tried on her feet or the voice of a singing girl trying the latest raga.

Ahmad knocked at a door and both friends were let into a hall where the daily performance took place. They seated themselves comfortably on the floor, reclining against large white pillows.

'I thought we weren't going to do anything immoral,' said Ghulam Rasool, as an old woman appeared with betel leaves covered with slivers of beaten silver paper.

'Mian, I would imagine you know me better than that. I promised you that nothing will happen which you could call immoral. I will keep my promise, but don't forget yours,' said Ahmad.

A little later, a teenaged girl emerged from a door facing them. With large eyes set in an oval face, and well-chiselled features, she looked strikingly beautiful. She was wearing a black dress with embroidered flowers of silver and gold, matching tight churidar and a white veil over her head.

As she advanced towards them with a proud lilting gait seeped in the consciousness of her beauty, Ghulam Rasool gaped at her, dumbfounded. He was about to ask who she was when Ahmad interrupted him.

'This is Yasmeen, my friend, the one I talked to you about. Remember?'

There was a short introduction by Ahmad and an exchange of pleasantries. Yasmeen's voice had a husky timbre which admirably rounded off her personality. Ghulam Rasool recalled that when Ahmad had first mentioned Yasmeen, his remarks about her hadn't been complimentary. He regretted what he had said, yet Yasmeen was undeniably a woman of the bazaar, created and trained to win men's hearts and empty their pockets.

A little later Ahmad signalled that it was time to leave. Out in the street and on the way to Ghulam Rasool's house, an uneasy quiet prevailed between the two.

'Mian, Yasmeen is the girl I hope to marry some day. You have to promise that you will take care of her in case something ever happened to me,' said Ahmad.

Ghulam Rasool hardly took notice of what Ahmad had said. He was sure that Yasmeen would always find someone to take care of her in the bazaar from which she earned her livelihood. She would always have a long line of admirers, including Ahmad, looking after her … so how would the need for Ghulam Rasool to do that ever arise. Ghulam Rasool was immersed in his thoughts when he heard Ahmad again.

'I am waiting for your promise, Mian.'

'I promise,' Ghulam Rasool replied casually.

Ahmad embraced his friend and, before Ghulam Rasool could pull himself together, disappeared from view down one of the numerous streets of Old Delhi.

Late in the afternoon the next day, Mohammed, a cleaning boy employed at the Royal Mosque came to Ghulam Rasool with a message from Ahmad's father. The imam wanted to see him immediately and suggested that he should come back with

Mohammed. Ghulam Rasool was apprehensive about what could have compelled the imam to summon him in so urgent a manner.

Ghulam Rasool met the imam in the main prayer hall of the mosque. The imam came to the point straightaway in an affectionate, fatherly manner.

'Beta, I am sorry to inform you that Ahmad is missing since last evening. We are all worried about his safety. I believe he came to see you yesterday. Did he say anything to you about leaving home when he met you? He is our only son ... his mother and sisters have been crying ever since we came to know that he is missing,' said the imam.

The news of his friend's disappearance shocked Ghulam Rasool. He also felt deeply anguished when he saw the imam's eyes glistening with tears. He realized that he had to think fast to tell the truth without compromising on the promise that he had made to Ahmad.

'Chachaji, I know Ahmad—he is my best friend. I do not think he would leave without letting somebody know where he was going. He did appear to be in some kind of a hurry yesterday but never said a word about leaving Delhi. I'll join you in your search and try to locate him and pass on any information that I may get to you,' said Ghulam Rasool.

Just then a servant appeared with an envelope. The imam hurriedly opened it and took out a letter which he began reading with extreme attention. Ghulam Rasool heard him sigh a couple of times as he read. He held out the paper for Ghulam Rasool to read. The letter was in Ahmad's writing:

Meerut Railway Station
Meerut
24 August 1916

Abbajan,
I am writing this letter on the way to my destination. I am sorry I left home in the manner I did, but there was no other way. I ask you, Ammi, the whole family, and my friends to forgive me for the worry and pain that my departure may have caused. I

am writing at the first available opportunity as the train stops here for thirty minutes. Please be reassured that I am safe, in good health, and have funds available with me for the time being.

The main reason for my leaving home was that I know I am too much of a sinner to be a muezzin at the Royal Mosque. I want to strike out on my own and make something of myself, after which I hope to return home to serve both of you dutifully for the rest of my life.

I promise that I will write regularly so that you are spared further pain and anguish. Believe me that I am,

Your most loving and devoted son,
Ahmad

'Chachaji, at least we know that Ahmad is safe which is good news.' Ghulam Rasool handed back the letter to the imam.

'I thank Allah for that but why must children be a source of pain to their parents when they are old. Ahmad could have remained here and made all of us happy but no, he had to leave home because he had already sinned too much. Everyone sins from the time one is born till the time one dies. That is why we have the houses of Allah for atonement. What sins could he have committed that couldn't be atoned? If only he had talked to me before leaving, we could have worked out something. When he comes back on completing his mission, his mother or I may not be around—who will he serve then?' the imam said ruefully.

Ghulam Rasool closed his eyes for a moment and envisioned Ahmad sitting in the train compartment, looking through its window at the sinking sun with its crimson halo over the horizon, headed for an unknown destination. The muezzin was already calling the faithful for the evening prayers from the northern minaret of the Royal Mosque where Ahmad was to take up duties from next month.

'I have to go and lead the congregation,' said the imam, shaking Ghulam Rasool's hand in a gesture of gratitude. 'Thank you for coming and I hope you will continue meeting me, Beta. If you hear anything about Ahmad please get in touch with me immediately.'

Saad Ashraf

Ghulam Rasool left the mosque, sombre, unsure of people, the best and closest of friends, and the motives which made them act impetuously. Who could have thought that Ahmad, who had visited Yasmeen in Chawri Bazaar with him only yesterday, would forsake his family and friends today and be where nobody could reach him?

During the succeeding weeks, Ghulam Rasool kept in touch with the imam and learnt that Ahmad was writing regularly. He never disclosed what he was doing or where he was but each letter said that he was in good health and engaged in completing his unknown mission. From the postmarks on the envelope, the imam learnt that he was in Madras but all his efforts to trace him, despite his connections, ended in failure. There were people who met the imam and said that they had sighted Ahmad in different cities and one informant even claimed that he had seen him near the Qutub Minar in Delhi a few days ago. The imam investigated each lead but to no avail. He enlisted the help of Mr Robertson, chief superintendent of the Criminal Investigation Department (CID) in Delhi, who wrote to his colleagues in Madras and Bangalore but without any success. Ahmad seemed to have vanished among the teeming masses of India, yet he was alive—an assurance given by the letters which the imam received with unfailing regularity. Ahmad's absence was like a festering wound for his family. Every letter they received brought hope and happiness but the interval that followed made the pain and anguish more intense. Ghulam Rasool could do nothing more than pray for Ahmad's safety and well-being every day after his daily prayers.

twelve

Noorani Begum was certain that Ghulam Rasool would be content to end his studies after having acquired the bachelor's degree and seek a job and start supporting the family on a full-time basis. The incessant struggle for survival for over a decade and a half had taken its toll on her. She had physically shrivelled and wanted some rest for her weary bones. She knew of only one or two families in Delhi whose sons had become graduates, and all of them were holding well-paid jobs. With a degree from the prestigious Missionary College, her son could also find something similar, maybe as a railway clerk, which would secure the family's future. Ghulam Rasool too had been in touch with Principal Thompson about the matter.

'Sir, I am seriously thinking of applying for a government job and would like to obtain your support in this regard,' Ghulam Rasool said to the principal one Thursday afternoon.

'Ghulam Rasool, you are aware that with a BA degree you will at the most be able to get the job of a clerk in some government office. That would be a sheer waste of your education. Why don't you apply for admission to the college in Aligarh or the Allahabad University which offer master's courses and thereafter get into government service as an officer?'

'Sir, you probably know of my circumstances. I have to start supporting my family. I cannot afford education outside Delhi for two more years.'

Principal Thompson started adjusting his half-moon glasses and looked thoughtfully towards the ceiling as if seeking the help of providence for a very complicated problem.

'Well, we'll have to do something about that, won't we? Why don't you come and see me the day after tomorrow in the morning before ten. I'll see whether something can be done,' he said.

Ghulam Rasool called on the principal promptly on the appointed day and time.

'Ghulam Rasool, I've given serious thought to our conversation two days ago. I don't want to tell you how but I will arrange that we somehow meet your tuition and hostel expenses at either Aligarh or Allahabad—wherever you are able to get admission for a master's course. But you'll have to give me your acceptance within the next two days, so that I can firm up the arrangements. As far as taking care of your family in Delhi, you will have to find the ways and means of doing that yourself,' said Principal Thompson.

'Thank you, sir! I don't know how to thank you, sir,' Ghulam Rasool muttered excitedly.

After the day's work at the library ended, Ghulam Rasool pedalled his cycle as fast as he could to get home and break the news to Noorani Begum. He parked the cycle in the alcove below the stairway in the house, rushed upstairs, and knocked loudly at the door.

'Ammi! Ammi, open up! Open up, it's me, Ghulam Rasool.'

Noorani Begum, who was preparing the evening's meal, left the pot of lentils on the fireplace and rushed to the door, alarmed at the urgency in her son's voice.

'What has come upon you? Is anything wrong, Beta?' asked Noorani Begum.

'Nothing is wrong, Ammi. There's only good news.'

'What good news? Have you managed to find a job as a railway clerk without putting in an application?'

'No, but I've got something better. Principal Thompson has agreed to bear all my educational expenses at a university for two years for an MA degree. I have to give him an answer in two days.' Ghulam Rasool was breathless with excitement.

But Noorani Begum did not quite share his enthusiasm. To her it appeared that her son was veering off the path she had laid out for him and her family's survival.

'And who may I ask will support and protect your mother and sisters while you are achieving academic laurels at a university?' Noorani Begum asked coldly.

'Ammi, Principal Thompson says that if I do my MA I will be able to get a government job as an officer, which is much better than joining as a clerk. As an officer I would be the boss of all clerks and would exercise real power. It is just a question of somehow finding the money to carry on for the next two years.'

'Is an officer higher than a superintendent?'

'Ammi, the lowliest officer is the boss of the superintendent.'

Noorani Begum was impressed. There had never been a government officer in her family, and her husband had reached the position of superintendent after slogging at work for nearly two decades. Undergoing hardships for another two years seemed worthwhile for the sake of long-term security for herself and the family, apart from the undeniable prestige that would accrue once her son made it as an officer. She would be restored to a position much higher in the eyes of society than she enjoyed when her husband died. Though antagonistic a moment ago to Ghulam Rasool's idea of studying further, Noorani Begum was now enamoured by the thought of her son going to a university and thereafter becoming a government officer. The only hurdle was the lack of money. Only last week when she had dipped her hand into the jar in which she kept all the money she had received on her husband's death, she found that she could touch its bottom. She had taken out all the coins and had found that she was left with a paltry sum. Unless there was a way of replenishing the jar with some more money, she was going to face hard times again and would have to resort to borrowing from the neighbourhood and raising credit from the shopkeepers. She

Saad Ashraf

needed at least two thousand rupees to get through the next two years while Ghulam Rasool studied for the master's degree.

'I'll pray to Allah to guide me as to how I can find the money. If I am successful, you will go to do your MA. If I can't, you will have to look for a job and support us. In the meantime, you tell your Professor Thompson that you accept his offer provisionally,' said Noorani Begum, picking up her prayer rug and setting it out on the floor.

Ghulam Rasool felt greatly relieved and made a secret pact with himself never to let his mother down as long as he lived.

The next day, Jahan Ara Begum, the wife of Noorani Begum's tenant Nawab Aziz Rehman, came to see her at about ten in the morning, just after Aziz Rehman left for his office.

'Noorani Begum, Allah has given me everything—fair skin, good features, a nice figure, and the culture of Lucknow—but deprived me of a large bust. Nawab sahib says it is his bad luck because that is the one thing he badly wanted in his wife. He has often said to me that he is prepared to sell all his ornamental furniture and his collection of handwritten books and spend the money he gets to find something, anything which would increase its size. I've heard of a new miracle cream manufactured in Bombay by the Pure Medicine Company which when massaged every night for three months is guaranteed to do that. The manufacturers are so sure of their product that they guarantee a refund of the entire cost of fifty rupees if it does not work. Do you think I should order this cream?' Jahan Ara Begum asked expectantly.

'Jahan Ara Begum, I cannot say anything about this cream but all kinds of frauds are being committed these days to make money. I don't think anything can change one's natural endowments. Instead of spending your money on miracle creams, why don't you pray to Allah to give you and your husband contentment with what you've got?'

Noorani Begum's reply did not satisfy Jahan Ara, who felt that it did not quite answer her query.

'By the way, Jahan Ara Begum,' continued Noorani Begum, 'how do you manage to carry on in these expensive times on the nawab sahib's salary? Add to that the money you spend in taking care of your body.'

'Ah behen, all this is the gift of Gittu Mal, the Hindu bania—may he live a thousand years. I must have told you that I inherited a small house in Delhi from my mother which didn't fetch such a good rent. The nawab sahib met Gittu Mal somewhere and mortgaged my house with him for a couple of thousand rupees. We pay back the mortgage over the next ten years with a nominal amount every month. If we want our house back earlier we have to pay double the amount we have taken. It is a good arrangement for us to meet our expenses,' Jahan Ara Begum explained in her soft Lucknavi accent.

'Can you tell me when and how I can meet Gittu Mal?' asked Noorani Begum.

'I hope everything is all right. I mean, you don't have any problems of the body that I have,' said Jahan Ara Begum, looking enviously at Noorani Begum's ample bust line.

'No, no, it is a minor problem, nothing much to talk about.'

'I will talk this over with the nawab sahib tonight and let you know how we can put you in touch with Gittu Mal. By the way, you didn't tell me whether I should or should not order the cream.'

'Jahan Ara Begum, tonight I will sleep after saying some special prayers taking your name. I've seen that whenever I have a problem, Allah gives me a hint in my dreams as to what I should do. So I'll let you know tomorrow morning of the directions that I receive.'

The next morning, Noorani Begum called Jahan Ara Begum to come to her window which overlooked her courtyard and shouted out the interpretation of what she had dreamt the previous night. She advised Jahan Ara Begum not to waste her money in ordering the cream from Bombay. In return, Jahan Ara Begum told her that Aziz Rehman was making all necessary arrangements for Gittu Mal to come to her that very afternoon.

Saad Ashraf

The bania called on Noorani Begum at the appointed hour, and by the time they had finished talking, she had mortgaged her house in White Haveli to Gittu Mal for two thousand rupees in silver coins. These were delivered to her an hour later and she carefully counted and placed them in the jar in the attic. A fortnight later, Ghulam Rasool took admission to the MA classes and boarded the evening train to Aligarh.

thirteen

Ghulam Rasool was fascinated by Aligarh College—its gabled buildings of red brick, the sprawling lawns, and the spirit of the Muslim elite that came to study here. The foundation of the college had been laid by the great Sir Syed Ahmad Khan some three decades ago to resurrect the Anglo-Muslim relationship which had deteriorated after the events of 1857. The hostel accommodation was good. Though Ghulam Rasool would have preferred doing his master's in a subject other than Arabic, it became inconsequential, fulfilling as it did the basic requirement for becoming a government officer. Besides, Delhi was not far away and he could go and spend every alternate weekend with his family.

While Ghulam Rasool was still trying to become proficient at spoken and written Arabic, three months after he had joined the college in Aligarh, he received a letter redirected from the White Haveli in Delhi. It was from Ahmad, written from the Prince of Wales Docks, Bombay, on 16 October 1916. He mentioned sailing on a troopship for war-torn Europe and asked to be forgiven for the haste in which he had to leave without saying a proper goodbye. He wrote about the meaning of love and how it overpowered one's self and made everything else in life insignificant. He said that he had thought about the contradictions in his life and had realized that he had to choose one of the two paths—the path of piety or of love. He had decided to choose the latter. He mentioned enlisting in the British Indian army as a common soldier to fight in Europe and reminded

Ghulam Rasool about the promise the latter had made with respect to Yasmeen if something happened to him and till such time that he returned.

Ghulam Rasool could not quite believe what he read. He could not imagine the suave, polite, English-speaking Ahmad, the pampered son of one of the most respectable families of Delhi, rubbing shoulders with illiterate men, most of whom, it was reported, joined the army to escape grinding poverty or the strong arm of the law. Ghulam Rasool had heard of some deposed European princes enlisting as soldiers in the armies fighting in the war, but this was the first time he had known of somebody from the Indian elite enlisting as an ordinary soldier. He did the only thing he could. He closed his eyes, prayed for his friend's well-being and safety, wiped his misty eyes, and departed for the college to attend a lecture. He decided that on his next visit to Delhi, he would go and see the imam. He wondered whether the imam knew that Ahmad had joined the army and had left for Europe. He also decided to visit Yasmeen to enquire about her welfare in fulfilment of the promise he had made to Ahmad.

During the next weekend, when Ghulam Rasool was in Delhi, he went to meet the imam on Saturday morning. The imam met him in his private quarters which were located on one side of the mosque's courtyard. He learnt from the imam that Ahmad had also written to him from Bombay about his joining the army and his impending departure for Europe.

'Ahmad's departure has affected our family and things have become worse ever since we learnt that he has left to fight in the war in Europe. His mother's eyesight has started failing and she cries when she misses her only son whom she may never see again,' said the imam, more than a trace of despair discernible in his voice. Ghulam Rasool noticed that the imam was walking with a visible stoop which was not there the last time he had met him.

Ghulam Rasool was perplexed by the ways of Allah. He wondered what sins a pious, noble, and well-intentioned man like the imam had committed to have to undergo a trial of this kind. The imam spent all his waking life in prayers or in leading congregations of Muslims in the mosque, so why did he and his family have to suffer the torment of seeing their only son leave home and go off to war. A family which had known only happiness till a year ago had been reduced to a state of helpless tears and anguish. Why did such things happen to good people? The more Ghulam Rasool questioned himself about the suffering that life imposed on Allah's beings in this world, the more difficult it became for him to rationalize on the causes of such suffering. Ghulam Rasool had no answer to his own questions.

Later that day, he visited Yasmeen at Chawri Bazaar. He walked briskly up the creaky wooden stairway and knocked at her door. The wrinkled, toothless face of an old woman peered out of the door.

'Who are you and what do you want at this time?' she asked.

'I am Ghulam Rasool, friend of Syed Ahmad, the son of the imam, and I have come to see Yasmeen Begum.'

After what seemed an endless wait, the same face peered out again. 'Come in,' the old woman said, opening the door and letting him in.

Ghulam Rasool found himself in familiar surroundings where he had once come accompanied by Ahmad. He was comfortably seated on the floor when he heard the soft rustle of bare feet and a few moments later found himself face to face with the overpowering beauty of Yasmeen. The faint smell of sandal emanated from her body. After an exchange of pleasantries, Ghulam Rasool came to the point.

'Yasmeen Begum, I came here specifically on the directions of my friend Ahmad to enquire about your welfare and to ask whether there's anything you need or anything I can do for you. I will give you my address in Aligarh where you can write to me,' said Ghulam Rasool, looking down shyly towards the floor.

'Bhaijaan, I don't need anything except news of Ahmad. He wrote to me from Bombay before departing for the war in Europe. I think about him all the time. The mistress of this house, Farida Begum, is my real aunt, so there is no risk of a letter not reaching

Saad Ashraf

me. She knows about my relationship with Ahmad. Not all the women of this bazaar are insensitive, though most people think that we sell our bodies and even our souls for money. But believe me, it is not like that. Some of us have feelings like any other woman outside this bazaar,' said Yasmeen.

Yasmeen did sound truthful and sincere. Ghulam Rasool had heard of stray cases of women in the bazaar sacrificing all for the men they loved, though he secretly hoped that the relationship between Ahmad and Yasmeen would end as soon as possible to avoid future complications and that Ahmad would return home safely and be reconciled with his family.

Ghulam Rasool wrote out his address on a small piece of paper and gave it to Yasmeen. Bidding her goodbye, he came down the stairway, unlocked his cycle, and pedalled his way to White Haveli to spend the rest of the day with his mother and sisters. He enquired about their well-being and about how they were coping in his absence.

'Everything is fine, Beta, although I have to struggle to keep this house going. I am waiting for the day when you become an officer and I get a few days of leisure and rest,' said Noorani Begum, a weary look in her eyes.

'I just have one more year to go before I complete my master's, Ammi. I am sure our days will turn for the better once I get a job. Once that happens I assure you that you will feel your struggle has not been in vain. The end of the road is in sight. If I have to I'll remain a lifelong bachelor and devote my life to looking after my family,' said Ghulam Rasool.

A few hours later, he boarded the passenger train from Delhi railway station for Aligarh. He had the satisfaction of meeting his family and being able to visit the imam and Yasmeen but the thought of his friend Ahmad kept bothering him throughout the journey.

By 1917, the Great War had entered its third year. Ever since it started, Indian newspapers had been full of unheard-of places with unpronounceable names in Europe where ferocious battles were fought with great losses of human life. For Ghulam Rasool, this was his last year at Aligarh and he was too involved in reading the original text of Ibn Khaldun in Arabic and becoming proficient in the Arabic language to let the war get on his mind. His personal involvement in the conflict in Europe was only to the extent of worrying for the safety of his friend Ahmad. He continued to receive occasional letters from Ahmad, in one of which Ahmad had written about his involvement in the Battle of the Ridge a month after he had landed in Europe. He wrote of how he had been ordered by his commander, a British major named Smith, to reconnoitre the enemy position by leading a party of half-a-dozen Indian soldiers in the pitch dark of the cold European night. He had been chosen as he could speak and understand English. Ahmad wrote of the fear and loneliness he had experienced while leading his men, and of the futility of war and his revulsion to the killing of human beings. He had returned to his trench with his men and found Major Smith badly wounded and groaning with pain. In his absence, their position had been overrun by the enemy. With screaming shells bursting around him and his own compatriots being killed, Ahmad had lifted his wounded commander on his shoulders and walked back three hundred yards. He had been lucky to fall in a trench still occupied by the Allies, thus saving his officer's life. He had done what he considered his duty. His superiors thought that he had shown exceptional bravery. He was decorated for this action and his photograph appeared in European and British newspapers. Unmindful of this honour and glory, Ahmad wrote of how he longed to be back in the warmth and sunshine of India and how he considered anyone who lived in his country and away from the cruelty of war to be truly fortunate. All his letters ended with the request that Ghulam Rasool should visit Yasmeen and tell her that if he survived the war, and the European cold, it would only be because he was madly in love with her and dreamt of marrying her as soon as he returned to India.

Ghulam Rasool copied portions of the letters he received from Ahmad and dutifully sent them off to Yasmeen in Delhi.

Saad Ashraf

Whenever he was in Delhi, he went to see Yasmeen in Chawri Bazaar, wary of being observed by anyone who might recognize him. It comforted him to see that Yasmeen was well and happy though fretful about Ahmad's safety. Ghulam Rasool conveyed her well-being to Ahmad in his letters and passed news about Ahmad to the imam who seemed to have gradually reconciled himself to his son's absence. His strong belief in religion and the inevitability of fate, coupled with the balming effects of time, seemed to have eased the pain of Ahmad's absence.

Ghulam Rasool appeared in the MA examinations in Arabic held in 1918. After the examinations were over, he made a farewell call on his professors, thereafter returning to his hostel room to pack his bags to take the afternoon train for the final trip to Delhi where he awaited the outcome.

When the results were announced in September that year, it transpired that Ghulam Rasool was the only candidate in his class who obtained a first-class in the examinations. He was happy that his academic career had ended on such a successful note. His delight was shared by Noorani Begum who felt that her long struggle had paid off. Now that Ghulam Rasool had completed his education she believed that he would shoulder the responsibilities of supporting the family financially and relieve her of a burden she had borne ever since she could remember. She could now afford to take things easy, relax and be the proud mother of an officer in the service of British India.

fourteen

An interlude of several weeks followed in which Ghulam Rasool basked in the praises that everybody showered on him. All of a sudden, Delhi seemed to have found a new celebrity that it could talk about—Ghulam Rasool, the poor, self-educated boy who had braved all odds to become a success. Women who made a living by arranging matches between girls with large dowries and young men with promise started eyeing Ghulam Rasool as a potential candidate. Noorani Begum had become so proud of her son's success that she made it a point to introduce him to such females with the words, 'Meet my celebrated son, Ghulam Rasool, MA pass.'

After a few months, Noorani Begum realized that her kingpin was getting used to lounging around, waiting for the next visitor to arrive and pay homage to him. He had become lazy, put on weight, and had started waking up late in the mornings, unmindful of the need to secure a source of livelihood. Noorani Begum had a more important reason to worry about Ghulam Rasool's complacency. The jar in which she had put the two thousand rupees she received from Gittu Mal two years ago had once more emptied.

One morning, when Ghulam Rasool was just getting out of bed well past nine in the morning, he found himself confronted by Noorani Begum.

'Beta, I think that the celebrations of your success must come to an end and you should start looking for a job. The day that you become a government officer would be the real day of jubilation for our family, especially for me. My tired bones are aching for a hard-earned rest,' said Noorani Begum.

'Ammi, I will start looking for a job next week, by which time the rush of the visitors coming to congratulate me will hopefully dwindle.'

'You will do no such thing! These visitors come and go. They also came when your father died seventeen years ago and would have kept coming had I not said that they had shared enough of my grief and that I wanted to attend to the more serious business of rearing my family and finding ways of keeping the kitchen going. The money we took from Gittu Mal two years ago is about to finish. I am afraid that we cannot go on any longer unless you start earning as soon as possible.'

Noorani Begum's words had a lightning effect on Ghulam Rasool who realized that time was indeed running out and that he would have to put in special efforts in finding a job if his family was to survive. That night he slept very little as he tossed and turned and made plans on how he should find a job. He decided to call on Professor Thompson, his mentor at Missionary College, and seek his help.

Early next morning, as if possessed, he was on his way to Missionary College to see the professor. Ghulam Rasool was acting on the advice given by the professor himself in an address delivered to the young graduates of his college some years ago. He had said that the best time for anyone to get favourable results from those who occupied a powerful chair was either early in the morning when that individual was fresh or half an hour before closure when the individual was exhausted.

'Well, thank you for coming to see me and congratulations on being the only one to get a first division in MA. As an old boy of this institution, you've brought honour to Missionary College by your performance,' said Professor Thompson, greeting Ghulam Rasool effusively.

'Sir, all this is because of the grounding I got from this college and because of the personal interest you took in giving me the financial support without which it would not have been possible for me to join the college in Aligarh. You have been like a father. There's no way I can convey my gratitude,' said Ghulam Rasool, his eyes welling with tears.

'Tut tut, my boy, I did my part and you did yours and let's allow the matter to rest there. What do you plan to do now?'

Ghulam Rasool was relieved that the professor had brought up the subject himself. 'Sir, I came to seek your support and advice in getting a job for the time being till I can take the next step of appearing in the ICS examination, which I believe is going to be held in India from now on,' he said.

'I think this is a good idea, though the final decision to hold the ICS examination in India has still not been made. In the meantime, I could talk to other members of the Missionary College's Trust and if they agree we could use you as a junior lecturer in Arabic on temporary basis. The pay won't be all that much but you would have access to the college library which is essential for preparing for the ICS examination.'

Once again, Principal Thompson's benevolent approach and Ghulam Rasool's string of lucky breaks had come to the rescue. He thanked the professor profusely and headed back for White Haveli to break the good news to Noorani Begum.

It took another month before Ghulam Rasool received a letter setting out the terms and conditions of his appointment as a temporary junior lecturer in Arabic. He was to work directly with Professor Ahad, the head of the Arabic department at Missionary College. He was to receive a salary of one hundred and twenty-five rupees a month, and his services were terminable without notice. Though this was not much of a salary for somebody with a master's degree, he was happy that he would be contributing towards the sustenance of his family and relieve Noorani Begum of financial stress.

A year later, one morning, just as Ghulam Rasool returned after delivering a lecture to the dozen students who had chosen Arabic for their bachelor's, Ghulam Rasool found a note on his small table in the office that he shared with Professor Ahad. Principal

Saad Ashraf

Thompson wanted to meet him immediately, it said. Ghulam Rasool's first reaction was to try and recollect any misdemeanour he might have committed in the past weeks which might have resulted in the urgent summons. Professor Ahad was quite happy with his work and treated him with extreme kindness, showering praises on him in front of Principal Thompson. His students respected him. Ever since he had been engaged by the college, they had shown considerable improvement both in written and spoken Arabic. He had had no interaction lately with any other staff member which could be the cause of complaint. All kinds of thoughts raced through his mind. Maybe the principal had decided to dispense with his services, a right he could exercise at any time. Ghulam Rasool unloaded the pile of the books he was carrying in his arms on the table and rushed to see the principal.

'Ah, Ghulam Rasool, nice of you to come. Please have a seat. It'll take me just a few minutes to get rid of this file,' said Principal Thompson, motioning Ghulam Rasool to the middle of the three chairs in front of him. After having finished working on the file, he turned to Ghulam Rasool.

'Well, Rasool there is some good news for you. The Missionary College Trust has awarded you an honorarium of two thousand rupees because of your hard work and dedication. All the five candidates who appeared in the BA examination in Arabic from our college in the last session have passed in the first division. The Trust has also confirmed you as a junior lecturer which means that you receive an increment of twenty-five rupees a month. You will receive a formal letter tomorrow.'

It took Ghulam Rasool a few moments to recover from the unexpected nature of the munificence.

'Sir, thank you. Thank you very much. Beg your pardon, sir ... did you say two thousand rupees? I don't think I have done anything to deserve this award. I was merely doing my duty,' said Ghulam Rasool, trying not to show his delight.

When Ghulam Rasool left the principal's office, he felt on top of the world. He wanted to jump with joy and shout at the top of his voice at every passer-by: 'I am Ghulam Rasool, son of

Ghulam Nabi, on whom fortune always smiles!' He felt blessed—only divine intervention could account for the fact that the honorarium amounted to exactly what his family owed Gittu Mal. He left his cycle in the college and hailed an exclusive tumtum to take him back home in style so that he could break the news to Noorani Begum and his family. He rushed up the stairs and knocked hard on the door twice with the chain installed on it. It was Noorani Begum who opened the door.

'Hai, hai, what's happened to my son!' exclaimed Noorani Begum, observing his excited condition.

'Ammi, this is a strange welcome for a son who brings good news for you and the family.'

'What good news? Have you been appointed the lieutenant governor of Delhi? Tell me, what is the good news? Tell me,' begged Noorani Begum excitedly.

'Ammi, the college has given me a special award of two thousand rupees for my work. This amount can knock off Gittu Mal's loan. The other news is that I have been made permanent in my job which means an additional twenty-five rupees per month plus chances of promotion.' The pride and joy in his voice were barely suppressed.

'What is it that you have done for the college for them to give you such a large sum of money?'

Ghulam Rasool had no answer to this question. He thought deeply and realized that he could not pinpoint the reasons for this award as he was just performing his duties as best as he could.

'Well, I am waiting for an answer,' said Noorani Begum.

'I myself don't know exactly, Ammi. Principal Thompson simply called me to his office and told me,' he replied, with a sheepish grin.

A couple of weeks later, Noorani Begum called Gittu Mal to her house in White Haveli and, with Nawab Aziz Rehman and Jahan Ara Begum as witnesses, paid back the two thousand rupees she had borrowed from him. She also took back all the papers of her house and had Gittu Mal sign an undertaking that

Saad Ashraf

nothing more was due from her on account of the loan. Noorani Begum knew that she had obtained a respite from financial worries. She had become so used to financial stress that she could not visualize an existence free of it. She felt like a caged bird who on being given its freedom had forgotten to fly. She was happy that her gamble, faith, and investment in Ghulam Rasool were paying off.

fifteen

Meanwhile, the Great War raged with all its ferocity in Europe. Ahmad would write about how his regiment had been pulled back for rest and recuperation, and the imam and Ghulam Rasool would receive several letters within a short time. This happy interlude would be followed by several weeks of silence when the regiment would be moved to the front to resume fighting.

In early November 1917, the imam received the distressing news from the War Office in London that Ahmad had taken part in the Battle of Ypres on the Western Front and had been reported 'missing in action'. In India, this was taken to mean 'killed in action' subject to confirmation. A large number of people who knew the imam converged on him before and after the five congregations at the mosque, and offered their sympathies for his missing son. Most said the Muslim prayer to bless his soul, raising their hands skywards and closing their eyes while a few offered hopes that Ahmad might still be alive. The imam seemed an exceptionally determined man and grief rarely showed on his face. He continued leading the prayers and listened to the long monologues on the virtues of his missing son, by people he had neither seen nor met before and who he was sure were Ahmad's passing acquaintances.

Ghulam Rasool went to see the imam when he heard the news.

'Chachaji, I am sure Ahmad is alive and will be found within a few days. He is too young and has too much to live for to leave this world so early,' said Ghulam Rasool.

'I know you are Ahmad's true friend, Beta. I pray for Ahmad's well-being in this world and the hereafter after the five prayers, as well as after midnight when silence reigns and man is closest to Allah. However, something inside tells me that all is not well. A parent's intuition is never wrong,' remarked the imam.

'Though I am much younger, Chachaji, and much less experienced, I have a feeling that everything will turn out well in the end.'

The imam sighed. 'I am a sinner and Allah has not answered my prayers for Ahmad's safe return but maybe Allah will listen to you if you pray for your friend.'

Ghulam Rasool promised to do so and took his leave. Disturbed as he was by this news, he felt that Yasmeen was one person who should know that Ahmad was missing in action. Ghulam Rasool had called on her twice in the last three years. On these occasions, he had reiterated that he was at her disposal for anything that she may need, but she had never asked him for anything other than news of Ahmad.

He visited her one afternoon having taken off early from his teaching.

'Bhaijaan, I hope everything is all right with Ahmad,' Yasmeen said in her husky voice. 'I've been dreaming of him for the last ten days or so. I have got an amulet from the fakir baba who sits under the evergreen tree behind the Royal Mosque. It will keep Ahmad safe from danger.'

She dipped her hand into her bosom, and opened her palm in front of Ghulam Rasool to reveal a small green sac containing the amulet which was attached to a cotton thread hung around her neck.

Ghulam Rasool's head hung low over his chest as he said, 'I am afraid that something is wrong. Ahmad is missing in war, and they are trying to find him.'

Yasmeen was visibly upset as tears filled her eyes and worry contorted her face.

'This will save him yet, you will see,' she said, clutching the amulet tightly in her hands.

An uncomfortable silence ensued.

'Nobody knows if he is alive … it may take a few weeks before we come to know what has happened. Only prayers can help Ahmad. I will let you know if I learn anything more,' said Ghulam Rasool, getting up to leave.

Ghulam Rasool left the room in whose silence only the muffled sobs of Yasmeen could be heard.

Despite extensive correspondence by the imam with the War Office in London on the fate of his son, it took some months for that office to confirm that Ahmad had been injured in action and taken prisoner by the Germans. He was advised that he could write to his son, Care of the War Office, Prisoner of War (POW) Section, London, without affixing any postage stamps— that being a privilege accorded to the next of kin of such prisoners. The War Office could not provide any information on the extent of the injuries suffered by Ahmad or his current state of health.

The imam and members of his family started writing almost a letter a day to Ahmad but there was no response. Whenever the matter was taken up, their proverbial reply was that Ahmad's condition 'was being investigated through the good offices of friendly neutral countries'.

It was not till the end of September 1918 that the War Office confirmed that Ahmad had been found in a German POW camp set up for the officers and men of the Indian army. The War Office wrote to the imam that while Ahmad was safe, he had been shifted to a special POW hospital in London to be provided special nursing care for injuries to his limbs and eyes which had been affected by a gas attack by the enemy. He was informed that Ahmad had been decorated a second time with the Special Military Medal and promoted to be a King's commissioned officer with the rank of a lieutenant. They notified that as soon as Ahmad regained his health, he would be demobilized and shipped to India with all benefits including the maximum pension of his rank. Everyone in Delhi of any consequence and close friends and relatives of the imam turned up at the Royal Mosque

Saad Ashraf

or at the imam's house to congratulate him and his family on their good fortune. Ghulam Rasool too went to offer his felicitations to the imam.

'Beta, your prayers and mine have been answered. But the majority of people who now come to congratulate me are those who had raised their eyes and hands to heaven in prayers to bless my son's soul. They were not even prepared to give him an odd chance of survival,' said the imam.

During the time that Ahmad was recovering from his wounds in the POW hospital in London, letters were written to him by those in Delhi, but only a few replies were received. The replies were in English and written by somebody else on his behalf. Ahmad thanked his well-wishers and informed them that he was regaining his strength and that he looked forward to the day when he would walk out of the hospital door and be on his way to sunny Hindustan. The imam would often call Ghulam Rasool to his house or to the Royal Mosque to translate and read and reread Ahmad's new and old letters to him and his visitors who would sit around and listen to their contents.

In November 1918, came the happiest tidings. The Great War had ended and Ahmad had been put on board the troopship *Battleaxe* which was due to dock at the Victoria Pier, Bombay, on 26 December 1918. The imam and his family rejoiced on hearing this by distributing pink, green and dark-brown sweets, made especially for the occasion.

Ghulam Rasool was overjoyed at the prospect of meeting his old friend and wondered what he looked like now after being in the inferno of the Great War. He had last met Yasmeen about a year ago when he had gone to convey the news of Ahmad missing in action. Now that Ahmad was returning, he decided to visit her and give her the happy news. He chose the morning hours for the visit. When she came out from the inner chambers to meet him, he observed that her face bore signs of a lingering sadness which he had never noticed before.

'Bhaijaan, you have come after a long time and I kept wondering what had happened to you. There was no way I could contact you although I did try once or twice through intermediaries. I wrote two letters to your White Haveli address which were returned undelivered,' said Yasmeen, taking two worn-out envelopes from the pocket of her dress. Ghulam Rasool held them in his hand and could read the postman's scribble saying that Ghulam Rasool no longer lived at the address.

'Don't believe the postman for what is written on the envelopes. I must have gone to the college and he may have misunderstood what was said to him. You know the quality of postmen being recruited these days. They can barely read the address on the envelope. In any case, the news I bring for you is joyous enough to overshadow whatever may have happened in the past. Ahmad is safe and alive and should be in Delhi in about six weeks from now,' said Ghulam Rasool.

Yasmeen's face lit up momentarily like the yellow flicker of a candle on its last legs before relapsing back into its sad mould. Her eyes were full of tears which she wiped with a small handkerchief. It struck Ghulam Rasool that the usual gusto she displayed in wanting to know and talk more about Ahmad seemed to be missing.

'Is everything all right? I mean, aren't you happy that Ahmad is coming home. Everybody who cares about him has been waiting for this day for two years now,' said Ghulam Rasool.

'Yes, deep inside I am very happy that he is safe and will be back home. I still wear the amulet the fakir gave ... it has saved him. Please tell him that I genuinely love him and shall always do so, since you will be meeting him earlier than I will,' said Yasmeen, gazing at the floor.

Though intrigued by Yasmeen's apparent lack of enthusiasm, Ghulam Rasool did not probe further. His objective of breaking the news of Ahmad's homecoming having been achieved, he took his leave, promising to keep her informed on further news of Ahmad's arrival.

Saad Ashraf

sixteen

The imam had reserved a bogie in the Bombay Mail leaving Delhi railway station on a cold December night of 1918, and had extended invitations to close male relatives and friends to travel with him to receive Ahmad. After staying for three days in a hotel, the party was to return to Delhi. Since Missionary College was closed for the winter vacations, Ghulam Rasool was among the first that the imam invited to join him on the trip. He looked upon the discomfort of an Indian train journey, in the company of twenty-five others who shared the bogie, as a small sacrifice for an old friend whose independent nature and raw courage he had come to admire.

As the hour of Ahmad's arrival at the Victoria Pier neared, the excitement among those who had come to receive him mounted. The majority hoped to see him as they remembered him when he had left India. There were a few muted voices of concern, though these were disregarded by the majority as those of perennial pessimism. It took over two hours for the troopship *Battleaxe*, carrying nearly a thousand men of the Indian army, to become visible since it was first sighted as a speck on the horizon. Its decks could be seen crawling with waving veterans. The din created by those on the deck and those waiting below as they sighted and recognized one another almost resulted in a melee. It became more peaceful once the ship was finally secured to the pier by ropes and cables, and the ramp for disembarking laid for the landing.

A platoon of British soldiers headed by an officer in uniform marched out of the ship to the music of a solitary bagpiper and stationed itself at the end of the ramp. As the name of a veteran was called out, he would walk over the ramp, haversack in one hand and a small steel trunk precariously balanced on the shoulder. The officer would shake the veteran's hand and give him an envelope containing some cash, discharge papers, and a railway warrant for travel to his home town. Many kissed the ground as they landed, and broke down on embracing those who had come to receive them. The process continued for a couple of hours during which the imam and his party waited impatiently for Ahmad to appear but there was no sign of him.

'Where could Ahmad have gone? I hope the authorities did not forget to put him on this ship ...' said the imam. He turned to Ghulam Rasool. 'Beta, why don't you find out from the officer if there's anything wrong?'

Ghulam Rasool approached the officer near the ramp and told him about their predicament. The officer went through the names of those who were yet to disembark.

'Doesn't seem to be among those who are fit to disembark on their own ... now let me see if he is listed in the wounded. Well, here's his name ... right here. It'll take another hour before we start disembarking the wounded. I'm sorry but you'll have to wait,' said the officer.

Ghulam Rasool went back to console the imam with the news. An hour and a half passed before the wounded men started disembarking. Some came out on stretchers carried by men of the medical corps, followed by coolies carrying their belongings on their shoulders. Some had their arms in slings, others pulled themselves slowly on crutches, and yet others had their faces encased in plaster with two holes for the eyes and another for the nose and were led like children by handlers. The wounded men wept aloud on meeting their relatives. The imam and Ghulam Rasool and others in their party wore expressions of concern on seeing these valiant wounded Indians pass in front of them.

Saad Ashraf

They saw a soldier in uniform leading a veteran by one hand. The latter held a white cane which he kept striking on the ramp as if to announce his arrival.

'Lieutenant Ahmad, 4th Garhwal Rifles,' the officer shouted aloud.

Both the imam and Ghulam Rasool moved swiftly in the direction of the veteran and his handler. At first sight, the man being led out did not look like Ahmad at all. He walked slowly with a discernible stoop, staring straight ahead with a vacant look in his eyes, and bore no resemblance to the agile and sprightly Ahmad, full of laughter and mischief, that people remembered. On a closer look, both could make out his unmistakable features. As soon as the officer delivered Ahmad's envelope to his handler, the imam sprang towards his son, holding him in an affectionate embrace, breaking down and crying like a child. Ahmad sobbed silently in his father's arms.

'Hold his hand and lead him slowly because he can't see ... and here are his medicines, prescription, and the file of his service papers. Good luck to all of you,' said Ahmad's handler, as the imam and Ghulam Rasool took charge. Ghulam Rasool held his friend by the hand and advanced towards the crowd of waiting relatives and friends. Everyone wanted to embrace Ahmad and the elders wanted to pass their hands over his head so that no evil should befall him. Echoes of 'Ahmad Mian, Ahmad Mian' sounded all around. Ghulam Rasool noticed that while it was apparent that Ahmad had lost his eyesight, he also seemed to have gone mute, giving no answers to the volley of questions that were being directed at him.

'Ahmad Mian, is Europe as beautiful as India?'

'Ahmad Mian, how many Germans did you kill?'

Ahmad nodded on hearing these questions, but whenever he attempted a reply, words would form in his mouth, his lips would quiver, tears would roll down his cheeks, but nothing would escape his lips. The only coherent words that one heard from him were 'please give me water', 'attack from the right flank', and 'abandon trench'.

Once the imam and his party were back in the hotel, Ghulam Rasool opened the voluminous file which Ahmad's handler had handed over to them at the quay. On top was an eight-page medical report which said that it might take another six months to a year for Ahmad to recover partial use of his eyesight and his memory to the extent that he may be able to look after himself. He was to take his medicines regularly, have plenty of rest, and, more importantly, avoid physical and mental stress. Ghulam Rasool called the imam aside and explained the contents of the medical report. He emphasized the importance of religiously following the doctor's instructions and passing the word around among the members of the reception party that Ahmad was to be pestered as little as possible.

The group left for Delhi by the Bombay Mail which departed from the Victoria Terminus railway station in Bombay. While the train traversed the plains of India at night, Ghulam Rasool lay half asleep on an upper berth, thinking about how much had happened in a day. From the corner of his eye, in the dim light glowing in the bogie, he watched the imam getting up unobtrusively, coming close to his son, kissing his forehead and passing his hand affectionately around his face, and thereafter raising his hands in prayer as if seeking divine help for his son's recovery.

Two days later, the train came to a halt at the Delhi railway station. Ghulam Rasool was surprised to see the large crowd at the platform that surged forward to receive the imam and his son. They were covered with so many garlands of roses and marigold that it became impossible to see their faces and they seemed like baskets of flowers moving on the platform among the crowd. Ghulam Rasool had to intercede by making appeals to the crowd that Ahmad was not well and must be spared the agony of being jostled any further. He cleared a path for them with the help of some of those who had travelled with him from Bombay, and escorted the imam and Ahmad into the black Austin car, decorated with buntings, which belonged to the imam's friend Seth Najmuddin. All along, Ahmad looked straight ahead, stony-eyed, a steady stream of tears flowing on his cheeks which the imam wiped with his cream-coloured silken handkerchief whenever he felt that nobody was looking.

Time went by quickly once Ahmad was back at home. The imam and his family devoted all their attention and care on him. He was given his medicines on time, and bothered as little as possible so that he could give his body and mind the rest it required to heal itself of the effects of the war. Ghulam Rasool made it a point to spend at least two hours every Saturday afternoon with him as there were no classes on that day. He spent this time talking to Ahmad and trying to restore his memory by making him recall past events. As a result of his efforts, spread over several months, there was a marked improvement in Ahmad's mental state. From a mute who merely listened, nodded, and shed tears in silence, Ahmad reached a stage where he would recall and narrate the major events of his past life in a slow and halting, but otherwise comprehensible speech. When Ghulam Rasool, through his tedious labour, brought Ahmad to that stage in his life where he had come across Yasmeen, he became uncommunicative. However, a few days more of his devotion to Ahmad's cause brought success.

His mental condition improved considerably although the previous agility and humour seemed to have disappeared. Ahmad eagerly looked forward to Saturdays when Ghulam Rasool would come and spend the evening with him. They talked about the years they had spent together at Missionary College, the whereabouts and vocations of their erstwhile colleagues and professors. Ahmad would invariably talk about the European war and places where he had seen action—Cambrai, Amiens, Bapaume, and St. Quentin. He spoke of the fear that struck a soldier's heart on a mission in the pitch dark and the cold of a European night far away from the comforts of home. He said that on such occasions he felt like a child—innocent, fearful, and totally at the mercy of nature. His faith in fate, reinforced by the loss of so many companions who were alive only a few minutes ago, became so strong that it had eventually driven fear out of him. And always in the midst of that cold and fear he found his love and Yasmeen's image omnipresent, egging him on to survive in spite of the odds.

'Mian,' Ahmad said to Ghulam Rasool one day, 'you must somehow inform Yasmeen that I am alive and arrange for us to meet. Surely you could do this for an old friend who has suffered so much in such a short time. It is my love for Yasmeen which kept me alive in trenches full of corpses, mud, and the terror of war. Even though darkness is my constant companion, I can see her all the time as vividly as I did when I saw her the first time.'

Ghulam Rasool had purposely steered clear of all mention of Yasmeen during the time Ahmad was recovering. He thought he had done this in Ahmad's own interest, sparing him mental stress, but deep inside Ghulam Rasool knew that he had hoped that Ahmad would somehow forget Yasmeen so as to avoid future complications in his life.

'Well, Mian, when are you going to arrange for my meeting with Yasmeen?' continued Ahmad.

'As soon as I feel that you are better and fit enough to bear the strain of such a meeting, and that may take a few months more,' Ghulam Rasool answered after thinking awhile.

Ahmad's insistence on meeting Yasmeen eventually led Ghulam Rasool to make a foray to her quarters in Chawri Bazaar. He was informed by those living there that Yasmeen had moved with her aunt to Bareli or Bombay a year ago, about the time that Ghulam Rasool had gone to see her with the news of Ahmad's return to India. There was no way of finding out whether the information was authentic and, in the absence of any definite address, Ghulam Rasool realized that tracing her would be next to impossible. He remembered that Yasmeen had appeared to be in state of deep depression when they had met last and wondered whether it had something to do with her impending departure.

'I think Allah must be punishing me for a grave, unforgivable sin. Though the only sin I have committed is loving a woman of the bazaar and ... killing human beings in the war,' remarked Ahmad, when his friend broke the news to him.

Saad Ashraf

Ghulam Rasool consoled Ahmad saying that many hopeless situations get resolved with time. There was reason to be optimistic that Yasmeen would eventually be traced and Ahmad would be able to meet her.

Although Ahmad's mental state had considerably improved, there was no such sign as far as his eyesight was concerned. He could move about only by striking a cane in front of him to ascertain whether anything was in his way. The imam consulted Dr Chatterjee, the Bengali doctor, who was famous all over India and practised in Daryaganj and who had specialized in this field by spending four years in England. But all he could say after going through his papers was that only time could tell whether nature would come to Ahmad's help and restore his sight because nothing known to medical science at that time was likely to be effective.

Apart from the doctors in Delhi, the imam consulted a variety of practitioners of other schools of healing—hakims, homoeopaths, hydropaths, Chinese herbal practitioners, German biochemists and Japanese practitioners of touch healing, Muslim fakirs and Hindu mendicants—to help restore his son's eyesight, but to no avail. Their medications, chants, concoctions, and balms did not lead to any improvement. The imam watched his son helplessly, hoping for some miracle but Ahmad still walked around the house, brandishing his cane and striking it on the floor in front of him. He was however confident that Allah would come to Ahmad's aid at the proper time. He strongly believed that his son could not have committed any sin for which Allah would punish him in this manner.

'Why don't you ask your son to offer prayers for himself? Allah likes direct communication,' suggested a devout member of the imam's congregation.

Though hesitant to make this suggestion to Ahmad because of his condition, the imam eventually brought himself around to broach the matter with his son.

'Beta, would you like a prayer mat and a cap, so that you can start saying your prayers? Of course you can say these while sitting in your chair or lying in bed,' the imam suggested one afternoon.

'Abbajaan, with darkness as my continuous companion, my head is always bowed in prayer before Allah. I pray every single moment that I am awake. Who would know more about my suffering than myself? You are an imam, well read in religion. Please tell me why I am being punished in this manner,' Ahmad said tearfully.

'I have no answer to your questions, Beta, but Allah knows best,' said the imam, clasping his son to his bosom.

A few months later, the imam decided to approach his son through Ghulam Rasool to suggest to him as discreetly as possible whether he would be willing to take up responsibilities as a muezzin at the Royal Mosque. The imam told Ghulam Rasool that this would keep Ahmad occupied in doing something useful and provide him an opportunity of getting out of the house which would be good for him.

Ghulam Rasool brought up this issue with Ahmad who agreed readily to the suggestion.

From the middle of January 1920, a new and beautiful voice pierced the heavens over Delhi in calling the faithful to prayers from the northern minaret of the Royal Mosque. Its musical lilt sounded loud and clear. Those in Delhi who heard this call said, 'What a beautiful voice! It almost seems that Allah is calling us to pray in the mosque.' And when word got around that it was Ahmad, they said, 'The beautiful prayer call is that of the blind muezzin, the imam's son, who has been endowed with special powers by Allah to call so melodiously.'

seventeen

'A re you going to spend your entire life teaching Arabic tenses to young men who have nothing better to do than learning a language which is not spoken in India? Am I going to go on like this and die as the mother of a teacher in a country where the bulk of people are illiterate and don't even know what a primary school looks like?' Noorani Begum railed at her son one evening.

'Ammi, you had yourself said once that teaching is a respectable profession no matter what one teaches, and Arabic is the language of the Quran though it may not be spoken in India. The pay at the college is good and we are comfortable, with all our loans paid off. I don't understand what could be troubling you,' replied Ghulam Rasool.

'I have two daughters and a son of marriageable age and no money or status which would help me get them married off. That is my problem.'

'What would you like me to do? I'm only waiting for the ICS examination to be held in India. If I qualify and become a big government officer you can be truly proud of me.'

'And suppose they never hold this examination in India? Will you keep waiting till you become old and I am dead? Your father also worked in the government though only as a superintendent and we had the status if not the money. Surely there must be another way to become a government officer ...'

'The only other way is to go to England and appear in the ICS examination which is held there but who will fund my passage to and stay in England. Only if Professor Thompson had not returned to England, I would have sought his help.'

'Beta, one has to live with the realities of life. Professor Thompson is no longer in India. Think of what you can do for your family that has sacrificed everything to get you educated. We only need to get some social status for this family so that we can all get ahead in life. If you get a government job we will get that status.'

Ghulam Rasool did not agree with his mother, but could only air his dissent couched in soft words.

'Ammi, if you think it is so important to get a government job for the sake of this family, I'll try and talk to the professors at the college as to how I can go about it.' He sighed with an air of resignation.

The very next day, Ghulam Rasool spoke to Professor Fitzpatrick, professor of history at Missionary College, who had been promoted to the newly created position of vice principal to assist Professor Pringle who had been appointed principal after the retirement of Professor Thompson. Ghulam Rasool explained how important it was in his domestic scenario for him to get a government job. Professor Fitzpatrick listened patiently and promised to talk the matter over with some people who mattered at the Chelmsford Club.

Professor Fitzpatrick did not forget his promise. His research finally led him to the conclusion that the quickest way was through the viceroy who had the authority to make such appointments. The professor did not let the matter rest at that and had Father Henderson, the Scotch padre at the chapel in the viceroy's house, put in a word for Ghulam Rasool after a Sunday service. The viceroy seemed receptive to the idea of helping this young Indian, particularly when he was told that Ghulam Rasool had a master's degree, was anglicized in temperament, and was the offspring of a late loyal servant of the British Indian government. The viceroy asked his military secretary to note Ghulam Rasool's name and particulars in the diary he carried around, and to remind him to talk to the concerned member of the viceroy's council at the next meeting for finding suitable employment for the young man.

Saad Ashraf

A few weeks later, when Ghulam Rasool had almost given up hope that he would be able to get into government service, he was pleasantly surprised to receive an envelope embossed with the gold seal of the viceroy of India. On opening the envelope he found a letter from the Military Secretary Colonel Edwards, asking him to appear for an interview before the special committee constituted for the purpose of considering an appointment for him. He was to report at the South Block secretariat buildings, New Delhi, for the interview.

Elated with this lucky break, Ghulam Rasool showed the letter to Professor Fitzpatrick the first thing next morning.

'Ghulam Rasool, I hope you get through with this interview and something good comes out of it for you since you said that it was so important for you to join government service. I don't know who will be on the panel but I am sure that you will get through with flying colours. I don't think they will do anything more than talk to you on general matters,' Professor Fitzpatrick said after reading the letter.

'Sir, I am grateful to you for getting me this interview. If I get into government service, it would only be because of you.'

'Aw, come off it, Ghulam Rasool. You have a claim on me—after all, we've known each other for years.'

Ghulam Rasool had not told Noorani Begum about the efforts he had been making to get into government service and about the call for the interview. He wanted this to come as a complete surprise to her in case he was successful.

Ghulam Rasool reached South Block on the day of the interview and parked his cycle in the stand. Holding on carefully to his file of personal papers, he climbed the stairs to reach the veranda of the first floor of the building. He located the committee room with the help of a babu and was informed that an interview was to take place at ten o'clock. He identified himself as the person to be interviewed and was told to wait outside the committee room.

As the clock in the tower of South Block struck ten, Ghulam Rasool found himself summoned and ushered into the committee room.

Three white sahibs, all bespectacled, were sitting at the end of the conference table. One of them wore a military uniform. Ghulam Rasool assumed that this would be none other than Colonel Edwards, the man who had signed the letter calling him to the interview.

Once Ghulam Rasool was seated, the colonel addressed him. 'Mr Ghulam Rasool, with your qualifications, why don't you just wait for a few months more and appear in the ICS examination which is going to be held in India? With a little luck you could become a member of the ICS.'

'Thank you very much, sir, for your suggestion but I'd prefer a government appointment now if that is possible. I could appear in the ICS examination, as suggested by you, whenever it is held in India, if I otherwise meet the criteria,' said Ghulam Rasool.

Colonel Edwards nodded. By now, Ghulam Rasool had settled comfortably enough to notice that one of the interviewers was looking at him intently. In the pause that followed his reply, Ghulam Rasool had an opportunity to look at him through the corner of his eye. The face seemed familiar and yet for some time he could not place it. He had to tax his memory quite a bit before he could recognize Professor Joseph Moses. The professor had changed a lot, having gained considerable weight and lost all the hair on his head. Ghulam Rasool wondered how the professor had come to be on the panel. He had resigned from Missionary College a couple of months before the World War began and it was rumoured that he had left for Europe. Nothing had been heard of him thereafter. And here he was. Ghulam Rasool felt ill at ease though he tried his level best not to appear so.

'Would you like to talk to this young man, Joseph?' asked Colonel Edwards, turning towards Professor Moses.

Professor Moses addressed Ghulam Rasool without the slightest indication of familiarity, and asked him a few questions about his life which he had no difficulty in answering. Ghulam Rasool thought he saw the professor wink at him ever so imperceptibly as to make him doubt that he had done so.

Saad Ashraf

The interview ended as Colonel Edwards got up to shake Ghulam Rasool's hand with the remark that he could expect to hear something from the panel very soon. Two weeks later, Ghulam Rasool received a sealed letter signed by one Mr Durand, the deputy postmaster general, Posts and Telegraphs Department, Delhi Circle, informing him that under the special dispensation granted to the viceroy it had been decided to offer him the post of deputy superintendent in that department.

Ghulam Rasool read and reread the letter, not quite believing that what it said could be true. It was indeed difficult, almost improbable, for a person like him, without an alluring family background or connections, to get a government post. Yet, when it came to being done, events had moved rapidly, sorting themselves out in a manner that seemed almost providential. He was however certain that Professor Moses had played an important role in his appointment, standing by a commitment given to him a long time back to be of help in time of need as a friend.

Needless to say, Ghulam Rasool's appointment as deputy superintendent put Noorani Begum on cloud nine. Her late husband had reached this position after putting in several years of service whereas her son was starting at that level at twenty-six years of age. She attributed her son's appointment to divine help and among the first thing she did was to spend as much time as she could spare for the next forty days, on the prayer mat, thanking the Almighty for fulfilling her desires.

Ghulam Rasool accepted the offer immediately and reported to the deputy postmaster general's office on 15 October 1920, on expiry of his notice period of four weeks to Missionary College. He was told that the deputy postmaster general wanted to see him. Ghulam Rasool knocked at his door and found himself face to face with a shrivelled-up old man with a mop of snow-white hair on his head and a matching moustache. Mr Durand shook hands with Ghulam Rasool and motioned him to sit, adjusting the thick black frame of his spectacles.

'So you are Ghulam Rasool, son of the late Ghulam Nabi. You probably do not know, but your father was the superintendent when I was postmaster at the Delhi GPO. I liked your father ... he was a good worker. I hope you are made of the same stuff and would work with the same kind of loyalty, devotion, and zeal,' said Mr Durand.

'I most certainly will,' Ghulam Rasool replied politely.

'By the way, Ghulam Rasool, I am posting you as deputy superintendent at the GPO, Delhi. This is a job your father had held many years ago. Remember that the post and telegraphs is a vital organ of British India and requires its staff to be constantly on the alert. The best way of doing so is to keep your eyes and ears open and your mouth shut.'

'Sir, I shall try and do my best.'

'You may collect your orders from my head clerk. I wish you the best of luck.'

Saad Ashraf

eighteen

A few days after Ghulam Rasool's appointment as deputy
superintendent, Jahan Ara Begum came to see Noorani
Begum for some late-morning gossip. She seemed very excited
and happy.

'Noorani Begum, a wonderful thing has happened to me,' said
Jahan Ara Begum.

'Why, have you become pregnant at this late stage in life?'

'No, no ... who wants to be burdened with bearing another
child. I have finally found something which has resolved the
problem of my bust.'

Noorani Begum looked unimpressed. 'I know that you ordered
a cream from a company in Bombay against my advice. Was it
the one that did the job?'

'No, Noorani Begum ... in the last six years I have tried
everything under the sun available in India—pills, creams, tablets,
potions, prayers, and black magic to increase my bust but to no
avail. Until I came across an advertisement, in the woman's
weekly *Niswan*, of a company in Calcutta which manufactures
padded brassieres guaranteed to arouse any man infatuated with
a woman's breasts. I was so desperate that I ordered a pair
immediately. It arrived five days back and I tried it on last night.
Oh, how the nawab sahib went wild! We didn't finish till the
early hours of the morning when we heard the call for prayers.
The nawab sahib has promised me a ring studded with rubies.
I'm so happy,' said Jahan Ara Begum, beaming with a smile that
comes only from a fully satisfied woman.

'Well, that you've been able to find something you were looking for is happy news indeed, but, Jahan Ara Begum, you haven't congratulated me yet on my son's achievement.'

'Why, what has he done now? Has he passed another examination? I thought that there was nothing higher than sixteen years of education and he had completed that some years ago.'

Noorani Begum clucked her tongue impatiently. 'No, no … he has been appointed deputy superintendent in the head post office of Delhi by the sarkar. This is a very big government post and he is probably one of the youngest persons to hold it. His father reached this post after having spent several years in government service. It is a great honour for the people of Delhi and everyone should be proud of my son's achievement.'

'But you never told anybody about this. In the past, whenever there was happy news, you would tell me and the neighbours. But this time nobody knows. How will anyone come to know if you don't tell us?'

'This time, everybody in Delhi will hear about it on their own. After all, don't people come to know when a new viceroy is appointed?' said Noorani Begum, raising her head proudly.

Jahan Ara Begum took leave of Noorani Begum. She resolved to pass this news to everyone she met including her husband. Nawab Aziz Rehman called on Ghulam Rasool the same evening to congratulate him on his appointment and presented him with a box containing four pounds of the best quality sweetmeats produced by a famous shop in Chandni Chowk.

As word about Ghulam Rasool's appointment got around, people started making a beeline for Noorani Begum's house. Rich and poor neighbours brought parcels of fruit, flowers, and sweets for Deputy Superintendent Ghulam Rasool, wishing him success in his new position and telling him that not only did he possess an exceptional brain, he also had Allah's blessings in full measure—a combination with which he was bound to rise higher and higher in service. Noorani Begum's relatives, many of whom so distant that she was meeting them for the first time, converged on her to congratulate her on her wisdom, planning, and

Saad Ashraf

determination that had finally resulted in her son becoming an important government functionary at such a young age. Noorani Begum was ecstatic with all the praise that came her way on account of Ghulam Rasool. Enormous pride would creep into her whenever she talked about her son.

One morning soon after, when Noorani Begum was busy in the kitchen, she heard a knock on her door. She left the ladle in the pot in which she was cooking some lentils for lunch and went to answer the knock. When she opened the door she was surprised to find Phool Begum, a distant cousin who lived in a large house in an affluent locality in the vicinity of the Royal Mosque. Phool Begum was a buxom woman, around forty-five years of age, short in height and fair of complexion. She had been widowed five years back but her husband had had the good sense to leave her with a substantial monthly rental derived from commercial property. Phool Begum had a good business head on her shoulders and had managed her affairs well. On account of her reticence and her wealth she was respected by all those who came in contact with her. Noorani Begum wondered what could have brought Phool Begum to her doorstep. They exchanged niceties and complimented one another on their appearances after which Noorani Begum conducted her guest to her living quarters.

'Apa! It is a great honour and privilege for me that you grace my humble abode. Please make yourself comfortable while I take the cooking pot off the fire grate. I was cooking some lentils for lunch,' Noorani Begum said to Phool Begum. The visitor took off her black burqa, placed it in a corner and seated herself.

Noorani Begum returned in a few minutes and sat on the other chair. She took out an ornamental silver box which contained paan and offered one to Phool Begum while putting one in her own mouth. She sat chewing on her leaf, waiting expectantly for Phool Begum to begin the conversation.

'Do you know, Noorani Begum, how I came to be named Phool Begum?' she enquired, raising her eyebrows.

Noorani Begum sat looking at her, clueless, her mouth in constant motion.

'I was named Phool Begum by my great-grandfather because our family owned the largest flower market of Delhi at the time of my birth. We owned no less than thirty shops in the market. Unfortunately, over the generations the property got divided but I still own half a dozen shops which we have rented out and the income from which is sufficient to support our whole family of four sons their wives and my grandchildren.'

'Oh! Really!' Noorani Begum feigned the amazement expected of her, while wondering as to the purpose of this prologue. Surely, she thought to herself, Phool Begum had not walked all the way to her house just to apprise her of her affluence of which Noorani Begum was already aware.

She offered Phool Begum another paan from her case which the latter gratefully accepted.

'Noorani Begum, my late husband concentrated on providing his children with one asset—education. He always said that circumstances could take away one's wealth and reduce a person to becoming a pauper but nothing could take away one's education. All my sons went to good schools and are matriculates. Two of them work as clerks in government offices and live in Delhi with their families. The third is in Bombay and works on a ship that sails the seven seas. My youngest son, Rehmat, is twenty-five years old, and works as a supervisor in the Delhi municipality and I am looking for a wife for him. Since you are a relative, I naturally thought of my nieces as the first choice since I have known them from the time they were little children.'

Noorani Begum's mouth started working faster on the paan. Of late she had been worried about her daughters Rehmani Begum and Sultana Begum who were getting on without receiving any suitable marriage proposals. However, in spite of her excitement, Noorani Begum sat with a straight face, not letting any emotion show.

'And, Noorani Begum, you don't have to worry about any expenses—we'll bring no more than a dozen relatives in the wedding party. You can offer them a simple cup of tea or a bottle of aerated water. There will be a nikah and I'll take my daughter-in-law to my house in the very clothes that she would be wearing. And there's no question of dowry either—if there's anything you would like to give to your daughter as all mothers want to, you can give her cash which will be strictly hers. We are your relatives, after all ... your grandfather and mine were first cousins ... your daughter will merely be moving from one home to another. I treat all my daughters-in-law as my own daughters since I only bore sons.'

Noorani Begum cleared her throat and spoke up.

'Apa, there are countless proposals for my daughters but your son Rehmat's will receive our utmost consideration simply because the boy is from our own family. We neither have to enquire about his ancestry nor about his character or his income. Your assurance that my daughter will be treated like your own is enough. But give me a few days to think about it. I will discuss it with my son when he returns from office this very afternoon and let you know in the shortest possible time.'

'O, Noorani Begum, I am sorry I forgot to mention that we are interested in your younger daughter Sultana Begum ... you know it is a question of physical compatibility, and from what my son has spoken to me about his preferences ...' said Phool Begum.

Noorani Begum was taken aback as she was under the impression that Phool Begum was interested in her elder daughter, Rehmani. She however decided not to urge Phool Begum on the matter. A bird in hand was better than two in the bush, she thought. There would be other proposals for Rehmani in the days to come.

When Ghulam Rasool returned home from office late in the afternoon that day and had sufficiently reinvigorated himself with a cup of tea, Noorani Begum broke the news of Phool Begum's visit. Ghulam Rasool was delighted to hear of the proposal for Sultana Begum though a bit disappointed that it was not for Rehmani.

'I think we should grab the proposal and you should convey word to Phool Begum tomorrow morning to fix a date for the wedding,' said Ghulam Rasool, beaming with joy.

'Beta, though we are lucky to receive this proposal for Sultana, in such matters it always pays for the girl's side to proceed slowly. Before I finally agree, I want you to use your contacts in the Delhi municipality to find out what his colleagues and superiors think of Rehmat,' said Noorani Begum.

Next day, Ghulam Rasool called on the superintendent of the Delhi municipality in person to enquire about Rehmat. He received such glowing reports about Rehmat's character and conduct that he took time off from the office to cycle back home to inform Noorani Begum about what he had learnt and advise her that as far as he was concerned his prospective brother-in-law was said to be an angel, and a wedding date should be fixed as soon as possible.

That very evening, Noorani Begum spoke to Sultana, who smiled coyly and retired to the other room, carrying happy thoughts of her future. Noorani Begum had some misgivings about how Rehmani would react to the news of the marriage proposal for her younger sister, but she was in for a pleasant surprise.

'Ammi, I am very happy about this proposal for Sultana,' Rehmani said, when her mother broke the news to her. 'I think we should convey our acceptance straightaway to Phool Begum now that Bhaijaan has confirmed from his office that Rehmat is so well spoken of there. I hope Sultana finds happiness in her home for all times to come. As an elder sister I'll always stand by her.'

Rehmani's reaction so overwhelmed Noorani Begum that she broke down, embraced her daughter, called her a woman from paradise, and promised that she would endeavour to find a husband of noble ancestry for her as soon as possible.

With everybody in agreement on Sultana's marriage proposal, Noorani Begum went to Phool Begum's house and conveyed her family's acceptance and fixed a convenient date within the week for the wedding.

In the presence of two dozen relatives and neighbours and a dower of hundred and one rupees, half of which was payable immediately in cash, the marriage of Sultana, Noorani Begum's younger daughter, was solemnized with Rehmat, Phool Begum's youngest son. Ghulam Rasool embraced his brother-in-law and, with tears in his eyes and parting words of 'may Allah be with you', gave away his sister as a bride.

A day after her wedding, Sultana returned to spend a few nights at her mother's home, as is the custom. She came back a happy, beaming and satisfied woman with nothing except praise for her husband, her new family, and her new home.

nineteen

A few months after Sultana's marriage, Ghulam Rasool was given an out-of-turn promotion on account of his hard work and loyalty, and transferred to the faraway province of Punjab. The development, though a happy one, worried Noorani Begum, not so much for herself—she after all would still have Rehmani with her—as for Ghulam Rasool who would be alone in the Punjab with nobody to take care of him.

One day, Jahan Ara Begum came to call on Noorani Begum, ostensibly to enquire after the latter's well-being but in reality to confirm what she had heard from others—that Ghulam Rasool had been promoted and had become an even bigger man. An element of intense jealousy had come to haunt Jahan Ara Begum ever since she had heard this rumour. Only a year ago, Noorani Begum had told her that Ghulam Rasool had joined government service, and so soon he had even been promoted. She wanted to know the secret behind Ghulam Rasool's incredible success in so short a time. Her own husband, in spite of having descended from a line of blue-blooded nawabs, remained a lower division clerk in the accountant general's office for well over twelve years of his service and had not been promoted even once. And here was a young upstart doing so well.

'Noorani Begum, I think one will have to start living with you to avoid missing the opportunity of congratulating you on your son's achievements. Either he has passed an examination or has been appointed to a high post or has achieved some other feat—his run of success seems unending. I have heard a rumour that he has been promoted …' enquired Jahan Ara Begum.

'It is true, Begum, my Ghulam Rasool has become the youngest Indian officer to be a superintendent in the dak department. It is all Allah's blessings and my son's hard work,' said Noorani Begum, mixing her pride and arrogance with a little humility.

Jahan Ara Begum smiled expansively in an effort to conceal the envy that pecked at her heart. 'Congratulations, Begum, may my nephew become the lieutenant governor of Delhi. Oh, we will all be so proud of him.'

'You have always supported me in my time of need, Begum, and I am sure that your prayers have contributed in getting Ghulam Rasool to where he is today. But there is a problem.'

'What problems can you have when things are going so well?'

'Unfortunately, there is a big problem. Ghulam Rasool has been transferred to the Punjab and he has to go there alone, leaving me in Delhi with my daughter.'

'Hai, but that's no problem. Why don't you get him married? I am sure that famous families of Delhi will be eager to give their daughters to such a highly placed person like Ghulam Rasool. If you like, I can start talking to some of the elders of the Lucknow families settled in Delhi. You know what good wives girls from Lucknow make. If I had a son like Ghulam Rasool, I would never send him alone to the Punjab without a wife. The women there will just grab him and you will never see him again.'

'I think my Ghulam Rasool will be grabbed anywhere, be it the Punjab or Lucknow. What's so unsafe about the Punjab?'

'The women of the Punjab … everybody talks of their bewitching physical beauty and their mesmerizing charms. It is said that they ensnare single, lonely men who go and work there, marry them, and then convert them into lifelong slaves,' Jahan Ara Begum informed with an air of authority.

'I am unprejudiced and do not believe all that is said about the people of one region or the other. My husband was from the Punjab and he was kind, gentle, and generous. The women of that province must be like those everywhere else—some naive and simple, others clever and crooked,' said Noorani Begum.

Jahan Ara Begum did not like being snubbed thus. When she spoke, her voice had more than a touch of asperity to it. 'You have a right to your own opinion but what I say is borne out by history. Alexander's generals, who had settled in the Punjab, mutinied on being asked to return to Greece with him. They told him that if he wanted, he could go back alone or go to hell for all they cared as they were quite comfortable in the Punjab. All because they were caught in the web of the beauty and charm of the Punjabi women.'

'It is not only the women of the Punjab who know how to captivate men ... it is women all over the world. Some years ago they used to talk of the women of Bengal practising their magic on the men they came in contact with. The women of Lucknow are no less. Now just look at yourself ... how you twirl the nawab sahib like a child around your little finger.'

A tribute of this high order, on the total control she could exercise on her man, not only assuaged her hurt but so elated Jahan Ara Begum that she decided to forego further conversation, deferring to the next visit the task of finding out what she had come for in the first place—that magic wand used by Ghulam Rasool to earn a promotion so quickly.

Noorani Begum kept thinking of all that Jahan Ara Begum had said and decided that her own future security lay in getting Ghulam Rasool married to a girl of her choice as soon as possible.

As 28 May 1921—the day for Ghulam Rasool's departure to Lahore—neared, a pall of gloom descended on Noorani Begum and her family. On the night prior to Ghulam Rasool's departure, Noorani Begum tossed and turned in her bed, disturbed by thoughts of unknown perils which would engulf her son so far away. Only a silent prayer, said to bring peace to disturbed minds and broken hearts, muttered in the early hours of the morning, brought the solace which lulled her to sleep. She woke up bleary-eyed and with a hangover clouding her mind, which haunted

Saad Ashraf

her the whole day. Sultana and her husband Rehmat had arrived early in the morning. When the time came to say goodbye, Noorani Begum and her daughters sobbed silently. The pain and anguish of parting showed on their faces. Ghulam Rasool tried consoling his mother and sisters.

'I'll always be with you,' he said. 'Delhi is only a night away by train from Lahore, so I can always come back on leave whenever you want me.'

Noorani Begum embraced her son as he got ready to leave for the railway station and tied an amulet around his right arm to solicit heavenly protection for him, beseeching Ghulam Rasool not to take it off for the next forty days. Against the backdrop of a last wail by his mother and sisters, Ghulam Rasool climbed down the stairs of the house, drying his tear-filled eyes with his handkerchief. He boarded a horse-driven buggy, accompanied by some men from the neighbourhood.

Although the sun had gone down it was still very hot, and people could be seen cooling themselves with small hand fans made of light-green reed. The muezzin's call for the evening prayers rent the sky. Loud, crisp, and clear, it pierced the dusk enveloping Delhi. It was the unmistakable voice of his friend Ahmad. Ghulam Rasool had gone to see him the previous day. Ahmad had enquired from Ghulam Rasool about the time of his departure for the railway station. When Ghulam Rasool had mentioned that it would be around the time of the evening prayers, Ahmad had said, 'I can't come to see you off at the railway station much as I would like to …'—he had paused briefly, as if pierced by a fresh awareness of his handicap—'… so I'll bid you goodbye through my call for prayers if you pass the mosque at that time.' As his best friend, Ahmad had fulfilled his promise.

On arrival at the station, Ghulam Rasool was received by a long line of his colleagues and juniors, including his successor. Each person was standing with garlands of fresh-smelling jasmine flowers in their hands. After being profusely garlanded by the large crowd who had come to see him off, he boarded the Frontier

Mail which started moving soon after and disappeared from view as it curved out of the Delhi railway station and melted into the dark wide expanse of India.

There was no news of Ghulam Rasool for the next ten days. The sadness of parting had descended like a dark cloud on Noorani Begum and her family, as she lay stricken with depression for two days after her son's departure. But thereafter she rose with her usual resilience of spirit and started attending to household chores.

On the eleventh day, they received a letter from Ghulam Rasool. He wrote that he had shared the railway compartment with three Englishmen, only one of whom was mildly friendly, and that at the break of dawn the next day he had looked through the windows of the train to see the sun embracing the lush green plains of the Punjab studded with patches of golden wheat as he hurtled towards his destination. He had disembarked at Lahore railway station which was a unique building designed like a fort, complete with turrets for placing guns to ward off the enemy. For the time being he was staying at the rest house of the postal department located near the railway station. He had met his boss, Mr Barnett, the postmaster general, Punjab and Frontier Province, who had assigned him as the superintendent of post offices in Lahore until an independent vacancy of a postmaster became available. His deputy was one Rashid who belonged to a well-known family of Lahore and who had proved to be an extremely genial and hospitable person, like the rest of the fun-loving people of that city. Rashid had invited Ghulam Rasool to his house for dinner and had introduced him to his family, which was a gesture of extreme regard among the people of Lahore who ordinarily kept their families away from strangers. Of course, Ghulam Rasool missed his family very much but would have felt even lonelier had it not been for the homely care and attention that his deputy had provided. He wrote about the beauty of the city of Lahore, its gardens, the Mughal fort, the mall, the fine sense and culture of those who lived there, and the

Saad Ashraf

amity that existed between its inhabitants. Ghulam Rasool ended his letter with the hope that Noorani Begum and his sisters would get a chance to visit Lahore while he was posted there.

Noorani Begum was happy to receive her son's letter but perturbed at his naivety in becoming too familiar too quickly with his deputy. Her late husband, Ghulam Nabi, had often said that it was best to keep official work, colleagues, and juniors away from home if one wanted peace and happiness both at work and at home. But more than that, Jahan Ara Begum's words—that Ghulam Rasool should never go to the Punjab without a wife—reverberated loudly in her ears. She could not understand why her son should be socializing with his junior within days of his arrival, and visiting his house for dinner and meeting his family. Did his deputy have comely daughters to whom her son may be attracted? She concluded that Rashid was either an angel or a Satan in the garb of a deputy superintendent. Only time would tell. Noorani Begum decided that her future security lay in finding a suitable bride for her son without further loss of time. Towards this end, she decided to enlist the services of Macho Begum, the famous matchmaker of Delhi.

twenty

Macho Begum arrived one morning at the request of Noorani Begum. She had earlier made the rounds of Noorani Begum's house immediately after Ghulam Rasool's appointment as deputy superintendent in the GPO about a year ago. She was a dark, buxom woman, about fifty years of age with silver-coloured hair which she tied in a short, tight six-inch pigtail with a bright multi-coloured braid. Only three of her upper teeth remained in her mouth and these were heavily encrusted with the deposit of betel leaf which she was in the habit of chewing continuously. Macho Begum's expertise lay in her immaculate manners and the god-given gift of polite speech delivered in a soft, hypnotic voice through which she was able to gain access into the closed circle of influential women in the most famous and wealthy families of Delhi. It was whispered in some prominent quarters that she was born the illegitimate granddaughter of a nawab in a principality of the former kingdom of Oudh, but nobody could confirm or deny this. It was claimed that she had made a thousand matches among boys and girls from wealthy and not-so-wealthy backgrounds for over two decades. There was not a single one that hadn't lasted.

The matchmaker sat on a chair in the drawing room which had been built for Ghulam Rasool but which was now used by Noorani Begum to receive guests. Macho Begum removed her large white burqa with a netted slit for a peephole and kept it aside. She took out a small silver case from the side pocket of her blue organdie shirt, from which she stuffed two leaves of betel full of condiments in her mouth and started chewing instantly.

'Noorani Begum, to what do I owe the privilege of these summons from you?' she asked in her trademark flowery speech.

'Macho Begum, how can I even think of summoning the greatest matchmaker of Delhi? It is my privilege that you grace my home. I wanted to meet you to discuss a matter concerning my son Ghulam Rasool. You may recall you had come to congratulate me on his appointment to the big post of deputy superintendent of the GPO in Delhi. Well, the sarkar gave him another promotion and now he is the superintendent of post offices in Lahore. He is the only Indian officer of this rank in the dak department. I am looking for a bride for him.'

Macho Begum smiled and nodded her head, acknowledging Noorani Begum's effort at sycophancy.

'My son is among the few Muslims in India who have passed sixteen classes and knows English like his mother tongue. That is why the government gave him this big job. You are already aware of our family background and the noble blood that flows through his veins, and you probably know that his father was the superintendent of the GPO, Delhi, before he passed away twenty years ago,' continued Noorani Begum.

Her eyes wide open, Macho Begum listened intently, taking in every word and chewing on the betel in her mouth.

'Is there anything else you would like to know about my son or our family which might help you locate a suitable bride for him?'

Macho Begum appeared to be in deep thought.

'Noorani Begum, I am delighted to know that your son is so highly educated and has done so well, but times have sadly changed. The parents of daughters these days like to see them move to more comfortable homes than their own. Gone are the days when they only looked at the pedigree of those whom their daughters would marry. By the way, what qualities are you looking for in your daughter-in-law?'

Noorani Begum was taken aback. She had expected that a matchmaker as famous as Macho Begum would be sufficiently overwhelmed by her exposition of her family background coupled with the official position of her son, and that she would start listing suitable brides from among the elite of Delhi, but this had not happened. Though a trifle unsettled, Noorani Begum did not let it show in the way she spoke.

'Well, I'd like my daughter-in-law to be good looking if not beautiful, fair-complexioned, devout, a good cook, efficient housekeeper, frugal, and, above all, be from well-known stock. As far as keeping somebody's daughter comfortable, it should be no problem for my son who earns a good salary with the facilities and the prestige that go with a high government position.'

'You want Delhi's most perfect woman as your daughter-in-law. No one can have all these qualities. You know, Noorani Begum, Allah made us all imperfect creatures.'

Noorani Begum looked expectantly towards the matchmaker, hoping that she might still say something about her son's prospects but she found Macho Begum sitting in quiet introspection.

'I will keep your son in mind for a suitable girl, one who meets the qualities you want, and come back to you in a few days,' said Macho Begum at last, even as she rose from her chair and prepared to leave.

A fortnight later, Macho Begum reappeared one morning. After exchanging salutations and having rested herself sufficiently to recover her breath she came to the subject.

'Begum, I have two suitable matches for your son. There is this girl, the twenty-year-old daughter of a factory owner of Lahore who makes and sells rat traps by the thousands all over India. The parents will give two houses in dowry and expect nothing from the boy's side. You could travel to Lahore to see their daughter and be their guests.' Macho Begum paused to fill another betel leaf with condiments, which she thrust into her mouth before starting to chew. 'Well ... what do you think of it?' she asked, looking expectantly towards her client.

'Macho Begum, I am not rejecting this girl outright because she may have many good qualities but I wouldn't like to have my son marry a girl who comes from a home where, most of her life, all she has been hearing is about rat traps of every shape and size. What about the other one?'

Saad Ashraf

'The other girl is from the famous Rattan family of jewellers. You know they are from among the wealthiest and oldest families of Delhi, their ancestors having settled in this city during the time of Emperor Bedar Bakht. I have seen their teenaged daughter Sara. She is beautiful and is said to be devout and an excellent cook. Haji Jaffar, her father, had received a marriage proposal for the Nawab of Zanjira's son, but the Haji rejected the boy. He didn't want his daughter to marry into a family of nawabs because of their bad reputation. They prefer a boy from a business background but I could put in a proposal for your son. This girl is not formally educated but can read and write,' said Macho Begum.

Noorani Begum had been listening to Macho Begum's monologue with rapt attention. She became more and more excited as Macho Begum elaborated on the qualities of the prospective bride and she became fixated in wanting this daughter from the Rattan family as a wife for her son.

'Macho Begum, I have made up my mind. This would be the ideal match for my son and I'd like you to propose his name for the hand of Haji Jaffar's daughter.'

'I don't think you should make decisions so quickly in matters of marriage on which the quality of your future generations depend. Marriage is not like taking a bath. In our society and culture it is a one-time deal. The least you can do is get your son's consent.'

'My son will do what I decide is best for him in these matters. In an arranged match he won't get a chance to see the girl himself and will have to depend upon the opinion of intermediaries like you and me.'

'In that case, if nothing else you should at least see Haji Jaffar's daughter yourself and meet her mother.'

'I think that is a good idea. I will meet the girl and her mother first and then send a proposal through you.'

Within the next two days, Macho Begum arranged for Noorani Begum to visit Haji Jaffar's house in Kucha Dehlavi to see his daughter Sara. Macho Begum accompanied her. Haji Jaffar lived in a big mansion which was formerly the palace of one of the principal courtiers of the last Mughal emperor. The courtier had been hanged for complicity with the mutineers. Thereafter, Haji Jaffar's forefathers had secured the property on a bid sealed by the auctioneer's hammer.

Noorani Begum found Sara even more attractive than described by Macho Begum. She had large brown eyes set in an oval face with chiselled features. Her skin had the glow, colour, and texture of freshly churned butter and she had an enticing body which would excite any man's imagination. Noorani Begum made some futile attempts to strike up a conversation with Sara but this was hardly a cause for concern as young, unmarried girls were generally uncommunicative and shy by nature. Sara did speak to her mother a few times—in what appeared to be 'businessman's Hindustani', a version of the language used mostly by the shopkeepers of Delhi. Noorani Begum considered this too as normal. After all, Sara was a merchant's daughter. In any case, a few small deficiencies on either side could always be rectified with some effort. Noorani Begum drank the piping-hot milk offered in mugs made from red baked earth and indulged in small talk with Sara's mother without dropping a hint as to the purpose of the visit.

On the way back home, Macho Begum asked, 'Well, what is your opinion of Haji Jaffar's daughter?'

'The same as I had without seeing her. Please go ahead with a formal proposal on behalf of my son for the hand of Haji Jaffar's daughter.'

'Wouldn't you like to think over this matter for a couple of days? It is always good to sleep over such matters for sometime before arriving at a decision.'

'No,' came the emphatic answer.

'If that's the way you want it, I would like to settle the terms. After all, I make a living out of making matches.'

'What are your terms?'

'I will take three hundred rupees, half payable in advance, one gold bangle of at least two tolas, a pair of brocade dresses,

Saad Ashraf

and an invitation to the marriage which is mandatory for the matchmaker,' said Macho Begum in a businesslike manner.

'I offer you four hundred rupees with a quarter in advance, two gold bangles of two tolas each, three brocade dresses, and an invitation to the marriage as a sister and not as a matchmaker if you can conclude this matter successfully.'

'Agreed.'

twenty-one

While Noorani Begum was arranging to send a marriage proposal for Ghulam Rasool to the Rattan family in Delhi, he had become the focus of attention for his deputy and his wife hundreds of miles away in Lahore. Rashid's children called him uncle and his wife Sumbul had, according to the custom, made Ghulam Rasool her brother by tying a piece of black thread around his left wrist. With each meeting, Ghulam Rasool came to admire Sumbul's housekeeping efficiency and her quiet charm. As time went by, he started the day waiting expectantly for an invitation from Rashid.

One evening, when Ghulam Rasool was at their home for dinner, he was introduced to Sabah, Sumbul's younger, unmarried sister. Sabah was a beautiful woman with a fair complexion and green eyes, auburn hair, and a well-proportioned body—a rare physical combination for an Indian woman. The more Ghulam Rasool saw Sabah the more beautiful she seemed to him. She spoke Hindustani tinged with a Punjabi accent which though harsh to the ears sounded like music to Ghulam Rasool. Rashid and Sumbul sensed that Ghulam Rasool was attracted to Sabah and often left them alone on one pretext or another.

While the intimacy between the two was still in its infancy, Mr Barnett, the postmaster general, had been getting reports of Ghulam Rasool's closeness with his deputy from one of the many spies he had planted throughout the department. His experience in the posts and telegraphs department had taught him that such intimacy between an officer and a subordinate, with the permissible exceptions of Europeans, was not desirable. As such, when he heard of a vacancy for a postmaster in Delhi he casually dropped Ghulam Rasool's name as an outstanding postal officer eminently suitable for that position. In that context, Ghulam Rasool was summoned one morning by the postmaster general to his office on Mall Road. After Ghulam Rasool was seated, Mr Barnett put aside the file he was working on, took off his glasses, and heaved a short sigh.

'Ghulam Rasool, I am sorry we haven't seen each other for sometime, busy as I have been with my work and touring. When they transferred you here I had promised you an independent posting as a postmaster. I have now agreed with the authorities, with the greatest of reluctance of course, to send you back to Delhi where you will be one of the four postmasters of the offices located in the Capital. This is a prestigious position and I am glad that they picked you up on my recommendation. I am sure you'll be happy going back to Delhi, your home town. Since you are urgently needed there, you may like to handover temporary charge of your office to your deputy till we can find a replacement for you,' said Mr Barnett.

If Ghulam Rasool was perplexed on hearing the news of his transfer he hid it well behind a straight face and a large but fake smile of gratitude.

'Thank you very much, sir. You are indeed my benefactor. I have been fortunate to have worked with you,' said Ghulam Rasool as coolly as possible and left his boss's office.

Deep down within himself, Ghulam Rasool was agitated at being transferred back to Delhi within three months when the normal tenure for an officer was three years. An even greater cause of his suffering was that Sabah, who had created a place in his heart, would be left behind in Lahore while he would have to nurse the wounds inflicted by her absence and the memories of her green eyes, auburn hair, and Punjabi-accented Hindustani.

The news of Ghulam Rasool's transfer spread fast throughout the postal circle and reached the ears of Noorani Begum in Delhi through the postman who came to deliver mail at the White

Haveli. Noorani Begum prayed to Allah that this be true but for the moment dismissed it as rumour. However, only a few days later, she received a letter from Ghulam Rasool confirming what the postman had said.

Rashid was deeply affected by Ghulam Rasool's transfer. He and his family had never been on such friendly terms with any superior officer and the relationship was deepening by the hour after Ghulam Rasool had met Sabah. Rashid and his wife held high hopes that the growing intimacy between Ghulam Rasool and Sabah would ultimately lead to their marriage which would cement their relationship even further and auger well for the future, but all their hopes seemed to have evaporated with this sudden transfer.

Rashid hosted a farewell dinner in honour of Ghulam Rasool a day before his departure for Delhi. It was a sad affair. Everyone tried smiling through their grim expressions except Sabah who had been crying ever since she learnt of Ghulam Rasool's transfer. She merely looked down at the floor, her green eyes now bloodshot, and sighed softly, recalling moments of her infatuation and trying her best to overcome her emotions so that her grief did not show on her face.

Ghulam Rasool left for Delhi the next day. Surprisingly, nobody from his office turned up to bid him goodbye except his loyal deputy and friend Rashid. After one tearful last embrace with Rashid, Ghulam Rasool boarded the train as it pulled out of the Lahore railway station.

Noorani Begum was, of course, overjoyed with this lucky break which had brought Ghulam Rasool back to Delhi just as she was taking the preliminary steps to get him married. She and her daughters waited with garlands of fresh roses in their hands to receive Ghulam Rasool at the lower landing of the house.

'Welcome, welcome home,' they sang in chorus as Ghulam Rasool arrived from the railway station. Noorani Begum put her arms around her son and kissed him on the forehead. Then they all went upstairs and sat down to a rich breakfast which

Noorani Begum had prepared. Even a casual look at Ghulam Rasool revealed that his countenance could best be described as dark and brooding. The substantial weight he had put on since leaving Delhi three months ago didn't help matters.

A few days later, Ghulam Rasool took charge as the postmaster of the New Delhi Post Office located near the secretariat blocks. It was a new and important post office catering to the requirements of the nerve centre of British power in India and its boss, the viceroy, the uncrowned king of British India.

Almost immediately afterwards, Noorani Begum went to work, pursuing her son's marriage in the Rattan family of jewellers by sending a message to Macho Begum to come and see her the next morning. Macho Begum attended to the summons promptly.

Noorani Begum tried to create a congenial atmosphere for the meeting by complimenting the matchmaker on the beautiful dress she was wearing and its fine fabric, but this had little effect on Macho Begum. The experienced matchmaker merely looked straight ahead, chewing on the remains of a betel leaf in her mouth.

'Macho Begum, I have troubled you today to find out how far you've gone with the proposal of my son in the Rattan family,' Noorani Begum said hesitatingly.

Macho Begum yawned with boredom, putting her right hand on her mouth.

'Noorani Begum, I told you right in the beginning that matrimonial matters take time and one needs to be patient. I have already dropped a few hints to Haji Jaffar's wife that an excellent proposal is available for her daughter. I will go in a day or two to find out whether it has registered with her and whether she has mentioned it to her husband.'

'But, Begum, can't you do something to speed up matters?' remarked Noorani Begum, a trace of impatience discernible in her voice.

'Noorani Begum, a marriage proposal is like a seed that you have to plant with care in the minds of parents and nurture it carefully so that it grows slowly but surely. If one tries to hurry things up by acting too vigorously, the parties start feeling suspicious that something is wrong with the match being proposed. You have to trust me and my experience. By the way, I hope you've informed your son in Lahore about this proposal.'

'I haven't yet, but I will tonight. My son has been transferred back to Delhi, as postmaster at the viceroy's house,' Noorani Begum boasted.

'Really ...! Why didn't you tell me earlier ... postmaster of the lord sahib's house, hmm ... that makes things even easier just in case Haji Jaffar wishes to meet your son. I'll see how I can push things with the family without making them feel that we are anxious for an early answer,' said Macho Begum, putting on a sly smile.

That afternoon, after Ghulam Rasool returned home from work and lay on the charpai, relaxing, Noorani Begum started hovering around him.

'Beta, Macho Begum came to visit me today,' said Noorani Begum, addressing her son casually.

Ghulam Rasool continued to lie still on the cot, his eyes closed. 'Macho Begum? Is she some relative?' he asked.

'I am surprised you haven't heard of Macho Begum. She is the most famous matchmaker of Delhi. She must have arranged the marriages of at least a thousand couples, if not more, in the last decade.'

'What has Macho Begum got to do with me?' enquired Ghulam Rasool, now looking at his mother.

'Well, I've asked her to propose your name for Sara, the daughter of Haji Jaffar who comes from the famous Rattan family of jewellers. I have already seen my prospective daughter-in-law. Even the fairies and angels in heaven would pale before her. She's got everything—the face, the complexion, the cooking skills, and the wealth. Oh, you'd be so lucky if they accept you,' said an overexcited Noorani Begum.

'Ammi, did you ask Macho Begum whether Haji Jaffar's daughter is educated?' interjected Ghulam Rasool.

'She has read the Quran and is from a devout background. She is a haji's daughter.'

Saad Ashraf

Ghulam Rasool was sitting up by now. 'But Ammi, you laid so much emphasis on western education for me right from childhood. Wouldn't you like to have a daughter-in-law who is educated like your son and perhaps knows a bit of English as well?'

Noorani Begum pondered over her son's words for a while.

'A woman doesn't have to be educated to make a good home. How much education did I have to survive without a husband and educate a son? In any case, if there are any deficiencies they can always be made up. You can always have an Anglo-Indian governess to come and teach your wife English,' said Noorani Begum.

'You should have at least asked me before proposing my name for marriage anywhere. After all, I am not a piece of furniture to be pawned off like this. Maybe I have other ideas, a choice of my own perhaps,' said Ghulam Rasool, summoning all the courage he could.

'A choice of your own, did I hear? And where did you make this choice—in the Punjab? And who gave you the right to make it after I scrubbed pots and pans for nearly twenty years and underwent all privations alone to educate you and look after the family, eh?' said Noorani Begum. Her eyes were alight and her face red with fury. She was like an angry tigress, ready to pounce.

Ghulam Rasool had never seen his mother like this before and kept his cool. He had learnt from his bosses at the post office that when tempers ran high, it was best to wait for a monsoon shower.

That night, as Ghulam Rasool lay on his bed, facing the corrugated tin roof over his head, he recalled his infatuation with the green-eyed, red-haired Sabah in Lahore, and wondered what she was doing at this very moment when he was thinking of her. If only he had had more time with her maybe their relationship could have developed into true love and a partnership for life. He had touched the boundaries of love and then had been forced to withdraw by the hands of fate that had intervened through his transfer. Maybe it was ordained that things should happen this way. He sighed at the thought of what could have been, turned over on his side, and went to sleep, having resigned to his destiny.

A couple of days later, when Ghulam Rasool had left for work, there was the sound of heavy footsteps on the stairway leading to Noorani Begum's door, followed by a loud knock.

'Open up! Open up quickly, Noorani Begum.'

It was Macho Begum.

Noorani Begum opened the door to find the matchmaker in a highly excited state.

'What is the matter? Hai Allah, I hope everything is all right with you, Macho Begum.' Noorani Begum took off the chain latch and ushered the matchmaker into the house.

'Noorani Begum, there's some good news for you. I have just been to Haji Jaffar's house, talking to his wife. They have provisionally accepted your son for their daughter, Sara, subject to checking on his character. More importantly, dowry is not an issue at all, and they impose no condition for it. My experience of arranging matches for over a decade has taught me that this is by far the most difficult stage, and the rest are mere formalities, that is if both sides are well intentioned,' said Macho Begum.

Noorani Begum got up from her chair, embraced Macho Begum affectionately, and kissed her on both her fluffed-up, betel-filled cheeks. 'Oh, Macho Begum, how can I thank you! You are not a matchmaker but an angel sent by Allah with the list of all the matches which have already been made in the heavens,' she said, putting her arm around the rotund shoulders of the matchmaker. 'So what happens now?'

'Now I'll keep in touch with Haji Jaffar's wife and keep you informed of further developments. If their enquiries do not bring out anything against your son, we should be able to fix a date for the marriage. Tell your son to keep his eyes and ears open for anyone making enquiries about him and make sure that only good words reach the haji's ears.'

Noorani Begum went inside her room and brought a large tin of perfumed condiments which Jahan Ara Begum had given her as a gift from Lucknow.

Saad Ashraf

'This is for you, Macho Begum, over and above everything else I've agreed to give you,' said Noorani Begum, handing the painted tin to her with an expression of gratitude.

'Begum, you should be distributing alms to the poor at the Royal Mosque and sweetmeats to your neighbours. The very best families of Delhi dream of getting a son married into the Rattan family. This is undoubtedly the most difficult match I have made in my whole life,' said Macho Begum.

Though immensely happy, as a matter of precaution, Noorani Begum decided to wait till a date was fixed for her son's marriage before distributing alms to the poor at the Royal Mosque and sweetmeats to her neighbours.

Macho Begum visited her again a few days later to confirm the happy news that Haji Jaffar and his wife had agreed to the match after their investigations had revealed that Ghulam Rasool was a man of good character. The wedding was fixed for 21 January 1922 in Delhi against a dower amount of a hundred and one silver rupees payable to the bride at the time of marriage.

twenty-two

I t was after Ghulam Rasool had joined Missionary College that he found his libido surface. Ahmad had introduced him to the irresistible spell that the red-light area casts over the human mind through the magical combination of the arts of music and dance expounded through the delicacy of the female voice and body. Ghulam Rasool could resist this spell because he knew that he had little to fall back upon. Ahmad was his window to bohemianism, gaiety, and friendship in which he could confide the secrets of his heart without the fear of anybody else sharing them. He had not forgotten the faint brush of Roshan Ara's breasts against his chest the first time Ahmad took him to see her sing and dance in Chawri Bazaar, nor the exhortations of love she made in the words of an unknown poet, her painted face held six inches away from his. Even though these incidents had not aroused him, they made him aware of the power a woman could exercise over a man. He wondered what influence a wife could exercise over a husband with sex, love, care, and cooking as her main weapons when she had most of the day and all night to put them to work. He decided to see Ahmad to share the news of his impending marriage.

'Our family has known the Rattan family of jewellers since time immemorial. They are a part of the history of Delhi. All I can say is that you are a lucky person to be getting married into that family and I am just as unlucky not to have the eyes which would enable me to see my best friend on the most important day of his life,' Ahmad said when they met.

'Ahmad mian, whether you can see or not is Allah's will but I assure you that there will always be a place in my heart and home for you. On my wedding day you will be right next to me, just like the best man at a Christian wedding.'

Ahmad's face lit up with a big smile.

'I know, Mian, I shall always have a place in your heart but it will be your wife who will rule your home and it would be her wish that would prevail once you are married as it does in all the homes of India. I will have a place in your home only if she chooses to, not otherwise.'

'You mean that after I am married I will have no say in my own house? How cruel can one be to a man!' exclaimed an amused Ghulam Rasool.

'Mian, I have more experience of women than you have. They are usually able to get whatever they want, sooner or later, having been endowed by Allah with intelligence and forbearance which no man can match. A husband eventually becomes a wife's slave in a successful marriage.'

'I am afraid that as far as I know, your only experience of women is with those who sit in the bazaar to entice men through their singing and dancing. What would you know about a woman as a wife? You've never been married.'

'It is true that I have no personal experience of married life but I am narrating what married men of different nationalities told me during the war in Europe. With death waiting stealthily in the trenches to strike any moment, men would speak the truth and the majority of them said that the voice and the will of the woman in their home were supreme. Surely, all these people from different cultures and nationalities couldn't be wrong if most of them said the same thing.'

'A woman's supremacy in the home does not mean that she wouldn't accede to a reasonable request from the husband. What else did they say which you think would be helpful to a friend who is getting married?' enquired Ghulam Rasool.

'Well ... the majority said that the wife was a reflection of her mother in everything. So if you have to select a wife you should see how her mother ran the home, interacted with her husband, relatives, and friends because her daughter would in all likelihood be similar.'

'I earnestly agree with this view, though in India, given that marriages are arranged, there is little possibility of knowing what the environment is like in a prospective mother-in-law's home. Is there any other advice you'd like to give me?'

'I think in this part of the world it is important for a husband to consummate the marriage on the wedding night itself, otherwise people start doubting your sexual capabilities,' Ahmad advised sagely.

'Ahmad mian, I ask you: is it a man who is getting married or a horse? What a husband and wife do on the wedding night should strictly be their personal business,' replied Ghulam Rasool.

'Mian, if you don't perform on the wedding night, you will be another martyr to the cause of emancipation and equality of the sexes in Indian society for which it is not ready, besides being the target of a scandal in which your partner may be the prime accuser.'

'I don't mind being a martyr to a good cause and I don't care what people say!' countered Ghulam Rasool. He thanked Ahmad for his sincerity and forthrightness, and left for home with thoughts of his wedding day in January.

21 January 1922 was cold yet sunny, with the clear blue sky stretching over the city like an endless canopy. When Ghulam Rasool looked at its unfathomable depths that morning, he felt this was nature's way of welcoming his wedding day. The house was brimful with female relatives who cackled with laughter and gossip, most of whom Ghulam Rasool had never seen before, some claiming to be his aunts.

'I am Macho Begum, your most important aunt here. I am the one who arranged this match. I always make it a point to see the bridegroom on his wedding day and wish him well. It gives one such a great feeling, bringing families together,' she said, placing her hand on Ghulam Rasool's chin.

Saad Ashraf

The proceedings of the wedding started from the Royal Mosque with the all-male ceremony presided over by the imam who announced the betrothal after reading portions from the Quran at four p.m., an auspicious time between the afternoon and evening prayers. Ghulam Rasool had undertaken to marry Haji Jaffar's daughter and keep her as a wife against a dower, as specified during the negotiations preceding the marriage, duly paid to the bride's father. This was followed by a dinner hosted by Haji Jaffar at his house.

Ghulam Rasool had invited about a dozen Englishmen and Anglo-Indians and their mems as his personal guests for the dinner. The white folk were the star attraction for the local guests who marvelled at the ease with which Ghulam Rasool mingled with them. With dinner over and the guests having departed with smiles of satisfaction on their faces caused by bellyful of curries, rice, and pudding, the groom was ushered into the zenana of Haji Jaffar's house and placed at the mercy of a group of female relatives of the bride. The only concession allowed to him while entering the zenana was that he could have Ahmad as an escort because the latter was sightless. Ahmad clutched Ghulam Rasool around his right arm with his sinewy fingers, as much to keep a hold on his friend as to make sure that he himself did not fall or lose his way. The women spewed their pent-up energy, which they saved for such occasions, by shouting, pushing, and pulling both Ghulam Rasool and Ahmad back and forth as if they were prized bulls let loose in the ring. Fortunately for them, Noorani Begum and Macho Begum saw them in this sorry state and came to their rescue. The traditional ceremonies—which seemed endless—finally concluded at around eleven in the night as Ghulam Rasool and Ahmad were pushed out of the zenana to await the arrival of the bride.

'Thank Allah, it's all over! I understand why a man gets married in his life only once. It is only the very brave who would dare go through all this a second time,' said Ghulam Rasool to Ahmad, wiping the sweat which trickled down his face in spite of the cold.

'It is not yet over, Mian. For you the night has just begun with the hardest part yet to come,' said Ahmad with a sly smile.

The wail of women that had arisen from the haji's house a little earlier rose to a crescendo as the time finally arrived to bid farewell to the girl who had been born and who had lived within its four walls for years. Ghulam Rasool was tense as he waited next to the imam's black Ford saloon car decked with flowers. The imam had recently purchased it and placed it at Ghulam Rasool's disposal for the wedding day. Ghulam Rasool thought of how difficult and cruel a moment this was for the parents and the bride, neither of whom knew what fate held for them in the shape of a son-in-law or a husband. His bride emerged fully covered with not a finger showing, laden with garlands of threaded flowers, silver and gold-coloured buntings. The haji stood at the door to bid farewell to his daughter.

'May Allah always be with you, Beti,' he said, tears dripping down his face. She could no longer control herself and let out a muted cry. The haji stood at the door with his arms wide open as if trying to retrieve his lost child and the wailing faded in the distance as the car pulled out of Kucha Dehlavi for its five-minute journey to White Haveli. Silence reigned in the car, punctuated by the sobs of Ghulam Rasool's newly wedded wife.

On the front seat next to the chauffeur, Ghulam Rasool found a woman in a burqa, her head barely reaching above the seat.

'And who may I ask are you?' enquired Ghulam Rasool.

She turned her head around, lifted the netted flap, and revealed her face.

'I am Mubarik Begum, the maid who brought up Sara right from the time she was born. She was weaned on my milk. I will settle her in her new home. You can call me Mubarik khala if you like,' she said.

Noorani Begum, her daughters, and some other female relatives had arrived in advance at the White Haveli to receive the bride and groom. They had converted Ghulam Rasool's sitting room into a temporary bedroom for the couple and had decorated the

Saad Ashraf

four-post silver bridal bed which the haji had sent to Noorani Begum's house the previous day.

A table lay in the room with a tray laden with fruits and two glasses of pistachio-filled milk.

A young girl came rushing up the stairs and shouted excitedly.

'The bride and groom are here.'

There was a rush of women down the stairs, as the black Ford car came to a stop before the landing of the house. Noorani Begum and her daughters came forward to receive Ghulam Rasool and his bride.

A cock was slaughtered at the feet of the couple to keep evil spirits away, and Ghulam Rasool was asked by his mother to carry his bride over the threshold of the house, a ritual meant to ensure their happiness for all times to come.

Once in their room, the throng of women continued unabated.

'She looks like a fairy descended from the heavens,' said one woman, holding Sara's chin up for all to see.

'Her skin is like butter, but it shines like gold,' observed another.

'Look at her nose, her mouth, the red lips, and kohl-coloured hair. Allah must have taken his time in creating her,' said yet another.

There was no stopping.

Sitting next to his wife, an increasingly embarrassed and fidgety Ghulam Rasool saw Macho Begum in the crowd of women and beckoned her outside the room.

'Macho Begum, you said you were the most important aunt I had here, so I'd like you to do me a favour,' he said.

'Anything, Beta, it is your wedding day.'

'Please get all these women out of my room. I would like to have some time alone with my wife.'

'I understand ... I'll do so immediately. Once I clear the room just bolt it from inside and don't let anyone come in no matter who knocks.'

Macho Begum went back to the room and whispered something in one woman's ear followed by that of another. Soon, all the women seemed to be whispering something to each other. A little later they were seen trooping out of the room.

Ghulam Rasool bolted the door.

He looked at his wife for the first time. She was young and pretty. Everything the women said about her beauty seemed to be true. She had a snow-white complexion, a round face, and high cheekbones, and her hair was dense and jet black in colour. She had pulled down the veil to cover her head which was bent low out of shyness or fear.

Ghulam Rasool realized how hard it must be for her to be in a totally alien environment with an unknown man and how undignified it was for a woman of beauty to sit with her head bent before a man.

'I won't hurt you, Sara. I am an educated man and education makes a person kind and sensitive to the feelings of others. You need not be afraid of me. If we talk to one another we will come to know each other better and faster and that will help both of us,' said Ghulam Rasool.

Sara sat quietly without budging and Ghulam Rasool kept trying, offering her fruits and pistachio milk in an effort to break the ice and make her talk. But all his efforts seemed to be in vain. Sara would not communicate and the only audible words he was able to get out of her were a yes or no. It was nearing one o'clock. The cock's crow and the distant sound of hooves on the metalled road around the Royal Mosque could be heard through the dark, cold night.

Ghulam Rasool felt too tired to continue. 'Sara, it has been a long and tiring day for both of us and we need some sleep. It may be best for you to change into something more comfortable, take off the jewellery you are wearing, and get some rest,' he said.

'What would people say in the morning if we were to go to sleep now without fulfilling the obligations of marriage,' remarked Sara.

This was the first time Ghulam Rasool heard her speak a complete sentence. Somehow, her voice seemed to bear a close resemblance to that of Roshan Ara, the dancing girl he had visited along with Ahmad as compensation for his private tutoring. His

Saad Ashraf

thoughts went back to the faint brush of Roshan Ara's breasts against his chest several years ago. Ghulam Rasool was mildly aroused.

'How would people know what happens here unless you and I tell them?' asked Ghulam Rasool.

'Women have a way of finding out such things from the way one talks, the facial expressions and mannerisms. There is Mubarik Begum who has looked after me ever since I was a child. She knows what I am going to say before I open my mouth. Besides, I will be going to my mother's house in the morning as is the custom and my mother will ask what went on in the night, and it is impossible to lie to a woman who gave you birth. She is bound to find out,' said Sara.

The more Sara spoke, the more Ghulam Rasool thought of Roshan Ara. He realized that he had kept his most intimate thoughts about Roshan Ara to himself. He had never told Ahmad how much he wanted to clasp Roshan Ara in his arms as she sat facing him and to kiss those lips through which words of devotion poured out in a song. He got up from the bed and stood in front of Sara. He thought that his mind was playing tricks on him, and it was only his imagination at work that Sara seemed to him to have become Roshan Ara. But as he looked at her closely, it seemed for a moment that Roshan Ara had indeed traversed time to come and sit on the bed as his wife.

Ghulam Rasool clasped her head and drew it to his midriff; she smiled and looked up at him and responded by placing her head willingly. He held both her hands in his and guided her from the bed towards him. She stood before him, her lips slightly parted, as a faint smile of expectation lit up her face. He found himself holding Sara in his arms. He realized that she was at least six inches shorter. It gave him an immense sense of power as he looked down on her. He squeezed her in a tight embrace and planted his lips on hers. She put her arms around him and he kissed the back of her neck. His hands felt her bare body under her dress, first her back and then her young and tight bosom. She let out muted shrieks as he massaged her. She seemed to be in a daze, intoxicated with pleasure. He put his head on her breast. He was doing with her whatever he might have wanted to do with Roshan Ara. There was no time to take off the jewellery or her gold bangles or the heavy necklace embedded with precious stones that she was wearing. He slipped his hand under the heavy brocaded dress, feeling for the knot of the cord that tied her trousers to her waist. Sara resisted his endeavours and pushed his hands aside, further stoking the fires of his desire. He tried again and succeeded this time, pulling her trousers down to her knees and guiding her down on the bed. He gave her a covetous look. She covered her eyes with her right arm, the last reaction of a woman who was going to lose her virginity. He lay on top of her and found her body cold. He could see the sweat that had broken out in small white beads on her forehead and face. He had already bared himself and pushed into her with all his might. Her face was contorted and she shrieked in pain as he kept going over and into her, breathing heavily with excitement. A few minutes later peace had descended on both of them. A deep sleep followed their encounter as they lay side by side, clasping one another in a tight embrace till they were interrupted by the muezzin's call for the morning prayers.

'Wake up for the morning prayers and don't forget to say two extra prayers to thank Allah for fulfilling our marital obligations, and I will do likewise,' Sara said to a sleeping Ghulam Rasool.

He got up half-asleep to perform his morning ablutions and offer his morning prayers.

twenty-three

Ghulam Rasool was overwhelmed by the hospitality of his in-laws when, according to tradition, he took Sara and her old maid Mubarik Begum to their house for the first time, on the day following the wedding. He and Sara were met by her parents at the entrance of their home and escorted to the sitting room located deep inside the maze of rooms in their mansion. A short while later, Sara and his mother-in-law disappeared and he was left alone with his father-in-law. Haji Jaffar was a tall, fair-bearded man with a slight stoop which became apparent when he got up to walk. He talked to Ghulam Rasool about the latter's job and its future prospects. He mentioned the turmoil that was seeping into India due to the rising wave of nationalism. The haji felt sure that at some point in time the British would have to leave India which would be governed by its own people. He could not say whether that would be good for the Indians and whether the peace that existed now, so essential for trade and prosperity, would continue. Ghulam Rasool abstained from being drawn into a political discussion, remembering Professor Thompson's oft-repeated advice to his students that for the sake of maintaining harmony in relationships it was best not to discuss politics and religion, both being subjects on which everyone held his own stringent opinion.

'Beta, now that you are here I'd like to discuss another matter with you. I have transferred the ownership of two of my houses to Sara. What would you like me to do with the rent that I will receive from the first of the next month for this property? Can I send it to you so that you can put it in your joint account and spend it in whatever manner you may want,' said the haji.

'Chachajaan, you didn't have to transfer ownership of the houses to her name. I am not rich but my salary is sufficient to take care of our expenses. Indeed, I was planning to give some pocket money to Sara to spend as she likes. You may like to keep the rent with you and give your daughter whatever you like when she visits you here,' replied Ghulam Rasool.

Haji Jaffar was impressed with the integrity of his son-in-law. Ghulam Rasool had also formed a good opinion about his father-in-law whose straightforwardness, hospitality, and a certain sadness in his light-brown eyes combined to make him an endearing personality. Ghulam Rasool felt that his father-in-law could go a long way to fill the emotional vacuum which had haunted him because of the absence of a father.

Sara came out with her mother, beaming with happiness.

'Ammi wants to know if I can stay here for the night ... I can come home tomorrow if it is all right with you,' said Sara.

Ghulam Rasool had no objections to the proposal. He shook hands with his father-in-law and left.

When Ghulam Rasool got back home, Noorani Begum opened the door for him.

'Well ... how did your visit to your in-laws go?' she enquired.

'Ammi, I am greatly impressed with my in-laws. They are exceptionally hospitable people. My father-in-law has already transferred two houses in Sara's name for her convenience. I think Ahmad mian was right when he said that I was lucky to be marrying in the Rattan family,' replied Ghulam Rasool.

'Haji Jaffar has transferred two houses to his daughter's name? Where are these houses? Are they lying empty or have they been rented out?' asked Noorani Begum, raising her eyebrows.

'I didn't ask where they are, I suppose they are in Delhi and rented out because Haji Sahib said that he would like to send the monthly rent to me. But I told him to keep it with himself and give it to his daughter whenever she visits them.'

Saad Ashraf

'You should have at least asked where these houses were and who they are rented out to and for how much—after all, you and Sara are married now and everything either of you owns belongs to both of you. I don't think there's any harm in you receiving the rent every month and passing it on to Sara.'

'Ammi, it would have looked downright mean of me to ask questions about somebody else's property. What impression would my father-in-law have gathered if I did that—a greedy and mean man who married into his family for money. If he wants to give some property to his daughter he is welcome to do so, the rent is hers to keep or spend as she wishes. My salary is enough to keep all of us going.'

Noorani Begum looked at her son quizzically.

'By the way, where is Sara?' she asked.

'She is with her parents. She wanted to spend the night there and I agreed.'

'Beta, you've just been married and already you are listening to her like an obedient servant. If you continue like this, what's going to happen a few years from now? You'll be standing in her presence like a slave with folded hands, waiting for her next command. I'd advise you to also say no once in a while so that everyone realizes that you are a powerful husband and a son-in-law with a mind of his own.'

Ghulam Rasool kept quiet and slid into his room.

When he slept he recalled all that happened the night before. He was already missing Sara's voice, the aroma of her body, the cold sweat on her forehead, her jet-black hair, and the contortions of pain on her face. How he wished she was here with him in bed. Maybe Noorani Begum was right. He shouldn't agree to everything she wanted. He clasped the pillow to himself and, imagining that it was Sara in his arms, went to sleep.

Within a month of Ghulam Rasool getting married, Noorani Begum had manoeuvred to get Sara to spend some time in the kitchen to help prepare the meals. As Macho Begum had described, Sara turned out to be an excellent cook. Her mother had trained her well in this art, believing that the way to a man's heart lay through his stomach. Sara knew of some old Mughal recipes which had been passed down her mother's family through the generations. She put this knowledge to full use by cooking a dish a day for Noorani Begum and her family. Everybody admitted that they had never tasted such delicious pulao, curries, lentils, and kebabs before. Noorani Begum tried once or twice to find out more about these recipes, but Sara managed to spurn her by telling her that as long as she was around, there was no need for her mother-in-law to waste her time in the kitchen.

In due course, Sara slowly but surely created a place for herself in Noorani Begum's household. She had become friendly with Rehmani. Jahan Ara Begum, the tenant downstairs, too seemed to be fond of her, and when she came for her gossip sessions with Noorani Begum, Sara would sometimes join them though she contributed little.

The months passed by quickly. Jahan Ara Begum came up one morning. She seemed to have something confidential to discuss.

'Noorani Begum, I do not hear of good tidings from you although more than nine months have passed since Ghulam Rasool got married. I say, is everything all right? By now your daughter-in-law should have been expecting. However, I have a recipe for the situation ...' whispered Jahan Ara Begum.

Noorani Begum heaved a long, sad sigh.

'Begum, I too am worried. You know Mughlani Begum who lives in the neighbourhood came to me for advice when her own daughter was not conceiving. When her daughter delivered a boy nine months later, she came to see me and said, "Begum, is it true that a medicine does not work on a doctor who prescribes it for others? You have helped so many women to conceive through your advice but have been unable to do anything for your daughter-in-law." Now, that remark really hurt. By the way, what is your recipe for such a situation?'

'Ask your son to go on leave and take Sara to Mehrauli for a few days. How do you expect him to impregnate her if he spends the whole day in the din of envelopes being defaced or hearing

Saad Ashraf

the squabble about parcels and money orders not reaching the addressee? On the way to Mehrauli they should visit the shrine of the naked fakir near the old fort. A niece of mine who wasn't conceiving went to this shrine and prayed for the fakir's help and, lo and behold, nine months later she delivered a baby boy! I don't see why Sara would not be able to do likewise if your son devotes full attention to her and the naked fakir's blessings are also with him.'

'Begum, I think you are right. I'll speak to my son this very evening when he returns home from work,' said Noorani Begum.

Later that evening, Noorani Begum approached her son when she found him alone in a rocking chair he had brought recently in which he relaxed when he returned from work.

'Beta, if your father was alive today I would have asked him to talk to you about this but I am deeply worried that there is no sign yet of you starting a family. You know that is what marriage is all about,' said Noorani Begum.

Ghulam Rasool continued rocking on his chair, unconcerned.

'Do you hear what I am saying!' continued Noorani Begum, her voice rising, as she felt slighted by Ghulam Rasool's silence.

'I hear you, Ammi! Here you are, bothering me with this question and there in Kucha Dehlavi whenever Sara goes to visit her parents, her mother and other relatives pester her with the same question. The other day she asked me to help her frame a reply which both of us can give to such a question. What can we do if there is no news—it is Allah's will,' replied Ghulam Rasool despondently.

'Well, you can take some leave and go and spend some time in Mehrauli where both the climate and the water are better than in Delhi. I am sure that would help. If nothing else, it would be a holiday and a change for both of you.'

'I just took a fortnight's leave to get married in January. Mr Bartlam, the new deputy postmaster general, may get annoyed if I ask him for some more now.'

'There's no harm in trying. If he is unwilling you can always withdraw your application by telling him that although you needed leave urgently for a personal problem, you will take it another time because duty comes first.'

'All right, I'll apply for a week's leave and see what happens. Anything else?'

'Yes. If you go to Mehrauli, visit the naked fakir's shrine near the fort which is on the way. Take Sara with you to the tomb of the naked fakir and pray for a child. You may find many naked disciples of the fakir at the shrine; distribute alms to them. It is rare if ever that one's prayers for conception are not answered at this shrine.'

'Ammi, do you really believe in the naked fakir! How can one say whether a human being is buried in that grave? You know as well as I do that it is Allah's will that prevails in all matters and it is to him that we should pray for what we want and not to a fakir dead for hundreds of years who was a human being like us.'

Her son's intransigence greatly perturbed Noorani Begum. 'You talk like a heretic at times, and I pray that you be protected from Allah's wrath. Even if you don't believe in the naked fakir and his powers, what would you lose if you spend half an hour on your way to Mehrauli? Neither you nor I know of Allah's ways. If visiting the shrine and praying there for a child didn't work, why do so many childless couples visit the shrine at all hours of the day and night?' she said.

'All right, Ammi, all right! I'll visit the shrine if I am granted leave and am able to take that holiday in Mehrauli.' Ghulam Rasool threw up his hands in despair.

He applied for one week's leave the next day. The leave was sanctioned by the deputy postmaster general to commence on 1 November 1922.

'Don't forget to visit the naked fakir's shrine and get his blessings on the way to Mehrauli,' said Noorani Begum, bidding her son and daughter-in-law goodbye as they sat in the car taking them from White Haveli on the balmy November morning. The car belonged to Sohan Singh, the transport contractor of the post offices in Delhi, who had developed an instant liking for Ghulam Rasool when he had met him for the first time soon after Ghulam

Rasool had taken charge of the New Delhi Post Office. Sohan Singh was a white-haired, sixty-year-old Sikh from the heart of the Potohar plateau of the Punjab. He was childless and his affection for Ghulam Rasool developed over a period of time into what it may have been for his own son if he could have had one. When Ghulam Rasool had mentioned in passing that he was planning to go for a week's holiday to Mehrauli with his wife, Sohan Singh had insisted that his car would transport them to the post office rest house in Mehrauli and bring them back after a week. Ghulam Rasool had resisted taking this favour but Sohan Singh's persistence finally won the day.

Sohan Singh's Ford convertible was soon out of the walled city on the road that linked the two Delhis—the Old Delhi of the Mughals and Luytens's New Delhi—separated by three hundred years of history. Between the two, in a small forest, lay the ruins of the old fort of Delhi, a witness to the past grandeur of emperors who resided there, their joys and their tragedies. Just beyond the fort, to the left, on a narrow, motorable dirt road was the naked fakir's shrine. Ghulam Rasool asked the driver to turn on the road to the shrine.

'Do we have to go? I don't believe that praying at a grave, even if it is that of a saint, is going to get us what we want,' said Sara.

'I don't believe in it either, but I gave my word to Ammi. So I'm fulfilling my promise,' said Ghulam Rasool.

As they got down from the car, they were surrounded by dirty, half-clad beggars holding out their hands for alms. The air was full of dust and the smell of human excreta mixed with an intermittent whiff of incense. A narrow path led to the shrine, a lime-plastered white building with a single large dome below which the naked fakir lay buried. The grave was covered with a thick, green cloth and was enclosed by a quadrangle of carved stone jali of intricate design. Those who believed in the powers of the naked fakir, prayed for his blessings for conceiving a child, by tying a piece of string on the jali, pledging to serve in the maintenance of the shrine or providing free food for his devotees.

The more ardent devotees promised to spend their entire lives collecting alms in his name, wearing the apparel of nudity. Ghulam Rasool saw many couples talking to these naked dervishes, filling their open hands with coins and in return receiving their blessings as they passed their hands over the head of the woman who was unable to conceive.

The week in Mehrauli passed quickly. Ghulam Rasool and Sara both realized that this was the first time they had one another to themselves since they were married. They walked together along the old tracks which led to ancient wells. The water in these wells was exceptionally cold and was said to be good for both male potency and female fertility. Whenever they were not outdoors they were in bed, making love, promising relentless devotion to one another as long as they lived, and talking of the children they would produce. Sara continued calling Ghulam Rasool her 'sartaj' till that one time when they lay entangled and Ghulam Rasool made her promise that she would call him 'sarkar' instead of sartaj as he felt more aroused whenever she did so.

On the morning they were to return to Delhi, Ghulam Rasool recalled the details of the many occasions during the past week when he had made love to Sara. He stood before the full-length mirror in the room and saw that he seemed to have put on weight because of too much food, sex, and inactivity. He imagined himself as a powerful vulture with Sara as a small, beautiful bird in his claws and found himself in bed again, making love, oblivious of the time. This interlude was interrupted by the honking of a car, a loud knock at their door, and the gruff voice of the caretaker of the rest house informing them that the driver was waiting with the car to take them back to Delhi.

On their return to Delhi, Noorani Begum welcomed them back with a broad, meaningful smile on her face as soon as they had climbed the stairs of the house.

'I hope you had a good time in Mehrauli. Ghulam Rasool's father had planned to buy some land there after he retired but it was not to be,' she said, with a long-drawn sigh and a distant look in her eyes.

Saad Ashraf

'Ammi, we did not forget to visit the naked fakir's shrine on our way to Mehrauli and we prayed at his tomb for his blessings.'

'Excellent! I am sure that something good will come of this pilgrimage. The fakir wouldn't have this kind of a following for centuries if visiting his shrine had no effect.'

Ghulam Rasool nodded and Sara smiled coyly as they both retreated into the sanctuary of their bedroom.

twenty-four

More than a year had passed since Ghulam Rasool and Sara were married. The year had been largely filled with marital joy and Ghulam Rasool's efforts to anglicize his wife. Six months after the marriage, he had persuaded Sara to take tuitions in English conversation from Mrs Chamanlal, whose home tuitions were said to work wonders. It was rumoured that within a month or two her pupils could speak in English well enough to be understood, as well as follow the general trend of a conversation even though they remained ignorant of the English alphabet. But Mrs Chamanlal gave up on Sara after four weeks, refusing even to accept her tuition fee of fifty rupees for the time she had spent on her. When Ghulam Rasool wanted to know why her well-tried system had failed to work on Sara, she demurred at first but on his insistence whispered that she thought Sara suffered from some psychological difficulty in learning English as she considered it to be the language of infidels.

Undeterred by Mrs Chamanlal's opinion, Ghulam Rasool decided to teach English conversation to Sara himself. He made her agree to religiously spending an hour every day with him to memorize the most common expressions of English conversation with their meanings. Within a few weeks, he had taught Sara enough English for her to be able to open a conversation by greeting others and introducing herself. Within another fortnight, he had graduated her to more enlightened remarks one of which was 'English education is necessary for the women of India'. Ghulam Rasool had rehearsed with her as to the sign he would make with his little finger when it was appropriate for her to say this in company. Ghulam Rasool instructed her that the best thing to do whenever she was unable to follow a conversation was to keep quiet and just keep nodding her head as if she was comprehending everything and at an opportune moment say 'please excuse me' and move away from the scene.

In another ten weeks, Ghulam Rasool felt that his wife had memorized enough English words and expressions to be exposed to English-speaking company. But he felt that before she could really be comfortable in such a crowd it was necessary to acquaint her with how she should conduct herself on the dining table. He told her how eating with one's hands and licking one's fingers after a meal was abhorred by the English and advised her about the dangers of belching on the dinner table even though she said that this was a call of nature. He taught her how to use the fork, knife, and spoon, and instructed her not to get up to greet a man but to do so only when she was being introduced to a lady. He cautioned her that in her conversations with English and Anglo-Indian ladies she should never pry into their personal matters and sex life and reminded her of the importance of talking softly, with a smile, looking into the eyes of those with whom she conversed, including men. After Ghulam Rasool had worked sufficiently on her, he conducted mock sessions to evaluate how she would fare in the company of white and brown sahibs and their mems. He concluded his endeavours at Sara's anglicization one evening.

'Sara, I think I have taught you enough of the English language and western manners for you to feel comfortable with both the white and brown sahibs. With time you will gain confidence and be a part of progressive Indian society. Now only one thing remains to be done: you should get rid of your black burqa and take to wearing a chador and shed any complex you may have in talking to men,' Ghulam Rasool instructed.

He had failed to notice the rage overtaking Sara which she was trying her very best to control but which became apparent from the contortions on her face.

'Sarkar, as a dutiful Muslim wife I have done whatever you wanted. I agreed to learn the language and manners of the infidels to please you even though I did not want to do so. But there is a limit to my tolerance. I cannot give up my burqa for the chador and expose my body and face for public viewing, nor attend mixed gatherings, let alone look into the eyes of men and try enticing them in a foreign language. I would rather die than do something which I feel is against my upbringing,' she said, her eyes aflame and her fair hands trembling more in anger than fear.

Sara's response shocked Ghulam Rasool. All his labour over the past months to teach Sara English conversation and manners seemed wasted and all his dreams of converting Sara into a modern, western-oriented Indian woman seemed shattered by her defiant reply.

Ghulam Rasool knew enough of Indian culture to give a befitting rebuttal to Sara, but he was aware that it would serve no purpose. She had neither the background nor the liberal education, to which he had been exposed, to be able to appreciate what he would say. He slumped down into the chair, shaking his head, still unable to come to terms with the reality that had dawned on him that an unbridgeable chasm lay between his views on life and that of his wife.

For days after this argument, Ghulam Rasool sulked, talked little, and stayed away from Sara. He abstained from getting into bed with her in spite of the overtures she made from time to time to indicate that she was in a good mood and willing. This situation lasted for some time until one evening Sara broke down in tears and begged him for his forgiveness.

'I will do whatever you say, sarkar, but only if you become your previous self again. Your silence is killing me. You remember when we went to Mehrauli we had both made vows to one another never to mix a lie with the truth. I merely followed that vow.'

Seeing her on her knees aroused Ghulam Rasool and he tenderly lifted her to the bed. He lay on top of her and murmured into her ears, 'You shall always be my only love, Sara. You will

Saad Ashraf

never have to do what you don't want to ... this is what the years at Missionary College and Aligarh and the English sahibs have taught me.'

Their lovemaking was interrupted by Noorani Begum's banging at their door with the announcement that dinner had been served.

twenty-five

The year 1924 commenced with Noorani Begum waiting in vain for some happy news from her daughter-in-law regarding a pregnancy. Nothing seemed to have worked—neither the visit to the shrine of the naked fakir, nor drinking the water on which the blind mullah at the Royal Mosque had blown his breath after saying special prayers. Not even gulping the smelly potions prescribed by a Delhi hakim who specialized in bringing about conception in infertile couples. As a result, Noorani Begum had reached a state of desperation made worse by the fact that the subject of her son and daughter-in-law's failure in starting a family cropped up in every conversation she had with the people she met. In course of time, the effect of all this gossip spilled over to vitiate the atmosphere of Noorani Begum's home. She decided to take up the matter directly with Ghulam Rasool on a Sunday morning when Sara had gone to visit her parents.

'Beta,' she began, 'you know people are talking all over Delhi that even after two years Sara hasn't been able to bear a child. It is our bad luck that this had to happen to such noble souls as yourselves, but both of you tried everything and were simply unlucky.'

'Ammi, why don't you tell the people who worry about my wife's conception and whisper things into your ears that something will happen only when Allah wills it. Surely you still have faith in Allah.'

'Beta, Allah knows best about my faith but how can I stop people from talking. They even talk of alternatives.'

'What alternatives?'

Noorani Begum hesitated a trifle. 'Well ... there are alternatives permitted to Muslims by their religion ...'

'What are you implying, Ammi?'

'I am not implying anything but in such circumstances the normal remedy is a second marriage,' said Noorani Begum, without beating about the bush any longer.

For the very few times in his life uncontrollable anger took hold of Ghulam Rasool. 'Ammi, you cannot be serious in suggesting that I take another wife after being married to Sara for about two and a half years just because she has been unable to conceive and that too in order to please people you meet socially,' he said, raising his voice in indignation.

'I am serious ... this is the only practical solution to the problem.' Noorani Begum was unabashed.

'To hell with the problem ... I cannot forsake a woman I have come to love and respect just because she is not having a child. I don't mind spending my whole life with her even if she remains barren. It is neither her fault nor mine that we do not have a child ... and ... and we are not the only childless couple in the whole world. The other thing is that I simply don't care about what people say and I urge you to never talk to me about this matter again.'

Having said his piece, Ghulam Rasool left the room in an angry huff while Noorani Begum sat bewildered that her dutiful and obedient son could be so insolent.

The gossip about Ghulam Rasool, postmaster, New Delhi, and Sara, the daughter from the famous Rattan family of jewellers, not being able to conceive kept raising its head like a multi-headed hydra. Although Ghulam Rasool and Sara refrained from lending their ears to this maliciousness, the little that came to their notice was enough to fray their nerves.

One mildly hot day of May 1924, as Ghulam Rasool lay on his bed recovering from the day's work, Sara came and sat on the only chair in the room and started playing nervously with her braid.

'What seems to be the matter, Sara? You look worried,' said Ghulam Rasool, observing her from the corner of one of his half-shut eyes.

'Well, sarkar, nothing really but all this talk of not being able to have a baby seems to have started playing on my mind. Wherever I go I feel that people are talking about one thing— why I am not pregnant. I wish we could get out of this city for a few years so that people can forget us.'

'You know something, Sara, I feel the same way. In any case, I've spent over three years in Delhi and I am due for a transfer. If only I knew of someone who could put in a word for me, this could come about in a few weeks. Those who had worked with my father have all retired or passed away. The other thing that worries me in a transfer is that my mother and my sister would be left all alone in Delhi.'

'But, sarkar, this is bound to happen one day. You'll have to leave Delhi sooner or later whenever we are transferred.'

The conversation between the two seemed to have been all but forgotten when two weeks later Ghulam Rasool climbed up the stairs of his house and sat down on the bed, recovering his breath.

'Colonel Knowles, ADC to the viceroy, called me to his office today about an extra-large parcel he wanted to send to a friend in Madras,' Ghulam Rasool said to his wife. 'Although I was just doing my duty, he seemed impressed with my suggestions. In the end he got up, shook hands with me, and said that he liked the way I explained everything to him and that if there was anything he could do for me I shouldn't hesitate to ask. I seized the opportunity and requested him to help me in getting a transfer. So let's wait and see if anything happens.'

Ghulam Rasool had almost forgotten his meeting with Colonel Knowles and his request for a transfer when he was delivered a sealed envelope with an acknowledgement slip at his table at the post office. On opening the envelope, Ghulam Rasool found a cyclostyled paper containing his transfer order. He was to report to Rawalpindi as postmaster with immediate effect

Saad Ashraf

and until further orders. It was dated 11 December 1924 and signed by the deputy postmaster general of the Indian Posts and Telegraphs Department, Delhi.

Ghulam Rasool read and reread his transfer order excitedly. He couldn't believe that this could happen after a chance meeting with Colonel Knowles. He kept the information to himself but repeatedly took out his transfer order from the drawer of his table and read it to reassure himself that it was indeed true. That day, after work, he pedalled his cycle furiously on his way back home to break the news to Sara. But every now and then he would slow down, worried by the thought of how his mother would react to the sudden news of his transfer.

Ghulam Rasool climbed up the stairs, knocked at the door which was opened by Sara, held her by the arm, and headed for their room.

'It's happened! My transfer order has arrived for Rawalpindi,' he said, slumping to the bed and handing the piece of paper to Sara.

'Rawalpindi! What place is that?' Sara enquired with an air of concern.

'It is a day and a night's journey from here into the Punjab. A clean and nice town, much colder than Delhi but you'll like it there. Don't break the news to anybody yet. I'll do that myself,' said Ghulam Rasool.

Sara was excited to hear about the transfer. Allah had heard her prayers. But after the initial euphoria she felt a certain twinge in her heart at the thought of leaving Delhi. She knew that she would miss the imperial city, her own and her husband's family, and even its slanderous women. She felt the ground slipping from under her feet when she realized that she would be all alone in a strange city where she did not know a single soul. She was fearful about the first train journey she would be making in her life. However, she concealed all these fears behind the broad smile she gave her husband to welcome the news.

After devoting a day in devising ways of breaking the news to his mother, Ghulam Rasool decided to broach the matter with her the next evening.

'Ammi, there is an important piece of news I want to give you,' he said, readying to deliver the coup de grace.

'I hope it is something good. I haven't heard anything to gladden my heart since you got married.'

'Well ... I am afraid that the news is neither good nor bad. I have been transferred to Rawalpindi.'

Noorani Begum went into a swoon when she heard this, but quickly recovered her bearings. 'These are bad tidings for us, Beta. Why do you have to leave us at this time?' she asked sadly.

'Ammi, I am a servant of the sarkar and have no choice. I get my orders and have to follow them whether I like them or not.'

'But this never used to happen in the days of your father. After all, he also worked for the same dak khana. He remained in Delhi right from the time he was transferred from the Punjab till he passed away.'

'Things have changed, Ammi. After the Great War the policy has been to keep an officer at one place only for three years and then move him to another place. This way, the government gets experienced officers and better administration because nobody has the time to make connections which could become dangerous,' explained Ghulam Rasool.

There was an uncomfortable pause in the conversation.

'I also wanted to raise some important matters with you, Beta. I have received a proposal for your sister Rehmani. There's too much going on for one soul to cope with, so what do I do?' Noorani Begum said with a look of desperation.

'I can't do anything to get my transfer cancelled, but I'm prepared to help you as much as I can with the family. By the way, whose proposal have you received for Rehmani?'

'Macho Begum brought the proposal for an engineer named Karim who has just returned from Africa after spending ten years there. His first wife died in Delhi some three years ago, fortunately without an issue and he wants to remarry. Although there is an age difference of fifteen years between your sister and the groom, I seem to have no choice. Bridegrooms are hard to find these days though Allah knows how hard I have tried finding one for her ever since Sultana was married. I spend sleepless nights when

I think of Rehmani and blame myself for not insisting that Phool Begum take Rehmani as a bride for Rehmat. With age on her side, Sultana could have waited a few more years for the right match. Rehmani is getting older by the day, and it will become more and more difficult to find a husband for her,' said Noorani Begum, tears welling up in her eyes.

'I know that the situation is worrisome, but desperation is not going to get us anywhere. One of these days Allah will send us a proposal of a noble gentleman for Rehmani, just as it happened for Sultana. Meanwhile, try to influence Macho Begum to keep the proposal of Engineer Karim on hold as long as she can while you continue with your efforts to find someone more suitable for Rehmani. If she insists on an answer, you can accept him provisionally which will give us some more time to look around.'

Noorani Begum sighed. 'I think I can manage to get this matter delayed for sometime but not forever.'

'Don't worry about anything, Ammi. No matter what happens, you'll always find me by your side. I'll send you the allowance of a hundred rupees on the first of every month and more whenever you need it,' promised Ghulam Rasool, relieved to find that his words had somewhat pacified his mother. She nodded her head as Ghulam Rasool went on, 'In case there is an emergency, all you have to do is send me a telegram. It will only take me a day and a night to get here from Rawalpindi.'

twenty-six

It was a cold evening in late December 1924 when the Frontier Mail carrying Ghulam Rasool and Sara steamed into Rawalpindi railway station. There was a fair turnout of employees of the Rawalpindi post office at the platform to receive Postmaster Ghulam Rasool, the first Indian designated for this post. Ghulam Rasool and Sara were taken in a horse-drawn buggy to the postal officers' rest house where they were to stay till such time that the incumbent postmaster, Mr James Jones, popularly known as JJ, vacated the official residence.

Early next morning, sitting on the chairs laid out in the lawns of the rest house, sipping a cup of steaming tea, Ghulam Rasool could see the range of the Murree hills, their snow-covered peaks glistening in the winter sun. The cleanliness of the town and the quietness of its morning convinced him that this town matched his temperament and that he would enjoy his posting here. Later, Ghulam Rasool walked down from the rest house to the GPO located off the Mall Road, carrying the portmanteau containing his transfer and relieving orders and an authorization to operate the treasury. He waited in the ante-room on being informed that Postmaster Jones was not yet in although it was after ten in the morning. An hour later, JJ arrived and Ghulam Rasool was ushered to his office by Head Clerk Niranjan.

Ghulam Rasool introduced himself and produced his transfer order for JJ to read.

'So you are my successor, eh?' said JJ coldly.

'Yes, sir,' replied Ghulam Rasool.

Ghulam Rasool had already learnt from his own sources at the rest house that JJ was not happy at being transferred to Amritsar, having to vacate his chair for an Indian. Not only was Amritsar hotter, dustier, and dirtier than Rawalpindi, but JJ would also have to make alternative arrangements for his family. As long as he was posted in Rawalpindi, they had preferred to stay in the hills barely thirty miles away and came down to Rawalpindi only after the sweltering heat of Punjab waned. Postmaster Jones could not understand the department's logic in replacing him, a thoroughbred Englishman, but then he was convinced from his experience of a quarter of a century in the postal department that most things were increasingly turning from illogical to stupid with the indigenization of the department. Though he swore on the purity of his blood despite being in India for so many generations, well-informed sources within the postal circles who knew the family spoke of the pink fingernails and freckles on the cheeks of the women in the Jones family which was a sure sign that he was not as pukka an Englishman as he claimed to be.

'So now that you have to take over my job what would you like me to do?' continued Postmaster Jones, feigning ignorance of the requirements for handing over his post.

'I suppose you have to sign the papers handing over charge to me after verification of the money in the treasury as well as the stamps and other valuable papers,' replied Ghulam Rasool.

Niranjan was summoned to get all the papers ready for signatures and to verify the amounts in the treasury and in the form of stamps. This having been done, papers were duly signed by both to complete the formalities of handing and taking over of the post.

Ghulam Rasool waited impatiently at the rest house, gnawing at his fingernails for further news of JJ's departure. The next afternoon, he was informed by the caretaker of the rest house that JJ had left Rawalpindi for Amritsar without telling anyone and that the official bungalow was vacant and ready to be occupied. Ghulam Rasool wasted no time in moving in with his wife, steel trunks, and holdalls.

The postmaster's bungalow was situated on the broadest and cleanest road of Rawalpindi, right opposite the British Officers Club. It had eight large rooms with eighteen-foot-high ceilings, attached bathrooms equipped with hot and cold showers, and thunder box commodes. There was a vast compound which stretched as far as the eye could see within which the bungalow stood like an island. The acres of cultivated fields surrounding the bungalow produced not only enough fruit, vegetables, and poultry for the postmaster's table but also a surplus that could easily sustain the ten servants who occupied the quarters built on its fringes.

'No wonder Postmaster Jones didn't want to be transferred out of Rawalpindi—who would want to leave luxuries such as free servants and food?' remarked Ghulam Rasool to Sara a couple of months after they had moved.

'What is the use of these luxuries when one is living in an icebox? I miss Delhi and hate the cold and rain of Rawalpindi. I can't even make out what the servants are saying here. They don't speak a Hindustani which I can understand. They tell me that they are at their politest but seem to me to be quarrelling all the time. Oh, how I wish I hadn't prayed so hard to leave Delhi,' remarked Sara, with tears in her eyes.

In the months that followed, Ghulam Rasool observed with concern that Sara was gradually withdrawing into herself. She lost her appetite and shed some weight. The colour in her cheeks disappeared and the glint in her eyes was replaced by a lurking sadness. She started showing signs of irritability and sometimes her voice, scolding the servants, could be heard above the din and clamour of pots and pans in the kitchen.

Ghulam Rasool, on the other hand, had been able to create a routine for himself which kept him occupied until late in the evening. He went to the office in the morning and came back in the late afternoon to have a light lunch and a short siesta. He then changed into a white towel shirt, shorts, and canvas shoes, and walked across the road to the British Officers Club for a game of tennis. On rare occasions, when the English officers

Saad Ashraf

were short of partners they would ask him to join them in a game of doubles.

The first time this happened was when Colonel Sanderson of the First Scottish Regiment and a high-ranking officer in the Northern Command had run short of a partner. He had gone up to Ghulam Rasool, who stood by the court drinking lemonade, and had said to him with a smile, 'Hello Blackie! I'm Colonel Sanderson of the First Scots. How about being my partner in a game against these two young majors?' Although Ghulam Rasool had not liked the way he had been addressed, he held back his reaction, proceeding to take out all his aggressiveness on the court with his thundering serves and backhand and forehand drives. Colonel Sanderson had stood in amazement and clapped when they won the five-set match, at the end of which the colonel had remarked, 'I must hand it to you, Blackie ... you are a good tennis player and I am lucky that I was your partner and not your opponent.' Thereafter, the colonel always sought Ghulam Rasool as his partner and thanked him profusely after every match but continued calling him 'Blackie'. Ghulam Rasool started considering this appellation as a big joke and when, once or twice, the colonel tried to address him as 'Mr Rasool' or 'Postmaster Rasool', Ghulam Rasool interjected by saying, 'Sir, call me by my nickname "Blackie",' which left everybody doubling up in laughter and sent the message across to the colonel.

Whatever time was left to Ghulam Rasool after attending office, having his siesta or playing tennis, he spent making love to Sara regardless of whether she was in the mood for it or not. It was as if he had developed an insatiable sexual urge.

As the months passed by, Ghulam Rasool found that Sara seemed to have somehow adjusted herself to Rawalpindi. The bleak winter months with their short days had passed and the spring of 1925 had arrived, bringing with it myriad multicoloured flowers which bloomed in every corner of the compound. The fields around the bungalow, which during winter had turned into hard black ground on which a plough would have dented, became a carpet of luxuriant green grass. The weather had turned balmy. Sara wanted to spend all the time she could outdoors, walking as much as two hours daily in the vast stretches of the compound. When she felt tired she would sit on a chair under the red concrete canopy Postmaster Jones had constructed within the compound to shield his family from the hot Rawalpindi sun. With the fine weather holding out for several weeks, the fresh air and regular exercise did much good to Sara's health and even more to her spirits. She came out of her depression and started communicating with the servants and their families, occupying herself with their welfare. This mental occupation reduced the feeling of loneliness and she felt genuinely happy for the first time since their arrival.

Saad Ashraf

twenty-seven

One morning in May 1925, Sara woke up with a terrible feeling of nausea and acidity in her stomach. She went into the bathroom and threw up and promptly felt better. She was sure that the pickles she had eaten at dinner the previous night were responsible for this episode. She took two pinches of a powder from a bottle her mother had given her when she was leaving Delhi. The powder had been prepared by a famous hakim in Delhi and was supposed to act like magic in settling upset stomachs. It proved true to its reputation. Sara considered this matter so inconsequential that she did not even mention it to Ghulam Rasool. Two mornings later, she got worried when the nausea reoccurred. This time it lasted longer and she felt that the ground was slipping under her. When Ghulam Rasool returned from office for his lunch and siesta, Sara couldn't restrain herself any more.

'Sarkar, I'm not well. Do something, take me to the doctor,' she said.

Ghulam Rasool looked her up and down.

'You look all right to me except that you've put on a little weight since I left you in the morning,' he said, smiling.

'I'm not joking, sarkar,' said Sara, worry clouding her face.

She explained her physical condition and Ghulam Rasool, who had never seen her in this state before in the three years of their marriage, decided that he had to get her to a doctor immediately.

He spoke to Colonel Collins, the civil surgeon, on the office telephone. The colonel suggested that, in the first instance, his wife should be seen by Lady Dr Anne Blyth, the gynaecologist in the district hospital. That presented a problem: how would Sara communicate her physical condition to an Englishwoman who had only recently arrived in India and who, it was said, did not know one word of Hindustani. Even the Anglo-Indian nurses who worked with her had a problem understanding her Scottish accent. Dr Blyth had in this short period acquired the reputation of being a short-tempered but exceptionally competent gynaecologist who punctuated her conversation with invectives which nobody could decipher.

There being no alternative, Ghulam Rasool took Sara to see Dr Blyth, handing her over to Miss Keane, an Anglo-Indian nurse. He informed Miss Keane that his wife knew no English and requested her to assist Sara in explaining her physical condition to the doctor. The nurse merely moved her head in despair and said that Dr Blyth preferred to see her patients in privacy, and assistance could only be rendered when the doctor so desired. Ghulam Rasool waited in the ante-room with his hands clasped and thumbs rotating one over another in nervousness as Sara disappeared into the doctor's consulting room.

When Sara emerged from Dr Blyth's clinic, after what seemed an eternity, he was astounded to see a broad grin across her face.

'I thought you would come out crying after having met the doctor but you appear to be happy. Whatever happened?' asked Ghulam Rasool, on their way back home.

'Oh, I don't know where to begin. When I entered the doctor's room she started off in fast English which I couldn't follow. So I put my fingers on my lips to ask her to quieten down and glared at her as if in anger. She stopped her jabbering. I then remembered the English you had taught me of which I could recall a few words.'

Ghulam Rasool listened with rapt attention as Sara continued.

'I told her how I feel very bad in the morning, and here I grimaced and made a face as if I was going to throw up. The doctor's eyes brightened to show that she understood what I

Saad Ashraf

was saying. She then moved her hands towards her private parts and made gestures to enquire whether everything was all right with me down there—I think she meant to enquire about my periods. I told her it was not good, as my periods have become irregular. She motioned to a table lying in the room and gestured that I should take off my trousers which I promptly did. After a short examination, the doctor smiled and made a gesture in front of her stomach to signal an increase in size. I understood this to mean that she thinks I am pregnant. She then took a bottle and gave it to me, making a shrill sound that I have seen mothers make when they want their infants to ease themselves. She gestured to a door which was that of a bathroom. So I passed some urine into the bottle and gave it back to her for which she thanked me. She pointed towards the door to indicate the end of the consultation. While I was leaving, I remembered the English sentence you had taught me for sophisticated company: English education is necessary for the women of India. I blurted it out. The doctor was taken aback and escorted me all the way out, shook hands with me at the door, and handed me this slip.'

Dr Blyth had written out Sara's next appointment with her a week hence. Her diagnosis was that, subject to confirmation, Sara was about eight weeks pregnant. The next appointment and the tests confirmed Dr Blyth's diagnosis. An elated Ghulam Rasool's started imagining what his son or daughter would look like and began to think of some famous historical names out of which he would select one for him or her. Ghulam Rasool wasted no time in informing Noorani Begum of his wife's pregnancy. His mother wrote back, welcoming the news, saying 'thank God everybody's efforts have been rewarded'—whatever that meant. She asked Ghulam Rasool about the plans for Sara's confinement, suggesting that it might be better if the delivery took place in Delhi where both their families would be available for support.

As time passed, Sara's stomach grew bigger by the day. The glow of happiness which appears on a woman's face when carrying a child started showing on hers but with each passing day she tired more easily. Sara's condition, however, had little effect on Ghulam Rasool's routine. He stuck by his office work, lunch, siesta, tennis, and sex, in spite of Sara's bulging stomach. He had decided to take a few weeks off in December and take Sara to Delhi for her delivery and thereafter to leave her there for a couple of months till the worst part of Rawalpindi's winter passed.

In the meantime, Sara spread the word around the servant quarters that she was looking for a young woman who could attend to her, give her a bath, comb and oil her hair, press and massage her body, and keep her company. A few days later, a middle-aged Christian woman named Kamini, who occupied one of the servant quarters, walked in with a young woman in tow.

'Begum, this is my niece Resham who worked in Deputy Postmaster William Sahib's house for about three years before he retired. She was his mem's personal attendant. She will clean your house, give you a bath, massage your body, and do anything else you want. She is called Resham because her hands are as soft as silk and can knead the body like dough. I brought her with me so she can give you a demonstration.' Kamini took a bottle of mustard oil out of the pocket of her shirt for Resham to use.

Sara looked at Resham from head to toe. 'Is Resham married?' she enquired.

Kamini shook her head. 'She was but it didn't work out. Her husband was a cruel man who used his shoe regularly on her. Fortunately, she didn't bear a child, and lives with me and is looking for work.'

'Send her tomorrow morning so that I can see what she can do,' said Sara.

Resham started work next morning. It became obvious to Sara that Resham was adept with her hands, massaging her mistress's body for an hour every morning and at night. Every session with Resham would leave Sara relaxed and the one in the evening helped her get a full night of blissful sleep. In addition, Resham was a congenial companion though there had been little happiness in her life. Her marriage of seven months was a continuous saga of the cruelty that a sadistic, near-insane husband imposed on her. The last straw had been his command that she become a part-time whore to augment his irregular income most of which he spent on country liquor. She had managed to escape from his clutches and ran to her aunt who had become her saviour.

As December approached, Ghulam Rasool made preparations for proceeding on leave. He was sanctioned four weeks of rest and recreation leave which carried the added benefit of a free railway warrant for the journey to Delhi for himself and his wife.

Over the past three months, Resham had become Sara's close confidante. She had got so used to the suppleness of Resham's hands that she now wanted Resham to accompany her to Delhi. Ghulam Rasool did not take well to the idea of transporting an unknown female servant all the way to another city. On Sara's insistence, he however agreed to let Resham continue in their employment to look after their home until Sara returned.

twenty-eight

Ghulam Rasool arrived in Delhi with Sara in the final stages of her pregnancy. He spent some time with his family and then decided to go and see Ahmad and give him a surprise. Arriving at the imam's house, he took their servant into confidence, asking him not to announce his arrival. He then ventured into Ahmad's room and found him sunning himself in front of an open window, staring into the space beyond.

'Who is there?' asked Ahmad.

Silence.

'I have a feeling that there's someone in this room—someone like my friend Ghulam Rasool who has come to see me all the way from Rawalpindi.'

Ghulam Rasool was stunned at the extrasensory powers of his friend.

'How did you know I was here, Ahmad mian?' asked Ghulam Rasool, embracing his friend.

'When Allah takes away one faculty he gives many more to make up for that loss. The light in my eyes has gone but I have been given the hearing power of the jinns. I can hear things miles away … sometimes I can hear you talk in Rawalpindi.'

Ghulam Rasool was not sure whether Ahmad genuinely believed that he had developed extraordinary powers of hearing but he had read somewhere that nature helped to develop the other senses among those who could not see.

The two friends filled each other on their lives.

'I am sure it must be great to feel that you will be a father within the next few weeks. I hope you have a son who will carry on your name,' said Ahmad.

Ghulam Rasool shrugged. 'I don't care whether it is a boy or a girl as long as he or she is born healthy and is blessed with good fortune. What is the use of a child if it is beset with misfortune and turmoil at every twist and turn of life? We human beings needn't procreate ourselves like pedigreed horses for our name. We don't have to run in a race.'

'Isn't life a race in which some are able to go ahead while for others fate interferes so that they fall behind.'

Ghulam Rasool surmised that Ahmad was talking about himself though everybody who came in contact with him admired the determination with which he had faced life alone without complaint and in solemn dignity.

'Mian, you know what keeps me going in life? It is my undying love for Yasmeen who seems to be with me all the time. I can't talk to anyone about her except to you. Do you understand what I say and do I make sense to you?' Ahmad asked, misty eyed.

'Ahmad mian, I have never experienced the kind of love you speak of—this malady for which there is said to be no cure—but I can appreciate your feelings for an individual no matter who that may be.'

'I have been trying to trace Yasmeen ever since I returned from the war. A reliable source from Chawri Bazaar has informed me that after her mother's death in Bareli, Yasmeen has moved to the bazaar in Lahore with a distant aunt. I think they call this place Heeramandi. Mian, why don't you track her down there, surely you can do this for an old friend,' beseeched Ahmad.

'I'll do anything for you, Ahmad mian. Let me get back to Rawalpindi after my wife's delivery and you'll hear from me in due course.'

'You won't forget? I mean you would not want me to remind you.'

'You don't have to remind me, I've written it on my heart,' said Ghulam Rasool, as he took leave of his friend.

The Postmaster   {185}

Sara was admitted to the Zenana Hospital on the morning of 19 December 1925. Late in the afternoon on the same day—with Mrs Roberts, the chief midwife of the hospital, in attendance—she delivered a girl who weighed six and a half pounds.

Though Noorani Begum and Sara's mother were disappointed that their grandchild was a daughter and not a son, Ghulam Rasool was overjoyed, more so because it had been a painless and uncomplicated delivery for Sara and the baby looked healthy and normal. After Haji Jaffar, her maternal grandfather, had loudly pronounced Allah's name in her right ear, the baby was named Nur Jahan.

Sara moved to her mother's house in Kucha Dehlavi to recover and to give the infant time to grow a little older in the milder weather of Delhi.

Ghulam Rasool boarded the Frontier Mail for Rawalpindi on the evening of 26 December 1925 so that he could rejoin his office on the expiry of his leave.

Ghulam Rasool returned to a home bereft of Sara where his loneliness was made worse by the cold, bleak December that Rawalpindi experienced that year. He soon resumed his regular routine, spending an hour or two extra at the office. In the afternoons he went for long sessions of tennis at the club, returning only at nightfall. He would then have a light supper and retire to his room, made comfortable by the coal fire in whose amber light and that of the solitary electric bulb he would either work on the files he brought with him from office or read the works of Shakespeare or Ghalib till sleep overtook him.

Ghulam Rasool observed that though the mistress of the house was missing, everything seemed to be working to perfection. The living rooms were cleaner than before, while the white-tiled bathrooms shone spick and span, smelling of lavender. He found himself being served with a variety of mouth-watering dishes, as a result of which he started looking forward to going back to the bungalow. He realized that he owed this eminently satisfactory state of affairs in the house to Resham, the maid.

Saad Ashraf

For the first few days after Ghulam Rasool's arrival from Delhi, Resham used to leave his meals on the table and disappear into the pantry or kitchen, but of late he observed that she had taken to silently standing behind him while he ate, removing and replacing the plate after every course. When a few more days passed in this manner, he found that she stationed herself in front of the dining table, her hands crossed in front and her eyes transfixed on the floor. Ghulam Rasool had never tried looking at her closely so far but now it became unavoidable. Resham looked younger than her twenty-five years of age, and was short and dark. Her face was rough and whorish, but if there was anything lacking in her features it was more than made up by her busty, voluptuous body and prominent hips. She tied her hair in a bun at the back of her head which was secured by a bright-coloured ribbon. When she went to fetch something from the kitchen she walked the breadth of the dining room with an attractive gait, swivelling her hips from side to side. Needless to say, she aroused Ghulam Rasool who wanted to know more about this woman who had begun to trigger his imagination thus. But the moment such thoughts entered his mind he remembered that he was a sahib who could have nothing to do with a servant woman. Through cold logic and self-discipline he was able to impose a check on himself, keeping his communication with her limited to the bare essentials.

Sometime later, Ghulam Rasool slipped on the tennis court in the club and fell while returning a low shot from his opponent, in the process hurting his right shoulder. He called off the game, apologizing to his opponent for any inconvenience caused. Though the only sign of the fall was a minor bruise, the right side of his body started aching as the hours passed. Soon enough, he was in excruciating pain. His groan could be heard beyond the compound, resonating in the silence of the cold empty rooms. He lay on the bed, tossing and turning, his eyes closed.

Ghulam Rasool was in deep agony when he heard Resham's voice.

'Sahib, whatever has happened?'

'I've hurt myself in the shoulder while playing tennis. It's painful but I'll be all right by the morning.' Ghulam Rasool tried to be as brave as possible.

'Sahib, I can help you in relieving this pain. I used to massage begum sahiba's head when she got those splitting headaches. I used the balm she keeps in the cabinet.'

Before Ghulam Rasool could reply, she had traversed the length of the room to a cabinet in the corner, pulled one of its drawers, and returned with a small bottle in her hands.

'Here it is, sahib. Begum sahiba told me that this balm is the cure for all pains in the body. It is made by the Amritdhara Company of Lahore,' said Resham, triumphantly holding the bottle in her hands. 'Now, sahib, if you allow me ... Tell me where you've been hurt.'

Ghulam Rasool pointed towards his shoulder. Resham unbuttoned his shirt from the front and exposed his arm on which a big blue bruise had made its appearance, and started applying the balm to this area using her nimble fingers.

Though the massage hurt, every passing moment brought relief. After half an hour Ghulam Rasool felt that his suffering had considerably reduced. Soon, the relaxation that follows relief from pain lulled him to sleep. The last words he could remember hearing were that of Resham.

'Sahib, I'll sleep on the floor ... just in case it begins to hurt again in the night.'

Sometime in the middle of the night Ghulam Rasool felt that somebody was trying to get into bed beside him. He knew that the only other person in the room was Resham. He made no effort to resist her initiative. He found that a warm body had wrapped itself around him and sensuous lips had implanted themselves upon his. A taut pair of breasts from which hot nipples protruded, pressed like burning coals on his chest and clouded his mind with desire. He positioned himself between her legs which he realized were bare and wanting. He bared himself similarly and immersed himself into this adventure. There was however no communication between the two beyond that of the

Saad Ashraf

body. While he was in a state of ecstasy, recovering from the triumph of his manhood, he realized that his bed had become cold once again as Resham left it to spend the remainder of the night on the floor.

Ghulam Rasool woke up in the morning and, after having dressed up for office, found Resham serving him breakfast like every other morning without any change in her manner or attitude, as dutiful and obedient as before, standing with her hands folded in front and eyes staring at the floor.

Over the next couple of months, this became a routine between the master and the servant. Within an hour of his retiring to bed, Ghulam Rasool would hear Resham tiptoeing to his bed for their nocturnal rendezvous, leaving in the early hours of the morning to take up her place as a dutiful servant.

Ghulam Rasool had so many pleasurable things to look forward to, he almost forgot that he had a family which was at that very moment making preparations to come back to Rawalpindi.

Sara and their daughter Nur Jahan arrived in Rawalpindi by the Frontier Mail on the morning of 16 April 1926. It was a cool but otherwise bright and sunny day in Rawalpindi and the hills could be seen in the distance, clothed in their newly born verdant green. Resham started attending to her mistress and the baby, and her relationship with the sahib receded into history.

twenty-nine

In May 1926, Ghulam Rasool received a letter from Ahmad mentioning the promise that Ghulam Rasool had made to him in Delhi to locate Yasmeen in Heeramandi—the red-light area of Lahore. Ghulam Rasool replied saying that he had been unable to visit Lahore so far because of the temporary charge of two or three other post offices located outside Rawalpindi which had been handed over to him and which made it impossible for him to get even a day's leave. He nevertheless hoped that he would be able to fulfil his promise. The opportunity presented itself when he was invited to attend the two-day postmasters' conference held in Lahore in September. He took leave for two days at the end of the conference to locate Yasmeen.

The day after the conference ended, Ghulam Rasool got ready in the morning and hired a tonga from the inspection bungalow, where he was staying, to take him to Heeramandi. The tonga driver welcomed him with a puzzled smile, surprised to get a customer for the red-light area so early in the day.

Dressed in grey slacks and a white shirt, Ghulam Rasool strolled along the deserted main street of the red-light area. The only place open was a wayside restaurant where a few stragglers from the night before hung around to finish their meals.

Ghulam Rasool approached the owner of the restaurant who sat on a chair next to the till.

'I am Ghulam Rasool from Rawalpindi looking for Yasmeen the dancer from Bareli. Can you tell me where she lives?' he enquired, displaying his official identity card.

Yaqub, the obese owner of the restaurant, who was a part-time police tout and professional wrestler tried sizing up his questioner. A babu dressed in western clothes and that too in the morning hours was a rarity in his restaurant. Being unable to read the English on Ghulam Rasool's identity card, Yaqub was certain that he was an agent for one of the many intelligence agencies of the sarkar.

'Babuji,' he said, 'there are several Yasmeens in this bazaar, all famous for their beauty and talent. I would not know one from another. If you meet one of them she may be able to direct you to the one you are looking for. One such Yasmeen lives across the street from here. You see that wooden stairway in front ... you will find her on the first floor. She will probably be asleep at this time, but maybe the matron of the house is awake and she could help you.'

Ghulam Rasool headed for the wooden stairway across the street and climbed up to the first floor where he knocked on the first door he came to. He could hear someone making strenuous efforts to get up from a charpai and this was followed by the appearance of two eyes in a narrow slit that opened in the door.

'Who are you and what is it that you want?' enquired a gruff female voice from the other side.

'My name is Ghulam Rasool and I am trying to locate Yasmeen who used to live in Bareli. She moved here a year or two ago.'

'Yasmeen of Bareli doesn't live here. Try knocking at some other door.'

The slit closed as abruptly as it had opened.

'Can you guide me to where anybody else with this name lives in this bazaar?'

There was no reply.

Ghulam Rasool hung around the door for another five minutes, repeating the question. He was disappointed but determined not to give up the search. He decided to see Yaqub again to enlist his help.

'Well ... were you able to meet the person you were looking for, sir?' Yaqub asked as Ghulam Rasool strode into his restaurant.

'No, and I was unable to get any clue either. The people in this bazaar seem to be ignorant of good manners and common courtesy.'

'Babuji, come and see them in the evening if you want to know what manners and courtesy they possess. The morning is not the proper time to visit Heeramandi,' said Yaqub, dropping some coins from a customer into the till.

'You look like a nice chap to me, Yaqub. I was wondering whether you could help me in a personal matter. I am prepared to pay for your services,' said Ghulam Rasool.

As Yaqub listened, Ghulam Rasool proceeded to relate his relationship with Ahmad and how much his friend had sacrificed for his love and how important it had become for him to locate Yasmeen.

'Sahib, I think the best thing you can do is to return this evening at about seven ... my cousin who helps me run this place arrives by that time. He'll look after the restaurant while we will go looking for your friend's beloved. As far as payment for my services are concerned, by Allah's grace this shop pays me enough to take care of my needs, so I am not going to accept a penny for doing someone some good.'

Ghulam Rasool reported to Yaqub's restaurant promptly at seven in the evening. He found the place full of the riff-raff of Lahore, the owner missing, and a rough specimen standing at the cash counter. Ghulam Rasool regretted having trusted Yaqub and wondered what had made him confide the personal matters of a dear friend to the unknown owner of a roadside restaurant in a red-light area. He was still in this state of mind when he heard himself being addressed by the man at the counter.

'Babuji, Yaqub bhai will be here in about fifteen minutes. Why don't you have a hot cup of tea meanwhile or would you prefer something else?'

Ghulam Rasool nodded in acknowledgement, refused the offer of tea, and went out. He preferred standing on the street rather than waiting in the noisy eating place.

Half an hour later, Ghulam Rasool saw the familiar figure of Yaqub approaching him. Yaqub was dressed in a white shirt and trousers and his lips were red with betel leaf. He was accompanied by a rather seedy-looking character.

'Babuji, this is my friend Sheeda who knows Heeramandi like the back of his hand ... all its dancing and singing girls. You can be sure that if anybody can trace Yasmeen in this bazaar, it's Sheeda,' said Yaqub.

Sheeda stood with one hand on his waist and his nose in the air, puffed up with the praises being sung of his knowledge of the red-light area and its residents. He asked Ghulam Rasool to give a physical description of Yasmeen as best as he could remember.

After Ghulam Rasool had finished describing Yasmeen, Sheeda stood still for a moment or two, as if weighing the words over in his mind. He shook his head. 'There are innumerable dancing and singing girls here, sahib, who go by the name of Yasmeen. The Yasmeen you are looking for may have adopted another name in this bazaar to hide her real identity. The only way out is to visit every bordello and find out if she is here. It is like looking for a needle in the haystack. If we spend a minute or two at each house we may be able to go through the entire bazaar in three hours.'

'Well, we can't stand here all night discussing how we should find Yasmeen. I think it is time for some action ... so let's go,' said Yaqub.

The three of them started moving from one house to another, stopping for only the shortest period at each place. After two hours of such frenetic activity, Ghulam Rasool was both physically and mentally exhausted. He had climbed up and down so many stairways, glimpsed so many beautiful, painted dolls performing the intricate movements of various dance forms, and heard snatches of so many songs to the beat of the tabla that he felt his body and mind needed some rest. But he knew that Ahmad was banking on him to discover Yasmeen in the bazaar. He knew that it would not be possible for him to come to the infamous Heeramandi again. He imagined Ahmad sitting in his room in Delhi, peering into the space beyond. He decided to continue with his mission regardless.

He climbed the next stairway as if possessed and couldn't believe his eyes—for there was Yasmeen, sitting right in front, oblivious of his presence. She was singing:

Everyone is here but you, my beloved,
to hear the cry of my heart.
But where are you, for whom I sing my songs
Waiting for me somewhere in the star-filled sky ...

'I can't believe my eyes, but this is Yasmeen,' whispered Ghulam Rasool in Yaqub's ears.

'Are you sure, babuji?'

'Absolutely, unless Allah created two identical Yasmeens.'

Yaqub and Sheeda murmured something to each other.

'Babuji, Sheeda and I feel that the best thing for you to do is to go and wait in the street below. As soon as this performance ends and the audience has departed we will come downstairs. We don't want to risk Yasmeen disappearing should she see you now,' Yaqub whispered.

Ghulam Rasool did as he was told.

About half an hour later, Yaqub and Sheeda climbed down the stairway.

'There's nobody upstairs, even the musicians have packed up and left. You had better hurry and see Yasmeen before she retires for the night. After you're finished you can join us at the restaurant,' said Yaqub.

Ghulam Rasool nodded, mustered all his courage, and walked up the stairway. Approaching the house, he knocked at its door. When Yasmeen came out to open the door, Ghulam Rasool could see the bewilderment on her face—a combination of amazement, fear, and happiness at finding someone familiar at the most unexpected place and time. She was still beautiful, her hazel eyes and jet-black hair hanging down well below her shoulders. Time had lent her features a grace and a halo of mystery.

'Bhaijaan, I can't believe my eyes! Am I just imagining things or am I really seeing you here in Lahore!' exclaimed Yasmeen, opening her hazel eyes wide in surprise. She ushered Ghulam Rasool in.

'Yasmeen, am I lucky to have found you!' said Ghulam Rasool, settling down comfortably on the mattress laid out on the floor. 'Frankly, I was just about to give up searching for you.'

'But how did you know I was here in Lahore, Bhaijaan?'

'Somebody found that out from Chawri Bazaar in Delhi.'

'I never expected to see you here or anywhere else again after we had left Delhi for Bareli. Oh, I can't even remember how long ago that was … may have been ten years ago,' Yasmeen cried with excitement.

'If one is determined to find something, persists long enough, and has luck on one's side, one may end up being rewarded even if it takes years.'

Yasmeen let out a deep sigh and sat with her eyes fixed on the floor.

'Do you know that my friend Ahmad's love for you kept him alive in the cold trenches of Europe even though he lost his eyesight during the war? It was his love that made me promise him that I would come and look for you here,' said Ghulam Rasool. He could see the contortions on Yasmeen's face as she tried to control her feelings.

'With or without sight, dead or alive, Ahmad is the only man I ever loved. My mother knew of this and wanted to avoid further complications, so she decided to leave Delhi for Bareli before he returned from the war. This was just after you came and told me that Ahmad was safe and returning to India. When my mother died I decided to move here with my aunt.'

'I don't understand, Yasmeen, if you are so deeply in love with Ahmad what stops you from meeting him.'

She sighed again. 'Bhaijaan, no matter how great our love, it cannot break the taboos of our society. I am a woman of the bazaar and Ahmad the son of the imam of one of the well-known mosques in Delhi ... any relationship between the two would be like the mating between fire and water. The fire dies and the water becomes murky.'

'But according to great poets, true love can transcend any barriers ... remember Shireen Farhad and Layla Majnun.'

Yasmeen did not answer for some time.

'Can you do me a favour, Bhaijaan?' she implored a little later. 'Let things be as they are. Both of us can spend the rest of our lives with the memories of our love. You can tell Ahmad that you were unable to find me here. I want you to promise me that.'

'I am sorry, Yasmeen, I cannot make such a promise. I have to tell Ahmad that I met you here ... I owe this much to an old friend. I have to respect his feelings too. Will it be possible for you to write to him even if you can't meet him?'

'But how will he read my letters when he cannot see?'

'An old, trusted servant reads out his letters to him, and also writes out the letters Ahmad dictates. I wonder if I can ask you for something?'

Yasmeen nodded.

'Promise me that whenever Ahmad writes to you, he will get a reply.'

'I promise,' said Yasmeen, her eyes brimming over with tears, as she sat on the floor like a deity—immobile, graceful, and proud.

It was time for Ghulam Rasool to leave.

Yasmeen raised her hand in a gesture of farewell, the tears now flowing unabated. With Ghulam Rasool's departure it seemed to her that the bridge that connected her with her past was about to collapse.

Ghulam Rasool climbed down the stairway, walked swiftly to the restaurant to say a hurried goodbye to Yaqub and Sheeda, and then hailed a tonga to take him back to the inspection bungalow.

Ghulam Rasool left for Rawalpindi the next morning. Soon after his arrival, he wrote a letter to Ahmad describing how he had managed to locate Yasmeen, and had obtained a promise from her that she would correspond with him. He passed on Yasmeen's address and asked Ahmad to let him know if there was anything more he could do for him in this matter.

thirty

On his return to Rawalpindi, Ghulam Rasool found Sara in a state of indifferent health. She seemed to be suffering from the same kind of morning nausea she had when she was pregnant. Ghulam Rasool was certain that she couldn't be pregnant again because ever since her return from Delhi she had been very cold towards him. It was only after every stratagem known to him had failed that he fell at her feet one night and begged her to sleep with him. He was sure that one stray encounter and that too in which one partner was cold couldn't result in a pregnancy. Unfortunately, Dr Blyth thought otherwise and confirmed that Sara was two months into her pregnancy. She also told Sara that if her husband really cared for her he would have been more careful.

The news of the second pregnancy did not unnerve Sara, as she had been brought up to believe that every child who came into this world with two hands and two feet brought his or her means of sustenance from Allah. Ghulam Rasool, on the other hand, was alarmed when he thought of the added economic burden and the risk to Sara's life in delivering another child so soon after the first.

When he conveyed the news to Noorani Begum in Delhi, he received a reply congratulating him on Sara's pregnancy along with a list of prayers from the Quran to be recited by her forty times a day which would assure that she bore a son. Noorani Begum also suggested that like Sara's previous delivery it would be best for everyone that the second one also took place in Delhi.

Ghulam Rasool dismissed the suggestion summarily at first but kept it in his mind for consideration at a later time. In the meantime, to keep his worries at bay, he buried himself in his office work.

The days became shorter with the onset of Rawalpindi's cold and wet winter. Sara had always dreaded this part of the year. The cold weather restricted her movements to the bungalow and brought on a state of depression. She imagined herself lying down on a charpai in the open in Delhi's balmy winter and getting herself massaged. If only her dreams could come true. As the days passed by, her girth kept on expanding till she found walking around difficult. Dr Blyth continued advising her on the importance of taking a brisk one-hour walk daily in her own interest and that of her unborn child. With only three months left before the scheduled time of delivery, Ghulam Rasool had still not made up his mind on whether Sara should have the baby in Rawalpindi or in Delhi.

One day, when Sara was taken to Dr Blyth on what appeared to be labour pains but turned out to be a false alarm, the doctor called Ghulam Rasool aside in her clinic and told him that from then onwards Sara must take plenty of rest and walk around the compound for no more than half an hour. She also pronounced that it would very risky for Sara to undertake any journey of any duration whether by rail or by road.

Returning home, Ghulam Rasool sought refuge in the loneliness of one of its rooms. He sat there with his head cradled in his hands, thinking of all the arrangements he would have to make for Sara's delivery to take place in Rawalpindi, when he heard somebody tiptoe into the room.

'Sahib!' It was Resham. 'You seem to be worried these days and I was wondering whether there was any way I could be of some help.'

Ghulam Rasool initially paid little attention to these words but he remembered Noorani Begum's oft-repeated advice: Never refuse an offer of help no matter how small or from what source it comes. He paused for a while before speaking.

'Thank you, but the way things are developing only God Almighty can help me. Nobody from my family is here in Rawalpindi and the doctor has forbidden your begum sahiba from travelling, which means that she cannot go to Delhi and she is due to have a baby in three months' time.'

'Don't worry, sahib. Resham is here to help you in whatever way you want. I will work day and night and take care of the begum sahiba such that you'll never feel the absence of your relatives. Besides, I'll pray to my Lord Jesus Christ in heaven to come to your help. You will see what Christian prayers can do and how worries disappear when prayers are addressed to Him.'

Even though this came from a domestic help in his employ, Ghulam Rasool found consolation in her words.

From that day onwards Resham could be seen at all times of the day or night in the bungalow. Most of the time she hovered around Sara, making sure that she exerted herself as little as possible. Whenever the sun was out, she accompanied her mistress for the half-hour walk as recommended by Dr Blyth.

With about a month left for Sara's delivery, Ghulam Rasool received a letter from Noorani Begum informing him that she was leaving for Rawalpindi within a fortnight to be with Sara at the time of her delivery. She wrote that she had arranged for one of her neighbours to take care of her household in the interregnum.

Noorani Begum arrived at Rawalpindi railway station one morning in June 1927. Ghulam Rasool was at the station to receive her. His heart missed a beat when he couldn't locate her in the melee on the platform, this being her first train journey on her own. He found her half an hour later next to the second-class European waiting room. He was expecting his mother to be nervous and ill at ease, sitting all alone, wrapped in a burqa. Instead, clad in a chador, she was chatting merrily with some porters.

Noorani Begum embraced her son effusively. 'Beta, I thought that some official business may have kept you from coming to fetch me, so I was trying to ask these porters the way to the postmaster's residence, but they don't seem to understand me.'

Saad Ashraf

'Ammi, I hope you had a comfortable journey,' Ghulam Rasool enquired with a smile.

'As comfortable as one can be with the sounds and smells in a second-class ladies' compartment and one's life in the hands of an engine driver for twenty-four hours,' Noorani Begum answered pleasantly.

On the way home, Noorani Begum enquired about her daughter-in-law's health and assured Ghulam Rasool that now that she was here he could put all his cares away.

That evening the mother and son found themselves alone with one another. She had been suitably impressed with the postmaster's residential quarters.

'I am lucky that my son is the postmaster of Rawalpindi. Look at the size and expanse of this house. I wish some of the nobles of Delhi who lay claim to large properties could come here and see for themselves what Noorani Begum and her son have achieved,' she said to Ghulam Rasool.

'Ammi, this is no great achievement. This house isn't mine—it's government property. It has been occupied by one postmaster after another for half a century or more. Thank God, I have so far not been affected by power which induces many in government service into thinking that they own the government houses they live in temporarily.'

'Whatever ... it makes me feel great. Your father never had it this way. Maybe if he had lived longer he too could have been posted in small towns and lived in this manner but I guess he passed away too soon.' Noorani Begum sighed. 'By the way,' she continued, raising her eyebrows ever so slightly, 'who is this sweeper Resham that you employ but who seems to be the queen of the house?'

Ghulam Rasool's eyes widened and he felt a shiver down his spine. He knew that his mother was an intelligent woman with an uncanny sense of reading between the lines. Earlier in the day, he had introduced Resham to his mother as the family's caretaker. He wondered if a naïve remark dropped by Resham during a conversation could have made Noorani Begum conclude that their relations had gone beyond that of a master and servant.

'Resham is no sweeper. She comes from a poor but good family, and she is devoted and hardworking.'

'I never said anything about her not being hardworking. I merely said that Resham runs everything here. Is there anything wrong in asking the master of the house a straight and simple question?'

'Well, Ammi, there were only two women in this house before you arrived. With your daughter-in-law in an advanced state of pregnancy and recommended bed rest by the doctor, it was natural that Resham took over the affairs of running the house. However, I am relieved that you are here now to take care of everything.'

Noorani Begum didn't take long to act on her son's directions. This came to be displayed by the growing tension on Resham's face. Noorani Begum ordered her around, not giving her a moment's rest. Ghulam Rasool felt guilty for having put her in this state, but he knew that there was no other way to keep peace in the house. The pleasant part of the whole arrangement was that it was purely temporary, lasting only as long as his mother decided to stay on in Rawalpindi.

Sara's labour pains started early in the morning of 13 June 1927, and she had to be taken to the district zenana hospital and Dr Blyth was summoned in some urgency. Noorani Begum waited outside the labour room, turning her worry beads around her fingers and calling aloud the names of Allah as the time for the delivery neared. In the afternoon, Sara delivered a healthy baby girl. When the news of the arrival of another granddaughter reached Noorani Begum, a pall of gloom descended upon her. She had desperately wanted a grandson because she believed that girls were a liability on their parents as long as they lived. Lately, her own experience with her daughter Rehmani had reinforced this thinking when she had refused to marry the engineer, Karim, and no amount of persuasion could make her change her mind. The end result was that instead of being the mistress of her own household, Rehmani had become a primary teacher in the newly established Bulbul School for girls. Noorani Begum's thoughts were interrupted when Ghulam Rasool made his appearance with a box of sweets in his hands.

'Why this long face, Ammi … here,' he said, pushing the box in her direction. 'I am grateful to Allah that both the mother and the daughter are doing well.'

Noorani Begum stayed in Rawalpindi for some more time, dismayed at the troubles that her son would have to undergo in raising two daughters. As soon as her daughter-in-law returned home and had recovered sufficiently to keep an eye on the running of the house, she announced her plans for returning to Delhi. She boarded the train for Delhi soon thereafter.

'I am sure that Sara did not say the prayers I sent to you. If she had, the result would have been altogether different,' were Noorani Begum's parting words to Ghulam Rasool.

thirty-one

Though Ghulam Rasool's tenure at Rawalpindi passed in comfortable routine, at least twice a year he was subjected to periods of considerable stress. This happened every time the postmaster general, Punjab, came for his half-yearly inspections. Whenever the inspection date became known, Ghulam Rasool would disappear for several days, working virtually round the clock to get everything ready for the visit. He could never forget the first time the postmaster general, Mr Herbertson, came down from Lahore. The formal meeting with the postmaster general had ended, followed by a cup of tea. Ghulam Rasool had heaved a sigh of relief that the inspection had gone by successfully when Mr Herbertson put on his bifocals and announced, 'Now let's get down to the inspection of the post office and the colony, but before we do that I'd like to inspect the lower-staff toilets. Their state usually indicates the quality of administration.'

Ghulam Rasool was flabbergasted. Ever since he had joined the department he had never once been inside these toilets in any of the post offices in which he had served. He thought that Postmaster General Herbertson must be mad to think of visiting one of these stink holes. Fortunately for Ghulam Rasool, his head clerk, Niranjan Babu, was familiar with the eccentricities of Mr Herbertson, having come across him during his previous posting in Peshawar, where he had insisted on seeing similar facilities in spite of strong protestations from the English postmaster. Without informing Ghulam Rasool, Niranjan Babu had got both the officers' and lower-staff toilets cleaned, disinfected, and sprayed with strong-smelling phenyl and lemon deodorant. Thus when Mr Herbertson entered the toilets, he was in for a most pleasant surprise.

'These are one of the cleanest staff toilets that I have seen in thirty years of my service in India, and I must congratulate you on attending to such small details. Well done, Postmaster Rasool,' he remarked.

Through this small lucky break, Postmaster Ghulam Rasool had managed to move to the top of the postmaster general's very brief list of Indian favourites.

In the meantime, there was some good news from Delhi.

Ahmad had been in touch with Yasmeen in Heeramandi. Their love for one another had blossomed into a full-blooded relationship in spite of the lost years. Ahmad informed Ghulam Rasool that there was now a daily exchange of letters between them.

The only disconcerting news came from his mother in April 1930. She wrote that that the family of one Abdul, a clerk in the school where Rehmani worked as a teacher, had visited her. Abdul's mother and sister had come to ask for Rehmani's hand in marriage. Noorani Begum had not been impressed by Abdul's family. His mother had bragged about her family background in a voice that reminded Noorani Begum of the cackle of a hen about to lay an egg. She had dropped names of many notables of Delhi of whom Noorani Begum had never heard. As soon as Abdul's mother and sister had left, Noorani Begum had got in touch with Macho Begum and had asked her to make enquiries regarding the family. Macho Begum's report confirmed Noorani Begum's worst fears.

'Hai, Hai, Noorani Begum,' Macho Begum had said excitedly, 'in all the years I've spent in Delhi, I've never come across such a family. Two of Abdul's brothers are opium addicts. The sister who came to see you with her mother is a divorcee with the additional qualification of being so callous as to abandon her newborn daughter with her former husband. How did you ever come across such people whose shadows should better be avoided?'

Subsequent to Macho Begum's visit, Rehmani seemed listless and the glow of happiness that had existed earlier had deserted her face. Noorani Begum feared that her daughter may have contracted tuberculosis.

One morning, Jahan Ara Begum said to Noorani Begum, 'Why don't you take Rehmani to Dr Ram Babu, the TB specialist, and have her checked out. Either this girl has a serious physical ailment or ... or ...'

'Or what?'

'Or it could be a malady of the heart. I have been through such an experience when I was only fourteen and fell in love with my cousin. I lived in a daze and used to dream of him day and night. Of course, for some reasons I couldn't marry him, but even today, after so many years of happy marriage, my heart cries out for him,' Jahan Ara Begum said softly, tears glistening in her eyes.

'So what do you suggest I do?'

'I think the best thing would be to somehow find out what is plaguing Rehmani.'

The next day, Noorani Begum decided to take her daughter into confidence and try prying her mind open.

After preliminary niceties with Rehmani, Noorani Begum started praising the graciousness of Abdul's family in coming with a proposal of marriage for her. At first Rehmani doubted her mother's sincerity but was soon taken in by her experience in camouflaging the real motives of her conversation.

'Ammi,' confessed Rehmani, 'the truth is I love Abdul, and he is the man I'd like to marry. He is kind, gentle and generous, and supports me in my job. Only the other day the old harridan Bilqis Begum, the principal, was scolding me for having dropped an ink pot in class, when Abdul interrupted her and whispered something in her ear after which she was all smiles. Later he told me that he had informed her that I was likely to become his wife and that he would feel agitated if his future wife was to be scolded in this manner. It is natural that I should develop feelings for such a man.'

Saad Ashraf

Noorani Begum felt it was time that her daughter was brought face to face with the realities.

'Rehmani, my dearest, I respect your feelings for Abdul. But do you know that two of his brothers are opium addicts and that the sister who came with her mother, bringing your proposal, is a divorcee with a baby girl whom she has left with her former husband? Abdul's family are not our kind of people. We have some values and a place in society. I think you should give some thought to that.'

'I want to marry Abdul and not his brothers … and what's wrong in the sister being a divorcee? Sometimes when things don't work out in a marriage it may be better to opt out of the arrangement. In any case, how do the personal matters of Abdul's brothers and sister affect me?'

'It is a pity, dear Rehmani, you don't realize that in our society marriage is not between two individuals but between two families. Please tell me how you expect to survive on a hundred and twenty rupees a month—which the both of you put together earn—except by living with your in-laws?'

'What's wrong in living with in-laws? They will be happy to give us one of the three rooms they have in their house. Ammi, I love Abdul and I wonder if that makes any sense to you,' countered Rehmani.

'Listen Rehmani, I'm your mother and I know what is good for you in life because of my experience. Love may be an important thing in marriage but eventually it wears off like the enamel on utensils. It is only thereafter that the loyalty of the husband and the family is tested. And loyalty has a direct link with the kind of background that one comes from.'

'Family background and values—you talk about it as if we are from the most blue-blooded family of Delhi! You have no concern for my happiness or my right to spend my life with the man I love. I suppose you'd like me to marry that old second-hand widower Karim whom I've already rejected.'

'He may have been a bit old but surely he came of good decent stock. He stood by his first wife who was ill with consumption for over ten years.'

By now Rehmani had come to the end of her tether. Infuriated that her mother had no respect for her relationship with Abdul, she said, with fire in her eyes, 'Ammi, you have always wanted to have things your way, even if it concerned the lives of your children. You got Bhaijaan married where you wanted and this is what you have always wanted to do with me as well. When I was younger and there was an opportunity to get me married, you proposed Sultana's name and I decently stood by my younger sister and abided by your decision. Now I am older and someone who loves me, and who I love, wants to marry me and you refuse to support me. How long should I continue to live on the hope that a husband meeting your requirements will become available one day? Truly, this is my last chance to get married before I am consigned to eternal spinsterhood—and come what may I am not going to miss this opportunity. I will marry Abdul even if I have to live on the steps of the Royal Mosque and beg for a living.'

Noorani Begum was deeply hurt by what she considered downright insolence on the part of her daughter. Rehmani's words seemed like a quiver of poisoned arrows aimed at her heart. At the same time, the sense of guilt for not having suggested Rehmani's name to Phool Begum all those years ago kept pestering her. She was trying her very best to put her experience to her daughter's use without any personal motive, while Rehmani was not even making an effort to understand. She thought of the years of hard labour that she had put in trying to see that her children did better in life than herself. For the moment, the struggle of several decades seemed to have been wasted.

In the days that followed, Noorani Begum made a few more concerted but futile efforts to dissuade Rehmani from continuing her relationship with Abdul, but the more she tried the more adamant she found her. Ultimately, she wrote an express-delivery letter to her son in Rawalpindi, explaining the compelling circumstances which were responsible for her having agreed to Rehmani's marriage with Abdul. The marriage would take place as soon as Ghulam Rasool could manage a few days' leave to come to Delhi.

Saad Ashraf

However, Ghulam Rasool could not attend the wedding. An epidemic of cholera had broken out in the vicinity of Rawalpindi and his leave was cancelled as he was asked to take charge of handling the emergency. Since it was not possible to call off the wedding, Noorani Begum decided to carry on with everything as planned. In the absence of her son, a cousin of Noorani Begum played the role of the major-domo at the wedding. Noorani Begum and the rest of the family sat listening to Abdul's mother patiently as she waxed eloquent about her family background and about how lucky Rehmani was in becoming her daughter-in-law. When the time for saying goodbye to Rehmani came, the whole family wept aloud and a neighbour remarked that it seemed more like an occasion of grief than of joy. As soon as the taxi carrying the married couple disappeared from view, Noorani Begum went upstairs and wailed in a fit of despair. It was several days before she was able to shake off her depression and recover her spirits.

thirty-two

Ghulam Rasool had remained posted in Rawalpindi for two terms of three years each. The second term was without a precedent in the Punjab postal circle and was entirely on account of the patronage of Mr Herbertson, the postmaster general, who had been greatly impressed by Ghulam Rasool's meticulous nature. Ghulam Rasool had come to know through his sources in the department that a number of postmasters in the circle had been trying to dislodge him. Their efforts had failed so far because of the resistance put up by the postmaster general. The question of Ghulam Rasool's transfer from Rawalpindi—because of the perceived ill effects of prolonged tenure at a station—had been agitated by interested quarters with the director general, Indian Posts and Telegraphs Department, the top boss of the service in New Delhi. Mr Herbertson had however dug his heels in and said that Postmaster Rasool could only be transferred when a suitable replacement was found. On account of this support for an Indian officer, Mr Herbertson had acquired a nickname— 'Herbert the Wog'—which his English subordinates used extensively behind his back.

It did not take long for word to reach the ears of the member of the viceroy's council who handled the portfolio of posts and telegraphs. A directive followed from the viceroy's council to look into this matter and restore the administrative norms of the department. Ghulam Rasool had kept himself apprised of the situation as it was developing and had cautioned Sara that she should start packing up her things and be ready to move at short notice.

'Where are we going?' enquired Sara on a hot morning in June.

'I don't know. They can throw us anywhere they like. We government servants are like puppets in the hands of our superiors—they do with us what they wish.'

'But can't you do something to move to a good station? Surely you have enough people on your side to manage that.'

'Herbertson Sahib is the one person I have talked to. Unfortunately, he is in trouble for having kept me at one station for over six years. I don't know how much of a say he would have in getting me to a good station.'

'It's not your fault that we remained here for six years. I have been quite fed up of this place—'

'Sara, in the government it is always the employee who is at fault. Officers who have spent their entire lives have still to discover the logic on which the sarkar works. According to them only those who can tolerate the worst remain happy in service.'

Ghulam Rasool didn't have to wait very long for what was coming his way. His order arrived one morning while he was in office, going over the accounts of the treasury for the previous day. It contained a two-line message posting him to Amritsar in lieu of Mr James Jones, the very person from whom he had taken over the Rawalpindi post office six years ago, and who was now being given charge of Rawalpindi again. A few days later, he received a letter from Jones saying that he would like to take charge personally from Ghulam Rasool within the next fortnight. Though not quite enamoured with the prospect of having an interaction with JJ once again, Ghulam Rasool knew that he would have to undergo the torture of exchanging official papers with him.

In order to be free to handle any tension that this may generate, Ghulam Rasool thought it best to move his family to Delhi till such time that he moved to Amritsar. He knew that the household goods were already packed and could be despatched at short notice. Once they were set up in Amritsar he could ask his family to join him there.

When Ghulam Rasool returned to the bungalow that day and broke the news to Sara, she seemed relieved. They had talked about their transfer so often that she was mentally prepared for the move. The uncertainty created by many months of rumour mongering had come to an end.

'What sort of a place is this Amritsar, sarkar?' enquired Sara.

'Much hotter than Rawalpindi, lots of mosquitoes, and bad water—I won't say it is better than this.'

'At least it will have milder winters and will be closer to Delhi. Oh, I am so happy to be getting away from the cold, dark winters of Rawalpindi even though Amritsar may turn out to be much worse in other ways.'

'You are going to Delhi first, not Amritsar.'

Sara couldn't believe her ears. Her eyes brightened at the mention of Delhi. She thought of all her relatives and her ailing father, and looked forward to this opportunity to be able to meet everyone. She would be invited to dinners and everybody would ask her what sort of a place Rawalpindi was and though she hated its winters she would praise the town sky-high, knowing that the best of the begums of Delhi had not ventured beyond the city walls.

'But what about you, sarkar?' enquired Sara.

'I'll finish up things here, then go to Amritsar and settle down before calling you there.'

Sara felt grateful to her husband for this gesture. He could very easily have asked her to remain behind with him till he moved to Amritsar.

'I'll worry about you, sarkar. While I'll be physically in Delhi, my mind and thoughts would be with you every moment of my stay there.'

That night she expressed her gratitude to Ghulam Rasool in bed as a woman would—even though he was not really in the mood for love.

'I am your slave, your whore or whatever you want to make of me,' she rasped in a voice choked with passion.

Saad Ashraf

'Sara, please control yourself. Please don't go wild. I am not going anywhere,' Ghulam Rasool said, trying to calm her down.

Sara, accompanied by her two daughters, left for Delhi three days later.

One morning soon after this, Head Clerk Niranjan Babu knocked on Postmaster Rasool's office door to inform him in a whisper that Mr James Jones, the postmaster designate, had arrived the previous evening from Amritsar, and had taken a room at the postal rest house.

At the moment JJ was in the bathroom and could be expected to make an appearance at the post office within the hour to take charge. Ghulam Rasool had mentally prepared himself for this from the very day he had received the letter from JJ. He had drawn up the necessary papers and had readied the treasury accounts so that no time would be lost in handing over charge.

A little later, JJ walked into Ghulam Rasool's office with a swagger, wearing a white suit and a brown felt hat with a parrot feather stuck in it. Ghulam Rasool stood up and they both shook hands.

'Well, Rasool, it took me six years to come back to Rawalpindi but in the end I got back the job you took from me, eh?' JJ said curtly.

'JJ, I took over nobody's job. The department posted me and kept me here for six years and that's it. If you have any complaints in this regard you can register them with the PMG's office in Lahore,' replied Ghulam Rasool.

'Please don't call me JJ. I am Mr James Jones or Jones Sahib to you! Only my friends have the right to call me JJ, and as far as registering complaints, I think I know where and with whom that should be done.'

It was obvious to Ghulam Rasool that James Jones was trying to pick a fight.

'All right Mr James Jones, you can say whatever you like but I won't react. I have readied all the papers for handing over this post office to you. The head clerk has these with him. I will leave for Amritsar the day after I receive a signed copy of these papers,' Ghulam Rasool said coldly. He called the head clerk and asked him to bring the papers for JJ's signatures.

JJ's face reddened with anger as he muttered an abuse under his breath, but Ghulam Rasool sat patiently working on a file. JJ seemed affronted, picked the papers placed before him, and strode out of the room in a huff.

As soon as he had left the office, Ghulam Rasool summoned Niranjan Babu.

'Niranjan Babu, please provide all necessary cooperation to Jones Sahib. If he wishes to go through the treasury accounts and wants to physically check out the balances, help him do so. If he wants me to come personally for something do not hesitate to call me regardless of the hour, but try and have him sign the papers as soon as possible so that I can vacate the bungalow and leave for Amritsar.'

When the office closed that afternoon, Ghulam Rasool walked back home to the empty bungalow, pondering over the day's events, his hands deep in his trouser pockets and the sound of his own footsteps resounding in his ears. He wondered what made JJ, who claimed to be a thoroughbred Englishman, blow his top. Ghulam Rasool was not in the best of spirits as he lay down on the bed spread out on the floor of his room. He took up a copy of *Wuthering Heights* which lay on a side table and started reading. Even as he waited for sleep to overtake him, he saw Resham standing in front of him with something in her hands.

'A cup of tea for you, sahibji,' she said, as Ghulam Rasool stood up from his bed to help himself to the cup that she held in her hands.

He wondered what made an uneducated and socially underprivileged person like Resham so gracious and thoughtful.

'Sahibji, can I say something?' she asked.

Ghulam Rasool nodded.

'Sahibji, can you hear the silence in this house as if it is mourning your departure. Only a few weeks ago it was full of life. Why must the Lord Jesus test us humans with the sorrow of parting.' Her eyes filled with tears.

Saad Ashraf

Ghulam Rasool was deeply touched.

'Resham, this is the way of the world. We come across people, make friends and when the time comes we depart in different directions never to meet again. Time heals the sorrow of parting; that is how one survives in life.'

Resham shed some more tears which she dabbed with a cheap, pink handkerchief.

Ghulam Rasool put his arms around her in an effort to console her. She turned to face him, put her arms around his neck, and gave him a long and passionate kiss.

'I shall remember you, sahibji, till the last breath in my body,' said Resham, as Ghulam Rasool felt her warm tears drip on his shirt.

She disentangled herself, took out an envelope from her pocket, and pressed it into Ghulam Rasool's hands.

'Sahibji, this is a small parting gift for you. It is of course not worthy of you but promise me that you shall open this only when your train departs for Amritsar.'

Ghulam Rasool clutched the envelope in one hand and clasped her in a tight embrace.

Next morning promptly at eight Ghulam Rasool was in his office. Niranjan Babu made his way into the office, clad in a sparkling white dhoti and a grey waistcoat.

'Sirji, Jones Sahib called me to the rest house at eight last evening and I was told to wait in the ante-room. The caretaker said that the sahib was alone and drowning himself in liquor. He signed these papers at four in the morning,' said Niranjan Babu.

Ghulam Rasool kept one copy of the papers for his record.

He left for Amritsar the same evening. On the train, he remembered the envelope Resham had given him and took it out of his coat pocket. It contained a silver-coloured oval-shaped double photo frame. One frame had a picture of Jesus Christ while the other contained a photograph of Resham with the words 'I shall always remember you' scribbled in Hindustani.

thirty-three

When Ghulam Rasool arrived in Amritsar he had expected that James Jones would follow him from Rawalpindi to handover charge of the Amritsar post office. When this did not happen for a couple of days, Ghulam Rasool got perturbed. After some more time elapsed he became panicky. He paced the floor of the civil rest house where he was staying, wondering what had happened. He could not contain himself any longer and made a telephone call to Niranjan Babu in Rawalpindi who informed him that JJ had left for Amritsar some three or four days back. He had not attended office for a single day since taking charge but had been spending all his time, drinking alone at the postal rest house and had asked the head clerk not to disturb him unless there was utmost urgency.

Alarmed at the abnormal delay in JJ's arrival in Amritsar, Ghulam Rasool sent off a telegram to the postmaster general in Lahore, informing him of this and requesting further directions. The postmaster general's office acknowledged the receipt of the telegram and ordered Ghulam Rasool to take charge and start administering the Amritsar GPO. They said that they were investigating JJ's disappearance.

The authorities launched a search at all stations en route and looked for JJ in the European-style waiting rooms but he was nowhere to be found. Thereafter, the railway police started looking through the green plains of the Punjab through which the rail line passed. A few days later, a gang of trackers found

JJ's bloated body in a ditch three hundred yards from the main line short of Gujrat Junction, five miles away from the nearest habitation. A half-empty bottle of whiskey and two empty vials of sleeping tablets lay close by which meant that JJ had got off the train and walked away, probably drunk, into the darkness of the night. The diary of the engine driver revealed that the Frontier Mail had made an unscheduled short stop in the early hours of the morning at that location to allow a herd of wild boars to cross the track. Nobody knew what had transformed JJ into a tormented man who would put an end to his life in this manner. His body was removed to Rawalpindi where he was buried in the Christian cemetery two days later.

Ghulam Rasool did not transact any cash from the treasury and requested an audit team from Lahore to go through its accounts. After four weeks of work the team was able to establish that there were innumerable instances in the treasury accounts where JJ had withdrawn government funds without any explanation. At the end of his last tenure of three years, the total amount due from him came to thirty thousand rupees.

Although Ghulam Rasool started on his tenure in Amritsar under the tragic shadow of the Jones suicide, he soon eased himself into the usual stride as an efficient administrator. He learnt from his Head Clerk Babu Sant Singh, that JJ had suffered on account of his family's insatiable demand for a better standard of living. The memsahib had become addicted to the rarefied air of Murree where she lived for most of the year in a hired chateau called the 'Heart's Reprieve'. There, in the company of her daughters who went to the Convent School, she could walk up and down the mountain slopes covered with white daisies. The nippy mountain air smelling of wet moss on which rain had just fallen, reminded her of her village back home on the Scottish border. Alone in the spacious postmaster's bungalow in Amritsar, JJ, an introvert by nature, had taken refuge in liquor. The maintenance of two establishments had become a strain on his pocket and the postmaster had started dipping his hand into government coffers to make his ends meet. A stage came when he could no longer replace what he had taken out and in the end there probably seemed to him no other alternative except to end his life.

When Ghulam Rasool took over the postmaster's ten-room bungalow in Amritsar he found two locked trunks and some other personal belongings of the late James Jones. In an almirah, he came across some tattered pages from an exercise book in which JJ had written some poems to describe his loneliness and the wounds that life had inflicted on him. He seemed to have painted as well and there was a large watercolour of the Jallianwala Bagh with the caption 'Here walk the spirits of innocent natives'.

Ghulam Rasool's admiration of the late postmaster grew for he seemed to be possessed of a high degree of sensitivity. Ghulam Rasool kept all of JJ's belongings separately in the corner of one of the bedrooms, hoping that one day his wife or daughters would come to claim them but the days turned into months and there was no claimant. Ghulam Rasool wrote several letters to Mrs Jones, c/o Heart's Reprieve, Murree, but there was no reply. It was Babu Sant Singh who informed him one day that according to reliable sources Mrs Jones and her daughters had departed for England for good.

On her return from Delhi, Sara had settled well in Amritsar in spite of the heat, the mosquitoes and the water.

'What is all this stuff doing in this room?' she had enquired from Ghulam Rasool when she saw the trunks JJ had left behind.

'They belong to Jones Sahib, the former postmaster. I am keeping them here until his family members come to take them away.'

'You mean the same sahib who committed suicide by walking off the train in the middle of the night when coming to Amritsar? He must have been a very selfish man and a coward to escape the rigours of life and leave his wife and children at the mercy of this cruel world,' remarked Sara.

'Jones Sahib was a sensitive man and no coward. His family was responsible for the suicide. They should have taken better care of their man.'

'You'll always blame the family for whatever goes wrong. Well, what are we supposed to do with a dead man's belongings?

Saad Ashraf

Maybe we should send them to an orphanage ... that may help wipe off some of his sins.'

This unfair judgement agitated Ghulam Rasool. The couple were soon into a heated argument. They sulked, not speaking to one another for days, until they made up for it all one night in bed with promises of undying love.

thirty-four

A hmad had been writing to Ghulam Rasool regularly and had kept him informed of how the relationship between him and Yasmeen had reached a stage where they found it impossible to live without one another. However, the storms of gossip and slander that such a union would create in Delhi and within the imam's immediate and extended family would be impossible to weather. They had therefore decided to get married secretly in Lahore with Ghulam Rasool as their confidant and witness. Ahmad wrote to Ghulam Rasool enquiring when he could come to Lahore for this purpose, cautioning him to keep this matter a closely guarded secret from everyone including Sara. 'Please be careful, even whispers can travel in the wide expanses of India,' he had written. Ghulam Rasool found that he had a meeting to attend in Lahore with the postmaster general on 12 May 1933 and advised Ahmad that he could stay for one more day to attend the marriage. In Delhi, Ahmad contrived with his father to take the trip to Lahore in the company of his trusted servant Ditta, ostensibly to meet his friend Ghulam Rasool. The imam agreed that, if nothing else, a change of air would do his son some good.

Arriving in Lahore, Ahmad and his servant checked in at the Broadways Hotel on the Mall Road and were met by Ghulam Rasool after he had finished with his official business. Since they were meeting after almost seven years, the two friends spent some time catching up with each other's lives and reminiscing about the old days, after which Ahmad broached the subject of his impending marriage.

'I've arranged for a maulvi to be here to perform the nuptials tomorrow at four in the afternoon which is an auspicious time. Ditta can act as my witness, while you can represent Yasmeen. You'll have to bring her here so that she can sign the papers. I have managed to speak to her on the telephone and she will be waiting for you to pick her up at three o'clock sharp at the foot of the stairs of the Badshahi Mosque opposite the Elephant Gate of the Lahore fort.'

'Ahmad mian, that is all very well, but what happens after you are married? Surely you wouldn't want your wife going back to her profession of singing for the public in the bazaar.'

Ahmad heaved a big sigh. 'I hope to have one of my houses in Delhi vacated by my tenant in a couple of months' time after which I will move her there, but until that happens I am afraid that she will have to live in Lahore the way she is doing presently.'

Ghulam Rasool failed to reconcile himself with the thought of Ahmad sending his newly wedded wife back to Heeramandi, no matter how compelling the circumstances. But when he thought deeply of the situation that Ahmad was placed in and took into account his disability and dependence, he realized that his friend had no other option available.

The next day, Ghulam Rasool waited at the foot of the stairs of the Badshahi Mosque at the appointed time. He paced back and forth along the length of the last of these stairs to overcome his nervousness, hoping and wishing that Yasmeen would turn up to redeem the pledge of love she had made with Ahmad. He thought of all the sacrifices that Ahmad had made in bringing matters to this stage. Ahmad's devotion to this woman of the bazaar had estranged him from his family and made him brave death on the battlefields of Europe. He glanced at his watch—it was already five minutes beyond the appointed time and there was no sign of Yasmeen. If she did not turn up it would be a great shock for Ahmad and yet Yasmeen would only be human if she refused getting into a lifelong relationship with a person who was blind. Another quarter of an hour passed and Ghulam Rasool was more or less certain that she wasn't coming. He decided to give himself another ten minutes before heading back for the hotel as the harbinger of bad news for his friend.

'Bhaijaan!' a familiar husky voice addressed him from behind a black burqa. 'I am sorry I am late. We had a visitor and until he had left I simply could not make an excuse to leave. There was no other way. Women like us are not free.'

'Well ...' said a visibly relieved Ghulam Rasool, 'let's not waste any more time. Ahmad mian must be worried to death waiting for you. I hope he has managed to hold back the maulvi to pronounce you man and wife.'

'I'll be seeing Ahmad after nearly twenty years,' remarked Yasmeen, as the tonga they had hailed picked up speed on its way to Broadways Hotel. 'I wonder what he looks like ... is he the same as he was when he used to visit us in Chawri Bazaar?'

'Twenty years is a long time ... everything changes ... though I dare say you'll recognize him. Don't express any shock at the vacant look in his eyes. In any case, it is what a person is inside that makes the difference. And he is an exceptionally good human being.'

'I think he is much more than that, I think he has the spirit of God in him. How many men in this world would love a woman of the bazaar in this manner and for this long and be ready to marry her?'

'My friend has had more than his share of suffering in his life. Yasmeen, you must promise me that you will always remain loyal to him no matter how pressing the circumstances.'

'I may be a fallen woman in the eyes of the society, Bhaijaan, ready to sing for anyone who walks up the stairs with a few coins in his pocket, but I assure you of my lifelong loyalty to your friend.'

Arriving at the hotel, the burqa-clad Yasmeen followed Ghulam Rasool as he made his way to the second floor where Ahmad had his room. He knocked at the door which was opened by Ahmad's servant.

'Ahmad mian has been waiting for you for the last one hour in a state of near panic, wondering why you hadn't turned up.

Saad Ashraf

He has arranged for the adjoining room for the lady. Come, I will open it ... she can wait there,' said Ditta.

Ghulam Rasool left Yasmeen in the room and hurried back to Ahmad who was closeted with a man sporting a goatee. Ahmad introduced him as Maulvi Hidayatullah—the man who would perform the nikah.

'Mian, I have had to persuade Maulvi Hidayatullah to stay for performing the nikah. You know he has other appointments as well,' said Ahmad, as the maulvi looked on.

Ghulam Rasool nodded quietly and tugged on Ahmad's arm to take him aside.

'There was a problem ... she turned up late and there was no way of informing you.'

'I'd like to meet Yasmeen before I go through with this. Please lead me to her.'

Ghulam Rasool held Ahmad by the hand and led him to the adjoining room. He left him there and withdrew from the room, leaving them alone. Yasmeen clasped Ahmad's hands in hers. They embraced. She discerned his features, recollecting distant times. Though he had aged, walked with a shuffle, had developed a slight stoop and had grey hair, she saw him as the vibrant handsome young man, lips red with betel, reclining against the white pillows at her house in Chawri Bazaar, love and admiration for her in his eyes as she danced late into the night. Her face was next to his and she looked into his listless eyes.

'You shouldn't have sacrificed your youth, home, family, and even your sight for someone like me, Ahmad,' Yasmeen said. 'I am not even worth the dust under your feet—I am fit only for the lowliest of men.'

She broke down and sobbed like a child, recalling their last meeting at the bazaar in Delhi. Ahmad pressed her close to his chest.

'Yasmeen! Don't say such words about yourself ever again. You are a deity in the form of a woman—the goddess who transcended time and distance to come and stand by me as the symbol of love and hope that kept me alive in frozen trenches through the barrage of bullets and bombs. I've suffered much for this day. Strange are the ways of Allah ... I am so close to you yet so far that I cannot see you,' said Ahmad, his cheeks sodden with tears.

He could vividly recall himself in a trench in which the frozen mud had become red with human blood, and the air was acrid with the smell of flesh ... he could hear the deafening roar of guns which had just relieved themselves of their parcels of death ... and through all the smoke and the din of battle and the groans of men in the throes of death, he could see the young pretty face of Yasmeen, dressed in white, a smile on her face, urging him to live for her sake and their love.

She put her arms around his shoulders and walked him slowly to the bed in the room. He sat on its edge and she sat at his feet, her head on his knees, as he stroked the strands of her velvety hair and then moved his fingers over her face.

'I'll love you to the last breath in my body,' Ahmad whispered with emotion.

Some lines from Ghalib came to Yasmeen's mind:

My dust is wandering in the lane where my beloved lives
It is a good thing, O wind, that it has now no desire to
have wings!

There was a soft knock on the door. It was Ghulam Rasool, wanting them to hurry up. Ahmad asked for a few more minutes.

'Are you sure you would still like to marry me? There's still time for you to say no if you want to,' said Ahmad.

'I came here of my own choice—a choice I have made for life. I want to be your wife and be with you every moment of your life and mine in this world as well as the next.'

Ahmad asked Ghulam Rasool to start readying the papers for the ceremony. Ghulam Rasool went out of the room and returned with the sheaf of papers.

'Ahmad mian, there are still a few columns that require filling up. I was wondering what to do about them. Maulvi Hidayatullah says every column has to be filled before he will pronounce you man and wife.'

'Why don't you read out the information you need so that we can provide you with the answers?'

'Well, the first column requires the name of the father of the bride.'

Ahmad looked in the direction of Yasmeen, waiting for her to say something. There was an embarrassing silence in the room as Yasmeen sat with downcast eyes.

'What difference does a father's name make to a marriage? After all, the two who are getting married must have come from somewhere. Just fill in that column with the words "not known",' interjected Ahmad.

'We can enter a hypothetical name here which will settle the legal requirements,' counselled Ghulam Rasool.

'And build a marriage based on love and truth on the foundations of fraud?' countered Ahmad.

'There is another column here which requires the address of the bride.'

'I think we should state the truth and give her address in Heeramandi.'

Ghulam Rasool filled the form and moved to the other room to show these papers to Maulvi Hidayatullah. Ahmad followed his friend.

The maulvi took his eyeglass out of the upper pocket of his long, black coat and started reading the marriage document.

When he had finished, he looked up, his narrow eyes blazing. 'I find that the name of the father of the bride is not known. Do you know what we call anyone born of unknown parentage? A bastard. I also find that the bride's home is said to be in Heeramandi—the infamous bazaar where women sell themselves. Allah forgive me ... I am a respectable maulvi used to performing the nikahs of the nobility and not of bastards and prostitutes. You have insulted me by calling me here.'

Ghulam Rasool could see that Ahmad was trying his best to control himself.

'Maulvi Hidayatullah,' said Ahmad, his face livid with anger, 'you are an uneducated oaf and a slur on the name of Islam. It is not your business to cast aspersions on the parties getting married. If the name of the bride's father is not known for some reason, should we put in a false name? And what does her living in Heeramandi have to do with her marriage. It is maulvis like you who have lowered the prestige of our religion in the eyes of the world.'

'And what do you know about Islam, you who are ready to marry a prostitute?'

Ahmad could restrain himself no longer. He flayed his arms in the air in an effort to punch the maulvi, while Ghulam Rasool placed himself between Ahmad and the maulvi to keep them separated from physical contact.

'You blind infidel! I'll break every bone in your body and throw your foul flesh to the dogs!' shouted the maulvi.

'You uneducated maulvi of the gutter!' retorted Ahmad.

Neither Ghulam Rasool who had known Ahmad since his youth nor Ditta the servant who had served with the family for twenty-seven years could remember having seen Ahmad in such a rage. Before anyone realized what was happening, Maulvi Hidayatullah dashed for the door and left the room.

'Well ... what do we do now?' said Ghulam Rasool when he had recovered sufficiently.

'Get another maulvi to perform the nikah,' snapped Ahmad, still seething in anger.

'There's a mosque a furlong from here. I can go and bring the maulvi from there to come and perform the nikah,' volunteered Ditta.

'I think that's an excellent idea, but it might be best if you were to explain to him in advance that the name of the father of the bride is not known and that she resides in Heeramandi so that there is no problem later. You can offer the maulvi fifty rupees more to get him here,' said Ahmad.

Ditta left and was back in half an hour with a maulvi in tow.

Saad Ashraf

'I am Maulana Hashmat from the mosque next door … your servant has explained some of the peculiarities of the parties concerned in the marriage. It is not the business of those performing the nikah to get into the personal details of those wanting to get married as long as the bride and the groom agree to the marriage and there are witnesses from both sides who can vouch that neither party is being forced and both belong to acceptable faiths. The nikah is a ceremony to formalize this relationship,' said the maulana.

Maulana Hashmat recited some verses from the Quran, got the signatures on the marriage deed, and pronounced Ahmad and Yasmeen man and wife. He congratulated the bridegroom, wished him well for the future, and prepared to leave. He refused to accept the bonus of fifty rupees offered by Ahmad saying that his conscience did not permit him to take anything over his usual fee. The whole thing was over in five minutes.

'There are good maulvis and bad ones, just like good and bad eggs one may buy from the market. Maulana Hashmat did not create any fuss like his predecessor,' remarked Ahmad, as soon as the maulana left the room.

After Ghulam Rasool had congratulated Ahmad and Yasmeen and wished them all the best for the future he took his leave. He wanted to get back to the rest house to pack his suitcase so that he could board the train for Amritsar the next morning.

Ahmad and Yasmeen spent their wedding night in the room in Broadways Hotel, filling one another on what had happened to them in the intervening years. Both of them broke down many times during the night, blaming themselves for not making efforts to establish contact with one another. Yasmeen promised to be faithful and loyal to Ahmad as long as she lived.

The next day, Yasmeen left the hotel to get back to singing for the public in Heeramandi while Ahmad and his servant took the train for Delhi.

thirty-five

It was the summer of 1936. Sara was tired of living in Amritsar. She found the servants incompetent and unreliable and her mornings were spent bickering with them. She found flies everywhere in the house as they took refuge from the heat outside, and no matter how many were exterminated by insecticide a greater number appeared the next morning. She was sick of the dust storms which raged every evening following the silent stillness of the hot afternoon. By the time the storm abated, the house lay covered with a thin layer of dust. The city's water had not suited her and she seemed to have a mild stomach ache continuously which became more intense after meals. The confrontation with these natural odds coupled with boredom made Sara seek solace in religion.

'Throw these carnal desires out of your body and mind. Sex is the evil work of the devil at play,' she said one night, spurning the efforts of her husband.

'There is nothing evil in this act,' he tried to explain. 'It is a natural human instinct which every man and woman possesses and wants to satisfy. Every religion of the world permits it between a man and his wife.'

Sara however remained adamant. Ghulam Rasool found her increasingly cold in bed, almost frigid. They seemed to be drifting apart as he began to spend more and more time after office hours playing tennis on the GPO courts. One of his partners in doubles was Hakim, the superintendent of post offices who, though headquartered in Lahore, spent more than twenty days in the month touring districts around Amritsar. One evening Ghulam Rasool found himself alone with Hakim, relaxing in the easy armchairs set around the courts, drinking iced lemonade after a particularly tough doubles tennis match against Mr Kemp, the Anglo-Indian telegraph master, and his assistant.

'Rasool Sahib, I believe you have a vacancy of a deputy postmaster in your office ... I was wondering whether you will consider one Purshottam, presently posted in Jalandhar, for this position. I've known Purshottam for many years now and can vouch for his loyalty, obedience, and obliging nature. I believe that his file is lying on your table. I would consider it a personal favour if you could transfer him here,' requested Hakim, drinking from his glass.

Ghulam Rasool nodded quietly. He remembered seeing the file. Purshottam was the last of the three in order of merit who had been recommended by the postmaster general's office in Lahore. It was Ghulam Rasool's prerogative to choose any one of the three.

'I will see what I can do,' he replied casually.

Next morning, he went through the file which contained a profile of Purshottam. All the reports in the file, both from British and Indian postal officers, spoke of the good qualities of the man. Ghulam Rasool had little hesitation in recommending Purshottam's name for the post of deputy postmaster, Amritsar.

Two weeks later, Head Clerk Sant Singh walked into Ghulam Rasool's office, leading a tall, fair-complexioned, middle-aged man clad in a spotless white western suit with a gold pen stuck in his coat pocket, and introduced him as the newly posted deputy postmaster. Both men shook hands as Purshottam presented his credentials. He had worked at three different post offices in the Punjab during his career and looked forward to a pleasant and useful stint in Amritsar. Purshottam informed his boss that he had already got hold of a suitable quarter where he would move his family from Jalandhar shortly. As his immediate supervisor, Ghulam Rasool gave Purshottam the usual advice of keeping an eye on his subordinates and their work and to report anything unusual that took place, and remain non-controversial both during and after office hours.

Ghulam Rasool came to know that Purshottam had moved his family to Amritsar when he came home for lunch one afternoon and was having mangoes for dessert.

'Begum, I have never eaten sweeter mangoes in my whole life. Where did you get them from?' enquired Ghulam Rasool.

'A boy brought a basket this morning and said it came from the house of one Purshottam who has been posted here as your deputy. I didn't want to accept it at first but what harm can a small basket of fruit do. In fact, this is the first time anybody ever sent anything to our house,' said Sara.

Ghulam Rasool nodded and kept devouring one mango after another without giving another thought to the matter.

Next morning in office, during one of his several meetings with his deputy, Ghulam Rasool thanked Purshottam for his gift.

'It is nothing, sir,' said his deputy. 'I have an arrangement with a friend who has a mango grove near Saharanpur. He sends me a few baskets which I distribute every year among my acquaintances.'

'That is very gracious of you, Purshottam.'

'By the way, sir, if you don't mind … my wife Kiran and I would like to call on you some evening to pay our respects.'

Ghulam Rasool knew that this was not an unheard-of practice in the post office though he had always refrained from such social contacts with any member of the staff mainly because Sara observed purdah and did not feel comfortable in the company of males. He thought of this request from someone who had fed him with the choicest of mangoes the day before and decided that no harm could come from accepting so minor a request.

'Certainly, Purshottam, it would be our pleasure to welcome you,' he replied.

Two days later, Ghulam Rasool and Sara awaited the arrival of their guests Mr and Mrs Purshottam. Ghulam Rasool had bathed after his game of tennis and had applied his favourite

Saad Ashraf

711 perfume while Sara had tidied the sitting room and was wearing a freshly ironed blue-coloured shirt and pyjama suit. After a great deal of argument with Ghulam Rasool she had agreed to sit barefaced in the company of a male stranger. There was a knock at the door promptly at seven. Ghulam Rasool opened the door and welcomed the couple, shaking hands with Purshottam. He introduced him to Sara while Purshottam presented his wife to his hosts.

Mrs Kiran Purshottam was much taller than the average Indian woman. She had a milky-white complexion, charcoal-black eyes and jet-black hair that cascaded over her right shoulder. Her well-proportioned body was clad in an orange and black sari whose end covered her head. She stood there with her manicured fingers and painted nails clasped together in a Hindu greeting. She reminded Ghulam Rasool of an idol he had once seen in a Hindu temple, perilously perched on a hill on the side of the river outside Rawalpindi whose devotees bathed her with milk.

Unknown to their spouses, something happened to Ghulam Rasool and Kiran as their eyes met. Both of them had the impossible notion that they had met somewhere before. They tried recollecting where this could have been but soon gave up, sure that it could not have been on this earth. It was Purshottam's voice which brought them back into the real world.

'It's our family tradition to bring a box of sweets when we visit someone for the first time,' he was saying, as he handed to his boss a box wrapped in silver paper neatly tied with a red-coloured ribbon.

Ghulam Rasool made a conscious effort to keep his eyes off Kiran as he conversed with her husband. Purshottam told him that he and Kiran had been married for five years and had no children, though Kiran had two from her former husband who had died in an accident. He had seen her for the first time while disembarking from a houseboat on a holiday to Srinagar and had fallen head over heels in love with her. Thereafter, seemingly possessed by her, he had pursued her relentlessly till he succeeded in marrying her two years later. His family had bitterly opposed the marriage because she was a widow and had two young daughters.

Ghulam Rasool watched Sara from the corner of his eyes and was happy to observe her in animated conversation with Kiran which meant that both of them were getting along well.

After Purshottam and Kiran had departed, Ghulam Rasool asked Sara what she thought of them.

'Kiran seems to me to be a very good human being. I felt like I was talking to my own sister though she belongs to another faith,' remarked Sara.

That night, Ghulam Rasool found sleep eluding him. Whenever his eyes closed, Kiran appeared from the mists of time with her hands folded together in a greeting, to pull him back. Ghulam Rasool wondered what had gone wrong with him. He was sure that this infatuation for another woman was temporary and would wear off by the morning after he had caught a few hours of sleep. He tossed and turned, lay on his back with his face towards the ceiling, tried changing sides, but no matter what he did sleep just would not come. The roosters in the neighbourhood had long stopped crowing when Ghulam Rasool woke up to find that he had been lying in his bed for a full two hours after his usual waking time. Bleary-eyed and weary, he had his bath, helped himself to breakfast, and went to office.

At office, he found that the same symptoms persisted. His body ached from lack of sleep. He could not concentrate on the files that were put before him and every now and then his thoughts drifted to Kiran. She seemed to be omnipresent and it surprised him that he could recall every moment of her presence from the evening before vividly—the way she sat down, the way she talked, and her quaint gestures with her henna-covered hands to emphasize a point. He scratched his head with the end of the pen and tried to explain to himself that this infatuation would wear off in a few days even though it had somehow persisted longer than he thought it would.

Saad Ashraf

The malady persisted. It motivated Ghulam Rasool to find ways of trying to get in touch with Kiran. He found out from the servants in the house that Sara's relations with Kiran were growing stronger by the day, and that they were spending many mornings together. They were exchanging recipes handed to them by their mothers, and the gossip concerning the neighbourhood. They were discussing their husbands, their children, their servants, their religious beliefs and to top it all, despite being a Brahmin, Kiran did not mind eating a meal in Sara's home.

When Ghulam Rasool came home for lunch one day he found Sara very happy.

'Kiran was here this morning and she told me that the day after tomorrow is their festival of Diwali which is like our Eid. She has invited us to tea at their home on the evening of Diwali. I said I'll speak to you and let her know,' she said.

Ghulam Rasool was delighted at this heaven-sent opportunity of being able to meet Kiran. Throughout his career he had made it a point not to socialize with those in the department because of its culture of gossip which made tales out of innocent social contacts which then made their way throughout the organization. However, with Kiran beginning to dominate his thoughts day and night he decided to break the stringent norms he had imposed on himself. He accepted the invitation and suggested to Sara that since they were going to visit somebody from his office for the first time it might be a good gesture if they gave Kiran and her husband a befitting Diwali present. Ghulam Rasool telephoned a Kashmiri arts dealer the next morning who arranged to deliver an ornamental table inlaid with flowers to his bungalow.

On the evening of Diwali they strolled across to Purshottam's quarters after their gift had been delivered to their house.

'Welcome! Welcome to our home! Thank you for your beautiful gift. We don't have the words to express our gratitude,' said Purshottam and Kiran as soon as their guests had stepped into their house.

Kiran looked ravishingly beautiful in a red sari, which matched the colour of the sindoor in the centre parting of her hair and the bindya in the middle of her forehead. Ghulam Rasool kept chatting with Purshottam but whenever he felt he was not being observed, he looked towards Kiran who he thought responded by giving him faint and meaningful smiles. When Kiran handed him his cup of tea, her fingers curled under the saucer touched his ever so slightly and he felt his senses tingling with the warmth of her touch.

By the time Ghulam Rasool and Sara left about an hour later, amidst repeated and profuse expressions of gratitude by their host and hostess, Ghulam Rasool was almost convinced that any overtures made by him towards Kiran would be reciprocated but some doubts still haunted his mind. He reasoned that the minor physical contact while passing the cup of tea may have just been an accident and he could be wrong in his interpretation of her smiles. He had to find out whether Kiran reciprocated her feelings even though this involved taking a risk.

The next day he wrote out an unsigned note for Kiran saying that he had fallen in love with her and all that he wanted to do day and night was to sit at her feet and sing songs of devotion for her. He begged her to let him know how he could do so. He put the note in an envelope and handed the same to his trusted orderly Chandu, saying that this was an urgent message from his wife for Mrs Purshottam and that it should only be given to her after he had made sure that nobody else was around. He sent Chandu over to deliver the note after he had confirmed that Purshottam had left for office. Chandu returned within half an hour and told his sahib that he had delivered the envelope to Kiran and that she had taken out the letter it contained and read it in his presence. He said that she seemed delighted on receiving the letter because her face had lit up with a big smile.

Ghulam Rasool waited for a couple of days just in case something adverse happened and his love for Kiran turned out to be one-sided after all, but when life continued normally he was convinced that he was right in assuming that Kiran reciprocated his feelings. Emboldened, Ghulam Rasool's mind started working non-stop on a stratagem by which he could meet

Saad Ashraf

Kiran alone without arousing suspicion. He knew that she met Sara every other day. As such he started visiting the bungalow in the mornings for a cup of tea to refresh himself and to browse through the morning papers. One morning he heard Sara engaged in conversation with Kiran in the adjoining room. He entered the room and exchanged greetings with both. He asked Sara whether he too could have some tea, and slumped into the only unoccupied sofa available in the room with the newspaper in his hand. Sara called for a servant but on getting no response from the kitchen she decided to go and do the needful herself. As soon as the sound of Sara's sandals had receded in the distance, Ghulam Rasool mustered all his courage to speak to Kiran, half-expecting her to reprimand him for trying to take advantage of his wife's absence.

'You got the letter I sent you. I am madly in love with you and cannot live without you. If you do not reciprocate I will leave everything and become a fakir and spend the rest of my life in the jungles. I must see you alone. We must find a way of meeting one another,' Ghulam Rasool whispered feverishly.

Kiran nodded but said nothing. He saw that her eyes had lit up with tenderness and sympathy. They seemed to be waiting to tell a story.

Disturbed by the sound of Sara's footsteps approaching the room, Ghulam Rasool could say nothing more. He collected himself and sat on the chair, pretending to be engrossed in the newspaper, while Kiran started browsing innocently through a Hindustani magazine.

'Here you are, sarkar, here's your cup of tea prepared by your most devoted wife,' said Sara.

Ghulam Rasool slowly sipped the tea, put the empty cup on the side table, and, taking leave of the ladies, left for his office, happy at the dawn of a romance with a goddess who loved him as much as he worshipped her.

thirty-six

Meanwhile, in Lahore, Mr Herbertson had retired and left for home in England, leaving a note in Ghulam Rasool's dossier. The note said that Ghulam Rasool was the most competent Indian postal officer he had come across during his service and the closest that an Indian could come to becoming an Englishman through education and training. Postmaster General Simms had read this note when drawing up a panel of names for the position of postmaster, Simla—a highly sensitive post considering that the viceroy, his entourage, and the elite of British India spent their summer months at this hill station. The panel contained six names, Ghulam Rasool being the solitary Indian. Sir Donald Gruggson, the director general in New Delhi had ticked his name after a great deal of thought. He had commented that this was an experiment to test the success of the system of developing Indians in the art of administration while subtly serving the purpose of satisfying the nationalist lobbies which clamoured to see more of their countrymen holding high public offices.

Ghulam Rasool was informed of this decision a few days later. When he reached home from his office and broke the news to Sara, she was delighted at the thought of leaving the heat, dust, and mosquitoes of Amritsar for the cool, green hills of Simla. As an afterthought she realized that the one thing she would miss would be her dear, loving friend Kiran.

'Isn't there some way we can take Purshottam and Kiran with us to Simla?' she asked her husband.

'I could take them with me if I was the viceroy of India. For your sake, I could get an envelope defaced twice if nobody was watching, but transferring a deputy postmaster is beyond my authority,' said Ghulam Rasool.

He wrote about his transfer to Noorani Begum in Delhi. She was happy at the news and hoped to visit her son as soon as he had settled in Simla, on the condition that he would try his best to see that when she came she could be photographed with the vicereine. At the same time she warned that he should be ready to receive a spate of visitors from Delhi comprising distant relatives and acquaintances he may never have heard of or seen before. She advised keeping two rooms in the official bungalow during the summers for such visitors with beddings spread on the floor in the traditional Indian style.

Sara got to work, packing the household goods with the help of her servants and before long she had everything ready in wooden crates or sewed in jute matting to await the availability of a railway wagon. Only the bare essentials remained which they would carry with them personally.

Ghulam Rasool handed over temporary charge of his office to Purshottam under instructions from Lahore that he proceed immediately to Simla. He and his family left for Simla on a warm day in April 1939. Among those who came to say goodbye were Purshottam and Kiran. The latter wore a black sari, a pall of sadness enveloping her face—the kind of sadness that is visible on a woman's face when parting from a lover she may never see again.

Simla, the summer capital of British India, the darling of the sahib log, was a quaint little town nestled in the mountains. It seemed to have been carved by the hands of God who had then balanced bungalows with bright-red and dark-green roofs precariously on its slopes. As far as the eye could see the whole town was covered with spring flowers—white, red, yellow, and blue—each rivalling the other, some planted and tended to by the town's municipal gardeners, yet others that grew wild but in equal abundance. The main road, the Mall, ran as a central artery from one end of the town to the other till it disappeared at its farthest end through the large meadow at the base of the town's cathedral.

Ghulam Rasool had hardly settled in his new office when he received an urgent telegram from Sir Donald Gruggson informing him that the entourage of the viceroy would start arriving from mid-May and that His Excellency, the viceroy, was expected to follow suit in a few days in his special train. The postmaster along with the head of the police and the district commissioner were expected to be at the railway station to welcome the arrivals above a certain rank.

Since these protocol duties occupied all his time, Ghulam Rasool did what all his predecessors had done before him: leave the working of the post office to his superintendent, Mr Basu, who through some administrative quirk of the department had found himself transplanted from the heat and humidity of Bengal to the cold and snow of Simla some five years back. Dark in colour, short in height, and wearing spectacles with round glasses in a thin, black, wire frame, Basu was the epitome of an Indian clerk with a prodigious memory, an uncanny ability with numbers, and an inexhaustible capacity for work. He had a few weaknesses too. His English required close scrutiny before one could decipher what he was saying, and he had a tendency to become unnerved and disoriented every time he came in contact with somebody important, particularly a European.

The viceroy's special train steamed into the Simla railway station in the third week of May 1939 on a cool but otherwise bright and sunny day at eleven in the morning as thousands of small Union Jacks hung over the building fluttered in the light breeze. The officialdom and notables of the city, dressed in their best, stood in long queues on either side of the red carpet, waiting expectantly for their lord and ladyship to emerge from their saloon.

The viceroy and the vicereine finally disembarked from the glistening white railcar surrounded by their personal staff, some of them in military uniforms with their chests covered with medals

Saad Ashraf

which sparkled in the sun. The lord and the lady walked down the line, shaking hands with those who stood there to welcome them. Being the junior-most in terms of protocol and tenure, Postmaster Ghulam Rasool was at the end of the last line. The viceroy shook hands with him, and moved on before he could even establish eye contact.

The arrival of the viceroy and the vicereine in Simla signalled the transformation of the summer capital of India from a town of a few middle-level functionaries to the bastion of British imperial power in India. Everybody who walked on the Mall did so with a swagger that betrayed their assumed importance. The royalty of the many Indian princely states—with their wives, mistresses, and concubines—thronged the main roads during the day and well into the late hours of the night, rubbing shoulders with and trying to get close to those who ruled India. They sat in restaurants, sipping coffee and munching roasted cashew nuts whose aroma drifted to and filled the streets below. A drizzle during the day led to the opening of numerous multicoloured umbrellas which gave the Mall the semblance of a Persian carpet rolled out to welcome the elite of India. The mountain air smelt of fresh flowers and Parisian perfumes, infusing the senses and making Simla the capital of intrigue and love and romance.

Whenever Ghulam Rasool stepped out in the open, he thought and longed for Kiran. Ever since his arrival, he had tried to find a way of getting Purshottam posted to Simla but there was no position of a deputy postmaster at this station. He had learnt that Purshottam was still temporarily holding the post he had vacated in Amritsar by virtue of which he had a telephone at his official residence. Ghulam Rasool had rung up Kiran one morning, aware that Purshottam would be at the office at that hour. The telephone operator at the exchange had connected him and Kiran had picked up the phone.

'I think of you all the time. Are we ever going to meet again?' she had asked.

He told her that life without her had no meaning for him and that he yearned for her. He suggested that she try to come to

Simla if she could, knowing fully well that it was impossible. He said that he would try to come to Amritsar, knowing that that too was impossible. There was no way he could leave Simla even for a day before the end of the summer season when the viceroy and his party would depart for Delhi.

Several weeks had passed by since that conversation but Kiran still occupied his mind, appearing every now and then through the mountain mists to haunt him whenever he had a moment to spare.

In the meantime, war clouds had been gathering over Europe. On 2 September 1939, sitting on the thunder box commode in the bathroom, Ghulam Rasool browsed though the *Simla Times*, the local English newspaper, to learn that Germany had invaded Poland. Three days later, Britain was at war with Hitler's Germany. The journey from Prime Minister Chamberlain's statement of 'peace in our times' to the stark realities of a conflict of worldwide dimensions had taken only a few months. Ghulam Rasool was astonished that even the super intelligent English could make serious errors in their judgement.

As soon as war was declared, the viceroy advanced his plans of moving to Delhi. He and his entourage departed in their special train on 4 September with only a few selected invitees from the administration coming to bid them goodbye at the station. Within a couple of weeks Simla stood denuded of the fashionable elite, much like the trees lining both sides of the Mall which only a short time back had been resplendent in their green foliage but now stood as bareheaded sentinels in autumn's mournful silence, watching over the sparse crowd.

By November, it started becoming dark by five in the evening as the winter sun dipped over the mountains. Coal fires had to be lighted in the afternoons in the main hall of the GPO to keep visitors warm.

'Soon they will have to keep the fires lighted the whole day long, sir. The Simla winter is long and terrible,' Basu told his boss one morning with an expression of impending doom on his face.

With the departure of the Government of India for Delhi, the activities in the GPO had been reduced to a fraction of what

Saad Ashraf

they were during the season. Ghulam Rasool observed with concern the increase in the incidents of squabbling among his staff.

'This happens every year and more so as it grows colder. An empty mind is a devil's workshop. Previous sahib log handled this situation by serving a few charge sheets and suspending the troublemakers,' Basu cautioned his boss.

Ghulam Rasool observed the situation for a couple of weeks and realized that Basu was right—indeed it was the lack of meaningful activity among his staff which was responsible for this unrest. He thought of various ways in which they could be occupied, and having failed to discover any, drew up a paper for Sir Gruggson, suggesting that half the staff should be given leave for two months followed by the other half when the first group returned, on the written promise that they would not avail leave during the summer season. Ghulam Rasool pointed out in his paper that this would bolster the morale of the staff by giving them more time with their families who lived in the villages around the hills of Simla.

No sooner had Ghulam Rasool despatched the paper to Delhi than he regretted his action, half-expecting a reprimand for making an inappropriate initiative which flouted all rules. Instead, he was surprised a few weeks later to receive a letter of appreciation from none other than Sir Gruggson himself, approving the scheme and calling it a 'most innovative breakthrough'. With half the staff on leave, peace descended in the office with enough work to keep the remaining staff busy. Ghulam Rasool wanted Superintendent Basu to avail this opportunity as well and raised the matter with him one morning.

'Mr Basu, everybody in the GPO, including myself, is going to avail winter leave for a month or two ... when would you like to go and meet your family?'

'Sir, I don't have much of a family left,' said Basu. 'My parents died in a famine in my home district of Barisal five years ago. I only have a widowed sister who lives in Calcutta.'

'Why don't you go and see her? I am sure she'll be happy to see you.'

Basu was wringing his hand nervously as if he wanted to say something.

'Sir, can I impose on your generosity to ask you for a favour?'

'Why not, Mr Basu, you have a claim on me. Both of us have worked around the clock for many months to keep this post office running.'

'Sir, I have only one problem and that is the seven-month-long and bitter winter of this place. The cold gets into my bones during the winter months and barely do I manage to get it out of my body when it makes its appearance again. It is only because I cannot tolerate the cold that I would like you to transfer me to any station in any province which has a milder climate.'

Ghulam Rasool considered this request for some time before answering. 'Mr Basu,' he said, 'I promise you that I'll try my very best to have you transferred to a climatically more moderate place but I am afraid you'll have to wait because it can't be done in a hurry.'

Basu thanked him for considering his plea, collected the few files on his boss's table, stacked them neatly in one corner, and left.

Saad Ashraf

thirty-seven

Ghulam Rasool proceeded on a month's vacation to Delhi with his family in early March, leaving the Simla office in the reliable hands of Superintendent Basu. He planned to return well in time to ready himself and his staff to handle the workload which invariably came with the shifting of the government machinery to Simla for the summer. Sara was delighted that she was leaving Simla's cold behind for the balmy weather of her home town. In her wildest of dreams she had never imagined that there could be a place as cold as Simla but having witnessed the snowflakes pouring down from the skies followed by the howling wind over a desolate town shrouded in white, she was convinced that this was no place for her to spend her winters.

On their arrival in White Haveli, the whole family sat around the fireplace in the kitchen, sipping salted Kashmiri tea laced with pistachio which Noorani Begum had specially prepared. Everyone was there except Ghulam Rasool's sister Rehmani.

'Where is Rehmani, I don't see her here?' enquired Ghulam Rasool of his mother.

An uncomfortable silence descended in the kitchen.

'She is busy with her own family and expressed her apologies for not being able to come,' said Noorani Begum.

'I hope she is happy in her own home,' remarked Ghulam Rasool.

'I think so,' said Noorani Begum, shrugging her shoulders. 'Beta, I presume that you must be meeting the viceroy every day,' she added in an effort to divert the course of the conversation.

'Ammi, the viceroy is like the king of India. He has no need to see petty officials like me every day,' said Ghulam Rasool, considerably deflating his mother's ego. 'I've shaken hands with him only once during the whole of the last year when I was in the queue with several others to receive him at the railway station on his arrival from Delhi.'

Later in the day, they had a chance to be alone in the living room with one another.

'Ammi, I want to know if everything's all right with Rehmani. Why wasn't she here today?'

Noorani Begum sighed, her face a picture of anguish.

'I was waiting for you to arrive so I could tell you. I didn't want to bother you with family worries while you were busy with your work.'

'So there's something wrong?'

Noorani Begum nodded her head. 'Nothing has been right with her since she got married.'

'What do you mean?'

'Her in-laws have confined her to their house. The mother-in-law hovers over her like a prison warden, and all my efforts to see her have been spurned on one pretext or another. You know that decent people like us cannot force their entry into somebody's house. I believe that she works like a slave from the crack of dawn to late at night and is being subjected to physical and verbal abuse and that this treatment has started telling on her health. Her mother-in-law has also forced her to take long leave from the school,' said Noorani Begum, holding back her tears.

'How long has it been since you've seen Rehmani?' asked Ghulam Rasool, trying his best to keep his cool.

'It is almost a year now.'

'I am really amazed that you can sit here and talk while your daughter is being brutalized perhaps at this very moment. The least you could have done was to tell me so that I could have informed the police in Delhi.'

Noorani Begum responded with sullen silence.

Saad Ashraf

'Say something ... at least tell me how you know that she is in this terrible state.'

'I sought Macho Begum's assistance and got a woman named Rashida through her who has taken up a job as a maidservant with Rehmani's in-laws. I give her twenty rupees a month in addition to the pay she gets from there and she gives me news of my daughter on a daily basis.'

'How can an illiterate servant woman like Rashida change things for my sister? I think we should involve the police in this matter straightaway.'

'What can the police do if Rehmani has got used to the treatment being meted to her and is not willing to make an effort to come out of this situation herself. You don't want a scandal, do you, if she goes to a court saying that she was happy living with her husband till her own family manipulated to break up her marriage.'

'Rehmani would never say such a thing against us—we are her family and her blood.'

'Beta, I am afraid you have no idea how the mind of a woman who marries for love works. She will try her best to salvage her relationship with her husband and her in-laws before she breaks down and asks for help.'

Ghulam Rasool could no longer control himself. 'And you will only offer a helping hand when she is broken in health and spirit. How can a mother be so cruel?'

Noorani Begum's face revealed the pain she was undergoing inside. 'We have to be patient. I have Rashida talking to her, trying to find out what she thinks of her personal situation and dropping hints that she would be better off in her mother's home. Once Rehmani is convinced about it, we'll step in and rescue her. Things are already in an advanced stage. It won't take more than a couple of days.'

'And what if she doesn't agree to come back?'

'In that case she has to put up with her lot ... nobody can force a woman to do things against her own will.'

'I won't let my poor sister be tortured for the rest of her life. I will get her back to this house no matter what happens before I leave for Simla.'

'A small, hasty step can wreck our plans of rescuing her from that hellhole. Rehmani's simple nature led her to fall in love with a devious man who simply plotted to ensnare her. I tried my best to dissuade her from this marriage but it was too late, love had possessed her like the devil and made her blind to reason.'

'What could Abdul get out of marrying my sister? We are middle-class people with nothing much to offer.'

'For people who don't even have what we have, wouldn't she be a prize? She comes from a background better than theirs and they get an educated woman in the house as a slave to clean, wash, stitch, cook, and obey the commands of the mother-in-law and if need be work in a school and earn some money too.'

'I can't believe that there are such sinister people in this world.'

'You better start believing what I say. The world is a huge jungle with human beings using one another to serve their own ends. Unfortunately, as I have sadly learnt from my own experience it is those who are simple, decent, and honest who suffer the most in life.'

A couple of days later in the afternoon Noorani Begum took Ghulam Rasool aside.

'Rashida came to see me today,' she whispered to him. 'She told me that she had a long talk with Rehmani while her mother-in-law had gone visiting her neighbours. Rehmani opened her heart out to her and told her that she realizes the mistake she has made by marrying Abdul but there is no option for her except to continue living with her in-laws till she dropped dead from work and ill-treatment. She broke down and cried like a child, cursing her luckless existence and asking Allah for forgiveness for her sins which had estranged her from her close ones. Rashida consoled her and promised to help her. I think that the time has come for us to act.'

'In my opinion, we should involve the police in this matter immediately,' said Ghulam Rasool.

Saad Ashraf

'The police is all you can think of! Your father always used to say that the friendship of the Indian police is worse than their enmity. I always trusted his perceptions. I think I'll handle it my way and if things do not work out we can think of involving the police in whom you have so much trust.'

Over the next few days, Noorani Begum finalized the plans for her daughter's escape from the captivity of her in-laws. Rehmani was to leave the house by ten in the night by which time her husband and her in-laws would be sound asleep. That night, however, Abdul did not go to sleep till after midnight. Something seemed to be disturbing him and he paced the rooms of the house while Rehmani feigned sleep. It was only after Abdul retired and started to snore that Rehmani moved out of the room, tiptoed downstairs, and took the duplicate key out of her home-made brassieres to open the heavy padlock with which the main door was locked. When Rehmani stepped out of her in-laws' house she found Rashida waiting at the street corner.

'Whatever went wrong? I have been waiting for you for over two hours and almost thought you had changed your mind,' she whispered.

'I am sorry I kept you waiting. I couldn't come out until my husband had gone to sleep,' replied Rehmani.

'Come, my child, we don't have much time to waste. Just follow me,' said Rashida, quickening her steps, with Rehmani on her heels.

Rashida meandered her way through the dark narrow streets of Old Delhi until they were in a neighbourhood mainly inhabited by milkmen and their animals. The stench of the excreta of cows and buffaloes pervaded the atmosphere and the quiet of the night was punctuated with the mooing of these animals. Rashida knocked at a door which was opened by an old woman.

'Everything is ready, the beds are laid out in that room,' the old woman said, pointing towards a small cubicle.

'You'll rest here for the night, child. Your mother will meet you in the morning and take you with her,' said Rashida, occupying one of the two beddings laid out on the floor.

Rashida fell asleep instantly, snoring like an old steam locomotive on its last legs. Rehmani tried her best to sleep but found herself agitated by the thoughts of the next morning when she would have to put her past behind her and meet her mother. She could imagine the scene in the house of her in-laws once everyone woke up in the morning to discover that she was missing. Her mother-in-law would scream at the top of her voice, not finding the hot cup of tea that her dutiful daughter-in-law placed on the side table next to her bed every morning. Her husband would be pulling the hair out of his head in desperation on discovering that his wife of many years had not laid out the clothes which he wore to the school every day, and had bolted from home.

Early next morning, at the crack of dawn, there was a knock on the door as Noorani Begum, clad in her white burqa made her way into the house. She embraced her daughter and broke down. They made loud protestations to one another, each blaming the other for her suffering, finally agreeing to forget the past and to look after one another as long as they lived.

After they composed themselves and Noorani Begum pressed five ten-rupee notes in Rashida's hand as a special reward and thanked her profusely, they sat in a tonga and rode for two hours to cover the ten miles to the Qutub Minar near which a cousin of Noorani Begum owned a small farm. Noorani Begum had made arrangements for Rehmani to stay with her cousin to tide over any reaction from her in-laws for the time being. She had already asked her son to take Rehmani to Simla for a few months to help her recover from the turmoil of her married life. Ghulam Rasool had no objections to the idea.

Ensuring that Rehmani was comfortably settled at her cousin's place, Noorani Begum rushed back home to break the news to her family.

'Praise be to Allah that my daughter has been rescued and is now safely out of the clutches of her evil husband and that witch, her mother-in-law,' she told Ghulam Rasool.

'God has indeed been kind. I must book my seats on the train for Simla so that I can take Rehmani with me. If all goes well, I

Saad Ashraf

should be able to leave in two days' time,' said Ghulam Rasool, his face glowing with happiness.

'Beta, you talked of asking the police for help in rescuing your sister and I held you back for an opportune time to involve them ... well, now is the time I would like you to bring them in the picture.'

'Rehmani is safe with our relatives and nobody knows her whereabouts—what help can the police provide us now?'

'I want you to contact the police and ask them to send a constable to Rehmani's in-laws and tell them that your sister has left their house of her own choice because of maltreatment at their hands, and that if they try to create trouble, they should expect to be dealt with accordingly.'

Ghulam Rasool had over the years acquired the tendency of not getting involved in anything controversial but he put caution aside and went ahead to meet the deputy superintendent of police, Mr Nibblet, at the Daryaganj Police Station. Mr Nibblet asked him to write out an application containing the gist of the matter. Within an hour, two uniformed constables called on Rehmani's husband and in-laws and informed them that Rehmani was in safe hands and it was best to keep emotions in check and let the law take its course. They were also told what could happen if they decided otherwise. As a result, peace prevailed in White Haveli as Ghulam Rasool and his family along with Rehmani made preparations to leave Delhi for Simla. But before he left, he had an obligation to fulfil—he had to meet Ahmad.

The day before his departure, Ghulam Rasool called on his friend. He found Ahmad looking well, though a few grey hairs had started showing on his head. He had put on some weight but his face emanated a youthful glow. They talked about their lives, the joys, hopes, and fears.

Ghulam Rasool enquired about Yasmeen.

'She lives here in one of my houses, a furlong from where the river has flowed peacefully since eternity. I imagine that she looks more beautiful than ever, being at peace with herself and her surroundings without the compulsion of getting ready every evening for a performance. Nobody knows that she is my wife. I go and see her twice a month,' said Ahmad.

'How long can you keep your marriage a secret? Someday, somebody is bound to find out.'

'What are you suggesting?'

'Nothing except that somehow you should prepare your family to accept your marriage before they come to know about it through some other source.'

'Mian, are you mad! Do you think that the imam of one of the most famous mosques in Delhi will accept a daughter-in-law who has been singing and dancing before the public in the red-light areas of three cities? I don't want my parents to die of shock. I have caused them enough pain.'

'Well, you can do what you like but I gave you my candid advice.'

Ahmad shook his head in despair as if looking for a solution to a problem that weighed heavily on his mind.

'Mian, in this part of the world one has to live with the tragedies of one's own life ... that's why this marriage has to be kept a secret. Everyone in India dies carrying some secret to the grave. If I too were to pass away carrying one with me, what difference would it make?'

'It would make a difference to Yasmeen who is your legally wedded wife and to her future.'

'I've tried to ensure her financial security by transferring the house she lives in to her name, and I'll do the same for another house by the end of next year so that she can live off its rental if something happens to me.'

'Ahmad, people don't crave only financial security, they also need social security. That's what I was suggesting you provide for Yasmeen.'

'You think breaking the news of this marriage to my family will provide social security for Yasmeen. I think it would have the opposite effect because neither they nor the society will ever accept her.'

Saad Ashraf

Ahmad lapsed in deep thought and Ghulam Rasool did not wish to belabour the point any further. There was a tense silence in the room, till Ghulam Rasool got up to leave. Both friends parted with an affectionate, though cold embrace while promising to remain in touch with one another.

On 30 April 1940, Ghulam Rasool and his family accompanied by his sister Rehmani boarded the train for the journey to Simla.

thirty-eight

Rehmani came to stay at her brother's house in Simla, uncertain about what the future held for her. She had not obtained a divorce yet and was at best living in separation. Though she considered herself fortunate to have a brother like Ghulam Rasool and a sister-in-law like Sara who had opened their home for her to live in till things settled down, she was unsure of her place in the household. From the day she arrived in Simla she tried making herself useful by lending a helping hand in the house, doing some of the things which Sara did previously. She woke up early in the morning and served tea to her brother at six. She pampered Sara by looking after the children and getting them ready for school so that Sara could sleep longer. Since she knew how much her brother and sister-in-law loved tasty food, she took over the kitchen, preparing special curries for them. If there was any spare time left she worked on the embroidery.

In spite of all the comfort she had in her brother's home, it was strange that she should still be missing the arduous and cruel routine of her husband's home. She missed her mother-in-law's nagging which started early in the morning and did not end till she went to bed at night. She remembered the physical violence her husband inflicted on her when she was late in doing something he wanted done. She remembered the first time he had struck her across the face. The sound of the slap was still fresh in her mind. It was so sudden and unexpected that she could do nothing but stand rooted to the spot in shock. Later that night, he had fallen at her feet and asked to be forgiven. She had forgotten the incident, but a couple of weeks later he slapped her again for not bringing his cup of tea as soon as he had ordered. This time he did not bother to apologize. That night she had cried in bed, reminding him that she had abandoned her immediate family for their love. He had consoled her without expressing any regrets.

Over the years Rehmani had got used to the routine of physical violence followed by her husband's entreaties that that was the last time such a thing would happen. But there had been no last time and the physical abuse continued. Despite all this and the hard time she had in her husband's home she wondered whether she had done the right thing in walking out on him. She wrote to Noorani Begum in Delhi to find out whether her husband or his family had enquired about her and was dismayed to learn that they had made no effort whatsoever to find out whether she was dead or alive. It seemed as if she had never existed for them.

Meanwhile, the summer season of 1940 was in full swing in Simla. The viceroy was in station along with all his paraphernalia. The British officialdom and the Indian nobility jostled on the Mall like they did every year. Multicoloured butterflies flew in lazy trajectories in the cool breeze and white daisies abundantly covered the green, grassy slopes. The smell of freshly baked cakes wafted from a fashionable hotel at one end of the Mall while restaurants beckoned their customers to afternoon-tea dances at four. Through all this, the *Simla Times* blared in big, bold type that the Battle of Britain was raging in all its fury over the dark skies of London. This horrible war seemed to be happening in another world so distant from India as to make its message of death and destruction unreal for those who walked the Mall in the cool summer breeze.

Rehmani and Sara had become close friends and frequently sat on the terrace of the GPO overlooking the Mall, watching a world of fashion pass by. They saw little of Ghulam Rasool who was busy with his official work and protocol duties. Superintendent Basu hovered around the house, taking care of the odds and ends. The inflow of guests whose names were approved by Ghulam Rasool as worthy of staying at his house continued. The news from Delhi concerning Rehmani was not good. Her husband had moved a case in the Delhi courts for restitution of conjugal rights under the law as applicable to Muslims. He had alleged that his wife had been kidnapped by her mother Noorani Begum and her accomplices.

Advocate Azmatullah who had pleaded Noorani Begum's case years ago had passed away. She now engaged his son Naimatullah, also an advocate, to represent her daughter in court. Noorani Begum had written to Ghulam Rasool that it might be best to send Rehmani to Delhi as soon as possible so that she could appear in court whenever summoned.

The false grounds on which Abdul had filed the case against her distressed Rehmani in no small measure. The remnants of guilt that she may have had for walking out on him disappeared as she mentally prepared herself to expose him and his family in court. Ghulam Rasool decided that it would indeed be best for Rehmani to be in Delhi before the hearing of her case started and accordingly booked a ticket for her on the Kalka Express.

Ghulam Rasool and his family came to see off Rehmani at the railway station. She had made a place for herself in their home and hearts by her cheerful attitude and willing disposition in spite of the tragic circumstances of her marriage, and they were sad to see her leave. Rehmani raised her hand in goodbye and in the blink of an eye disappeared from their view as the train gathered speed in its journey towards Delhi.

While the nations of Europe battled one another on their home grounds, the deserts of Africa and even at the doorsteps of India when the Japanese entered Rangoon, Ghulam Rasool remained singularly devoted to his work. Sir Gruggson had been receiving such good reports about the manner in which the post office in Simla was being run that he decided to make an official visit to study the management techniques that the postmaster was using to achieve that level of efficiency. He visited Simla in August 1941 and interviewed Ghulam Rasool at length, hoping to

Saad Ashraf

discover some novel management technique used by him. He was disappointed when he found none but was sufficiently impressed by the man to make up his mind to transfer him to Delhi in a position of responsibility at an appropriate time in the future. Sir Gruggson hinted at this possibility to Ghulam Rasool before leaving for Delhi. A year passed but before the summer season of 1942 commenced and precisely to the day that he completed his three-year tenure in Simla, Ghulam Rasool received a telephone call from Sir Gruggson's office telling him to hold himself ready for transfer to a post in Delhi that was being specially created for him.

Superintendent Basu learnt of his boss's transfer on 6 May 1942 as he opened the official mail that morning and read the cyclostyled order that he removed from the coarse brown official envelope. Ghulam Rasool had been appointed special postmaster of Delhi. Basu realized that his boss's departure was imminent and that if he did not manage to get himself transferred now he would be left behind to brave Simla's cold and snow forever. He felt that the most important factor to effect a transfer, namely his boss's inclination, was strongly in his favour. Postmaster Ghulam Rasool held him in high esteem and had deep regard for his integrity and efficiency. More than anything else he felt he was Ghulam Rasool's personal confidant.

As soon as Ghulam Rasool had walked into his office that morning and had made himself comfortable, Basu strode up to him with a broad smile across his face.

'Sir, there's some good news this morning,' he said, handing him the file cover on which his boss's transfer orders were clipped.

Ghulam Rasool read the four-line order but displayed no emotion.

Embarrassed, Basu managed to mumble, 'Congratulations, sir! I wish you and begum sahiba all the best on your transfer to Delhi.'

'Thank you,' replied Ghulam Rasool, busying himself with the sheaf of papers lying on his table. Basu stood his ground and mustered all the courage he could to address his boss.

'Sir, I ... er ... em ... have a request to make.'

But before Basu could say anything more Ghulam Rasool interrupted him. 'I know, I know, Mr Basu, you'd like to remind me about your transfer. I remember I promised to help you in your transfer from Simla and I'll try my best to get that done, though as you are aware the matter rests entirely with the competent authorities in Delhi.'

Deep inside, Ghulam Rasool was overjoyed at receiving his formal transfer order. Though there had been a year-long wait from the time that Sir Gruggson first hinted at the transfer, he considered himself lucky that things had turned out well for him in the end. This transfer would not only give him an opportunity of being stationed in India's capital and his own home town but could also be the springboard for advancing to the pinnacle of his career—the position of a postmaster general of one or more provinces, a position to which only a few Indians had risen before him in the history of the Indian postal services. Ghulam Rasool was already looking ahead and realized that one of the first requirements for success in the new position would be a subordinate who enjoyed his full confidence and who could be his eyes and ears in the organization. What better choice could there be than Basu, whom he had thoroughly tried over three years. Not a word had ever leaked out from their personal or official discussions, and nobody had ever come up to him to say that Basu had uttered an uncomplimentary word about him behind his back. Above all, Basu was the only individual other than himself who had an inkling of his feelings for Kiran. With this in mind, Ghulam Rasool decided to do everything possible to get Basu transferred to Delhi with himself. He sent an urgent telegram to Delhi making this request and was pleasantly surprised to learn two days later that the department was working hard to process a case for Basu's transfer.

Needless to say, the news of the transfer made Sara very happy though she realized that she would miss sitting on the terrace in Simla's lukewarm summer to witness the yearly pageant of India's elite walk past on the Mall and fade into history. She thought that she must have done something good which had registered

Saad Ashraf

with Allah for which she was now being rewarded with a transfer to the city of her birth. She wondered how the begums of Delhi, proud and political in their outlook, whose principal pastimes were intrigue and chewing betel leaf, would react to her presence and whether she would be able to adjust to living with her relatives. Regardless of the difficulties she was afraid she might have to face, she was sure that life in Delhi would be much better than a lonesome existence in the towns and cities of the Punjab and suffering the inconvenience of a transfer after every three years.

Several hundred miles away in Delhi, Noorani Begum learnt of her son's transfer from Jahan Ara Begum when she walked up one morning for a session of gossip.

'Begum, you and I have known each other for several decades but it saddens me to say that when it comes to sharing the latest news I find that you hardly trust me,' she said.

'Jahan Ara Begum, do you realize what you are saying? An old neighbour is dearer to the heart than a blood relation. I've shared everything about my life with you ... even the delay in my daughter-in-law's first pregnancy, my financial affairs and what not ... and here you are taunting me about not sharing everything with you. Tell me, what have I not shared with you?' Noorani Begum said in admonishment.

'The latest news that your son Ghulam Rasool has been transferred to Delhi to a very high post.'

Noorani Begum was taken aback because this indeed was news to her; she had heard nothing about it. Only two days ago she had received a letter from her son but there was no mention of a transfer.

'These are rumours, dear Jahan Ara, pure rumours! You know the dak khana is full of rumours. If they had their way they would even say that you and I were sleeping with the viceroy. Don't pay any heed to such loose talk.'

'Arré Begum, the postman Bijju Lal told me and whatever he says usually turns out to be the truth. I am really surprised that you don't know about your own son's transfer.'

This comment offended Noorani Begum.

'What do you mean I don't know about my own son's transfer,' she said curtly. 'I am not duty-bound to tell you everything I know about my son, am I? If I do so it is my generosity. I don't go around prying information out of you, do I? You have no right to be vicious just because you are my tenant.'

An uneasy curtain of silence drew up between the two women. They sat like old cats grimacing and eyeing one another without saying a word, till Jahan Ara Begum got up and, sticking a betel leaf in her mouth from a silver case she carried in her hand, slunk towards the door which would take her downstairs to the sanctuary of her home.

As soon as Jahan Ara Begum left, Noorani Begum, angry with her son, sat down with a foolscap paper and started writing an urgent letter of admonishment to him. She upbraided him for not treating her like the mother who had done everything for him and who had brought him to this position in life ... and that now, despite all this, she was having to bear the insult of learning about his transfer from outsiders. Nevertheless, she wrote, she was happy for him and his family and would keep two rooms in the house ready for them. Meanwhile, she wanted Ghulam Rasool to inform her of the position he would hold in Delhi and whether he would have an office in the viceroy's house.

On 12 May 1942, Superintendent Basu received the formal orders transferring him to Delhi. He knocked on the polished door of the postmaster's office and on being admitted stood in front of Ghulam Rasool with the paper in his quivering hands.

'Sir, I have no words to thank you for your kindness. Even my father may not have been able to do more for me. I hope God gives me an opportunity to do something for you in my life,' he said in a voice trembling faintly with emotion.

'Come off it, Mr Basu. You and I have work to do. We have to move to Delhi, get settled, and start working there,' said Ghulam Rasool, extending his hand in congratulations.

For the next week, Basu was to be seen everywhere. He was at his boss's house, getting the postmaster's household effects

Saad Ashraf

sewn in jute matting, or in the office, getting personal papers ready for handing over charge, or making arrangements for the journey to Delhi. Ghulam Rasool's successor was one Mr Griffin, a pot-bellied Englishman, who had been the postmaster in Ambala. He was due for retirement within a year and hoped to return home as soon as the war ended. Mr Griffin arrived in Simla on 20 May 1942 and on the same day took over as postmaster.

The next day, Ghulam Rasool and his family boarded the train for Delhi. They were seen off by a crowd which packed every inch of the railway station. A few tear-filled eyes bore witness to the postmaster's popularity and the kindness he had shown and little favours he may have done for various members of his staff on different occasions.

In a second-class compartment, a few carriages away from the one occupied by Ghulam Rasool and his family, sat Superintendent Basu. As the train started moving, he opened a small attaché case he was carrying with him, pulled out two worn-out sweaters and headed for the compartment door. The cool nippy mountain air hit his face.

'Goodbye forever, Simla! I hope I never have to wear these damned sweaters again,' he said, flinging the apparel through the compartment window, towards the receding landscape of hills dotted with yellow and white wild flowers.

thirty-nine

On their arrival in Delhi, Ghulam Rasool and his family moved into the two rooms provided by Noorani Begum in her house in White Haveli. He found his mother still aggrieved at not being the first one to be informed of the transfer. There was some good news concerning his sister. After several months of legal wrangling, she had won the court case filed by her husband for the restoration of their marriage. When she was put in the witness box by the judge, she had truthfully stated that Abdul had made a false charge. She informed the court that she had left her husband's house of her own choice. She also said that she did not wish to live with him any more and wanted to lead an independent life. She had given vivid details of the way she was ill treated in her husband's home, saying that she was providing these for the benefit of Indian women who should no longer bear such cruelties. In his judgment, the magistrate had ruled in Rehmani's favour, granting her a divorce and providing her protection from further harassment from her husband or his family.

Soon after the judgment had been announced, Rehmani Begum applied for the job that she had many years ago at Bulbul School. As soon as Abdul learnt that his former wife was likely be re-employed at the school he had protested to the principal, Bilqis Begum, and gave her the option of choosing between him and Rehmani. Principal Bilqis Begum had accepted his resignation and employed Rehmani as a teacher.

The day after he arrived, Ghulam Rasool sought an audience with Sir Gruggson in the latter's office at South Block of the Delhi secretariat to find out what he was supposed to do as special postmaster, Delhi.

'Well, Mr Ghulam Rasool,' said Sir Gruggson, puffing away at his pipe, 'we have four postmasters in position to handle the postal work of each of the four districts in which we have divided Delhi. One of these postmasters may be transferred out shortly in which case you could take his place in addition to handling any special assignments with which you are entrusted.'

Ghulam Rasool learnt through his contacts that Sir Gruggson had originally wanted to appoint him to oversee the work of the four postmasters. However, one of the postmasters, an Englishman named Alfred, at the GPO in Old Delhi, had preferred a transfer rather than serve under an Indian officer. This had compelled Sir Gruggson to modify his plan.

When that vacancy came about a week later, Ghulam Rasool took charge.

The yellow building of the GPO at Kashmiri Gate in Old Delhi, with its big clock at the centre, was a familiar place to Ghulam Rasool. Both he and his father had worked there. Situated close as it was to the railway station, the cacophony created by the shunting of wagons and carriages by tired steam engines as they spewed grey-white steam on the rusted rails was within hearing distance of all those who worked at the GPO. A few hundred yards away from the building stood the obelisk which the British had built in the memory of those killed in this area in 1857. Inside the GPO, hundreds of electric bulbs irradiated their luminescence through the cream-coloured glass globes suspended by long polished brass rods from the high ceiling, while the postmen pounded away, stamping the post and parcels from all parts of India. In this din, Special Postmaster Ghulam Rasool installed Basu as the superintendent on 1 June 1942.

In the meantime, Ghulam Rasool had been allotted an official residence at Kashmiri Gate.

'Why do you want to leave your mother and stay at Kashmiri Gate when you could happily live here?' Noorani Begum asked when she came to know that her son intended to move there shortly.

'Ammi, the new residence is situated atop my office and I won't have to cycle four miles a day back and forth. Besides, you'll have another home in Delhi which you can visit whenever you want and where you can stay as long as you like,' replied Ghulam Rasool, pacifying her.

Unknown to Noorani Begum, there was however another reason which was prompting him to move out of his mother's house. On two occasions during the three weeks of their stay at White Haveli he had found Sara and Noorani Begum involved in squabbles over trifle matters. He did not know how it all started or who was at fault but he had to mediate to bring peace between them. He had tried counselling his mother.

'Ammi,' he said, 'why don't you be a little more patient with your daughter-in-law? After all, she's a guest in your house and we will all be moving out of here shortly.'

Noorani Begum had let out a doleful sigh. 'Of course I should have realized that times have changed … now a son and his family consider themselves guests in their mother's house. When the sons get married they are possessed by their wives, forgetting that it was the mother who had begotten them and the wife appeared later on the scene.'

Ghulam Rasool had also tried reasoning with Sara.

'Sara, why don't you be slightly more accommodating towards my mother?'

'Of course, the wife who has stood by you and your children, living in the dust and heat of those silly towns all these years is required to be accommodating when it comes to your mother,' was the indignant reply.

Ghulam Rasool knew that prolonging his stay at White Haveli would only lead to more skirmishes and could damage the relationship between his mother and his wife. He wasted no further time in occupying the official quarters and moved in as soon as the outgoing postmaster vacated the premises. It consisted of five large bedrooms with attached bathrooms, big halls, and

Saad Ashraf

an open space on one side of the living quarters which ran as far as the eyes could see. Old neem trees which marked the perimeter of the building had grown to phenomenal heights and hung on to the roof, weighed down with their heavy foliage of green and brown leaves.

A year had passed since Ghulam Rasool's transfer to Delhi. Though he had settled well in his new position and was as always earning laurels for his performance at work, the same could not be said of his personal life. He realized that he and Sara had drifted apart. There had been a slow but perceptible breakdown in their communication till they hardly spoke to one another. No longer did Ghulam Rasool find Sara physically attractive or her company stimulating. Her religiousness had grown into an obsession and she occupied a room at one end of the living quarters where she spent all her time in prayer, turning the beads and atoning for her sins.

On the rare occasions when they both sat on the dining table, an uneasy silence descended between the two broken only by acrimonious exchanges on the quality of the cooking.

'Begum, this food is so tasteless that I can hardly get it down my throat. You know wholesome food is the only pleasure left in my life and I am being deprived even of that. I can't imagine you cooking such an awful meal,' Ghulam Rasool said one day during lunch.

'Sarkar, it is obligatory on me to fulfil my religious duties first after which there is not much time left to cook a meal, so I ask the cook to make the dishes. If he can't do a good job of it that's your bad luck and mine. It's shameful that the government cannot provide a better cook. Even otherwise according to the tenets of Islam we should eat to live, not live to eat,' Sara retorted haughtily.

'Don't give me your interpretation of Islam. What has serving tasteless food on the table got to do with Islam?'

This exchange of words was followed by a prolonged breakdown of communication between the two. In the past, such situations would be repaired in bed but the flame of love having gone out there seemed no way to resuscitate their relationship. When Ghulam Rasool lay alone on his charpai in the terrace of his house and peered at the cold, bright stars in the dark sky and heard the rustle of the neem leaves in the light summer breeze, his thoughts turned to the one and only woman he loved: Kiran.

He recalled the first time he had set eyes on her in the flaming orange and black sari. The memory of that brief encounter aroused him but there was no Kiran to satisfy his wants and trowel his fantasies. He had tried his best to keep in touch with her, calling her up on the telephone whenever circumstances permitted. Purshottam had still not been promoted to a grade where he could be stationed as the postmaster of a major city. At the moment he was the postmaster of Sialkot, a small town in the Punjab, bordering Kashmir. When Ghulam Rasool had spoken to Kiran a few days ago from Delhi telling him how well he was settling in his new position and how much he was missing her she had suggested that he could try to have Purshottam posted to Delhi so that they could both be together.

Ghulam Rasool started looking into the matter and entrusted Basu with the responsibility of investigating if such a thing was possible. A couple of days later, Basu had reported on the situation—in about a month's time the postmaster at Qutub would proceed on retirement.

Ghulam Rasool thought that Qutub would be an ideal place for Purshottam. Qutub was the scenic suburb of Delhi, well known for the famous minaret built by the Aibaks as a part of the mosque complex. Small rivulets dotted the landscape and fed sweet water to ancient wells dug during the period of the Sultans.

'Can a postmaster from the Punjab circle be posted there?' enquired Ghulam Rasool.

'Not as a rule. But there are many exceptions. Such transfers are decided by the director general's office,' said Basu.

Ghulam Rasool realized that the exception Basu was referring to was none other than Ghulam Rasool himself. He made a note in his diary that he would have to take up the matter of

Saad Ashraf

Purshottam's transfer with Sir Gruggson when he met him in their next weekly meeting.

At the meeting a week later, Ghulam Rasool was able to find Sir Gruggson alone and at an opportune moment, when he sensed that the director general was in an amiable mood, he made the request.

'Well, Ghulam Rasool, since you sing so many praises of this man Purshottam, he must be really good. Leave a note with my personal assistant and ask him to remind me. I'll go through his personal file and if the man is clean we'll get him here,' said Sir Gruggson.

Ghulam Rasool realized the immense risk he was taking in asking for Purshottam's transfer. Should anything ever go wrong with the way Purshottam performed, Ghulam Rasool's image would be tarnished forever.

A couple of days later, he received a telephone call from the director general's office informing him that Purshottam's transfer order had been issued and a copy was being sent to him. On hearing this, Ghulam Rasool's elation knew no bounds. He longed for Kiran to be there with him at this moment and imagined her in his arms, yielding to him in gratitude. It didn't take him long to recover and make a call to the residence of the postmaster, Sialkot. He recognized Kiran's voice at the other end in spite of the static, and informed her of Purshottam's impending transfer. Despite the disturbance over the line, the excitement in Kiran's voice was unmistakable.

That afternoon when Ghulam Rasool went upstairs for lunch he broke the barrier of silence between Sara and himself that had existed for three months now.

'Purshottam has been transferred from Sialkot to Delhi. He and his family should be here within the next few weeks,' he announced, sitting down for lunch.

Sara's face brightened up for a moment but then froze into the morose mask that it had become over many months now.

'My kafir friend will be with me again. Maybe this time I will be successful in completing my mission of converting her to my religion,' Sara said.

Ghulam Rasool wondered whether she seriously meant what she was saying. He knew that in the good old days when she was more tolerant on matters of faith, this remark would have been made with a big laugh to indicate that it was nothing but a joke.

Purshottam and his family arrived in Delhi by the Frontier Mail on 4 September 1943, a day after Italy had signed the armistice and the tide of the war had turned in favour of the allies in Europe. Sara laid out a warm welcome for Kiran. The years in between, during which there had been no contact between the two, seemed inconsequential as they picked up the lost threads of their friendship from the moment they met again. Sara was generous and offered Kiran and her family two rooms in her home till such time that Purshottam was allotted government accommodation, an offer which Kiran politely declined after talking to her husband who felt that staying at the house of someone who was technically his boss would make tongues wag in the department. Purshottam and his family stayed at the postal rest house which was located within the compound of the GPO. He took over as postmaster, Qutub, a week later and was allotted quarter number 12G in the postal colony, barely two hundred yards from where Ghulam Rasool and Sara lived.

Saad Ashraf

forty

Sara helped Kiran to settle down in her new home. She had her cook prepare special vegetarian meals and sent them in a tiffin carrier with a servant and a note asking Kiran to let her know if they needed anything else. She bought some cooking utensils and curtain cloth from the bazaar and sent them over as presents for Kiran's new home. She sent her maidservant Anwari to make a tracing of the left foot of each of Kiran's daughters on paper and then bought white, black and golden sandals for her children as gifts.

After a couple of weeks, when Kiran had somewhat settled in her new home, she came to see Sara, reciprocating her generosity with a large box of sweets made by the famous halwais at Chandni Chowk, and bangles of bright green, red and blue for Sara's daughters. She put these on their wrists and said that they should henceforth consider her as their mother. Sara and Kiran talked for several hours, sharing news of their lives during the years they had been away from one another. Kiran spoke about the hard stations where she had lived and expressed her gratitude for the favour that Ghulam Rasool had done to them by getting her husband transferred to Delhi.

Ghulam Rasool had meanwhile managed to establish contact with Kiran. Purshottam had called on him in the office to thank him for initiating his transfer and had informed him that he had taken charge of the Qutub post office. The only inconvenience in his posting in Delhi was the time it took for the journey to and from Qutub, which resulted in his absence from home from seven in the morning to about five every evening.

'I worry about Kiran and the children being on their own the whole day. You know how the situation is deteriorating all over India, the tension is mounting and there has been communal rioting in other cities,' Purshottam had said to Ghulam Rasool.

'Purshottam, you don't have to worry about the safety of your family. One couldn't be safer in heaven than in the postal colony of the Delhi GPO. However, if this is a source of worry, why don't you get a private telephone installed in your house, so you can remain in touch with your family? It won't cost much,' Ghulam Rasool had suggested.

Purshottam thought this an excellent idea and had got a telephone installed in the house that very day.

Ghulam Rasool was the first person to make a telephone call to Kiran. He ensured that Purshottam had taken the bus for work that morning.

'Gullo, I am dying to meet you,' said Kiran.

'Don't ever act impetuously, Kiran. Now that you are living a stone's throw away we have to be very careful. We must never see each other either in the postal colony or in my house. If anybody ever comes to know of our love for one another we'll have a scandal of a magnitude that has never hit India before. Our photographs will be on the front page of every newspaper, and we will both be destroyed,' said Ghulam Rasool.

'It may destroy us but it cannot destroy our love. There's only one way out. We must find a way of being together. How I wish I could be a part of you, your life. You'll never know how my heart has pined for you and how many tears I have shed in longing in the days that I remained separated from you. I long to be with you till the very end—till you carry me to the funeral pyre and set fire to my lifeless body.' She sighed deeply and after a pause continued in a voice choked with emotion, 'I wish it was possible for us to get married somehow.'

Ghulam Rasool tried pacifying her but it didn't seem to work. On the contrary, what she perceived as vacillation on his part only irked her, and when she spoke next her words had more than a note of asperity to it.

'I want to know whether you are prepared to marry me for the sake of our love.'

Ghulam Rasool was in a quandary. He had never broken a word he had once given or gone back on a commitment he had made. He attributed all his success in life to this aspect in his character. For the first time he was in a fix, not knowing what to say. Needless to say, his silence further infuriated Kiran.

'Well, what is it going to be? Are you going to say yes and honour our love by marrying a Hindu or are you going to be a gutless man—' she stopped short, suddenly ashamed of her outburst. 'I didn't mean that, dear. I hope you understand what I am going through.'

Ghulam Rasool hesitated for a moment and then spoke into the mouthpiece of the telephone.

'Kiran, I'll honour my love and marry you but give me a few months to find a way of doing so. Meanwhile, promise me that you'll take no hasty steps which may become the cause of embarrassment for us or our families. You understand?'

'I understand,' said Kiran and disconnected the line.

Ghulam Rasool sat in his office, trying to size up the impact of the commitment he had just made.

For the residents of the housing colony where the staff of the GPO, Delhi, resided, the next couple of years passed quickly. The war had ended and though the Union Jack still fluttered over the post office, everybody said that the conflict had drained the strength out of Great Britain as a world power.

Ghulam Rasool had been unable to fulfil his promise of marrying Kiran, though he still stood by her and his commitment. They talked on the telephone at least half a dozen times a day with most of the conversation devoted to professions of undying love for each other. He said that he was still trying to find a way of getting married to her which would have the least impact on both of them and their families.

'More than that I am trying to find a way by which undue publicity could be avoided which may otherwise attract the displeasure of the government and leave me without a job in these uncertain times,' Ghulam Rasool had said.

Kiran believed every word that he said but though her love was steadfast, her patience was wearing out. She realized that unless providence came to her rescue it would be impossible for her to marry Ghulam Rasool. She decided to seek the intervention of the gods.

It was past midnight on the festival of lights, the Diwali of 1946. Kiran was dressed in a red sari with a long red tilak on her forehead. She had illuminated her home, placing small oil-filled lamps on its walls in which the flames flickered in the evening breeze. Her husband and daughters had gone to bed, tired after a hectic day. Kiran was awaiting the arrival of Swami Mohanji, a renowned Hindu ascetic with whom she had established contact through a clerk who worked in the GPO.

Swami Mohanji spent most of his time in meditation and prayers in the forests at the foothills of the Himalayas but trekked all the way to Delhi to be present in the city on this festival every year. He was said to possess supernatural powers and was reputed to have the ability to make dreams come true by offering special prayers in which he recited secret mantras.

The swami arrived at Kiran's home. He was a dark man of medium height with a rough weather-beaten face which sported a conical beard and a conspicuous pigtail in the middle of a clean-shaved head. Though he was said to be seventy he looked at least twenty years younger. He was clad in a long saffron cloth and carried a staff in his hand. As soon as he entered the house, Kiran touched his feet in greeting and motioned him to an adjoining room where he sat on the floor in a yogic posture.

'Beti, I will explain how we will hold this session of prayer and meditation. You will sit facing me. I shall place a tray containing sweets in front of you and light four lamps around its corners and then start chanting the holy mantras which will put me in a trance. As soon as that happens, you should close

Saad Ashraf

your eyes and concentrate on what you want to get done. If one desires somebody's love it is best to have him or her eat these sweets,' said the swami.

Both the swami and Kiran took their positions and the session started with Swami Mohanji reciting the mantras, swaying from side to side. Soon his renderings became an incomprehensible hypnotic drone. Kiran felt that the mantras were taking effect for she had the sensation that she was sitting far above the world on a drifting cloud. She looked at the swami who seemed to have turned into a stone idol like one of the many that she saw in the temple where she went for her weekly prayers. She started concentrating on the one desire she wanted desperately to be fulfilled. To marry the only man she had loved in her life— Postmaster Ghulam Rasool. She knew that it was not a simple matter for him—a married man with children—to wed a woman of another faith but there were similar difficulties for her and she had the courage to do so. It must be that wife of his, Sara, who was keeping him away from her, thought Kiran. As such, she wished Sara an exit from her world. Surely, the gods could do something to separate Sara from her husband, so that she and her lover could live in peace forever.

While Kiran was concentrating her hardest on these thoughts, Sara was fast asleep in the postmaster's residence hardly a furlong away, dreaming. In her dream she saw a swami dressed in saffron emerge from the cemented floor in the centre of her room accompanied by a whole army of similarly attired clones. They were grimacing at her, making scary faces and threatening her, mouthing gibberish. She woke up with a shriek and noticed that she was covered in sweat and was cold with fear. She pinched herself to make sure that she was awake.

At ten the next morning, while she was still trying to catch some lost sleep she heard the soft footsteps of her maidservant Anwari in her room.

'What is it, Anwari?' she enquired, watching her from the corner of her eye.

'Bibiji, it is Kiran Bai's servant with a plate of sweets.'

'Put them on the dining table, the sahib and the children may like to eat them. I am too sleepy to get up from the bed right now,' said Sara, dozing off.

Anwari did as she was told.

That afternoon when Ghulam Rasool came home from office for lunch he noticed the plate laden with sweets on the dining table. He couldn't help eating two pieces and finding them delicious ate another two.

Sara got out of bed late in the afternoon feeling extremely unwell. Her appetite had left her. This condition persisted for some time which led to her becoming haggard and sick in appearance. As she was not on talking terms with Ghulam Rasool she never thought of discussing this matter with him and sent her maidservant Anwari to her mother with a note asking her to visit her urgently.

'Oh, my poor child, what's wrong with you? You look very sick,' remarked her mother, embracing her when she arrived.

Sara broke down and wept like a child in her mother's arms.

'I don't understand what's happening to me. I can't eat and I can't sleep. It all seems to have started from the night when a swami and his army of clones appeared in my dreams. The unfortunate thing is that they still make their appearance at all odd hours and are as real as you and me sitting here.'

Her mother suggested that Sara come and stay in her house for a few days. When Sara hesitated, she consoled her by telling her that she would bring a doctor or a hakim to examine her. Before leaving, she recited Quranic verses and blew her breath on some water and asked Sara to drink this in small doses to help overcome her fears.

Early next morning, Sara's mother brought with her an old man in tattered clothing, bent over with age, and wearing sandals made of rope and jute matting. She took off her burqa and settled herself in her daughter's room.

'Sara, my dearest, I've brought somebody with me who can help you. You will see how quickly your health, appetite, and spirits are restored after he treats you,' she said.

Saad Ashraf

'Who is he, Ammi?'

'He is Fakir Jami, the famous mendicant, an expert in exorcizing evil spirits or nullifying a spell cast by somebody. I haven't told him a thing about the swami.'

Fakir Jami sat on a chair behind the door which opened into the adjoining room, observing the protocol of purdah in a Muslim household.

'Beti,' he said, 'tie this piece of black thread on your left wrist and pass the other end to me.'

Sara did as she was told.

There was a prolonged pause as the fakir recited Quranic verses and blew his breath in the direction of the door.

'I see evil spirits residing in you and spells cast on you through black magic performed by a swami. The magic has failed in its mission of driving you insane. I will write out some Quranic verses for you to recite whenever the swami or his clones appear. In addition, you will only drink water from a separate pitcher in which you will soak neem leaves from a tree which grows closest to your home. If Allah wills you should be fully cured in a couple of months,' the fakir continued.

Having written out the Quranic verses on a piece of paper, Fakir Jami departed, reciting the ninety-nine names of the Almighty.

Sara memorized the verses, and decided to try their effectiveness the next time the swami appeared. She didn't have to wait very long. On a Thursday morning, when Anwari was busy in the kitchen and Sara was dusting her room, the swami appeared right in front of her. Sara kept her cool, recited the verse and blew her breath in his direction. The effect was instantaneous. The swami melted right in front of her eyes, disappearing into the concrete floor, extreme agony writ on his face. In accordance with the directions given by Fakir Jami, Sara started drinking water from a separate pitcher containing neem leaves from the tree that hung over her house. In the days that followed she began to feel better.

forty-one

Even as Sara was beginning to recover from the effects of the spell cast on her, Anwari brought her son Niazoo, a strapping young lad, to her master's house one morning.

'Bibiji,' Anwari said, 'my son has been pestering me to ask you if he could come and see you. He won't tell me why. But he says it's urgent. He's waiting outside, if you want to meet him.'

Sara asked her to produce her son immediately.

'Well, what is it you wish to talk to me about so urgently, Niazoo?' asked Sara, as Niazoo stood behind the door, shy and fearful.

'I want to tell you that a fakir came to Kiran Bai's house on Diwali night and they held special prayers till early in the morning. Their servant told me that he had carried some sweets to your house the next morning,' said Niazoo.

Sara recalled that a servant from Kiran's house had come to deliver a plate of sweets the day after Diwali.

'Is that all you wanted to tell me in such secrecy? Kiran Bai is a respectable woman and Hindus have a special puja on Diwali night. I don't see what is wrong with that and in sending a plate of sweets to me.'

'I have something more to tell you,' said Niazoo, fear clouding his face. 'A few days later, while I was lying on my charpai in the courtyard, I heard a loud whistle early in the morning. At first I thought it was a bird but this was followed by some clatter in Kiran Bai's house. I looked over the compound wall and saw Kiran Bai all dressed up, talking in whispers with somebody. I came out of the quarter unobserved and got a full glimpse of a man at her door. I fear for my life in saying this but it was the postmaster sahib bahadur in his suit. Kiran Bai and the sahib bahadur then held hands together like children and started walking on the unfrequented dirt track that runs from the colony to the Yamuna.'

Though deeply shocked, Sara kept her cool and displayed no emotion.

'Did this happen only once or more often?'

'It happens every other day since I first saw them that morning.'

'And what does her husband do while Kiran Bai is busy in this manner?'

'I suppose he is not aware of what is happening as these meetings take place before dawn, much before Purshottam sahib wakes up.'

'Listen, I see that you are an intelligent young man and faithful too. Keep an eye on Kiran Bai and her meetings with the postmaster sahib and come and tell me everything you hear or see. Make sure though that you are not discovered in this process,' said Sara, pressing an eight-anna bit into Niazoo's hand.

After Niazoo left, Sara sat on the chair and wept uncontrollably. She could never imagine Kiran, whom she considered a close friend, destroying her home and family. She summoned Anwari and sent her for her mother who arrived within the hour. Sara told her mother about Ghulam Rasool's early-morning trysts with Kiran, and how Fakir Jami's insight into the magic spell cast on her by a swami on Diwali night stood substantiated.

Alarmed at this development, Sara's mother said, 'Beti, we have to find a way to end this relationship before it devours your whole family.'

The mother and daughter thought and talked of many schemes, from getting Kiran poisoned or murdered to confronting her with the truth, but realized that nothing could be achieved until Ghulam Rasool had been weaned to their side.

As the months passed, the news from Niazoo became more and more discouraging. The postmaster was continuing with his pre-dawn calls on Kiran. One day Niazoo came to see his begum sahiba earlier than usual. He seemed excited and out of breath.

'Begum Sahiba, this morning the sahib bahadur came very early and he and Kiran Bai walked hand in hand in the dim light ... I was only a few paces behind them. On the way they decided to rest on a mound. I hid myself behind a clump of bushes so that I could overhear whatever they were saying. Kiran Bai said something about marriage and that she couldn't wait any longer. The postmaster sahib was pleading with her to wait as the matter was in its final stages. I couldn't make head or tail of their conversation but I thought I should come and tell you whatever I had heard.'

Sara pressed a rupee in Niazoo's hand and encouraged him to continue with the good work. She then summoned her mother.

'Ammi, Ghulam Rasool may be thinking of marrying Kiran. We had better do something fast otherwise ...'

'Why don't we approach someone ... someone who has experience of dealing with such matters?'

'Where are we going to find such a person, Ammi?'

'I've an idea—why don't we ask Macho Begum for help. After all, she is the one who brought Ghulam Rasool's proposal for you. Macho Begum is a clever and ruthless woman ... maybe she can find a way of saving your home for a fee. I have heard that she is an expert at handling extramarital affairs.'

Sara thought that the idea was worth a try. In the days that followed, Sara's mother briefed Macho Begum on her daughter's marital problems. Macho Begum settled a fee of three hundred rupees, to be paid fifty per cent in advance and the rest on successful completion of the work. She obtained an assurance from Sara's mother that she would have a free hand in choosing her tactics for destroying the love affair between Ghulam Rasool and Kiran.

Macho Begum called on Noorani Begum soon after.

Saad Ashraf

'To what good deeds should I attribute the privilege of your visit to my poor home?' said Noorani Begum, welcoming her with traditional courtesy.

'You've always been kind to me, Begum, both in words and deeds,' replied Macho Begum.

'Well, are you here with a proposal for my daughter Rehmani? You know she has all the qualities any husband would want in a wife except that she is a divorcee. Macho Begum, I cannot forget that it was you who gave us Sara, my daughter-in-law, and I am sure if you put your best efforts you can find a suitable match for my daughter too.'

'I always keep your daughter in mind and you can be sure that when I find a good match you will get to know immediately. You talked of the match I had arranged for your son with Sara. Well, there is something regarding the same which I would like to discuss with you. The matter is so grave and secret that I can only whisper whatever I have to say in your ears.'

Noorani Begum's eyes opened wide in apprehension as the matchmaker began her narration.

'I am not going to believe a word of what you have said till I check out the whole story. But even if a quarter of it is true, there is a lot to worry about,' Noorani Begum said after Macho Begum had finished.

Noorani Begum made discreet enquiries regarding her son's affair with Kiran from some people she knew in the postal colony and was surprised to learn that it was one of the current topics of discussion among the women in the colony. On being convinced that there could be no smoke without fire, Noorani Begum donned a cloak of silence which she felt would suit her best till such time that the whole thing blew over.

A few weeks later, Macho Begum visited Noorani Begum again to find out whether her enquiries had revealed anything and, if yes, what she proposed doing about it.

Noorani Begum could not look the matchmaker in the eye. She glanced at the floor and then at the roof of her home in an effort to find something to say to her.

'Macho Begum, I don't know what to say, since I've not been able to establish the truth of the matter but even if it was true I don't see what is there to be so concerned about. After all, there are so many examples in our history where people of one faith have had affairs with and even married women of another faith. The royal Mughal house itself is one shining example,' Noorani Begum said apologetically.

Her response enraged Macho Begum. In all her life she had never come across a woman who instead of trying to save her son's marriage was trying to justify its ruin.

'Noorani Begum,' said Macho Begum, irritation showing on her face, 'I would like you to talk to your son to break his affair with this woman immediately and honour his marriage. Otherwise, I shall have to take steps to save Sara's home since I was the one who arranged this match.'

Having said her piece she picked up her burqa, wrapped it around herself and left.

Noorani Begum was in a quandary. The matter was too sensitive to be discussed with her son—she did not want to risk an estrangement with Ghulam Rasool—and yet Macho Begum's threat could not be ignored. She was an influential matchmaker with contacts all over Delhi and the potential to create trouble for anyone if she set her mind to it.

While Noorani Begum was still pondering on how to tackle the dilemma, Macho Begum made her next move. She addressed a letter to the postmaster general, informing him of the affair between Special Postmaster Ghulam Rasool and Kiran, the Hindu wife of his junior. She pointed out that with Hindu-Muslim tensions running high in Delhi and elsewhere in India, if the affair became public, it could lead to violence. She suggested that it may be in the interest of the department to transfer Mr Purshottam out of Delhi forthwith. For good measure, Macho Begum volunteered to make an appearance before the authorities if required.

Saad Ashraf

forty-two

The letter reached the postmaster general's office the next day. When Harold Hubert, the postmaster general, Central Circle, read it, his first reaction was to ignore it and file it without any further action because it was a personal matter between two individuals. On second thought, however, he weighed the implications pointed out in the letter and decided to take action.

'Sidney,' he said, handing over Macho Begum's letter to his personal assistant, an Indian Christian with an English name, 'here's a complaint I have received this morning which I would like you to investigate without the parties getting to know what we are up to.'

Sidney was essentially an employee of the Indian intelligence department on secondment with the postal department. The Second World War had seen more and more such personnel placed unobtrusively in many offices, their presence known only to their supervisors in the intelligence department. Sidney spared no time in handling the matter and confirmed within a week that Special Postmaster Ghulam Rasool was indeed having a fully-fledged affair with Kiran, the wife of the postmaster, Qutub.

When Sidney's report reached Harold Hubert, the latter made out his written assessment, clasped the file in his hand, and sauntered across the long corridor between his office and that of the director general, Sir Gruggson, for his morning meeting.

'Harold,' said Sir Gruggson after he had been briefed on the matter, 'I've known Ghulam Rasool for over a decade and nothing against him has ever been brought to my notice. You know he is one of the finest Indian officers we have and, with all this talk of independence, I would hate to see his career end post-haste. Each one of us has committed some indiscretion in our lives, and in view of his services to the crown I feel we should give him a chance. As far as Purshottam is concerned you can give him his marching orders whenever and wherever you wish.'

Postmaster General Hubert knew that this meant letting Ghulam Rasool off the hook but long years of service had taught him not to betray his disappointment on his recommendation being overturned by the boss.

Early next morning Ghulam Rasool received a frantic telephone call in his office from Kiran. She seemed overwhelmed with emotion.

'The worst has happened to us! We've been transferred to Ferozepur. A man delivered the order last night. Purshottam thinks there is a big mistake somewhere and that the order was meant for someone else. He has gone to his office to check. If we've really been transferred, be ready to light my funeral pyre because I'm not going anywhere without you.'

Ghulam Rasool listened patiently, his sixth sense warning him that something serious had happened. He rang the bell for his trusted superintendent, Basu, and put him on the task of investigating the matter. Basu reported that there was no mistake in the order.

Ghulam Rasool could do little in his office, except brood over the impact of Purshottam's transfer. He kept doodling on official files while his mind strayed to Kiran. He could not bring himself to imagine how devoid and empty his life would be without her. Later that night, as he lay on his bed, peering at the stars in the summer sky, his mind clouded with dark thoughts of the misfortunes that had been piled on him by nature in the only love he had experienced in life.

Kiran rang him up the next day. She was in tears and sounded desperate.

'Purshottam left for Ferozepur by the morning train. He has told me to start packing and follow him there as soon as possible.

Saad Ashraf

I pleaded with him to at least go and see you—after all you have been his benefactor—but he seemed hesitant and unnerved. He kept repeating "they are hell-bent on having me leave without delay".'

They decided to meet early next morning. While the stars still twinkled in the dark night, they walked on the solitary track they had treaded many times before in the direction of the Yamuna. They came to the forest clearing and sat on the mound where they had made many a promise to remain united in their love for one another.

Kiran wept like a child, her head placed on Ghulam Rasool's shoulder. He could feel her warm tears on his chest and tried to console her but to no avail. An air of uneasy sadness hung around the place. Both of them knew that Kiran would have to leave Delhi soon, no matter what he did. This was to be their last meeting. He considered himself guilty on all counts—for the trouble he had caused her by initiating Purshottam's transfer to Delhi to have Kiran by his side.

They made love on the pristine earth with its blanket of wet, wild grass covered with glistening pearls of early-morning dew. As their lovemaking reached its climax and the sun emerged with its golden radiance, they professed to remain true to one another and be united in spirit in this world and the next. When the faint chirping of the birds could be heard, they started back home, their arms around one another. Every now and then they stopped, recalling an incident from the moments they had shared together.

By the time they reached Kiran's quarters, morning had broken. One could hear the faint barking of stray dogs in the distance and the sound of the bugle from the Red Fort, summoning the soldiers to rise from their slumber for another day of service with the Raj.

After one last embrace, Ghulam Rasool headed in the direction of his home, broken in spirit, his shoulders drooping. Kiran stood at her door till such time that Ghulam Rasool's silhouette disappeared up the incline from her house in the direction of the GPO.

The Postmaster

When Ghulam Rasool rang up Purshottam's house next morning there was no response. Even an hour later nobody answered the telephone. Worried and expecting the worst, Ghulam Rasool deputed Basu to find out what was wrong. Basu reported that Purshottam's house was locked and his wife had given the key to a neighbour for delivery to the estate officer. The neighbour had told him that she had left for the station to board the train to Ferozepur.

Ghulam Rasool told Basu that he did not want to be disturbed, bolted the doors of his office from inside, laid his head on the table, broke down and wept uncontrollably from the kind of grief and desperation that comes to a man when he loses the only love of his life.

For the next few months, Ghulam Rasool moved around like a zombie, broken in spirit, sunk in the depths of melancholy, without a purpose and objective to his life. He contemplated suicide but gave up the idea when he thought of the stigma his daughters would have to bear throughout their lives for no fault of theirs. In the office he would sit for hours, recalling his romance with Kiran. He made some attempts to contact her in Ferozepur but every time he got through to her, she hung up on him. He left the working of his office to Basu and attended only to the essentials that could not be avoided. His brown eyes which had shone with intelligence in the past were now dull. Many times during the day he found himself crying uncontrollably. He would bury his face in his handkerchief and weep his heart out. Kiran haunted his thoughts every agonizing moment of the day. In a matter of months he seemed to have aged years.

Noorani Begum had not made any serious effort to try and stop or break her son's affair with his subordinate's wife. She had investigated it and left it at that. Her own relationship with her son was all that mattered to her and she had been marking time, waiting for the affair to settle one way or the other. Now that it was over, she was happy that it had ended without her involvement.

Saad Ashraf

It was Macho Begum who had brought to her the glad tidings. She had come one morning, clutching a box of sweets which she handed over to Noorani Begum.

'What are these sweets in celebration of, Macho Begum?' Noorani Begum had asked. 'Eid is still far away.'

'You mean you don't know? Thanks to Macho Begum your son's home has been saved. I have not acquired my fame as matchmaker for nothing. And mind you, this was only the first arrow from my quiver that I had fired. The vixen has been made to leave Delhi forever,' was the answer.

'And pray what was this first arrow from your quiver which did the trick?' queried Noorani Begum, offering a betel leaf to the matchmaker and stuffing one in her mouth as well.

'One single letter to the postmaster general was all that was needed. If required I would have used my contacts at the viceroy's house. I had arranged a match for the daughter of the matron who waits on the vicereine and praise be to Allah, like all the other matches I have arranged so far, that one lasts too,' said Macho Begum proudly.

'I am truly thankful to you, Macho Begum, for saving my son's home,' said Noorani Begum, now quite content to humour the matchmaker.

'You are not the only person who is thankful to me. Talk to your daughter-in-law and her mother as well and see how grateful they are. Macho Begum knows how to protect the matches she makes.'

forty-three

By early 1947, India had become an abattoir for its poor and innocent masses with communal riots erupting in Bengal, Bihar, and the Punjab. The spectre of death stalked its cities, towns, and villages, sparing neither Hindus nor Muslims nor Sikhs. People who had for years lived peacefully with one another as brothers went on a rampage of killing, arson, and rape. There was no one to comfort the widow whose breadwinner had been disembowelled during the day, nor anyone to wipe the tears of orphans who saw their parents butchered before their very eyes. The British government, a mere shadow of its previous might and political power, looked on haplessly for a way to save its face.

While Ghulam Rasool was stuck in the mire of acute depression resulting from the loss of Kiran, an announcement regarding the partition was made by the new viceroy of India. Ghulam Rasool was soon confronted with an official piece of paper asking him to make a choice between serving India or the new Muslim state of Pakistan. Confused, and not sure of what to do, Ghulam Rasool decided to seek the advice of his friend Ahmad.

Ahmad was of the opinion that despite the apparent hatred that had developed between Hindus and Muslims, the majority of the enlightened people in both the communities could see no genuine reason why India should be divided into two countries. He believed that this hatred was bound to die down.

'This land has been one since time immemorial, regardless of the faith of its rulers. The people of India have learnt to live with one another and have been used to each other's company over the centuries. I'd like to live for another twenty years just to see what happens,' said Ahmad.

Ghulam Rasool did not quite see it that way. He knew that tragic though it was for the country and its people, partition was a reality which everybody would have to accept.

'What worries me is how a peaceful transfer of population between the two countries can be ensured,' said Ghulam Rasool.

'Mian, I don't think there will be a mass migration. An artificial boundary cannot keep people away from one another. I think people will be able to travel freely and do whatever else they want except that the government will be run by brown people instead of white.'

'Ahmad mian, the British *are* partitioning India. There will be two countries, India and Pakistan, and you may need a passport to travel between the two. In all probability these countries will be at loggerheads with one another from the day they are created. This will be the biggest change that has ever occurred in the history of the Indian subcontinent in a thousand years.'

'There you go again, Mian, who has seen that day yet and how is it going to affect you and me. I'm not going to abandon Delhi no matter what happens, though I don't know about you.'

'Well, that's what I came to discuss,' said Ghulam Rasool, as he explained the pros and cons of staying on in India or migrating to Pakistan.

'Hang on in Delhi. This is where your roots are, this is where people know you. Settling in Pakistan would be a big risk. Besides, you'll be retiring in a few years' time. I wonder what you will do alone in an alien country without friends and relatives,' Ahmad reasoned.

Ghulam Rasool thought about this for some time. It was possible that his friend was right. Ghulam Rasool had never talked to Ahmad about his affair with Kiran or his relations with Sara which had deteriorated to the extent that there was no communication between the two. Ahmad did not know that the home to which Ghulam Rasool returned every day provided him with little happiness. For him, Delhi was as lonely a place as any there could be in Pakistan.

'It is true, Ahmad mian, that I won't have friends like you in Pakistan if I decide to work in that country, but any new country offers opportunities and it might be well worth taking that into consideration. With an artificial border dividing the two countries, as you put it, I could always travel to Delhi and be with you or come and live in Delhi and spend my retirement in your company,' said Ghulam Rasool.

'Only time will tell what Allah holds in store for all of us,' Ahmad said with a sigh.

To Ghulam Rasool, Ahmad's point of view, that things would continue as they were, was the only ray of hope in an otherwise dark scenario brought about by the hasty and imprudent decision of the British to partition India.

In spite of thinking over the matter intensely, Ghulam Rasool could not arrive at any definite decision to opt for India or Pakistan. Suddenly, it occurred to him to talk this matter over with Sir Gruggson whom he considered his mentor. He fixed a time with Sir Gruggson's secretary and went to see him in his office.

'Really, it's a personal decision that you'll have to make yourself,' said the director general, taking a few puffs at his pipe in an effort to get it going. 'It is hard to perceive the future of these countries, particularly Pakistan. There might be greater opportunities in Pakistan for Muslims, naturally, but service conditions may be better in India with everything running the way it is.'

Sir Gruggson paused for a while. There seemed to be something on his mind which he did not know exactly how to put across.

'You know, Ghulam Rasool, I have not had the time to talk to you lately, but starting out in a new country with a clean slate may be better simply because people who are here won't be there. The partition of India will be the shroud in which the indiscretions of many people, big and small, would be buried forever.'

On the face of it, Sir Gruggson's advice was non-committal but Ghulam Rasool could read between the lines. He realized

Saad Ashraf

that there was a message for him in what Sir Gruggson was saying. Pakistan may just be the escape he needed to wrench himself out from the realities of his personal situation and help him expunge Kiran's thoughts from his system.

By the time Ghulam Rasool left the director general's office he had made up his mind. He came back to his office, took out the official paper, and signed it opting to serve Pakistan. He folded and placed it in an official envelope and despatched it by special messenger to the director general, Posts and Telegraphs, New Delhi.

When Ghulam Rasool informed Noorani Begum that he had decided to serve Pakistan, he was greeted with cries of anguish from her and his sisters, both of whom were now living in White Haveli. Rehmani had obtained her divorce from Abdul a few years ago while Sultana had been recently widowed and was childless.

'This is not fair … have a heart, Ghulam Rasool … imagine leaving your mother alone in Delhi in her old age,' said Noorani Begum.

'Bhaijaan, are you going to leave us all alone here at the mercy of others while you push off to Pakistan?' his sisters said in chorus.

Ghulam Rasool asked all of them not to get panicky over his decision and to listen to him patiently.

'Going to Pakistan is just like a transfer to another part of India. The partition of the country does not mean a partition of the people, it does not mean that we won't be able to move around freely across the boundary dividing India and Pakistan and meet one another. Pakistan isn't going to be so faraway … in an emergency I could always be with you within a day or two.'

Ghulam Rasool spoke separately to his mother.

'Don't worry, Ammi, you'll continue receiving a hundred rupees by the fifth of each month. If I get a promotion after going to Pakistan and my salary increases, I'll increase your allowance as well.'

This remark pleased Noorani Begum even more and made up for any misgivings she may have had regarding her son's migration to Pakistan. With a few more similar pep sessions Ghulam Rasool managed to allay the fears of his mother and sisters and they agreed to stay back in Delhi.

But Ghulam Rasool had a greater hurdle waiting for him to surmount. He had to break the news to Sara with whom his relation remained distant. He felt that it was time to break the ice.

A few days later, when Ghulam Rasool had finished his lunch of rice and meatball curry and was getting up from the dining table, he asked Anwari as to the whereabouts of her mistress. When told that she was in the next room, he walked in to find Sara sitting on her bed.

'I came to tell you that I have opted to serve Pakistan. It may take some time before I get my order to proceed but I thought I'd let you know as much in advance as possible. You'll have to get the household goods packed and everything ready for the family to move,' said Ghulam Rasool.

He waited for an answer, expecting her to say something rude and irritating.

'All right, sarkar, I'll get ready to leave, but where is this Pakistan?' Sara asked softly.

Ghulam Rasool was taken aback by the sensual politeness of her voice. It was almost like her old self—an innocent question delivered in a loving tone. He, however, had no answer to her question. A map of India hung on one of the walls in the room and Ghulam Rasool wondered where Sir Radcliffe would draw the line carving two countries out of one.

'We will come to know where exactly Pakistan is going to be very soon, but in the meantime we must ready ourselves to move at very short notice,' said Ghulam Rasool.

He waited for her to say something more but she remained silent. He walked out of the room, climbed down the stairs to his office, settled himself in his chair and started working on his files.

Sara was delighted that her husband had at last broken the spell of silence by speaking to her. Perhaps Allah had heard her

Saad Ashraf

prayers and was going to restore her relationship with her husband. This conversation and the decision to move to Pakistan were probably the first signs. She was so excited that she despatched Anwari with a note to her mother asking her to come and see her immediately so that she could share the happiness of the possibility of an unexpected reconciliation with her husband.

Ghulam Rasool received his order to proceed to Pakistan on 1 August 1947. He was to report to the postmaster general, Punjab, in Lahore for a posting. He had two alternatives available: either to travel by the special government trains leaving Delhi for Pakistan daily or to travel privately. Ghulam Rasool chose the latter. The news of his impending departure for Pakistan spread like wildfire among those who worked in the GPO. In spite of the communal tension and the uncertainty which prevailed in the country, many babus called on Ghulam Rasool in an effort to dissuade him from proceeding to Pakistan when he was doing so well in India. Superintendent Basu did likewise.

'Sir, I hope you won't mind if I take the liberty of talking to you on a personal matter because of my association with you over many years. India will need capable officers like you, and there are bound to be good prospects for advancement here. It is still not too late to withdraw. If you just give me the nod I'll go ahead and get all the paperwork done,' said Basu.

Ghulam Rasool sat quietly, glancing through his files. 'Thank you, Mr Basu, I greatly appreciate your kind words but you know that my order has already been issued and I will have to leave for Pakistan. I hope partition works to the benefit of everybody and the people of both countries live peacefully with one another like brothers,' he said.

A few days before his departure, Ghulam Rasool visited the branch post offices to bid goodbye to those who worked there. He sat with the assistant postmasters and then addressed the staff, asking them to be as loyal to the new countries as they had been to the British sarkar. He appreciated the cooperation that they had provided to him and asked them to forgive him for whatever he may have said or done in the line of duty that may have caused offence.

On the day of his departure, Ghulam Rasool woke up early, an hour before dawn, dressed himself in a three-piece suit, took his walking stick, and, stepping down the stairs, walked in the direction of the postal colony. His decision to opt for Pakistan was weighing more heavily on him by the hour as the time for his departure neared. This was his last day in Delhi. He walked as a man possessed towards the quarters where Kiran had lived not too long ago. The night had not yet passed and it was dark and silent and there was not a soul around. He stood outside the door of her house from where he used to beckon her to come out. He waited a while, half expecting her to do so now. He then proceeded in the direction of the lonely track towards the river where both of them had often walked hand in hand. He stopped from time to time to recollect a moment of their romance. He wondered what Kiran was doing at this very moment. He continued in this manner for well over an hour and returned home exhausted. He lay down on the bed without caring to change from the three-piece suit he was wearing.

Later in the day Ghulam Rasool arrived at the Delhi railway station along with his family to board the Frontier Mail for Lahore. The newspapers had carried an account of the Hindu-Muslim riots which had reportedly taken place on the outskirts of the city. A few people had come to see him off and everyone was a bit tense. When the guard blew the whistle for the train to depart, his mother, sisters and his mother-in-law, clad in their burqas, gathered around him and Sara to bid them goodbye. Noorani Begum embraced her son and daughter-in-law and tied an amulet around their arms, holding back her tears.

'Be in touch, children,' she said as she embraced them and moved away.

Others were waiting in line to say goodbye.

'I hope we meet again very soon,' said Ahmad, Ghulam Rasool's friend of many decades.

'Goodbye sir,' said Basu, his eyes misty.

Saad Ashraf

As the train left the station and gathered speed, Ghulam Rasool could see those on the platform receding in the distance till their arms raised in farewell appeared as specks above their heads. When the train passed below the ramparts of the Red Fort, Ghulam Rasool sighed deeply. He had passed that way hundreds of times, toiling on his cycle in the direction of Missionary College or the GPO. He knew that he was leaving the better part of his life behind in the city of his birth as the train hurtled towards its destination—his new homeland called Pakistan.

forty-four

Ghulam Rasool had served in Lahore before and was familiar
with its fun-loving people and the city's bohemian culture,
but the Lahore that he arrived in now was totally different.
Though the verdant green of the Lawrence Gardens provided
solace to the eyes, the once fathomless blue sky wore a continuous
dark grey haze from the smoke of Hindu and Sikh houses which
had been set on fire by large crowds of unruly ruffians. As night
descended, the horizon acquired a crimson hue from the bright
embers that flew skywards from these houses. Those who lost
their homes through arson were unable to fathom how their
neighbours with whom they had lived in peace for generations
could have become so treacherous and evil overnight. Similar
events were taking place on the other side of the border in India
with unprecedented massacres of Muslims. Ghulam Rasool could
not help wondering what the people of the subcontinent had
gained by its partition and what kind of independence this was,
baptized in blood and fire, and at whose altar innocent people,
unconnected with the politics of the subcontinent, were being
made to pay a price with their lives, honour, and property.

On his arrival in Lahore, Ghulam Rasool had been appointed
special postmaster and allotted eight rooms on the first floor of
the GPO as his official residence. The large accommodation was
proving helpful with the influx of relatives from Delhi who stayed
in the house for a few days before moving on to other cities and
towns in Pakistan.

At the end of August, the English governor of West Punjab had appointed a number of officers including Ghulam Rasool to allot accommodation left behind by the Hindus and Sikhs in Lahore to the Muslim refugees. These allotments were provisional till such time as India and Pakistan could exchange records pertaining to the property left behind by the refugees from either side.

Ghulam Rasool took up the work of allotment of property with unusual zeal. He decided to dedicate his evenings to the task so that his duties as postmaster did not interfere with this noble work. The procedure for allotment of property had been made very simple and required that applicants appear in person before him with two sureties who could certify to the ownership of property left behind by the applicant in India.

One day, a venerable gentleman with downcast eyes, drooping shoulders and a worried expression accompanied by his two sureties walked into his office.

'I am Sheikh Mohammed from Saharanpur in India,' he said dourly, introducing himself, as Ghulam Rasool got up to shake hands with him.

'Sheikh Mohammed was one of the wealthiest men in Saharanpur, owning several houses and commercial buildings in that city. He is presently without a roof over his head and his family shares a makeshift tent with another at the Walton camp. We came here to vouch for the truth of his statements as we were his tenants in one of the houses he owned in that city,' said one of the witnesses who accompanied him.

Ghulam Rasool raised a few questions about what the Sheikh claimed to have left behind in Saharanpur to which he thought he got honest answers. In the absence of any records it was impossible for him to verify the correctness of what was said and the decision to allot or not to allot a property was to be made purely on his personal assessment. Ghulam Rasool decided to allot Sheikh Mohammed a bungalow near the university grounds which had recently been abandoned by a Sikh engineer who had migrated to India.

A few days later, when Ghulam Rasool was out for an evening walk, he passed by a bungalow which attracted his attention by its meticulous upkeep. Tall eucalyptus trees stood on one side of the large manicured lawn while wafts of the evening breeze, smelling of rose and lavender, enthused those who passed by the flower-filled beds laid out in the garden. A plate on the gate bore Sheikh Mohammed's name. Ghulam Rasool decided on the spur of the moment to enquire about his welfare and was ushered into a spacious sitting room furnished in cool, blue colours with matching sofas, cushions, and curtains. It assuaged his ego that the power of his pen had been able to place a roof over the head of at least one unfortunate soul who had lost his property in the turmoil of partition. Everything in the room exuded taste except for a long bamboo which stood in the middle of the room as a solitary symbol of ugliness inserted between the blades of the ceiling fan for some unknown reason.

Sheikh Mohammed made his appearance dressed in a cream-coloured flannel suit and greeted Ghulam Rasool with a broad smile. Ghulam Rasool could see the marked improvement in his health since their last meeting. From a man broken in spirit he had been miraculously transformed into someone with confidence and command over matters at hand.

'I am sorry to have barged in like this without informing you Sheikh Sahib. I just noticed your name outside the gate and couldn't help coming in to enquire about your well-being,' Ghulam Rasool said apologetically.

'Well, I owe everything to you, Postmaster Sahib, for allotting me this house. The sardar who owned this place left everything behind for me to use—cars, furniture, household articles and innumerable suitcases full of clothing. I am still trying to make an inventory of his belongings. It seems that he had a daughter who was to be married soon because we found her jewellery and her trousseau in a large steel trunk. It is a strange coincidence that the clothes fit my wife perfectly and the jewellery too looks good on her, just as if everything was made for her.'

Saad Ashraf

Ghulam Rasool felt sick on hearing such remarks. Suddenly the man appeared to be emerging in his true colours—an uneducated and corrupt individual devoid of sensitivity who felt no qualms in grabbing and using the wealth of others as his own.

'Don't you think you should turn over everything you've found in this house to the Pakistan government?'

'I am prepared to do that if the Pakistan government can get me back what I have left behind in India.'

Ghulam Rasool could see that there was some merit in the point the man had just made.

'And pray what is the purpose of this bamboo stuck in the ceiling fan,' he enquired of the Sheikh.

'Ah, this too is a reminder of the hurry in which the sardar left this house. When I entered here I found the blades of the ceiling fan whirling non-stop day and night and there seemed to be no way of stopping it. Finally we had to find a bamboo to do the job for us,' said the Sheikh, quite amused with the remark that he had just made.

'Why don't you use the regulator to stop the fan?'

'Regulator? What regulator?'

Ghulam Rasool got up and strode to the small regulator on the wall behind the sofa and turned the knob. He came back to the middle of the room, pulled the bamboo away, and laid it on the floor.

'See, Sheikh Sahib, when you want to put on the fan, all you have to do is to turn the knob in the other direction like this,' said Ghulam Rasool, conducting a demonstration.

'Amazing!' chirped the Sheikh, relaxing on the sofa with a cigarette between his lips.

It was obvious that wherever he had come from, the Sheikh had no idea about electricity. It was more than likely that the story of his owning all the property in Saharanpur was false. But who could say what the truth was in the absence of records.

Ghulam Rasool left the Sheikh's house in a huff.

He spent a sleepless night, thinking about his own inadequacy in judging others and wondering how people like the Sheikh and his progeny would build and run the new state of Pakistan.

In October 1947, out of the blue, Sara's brother Ghazi, accompanied by his family, turned up at the special postmaster's residence in Lahore. He had fled from Delhi, abandoning two of his shops at the foot of the Royal Mosque. Ghazi related how he was chased out by a crowd of Hindu and Sikh refugees who had been meted the same treatment in their home towns in the Punjab by Muslims. Ghazi had escaped with his life after throwing the keys of his shops among the crowd. This led to a melee thus providing him an opportunity to disappear from the scene. He had dashed for home and ordered his family to rush to the railway station with whatever cash they could lay their hands on. They had managed to get on the next passenger train leaving for Lahore by bribing the railway guard in whose cabin Ghazi and his family spent the next twenty-four hours in utter discomfort before reaching Pakistan.

'Ghazi Bhai has left everything behind in Delhi including his two shops. Can't you allot at least one shop to him in the bazaar?' Sara said to her husband shortly after her brother's arrival. She had mustered all her courage to make this request because of the estranged relations between them.

Ghulam Rasool shook his head emphatically. 'What will people say once they hear that I have allotted a shop to my brother-in-law? I am sorry I cannot do this.'

'But everybody from Delhi knows that Ghazi Bhai had two shops at the Royal Mosque,' remonstrated Sara.

'I am sorry but he'll have to find somebody else to do this for him.'

'Somebody else? Who?'

'I don't know,' said Ghulam Rasool, shrugging his shoulders.

'Influential people are helping their relatives who have arrived from India as refugees while you are doing just the opposite,' remarked Sara angrily.

Saad Ashraf

Ghulam Rasool walked away without responding. Sara realized that she had very little influence left on her husband. Ghazi moved out of the special postmaster's residence a few days later, bitter with the non-cooperative attitude of his brother-in-law and managed to get a shop allotted to him in the Lahore Cantonment through some other contact.

Every day provided an education for Ghulam Rasool in the new societal order emerging in Pakistan. He realized that in this country one had to acquire the subtle art of sycophancy and attach oneself as a courtier to someone who wielded power. He wondered if he was capable of learning this new technique in a homeland that was created to provide equitable treatment for all who chose to live in it.

forty-five

'Sir, members of the staff at the GPO frequently ask me whether you are a Punjabi or a refugee from Delhi,' said Deen, Ghulam Rasool's personal assistant, one morning. Deen was a soft-spoken man, pliant and obedient, a quality common among most personal assistants in government service. Ghulam Rasool remembered Sir Gruggson's comment that a personal assistant was an important source of information for an officer on the state of affairs prevailing in his organization.

'And what do you tell them?'

'I tell them I don't know.'

'I think that is a forthright answer, Mr Deen ... though I can't understand the purpose behind such a question. What does it matter if one is a local or a refugee from India or an Englishman? We are all human beings equal in the eyes of Allah.'

'That is true, sir, but in this part of the world it is normal to ask those who work with you where they come from.'

'You can tell them what you like and if you want to be precise you can say I'm fifty-fifty—half Punjabi, half Hindustani.'

The authentic version of his boss's ethnicity did not clear the situation as far as Deen was concerned. Fifty-fifty was neither here nor there, he thought as he left. The next day Deen informed Ghulam Rasool that those who enquired about his ethnicity were holding regular meetings to arrive at some consensus on his origins.

'Mr Deen, don't they have enough work to occupy themselves to be wasting their time in working out my ancestry. I think this is a very serious matter and needs to be sorted out.'

Ghulam Rasool convened a meeting of the staff and told them that they were to concentrate all their energies on building the Pakistan postal services into an organization whose hallmark was to be efficiency and hard work which required that no time should be wasted in idle talk. He issued a few written warnings to some of those he addressed.

The following day he received a summons from his immediate boss—a retired army man, Colonel Farouk, the first non-white postmaster general of the Punjab Circle—to see him urgently in his office. Colonel Farouk had been inducted into the Indian Posts and Telegraphs Department after his demobilization from the Indian army at the end of the Second World War in 1945 and was thought of as an officer whose only objective was his own survival.

'Postmaster Ghulam Rasool, a delegation of your staff came to see me yesterday and I thought we'd meet and I'll bring this to your notice,' said the postmaster general.

'That's very kind of you, sir,' replied Ghulam Rasool.

'Well, those who came to see me complained that the working environment in the post office was not as good as it should be. I believe you have issued warning letters to some members of your staff. I am sure that there must have been good reasons for doing so.'

'Sir, I am certain that those who met you must have given you their version of why the warning letters were issued to them. They were given the warnings because they were creating indiscipline by wasting time in idle gossip. I am sure you'll agree that the action taken was appropriate.'

'I agree, but I thought you may want to take steps to bring about a ceasefire on this front.'

'Doing what?'

'By withdrawing the letters you have issued,' said the postmaster general.

Ghulam Rasool was seething inside. Never in his service of nearly three decades had he been put under this kind of pressure. Never had he been asked to take back an order which he had passed in good judgement. Yet, service discipline stopped him from retorting rudely to his boss.

'Sir, you are my boss and you have the authority to overrule me and withdraw whatever orders I have given. I am sure that you could find it convenient to do so,' said Ghulam Rasool politely.

Colonel Farouk was taken aback.

'Postmaster Ghulam Rasool, we have a country of our own now. We are no longer a British colony. We are all brothers. Why should we try to create problems for one another,' he said in a conciliatory tone.

'But surely nothing is more important than building a strong Pakistan. Unity, faith and discipline—that is the message of the founder.'

The room seemed to be charged with tension which exhibited itself in the restlessness of the two officers in their chairs.

'Nevertheless, you may want to think about what I've said,' remarked the postmaster general.

'I've already thought about it,' said Ghulam Rasool, taking his leave and walking back to his office.

There were fourteen months left before he reached fifty-five years of age and retired from government service. Ghulam Rasool now began to eagerly wait for the day when he would become a free man after thirty years of servitude.

Ghulam Rasool worried about his family, friends, and acquaintances in Delhi every time he heard of communal rioting in that city. He missed the unsolicited advice his mother Noorani Begum gave when he found life too stressful. He longed for the company of his childhood friend Ahmad. He recalled with nostalgia the narrow streets of the old city. He yearned for Kiran, the only love in his life, and suffered from remorse for not having had the courage to marry her and face the world in spite of the complications that may have followed. He wondered if relations between the two countries would ever improve to enable him to visit Delhi again. He wrote regularly to Noorani Begum and his sisters and received their letters. They wrote that all was well at White Haveli though Delhi was not totally at peace even a year after partition. There too, magistrates had been appointed to pinpoint property abandoned by Muslims and to make an allotment to those who had migrated from Pakistan. The staff of one such magistrate had visited Noorani Begum's house in White Haveli to ascertain whether the owner was alive, had not migrated to Pakistan, and was still in occupation of the property. Noorani Begum had proudly showed her ownership deed which had yellowed with age and loudly proclaimed, 'Can't you see me standing before you in flesh and blood. What more proof do you want that I am alive and have not migrated to Pakistan?'

In mid-1948, Ghulam Rasool was promoted to be the new postmaster general of the Punjab. Though the news elated Ghulam Rasool, it made little difference to his relationship with Sara.

'I've been promoted, Begum!' he announced excitedly on returning home from office the day he received the official paper.

Sara gave no response.

'Well … don't you have anything to say to your husband who has reached the top after struggling for three decades without anyone's support.'

'What do you want me to do and why do you say you had no support? You had Allah's support without which not even a leaf moves in this world. You should be offering prayers to thank the Almighty for what has been bestowed on you.'

Ghulam Rasool listened to Sara's sermon with a sense of resignation. He wrote a letter to his mother and sisters, giving them the news about his promotion and in a separate, private note informed his mother that she could expect an increase in her allowance once his new salary became known to him.

This happiness was followed a few weeks later by disturbing news from Delhi.

Ghulam Rasool received a telegram from Rehmani, saying that their mother was in a serious condition following a fall in the bathroom and that he should try to get to Delhi as soon as possible. Ghulam Rasool had taken charge as postmaster general only a few weeks earlier and realized that a request for leave at this time to go to Delhi wouldn't be viewed favourably, more so because relations between the two countries were deteriorating by the day. With this in mind, Ghulam Rasool decided to forego the idea of going to Delhi. But whenever he was alone in the office, working on his files, or in bed trying to catch some sleep under the cloudy monsoon sky of Lahore, he thought of his mother in Delhi and felt sorry that he could not be with her at a time when she needed him most.

One day in September 1948, while Ghulam Rasool was busy in his office, he was handed a telegram. It read:

MOTHER EXPIRED EARLY THIS MORNING. FUNERAL TOMORROW MORNING. COME IF YOU CAN. REHMANI BEGUM.

Ghulam Rasool refused to believe that Noorani Begum could have left this world without so much as saying goodbye to her favourite child. He recalled the events of the last five decades, as his eyes welled up with tears. He knew that whatever he had achieved in life was because of the trials and tribulations that woman had endured during the best years of her life. Suddenly, he was aware of a vacuum in his life though he had not seen her for over a year, and had indeed stayed away from her for the better part of his service life.

He called his personal assistant to his office and dictated an express telegram to his director general in Karachi, requesting a fortnight's leave to India on account of his bereavement. Overwhelmed with grief he decided to call it a day and walked back to his living quarters.

'Noorani Begum—she's gone,' Ghulam Rasool announced to Sara who was busy with her sewing. Sara muttered a short prayer under her breath and immediately took to the prayer mat to offer prayers for the departed soul.

The next morning, Ghulam Rasool's personal assistant brought to his attention a telegram received from Karachi which read as follows:

Saad Ashraf

DEPARTMENT CONDOLES WITH YOU ON THE LOSS OF YOUR
MOTHER STOP BUT REGRETS THAT IT IS NOT POSSIBLE TO GRANT
IMMEDIATE EX PAKISTAN LEAVE IN INDIA AS ALPHA NOT POSSIBLE
TO ARRANGE FOR A REPLACEMENT FOR YOU ON IMMEDIATE BASIS
BRAVO ALL APPLICATIONS OF EX PAKISTAN LEAVE IN INDIA FOR
GOVERNMENT OFFICIALS ARE APPROVED BY A SPECIAL INTER-
MINISTERIAL BOARD WHICH ALLOWS OR DISALLOWS SUCH REQUESTS
STOP REMAIN ASSURED WILL TRY TO FIND REPLACEMENT AND PUT
YOUR APPLICATION BEFORE THE BOARD AT ITS NEXT MEETING
STOP FAROUK DG POSTS KARACHI.

Ghulam Rasool lamented the callousness that had developed in
a department which was once known for how well it catered to
personal problems of its employees. He reflected on the partition
of India—the riots and the arson would be talked about in history
for long, but what of the individual 'lesser' tragedies, like the
one he was faced with. He knew that by the time he received the
permission from the department to proceed to Delhi, Noorani
Begum would have long been buried. He decided to give up the
idea of going at all.

A few days later, he received a detailed letter from Rehmani,
describing the last days of Noorani Begum. Two days before she
died, she had become delirious with fever, describing events of
her childhood and her youth and calling out the names of half a
dozen women she wanted to see. With great difficulty, Rehmani
had got together those who were available in Delhi. From each
of them Noorani Begum had asked for forgiveness for some
minor thing or the other she might have said or done years ago,
none of which they could remember anyway.

On the last day of her life, Noorani Begum had uttered
Ghulam Rasool's name almost every half hour, and said that
she was waiting for him to come from Pakistan. A sudden calm
had descended on her in the late afternoon when she claimed
that she could see him walk up the stairs to her with a garland of
marigold flowers which he put around her neck. She had talked
of someone by the name of Sir Wilbur Bright who was waiting

to receive her outside the door. Rehmani thought that it must be some Englishman whose name her mother had remembered from a newspaper or magazine. A couple of moments later, eternal sleep overtook Noorani Begum as she left this world for her permanent abode.

Saad Ashraf

forty-six

A few months later, Mr Yakoob, Ghulam Rasool's deputy, who was responsible for the administration of his office, came to see him to discuss an official matter. After the meeting had ended, Yakoob told Ghulam Rasool that he had worked in the Rawalpindi post office as a clerk when the latter was the postmaster back in 1924. Though Ghulam Rasool could not recall him from those days, the awareness of a shared past created a familiarity between the two men and they got talking to one another.

Yakoob asked Ghulam Rasool about his plans after retirement from service.

'I have not made any plans so far,' replied Ghulam Rasool.

Though retirement was only a few months away, he had not given much thought to how he and his family would survive once his service ended. He had a vague idea that like others who had retired before him, he would build or buy a house with the lump sum money he would receive as gratuity and thereafter live on the monthly pension he was entitled to. For the moment, he had got a house on McLeod Road, abandoned by a Hindu barrister, allotted to his name by the refugees rehabilitation department for which he would have to pay a hundred and fifty rupees as monthly rental. He had moved to this house as soon as the allotment was made and had vacated the living quarters at the GPO.

'Sir, you could do a few things to make life more comfortable for yourself after August,' continued Yakoob.

'Such as …?'

'You could get permits for cars that are being given to government officers these days. You may recall that I circulated a notice from the home department a few weeks ago asking for applications for these permits.'

'And then? I believe these permits are being given to government officers for buying cars for their personal use at the control price?'

'Sir, you could sell each of these permits in the market for a premium of five thousand rupees and earn a profit without investing a rupee of your own. The sale of ten such permits would equal the total lump sum amount that you may receive at the time of your retirement.'

'You mean that I become a permit trader at the fag end of my career, and soil my integrity with ill-gotten gains.' The disgust in Ghulam Rasool's voice was barely disguised.

'Sir, the government has created this scheme for the benefit of its employees … we aren't the ones to initiate it. The government has placed no restriction on the number of permits one wants to apply for nor is there a restriction on their sale. If you call the profit earned by selling car permits as ill-gotten, why does the government act as a silent bystander when these gains are being made,' remarked Yakoob.

'I agree, Mr Yakoob, that the law and its implementation should be more stringent but it is totally up to one's conscience whether one considers the gain from selling car permits to be unfair or not.'

'Sir, Pakistan was not made for angels but for human beings with all their failings. It was made for the deprived Muslims of the subcontinent, to improve their lot. The poorer you are the richer you want to be in the quickest possible time, and the sale of car permits is one such way to make quick money.'

This viewpoint was reiterated when Mr Zaman, a postmaster who had retired from service some ten years ago and was looked upon as a venerable elder by the officers of the post office, called on Ghulam Rasool one day.

Saad Ashraf

'You know, Ghulam Rasool, there was a time when senior citizens didn't have to work after retirement. One built a house with the money one got from the government and survived with his family on the monthly pension, but unfortunately it is no longer like that. While the cost of living has gone up, the respect with which people looked upon retired government servants in the past has disappeared. After partition, money has become the most important factor in life, and money no longer lies in government service but in business,' explained Zaman.

'So, Mr Zaman, can you suggest a business I could engage in after I retire?'

'I have a small bookshop at Anarkali Bazaar ... I can offer you a partnership in it for five thousand rupees. That should be a respectable retreat for a retiree like you.'

'Done,' said Ghulam Rasool, getting up to shake Zaman's hand.

After Zaman had left, Ghulam Rasool pondered over the commitment he had just made. He realized that he may have been a bit hasty in accepting Zaman's offer without checking whether Zaman's bookshop was doing well enough to give him a profit on his investment.

But Ghulam Rasool had faith in the camaraderie of the serving and retired employees of the postal department. He believed that anybody associated with the post office was a gentleman and Zaman had retired with honour after serving the organization for thirty-five years. He was happy that he had found something useful to do once he was out of office. What greater pleasure could there be than the company of books. Without a nine-to-five routine, he would be able to read the works of Shakespeare, Shaw, Russell, and Rousseau as late into the night as he wanted. He would keep himself physically fit and occupy himself by looking after his investment in Zaman's bookshop, devoting whatever time was left to providing the much needed attention to his family.

With such idyllic thoughts racing through his mind, Ghulam Rasool looked forward to the day of his retirement a month hence. Though it was sad that Jinnah had passed away and an undeclared war with India was being fought in Kashmir, one could sense that Pakistan as a country and a nation had come to stay. Ghulam Rasool knew that he was to live the remaining part of his life in this new country regardless of what happened and was prepared to brave all odds that came his way.

And then came the day every government employee in the subcontinent dreads—the day of one's retirement from service. For Ghulam Rasool this day fell on 20 August 1949, his fifty-fifth birthday. He couldn't sleep the night before, thinking of what lay in store for him in the future. At eight in the morning, for the last time, he rode in the official black Wolseley car to his office in the GPO on the Mall. As soon as he had settled in his chair, those who worked with him started dropping in to see him. They offered guardedly worded congratulations on his honourable retirement and gave him advice on how best and most profitably he could spend the rest of his life.

'It is Allah's favour if one reaches the age of retirement in sound physical and mental health. In the subcontinent, every day of one's life after fifty-five should be considered a bonus,' said one colleague.

'Sir, retirement does not mean that you will be out of our hearts and minds. Everyone who has worked with you considers it a privilege. You can come to this office whenever you like and give us the benefit of your advice and experience. When you visit me I shall consider it a great honour if you sit in my chair,' said Ghulam Rasool's deputy who was to take over as postmaster general temporarily.

Ghulam Rasool was not taken in by all this adulation. He knew that the training and experience of those who worked for the government sealed their hearts and lips and prevented them from speaking their minds freely. He knew that once he left his office he would be forgotten as quickly as the hundreds of other faceless individuals who had worked in the postal department since it was created by the British nearly a century ago.

Saad Ashraf

By midday, Ghulam Rasool had received a dozen boxes of the most popular sweetmeats of Lahore wrapped in ornamental silver paper, from the delegations of the lower staff. No sooner had the clock in the tower of the GPO building struck one in the afternoon, than Ghulam Rasool signed the report relinquishing the charge of his office. He could hear the rising din of voices of the staff who had gathered outside his door to bid him farewell. The poignancy of the day and the moment showed on his face. Three decades of service in the postal department was coming to an end.

Ghulam Rasool came out of his office and shook hands with those who had gathered outside. He was profusely garlanded as he made his way down the stairs from the first floor of the GPO building to the Wolseley car in the porch. The fifty-odd employees who had come to see him off waved after him as he sat in the car and raised his hand to his forehead in a gesture of goodbye, before disappearing in a cloud of dust raised by the speeding vehicle heading in the direction of his home on McLeod Road.

When Ghulam Rasool reached home he found the house clothed in silence. His daughters had gone to their colleges and Sara was busy with the afternoon prayers. He pulled a chair and sat down, waiting for her to finish. His happiness at having retired with honour was tinged with sorrow that there was nobody to share this moment and its loneliness with him. How he longed for Noorani Begum to be around to bolster his ego with lengthy speeches on his qualities as an officer and a gentleman. She would have made him feel like a king even though he had just lost his kingdom. He sorely missed his friend Ahmad but above all he missed the presence of Kiran on whose bosom he would have laid his head and unburdened himself of his heavy heart. But the sad reality was that while Noorani Begum had passed away, Ahmad and Kiran were so distant as to have been cenotaphs of a bygone era.

Sara sat turning her prayer beads having finished with the prayers.

'You've come early from the office today, sarkar. Is everything all right?' she asked.

'I've retired from service; today was my last day in office. From tomorrow I won't have to go to office,' said Ghulam Rasool, heaving a sad sigh.

'You mean, never again?'

'Yes … never again.'

Sara muttered a short prayer under her breath.

'Well, it's not the end of life you know,' she said. 'There are many beautiful worlds beyond this one, and many better things to do than devoting time to a man-made office. Allah will show you what you have to do next. I'll lay lunch on the table for you.'

Ghulam Rasool said he didn't feel like eating and, excusing himself, went to his room where he spent the rest of the afternoon in the company of his thoughts.

Saad Ashraf

forty-seven

Ghulam Rasool spent the first week of his retirement trying to make up for the sleep he thought he had lost in the thirty years of government service. Thereafter, he started taking an hour-long morning walk in the Lawrence Gardens, came back home, and read Kipling's *Civil and Military Gazette*, making sure that he did not miss any news. He then got out of the house to attend to the most important items of his future existence—his gratuity and pension.

Over the next few weeks, Ghulam Rasool devoted himself to chasing his papers in the accountant general's office. He found himself being shunted from one clerk's table to another in a veritable merry-go-round till the whole process began to sorely test his patience. The entire office appeared to be full of shirkers whose main occupation was drinking tea, indulging in gossip, and finding pretexts for not doing an honest day's work.

'Mr Retired Postmaster General,' volunteered one clerk, 'you have been a senior officer of the government ... it does not become you to be sitting with one clerk after another. Why don't we settle for a small baksheesh, payable when I get all the paperwork done for you? I promise you that in two weeks' time you'll have your gratuity and pension book.'

'You mean, give you a bribe to get what is my due? I'll never do that even if I don't get a rupee in my lifetime. There is nothing undignified about chasing one's pension papers,' thundered an indignant Ghulam Rasool.

His papers finally landed on the table of a middle-level functionary named Abbas, who to Ghulam Rasool's relief and surprise turned out to be genuinely interested in his cause.

'Sahib, I feel ashamed of the way this office has treated a retired government officer like you. We all seem to forget that one day all of us will have to retire and be the victims of the same red tape we have created for others. From now on I'll do everything for you and get you your gratuity and pension as soon as possible,' assured Abbas.

In about a week's time, through the efforts of Abbas, Ghulam Rasool was able to get a cheque of ten thousand rupees as his gratuity. He also received his pension book with which he could draw his monthly pension.

The state of affairs in the lower echelons of the government shocked Ghulam Rasool. He noted with regret the rot which had set in and which he was sure would eventually consume the iron frame which the British had taken such pains to build for over a century.

Ghulam Rasool cashed his gratuity the next day and travelled to Anarkali Bazaar to meet Zaman.

'Aha, there you are, Ghulam Rasool, I was wondering where you had disappeared. I was thinking of visiting you. Well, how is retired life treating you?' asked Zaman.

'I am all right, sir, and I've finally been able to collect my gratuity and pension book from the accountant general's office after undergoing three months of forced penance.'

'Did you have to pay money to the clerks to get the documentation done? I believe that is the custom these days.'

'No, I didn't pay any money, though there was a demand at one stage to do so if I wanted to get things done in a hurry.'

'Good! I am glad there are some people around who will not give in to the way things are changing here.'

Ghulam Rasool next broached the matter of the partnership in the bookshop, informing Zaman that he had brought the requisite amount of five thousand rupees with him.

Saad Ashraf

'Ghulam Rasool, I'd like you to think about this matter before making an investment. When I mentioned this possibility you didn't ask me a thing about the business I owned and made a decision on the spur of the moment. The days when one could trust people implicitly have gone. People have changed ... just like the geography of the subcontinent,' Zaman remarked wistfully.

'I trust you fully ... you have the reputation of being a man of unimpeachable integrity.'

'It is kind of you to say these words, but I thought I should caution you against possible business losses. You know, business is a totally different ball game compared to government service. Unlike service where one gets a salary on the first of each month and the family knows that one has to make do with that, in business things are uncertain ... a college may buy three hundred books from us one day and thereafter there may be no sale for weeks.'

'Sir, the fact that you have survived in this business for so many years proves that you have done well.'

'I would say that this shop supports me and my family. Naturally, if we put more money into the business we shall be able to earn more. My son Yusuf runs the shop ... I just come and sit here in the mornings a couple of times in a week.'

Zaman then called Yusuf who was busy at the back of the shop and introduced him to Ghulam Rasool.

'We do our accounts every six months and that is when we come to know how much money we have made or lost,' remarked Zaman.

'I am sure we will do very well. Would it be all right if I were to come from tomorrow and spend a couple of hours at the shop to keep myself occupied?'

'I don't think that would either be necessary or helpful. Customers shy away when they see too many people hanging around. I think Yusuf manages this business well enough on his own. He objects to my presence at times too, though you are more than welcome to come every week and borrow books for your reading. After all you are going to be a fifty per cent partner.'

Ghulam Rasool felt aggrieved at being denied a more active participation in the business in which he was making an investment but decided not to make an issue of this. Zaman prepared a receipt on a plain piece of paper through which Ghulam Rasool became a fifty per cent partner in Zaman Book Company.

For several months after this, Ghulam Rasool would visit the shop once or twice a week, browsing through the latest books that had arrived. He would borrow half a dozen books by writers he liked best and carry them home. He had prolonged the duration of his morning walk since the morning he ran into a seventy-year-old retiree who had advised him that in order to live long 'you must keep yourself so busy that you don't get time to think and the best way to keep yourself busy is to keep walking'. Ghulam Rasool had followed this advice in earnest. He had discarded his cycle in favour of his legs and walked to attend to household chores such as paying the monthly bills or buying groceries.

Walking more and more each day, however, made Ghulam Rasool very tired by the afternoons. He would eat a heavy lunch and sleep long hours to recover from the physical stress of the morning. In a couple of months he had put on weight and developed a sizeable paunch. Ghulam Rasool could feel indolence creeping up his bones. He kept deferring the physical examination by the government medical board which would approve or disallow his receiving the lump sum pension money which was vital to his and his family's future.

With more time at home, he started interfering in Sara's household routine. Things came to a head one day. From where he sat on his bed, he could see Sara cooking.

'You are putting too many chillies in the lentils ... the whole house is smelling and will soon blow up!' Ghulam Rasool shouted from his bed, as she adjusted the firewood and blew into the iron pipe in her hand to get the flames going.

Saad Ashraf

'You've been pushing a pen and blackening paper all your life ... what do you know about chillies and lentils. Why don't you get out of the house and try and get a job somewhere?' Sara snapped.

'I worked for three decades and rose to the top in the dak khana, isn't that enough?'

'A man should work till the end—that's what Allah has created him for.'

'You are an insolent woman and have no respect for your husband! If you keep behaving in this manner I'll have to exercise the Muslim prerogative of another wife and remarry.'

'O yes! And where will you find a woman willing to marry a discarded envelope such as yourself, incapable of fulfilling marital obligations and unable to support a family on a meagre pension,' came the sharp rejoinder.

'You call five hundred rupees a month a meagre pension? Most people don't even get that as salary. You are an illiterate and ignorant woman who knows nothing about the world!' bellowed Ghulam Rasool.

The hot exchange of words and the volatile environment at home was more than what Ghulam Rasool could bear. He undressed quickly, changed into the ten-year-old grey flannel suit he used to wear to the office, and left in a huff.

In this state Ghulam Rasool roamed the streets of Lahore deep in thought. He had always considered himself fortunate in the way life had shaped up, particularly with his career. It was as if Allah had watched over him every step of the way. He wondered why luck had deserted him at a stage in life when he needed it most. He had lost Kiran, his marriage was in shambles, and his plans to secure the future of his family once he had retired hadn't materialized. He knew that he had tried to be a good man throughout his life by being honest, upright, humble, and helpful. He had prayed five times a day, seeking redemption for his sins ever since he could remember, so what could have offended Allah, he questioned.

Ghulam Rasool's thoughts turned to his daughters who though highly educated remained unmarried. He had never been financially savvy and had not bargained for a society where money would be the most important criteria for gauging the worth of a person. Sara's words that he was a discarded envelope had embedded themselves in his mind and kept haunting him.

In the last few weeks, Kiran seemed to have possessed his mind and heart again. With each passing day he found himself missing her like never before—physically, mentally, and spiritually. He wondered what it was in Kiran that attracted him so much as to haunt him all the time. The more he thought of her the more he realized that she had all the qualities that he innately desired in a woman. She was beautiful, had a fiercely independent nature and possessed more patience and forbearing than any woman he had ever known. But above all he acknowledged her superiority as a human being for her secular outlook and the dignity and grace with which she had borne all that fate had inflicted on her in their relationship—for much of which he blamed himself. He realized that in spite of an arranged marriage he had been physically attracted to Sara for the first decade or more and there was some mental compatibility between them but then they had slowly drifted apart and Kiran had come to fill in the vacuum. Before long, his affair with Kiran had completely overpowered him and alienated him from Sara who had become a recluse seeking refuge in religion. He wondered whether Kiran ever thought of him and her lost love and whether she could ever imagine how besotted he was with her as he walked up and down the roads of Lahore in his make-believe world where only the two of them existed.

Ghulam Rasool walked briskly on the sidewalk, passing a crowd of the perpetually unemployed watching a juggler performing his tricks, and yet another group listening to the harangue of a fraudster selling aphrodisiacs. He paid no heed to either but kept walking, hands in his trouser pockets, thinking of Kiran. He wanted to have her here with him in Lahore by his side for every remaining moment of his life. Had she passed

Saad Ashraf

away into another world and was her spirit haunting him? Was that why she was constantly on his mind? Had she reincarnated into that mynah, twittering on the branches of the mulberry tree in front, looking him up and down, disappointed that her Gullo was unable to recognize her? Thus obsessed he roamed the streets, muttering to himself.

An omnibus overloaded with passengers tore down the road at breakneck speed.

'Out of the way, old man, before you get hit,' said one passenger, hanging on to the handle by the door, stretching out his leg and missing Ghulam Rasool's body by inches.

What had the world come to after partition? In a few short years all respect for old age had vanished, thought Ghulam Rasool. He reached the Lawrence Gardens and walked down to a spot where it was dark and quiet and soft, green algae covered the wet earth and snails made their homes under mounds of earth. He imagined that he was holding Kiran by the hand as he walked under the old trees on which flying foxes hung upside down. Hadn't he walked in the same manner on the sodden soil of the banks of the Yamuna, hand in hand with Kiran, only a couple of years ago?

Two years back Ghulam Rasool had received a letter from Basu in Delhi, the only outsider who had an inkling of his affair with Kiran. He had written that Purshottam had been promoted and posted to Lucknow but he was suffering from cancer. His wife had taken up a job with the government organization for the recovery of abducted women. Ghulam Rasool had written a letter to the head office of the organization in Delhi wanting to know the whereabouts of Kiran. He had received a reply after a few weeks that they could not divulge the whereabouts of any of their employees due to the nature of their work and for fear of retribution. What retribution and by whom, Ghulam Rasool had wondered.

How long was one supposed to nurse the wounds of lost love? Ghulam Rasool broke down and wept aloud. A young boy with a yellow kite on a string ran past but stopped on seeing a grown-up crying. He came up to Ghulam Rasool.

'Why do you cry, Baba? Have you lost something? Here, take my kite—it will make you feel better,' he said, offering an end of the string to him.

Ghulam Rasool shook his head in despair, passed his hands affectionately over the boy's face, and walked to a bench nearby to rest his weary bones and reminisce.

Everything had not changed in the subcontinent. Some things had remained the same. The innocence of children for one. There was still some hope. After a while, Ghulam Rasool got up and walked back in the direction of his home on McLeod Road.

Saad Ashraf

forty-eight

One day, late in the evening, there was a knock on Ghulam Rasool's door. A man introduced himself as a neighbour of Zaman. He said that he had been sent by Zaman's son Yusuf with the news that his father had died suddenly and was to be buried the next day at ten in the morning. Ghulam Rasool was shocked by the news. Only last week he had been to the bookshop and had met Zaman who looked every bit in good health and spirits.

As Ghulam Rasool was leaving the shop with his quota of half a dozen fresh books, Zaman had said to him, 'Ever since you've become our partner the shop has prospered. You must have been born under a lucky star. Our auditors tell me that our sales have tripled and expect a significant rise in our profits. I am going to receive a final word from them next week. Half of what we make after expenses will be yours. You may well end up recovering your entire capital in less than a year.'

Ghulam Rasool had been delighted to hear about the profit that would accrue to him from the bookshop and had decided to give all of it to Sara. This supplementary income together with the allowance he gave her from his monthly pension should be more than sufficient to keep her and the whole family comfortable. Sara wouldn't have much to crib about thereafter. And now, out of the blue, this bad news had come.

The next day Ghulam Rasool made his way to the century-old graveyard of Lahore. After the prayers for the deceased had been said and the formalities of a Muslim burial done, those who had come to bury Zaman threw three fistfuls of dust over his grave and started leaving one by one while Ghulam Rasool and Yusuf remained by the side of the freshly dug grave. They stayed there for what seemed an eternity. Then, just as the sun was about to plunge into the ocean of colours that the sunset had produced on the horizon that day, they too left.

Ghulam Rasool did not contact Yusuf for the next forty days, but as soon as this period of compulsory mourning was over he went over to the bookshop, carrying the receipt that Zaman had given him. He found Yusuf sitting at the counter of the shop all alone.

After they had exchanged salutations and a few remarks about the late Zaman, Ghulam Rasool said, 'Yusuf, you are aware that I am a fifty per cent partner in this shop. I've come to discuss the future of this arrangement. Your father's sudden death has shaken me. I am not so young myself ... I'd like to do something so that both your interest and mine can be protected for the future. You can talk to me as freely as you would have talked to your father.'

Yusuf thought for a while before he spoke.

'Chachaji, since you say that I can talk to you as I would have to my father I'll do so. I must tell you that I was not in favour of your partnership in our shop. I have the utmost respect for you but I believe that partnerships do not survive in the long run in this part of the world and when they end, friendships quickly turn into animosities. I advised father accordingly but he wouldn't listen and said that he had given you his word and that was it. I'd like you to give me a week to think about this matter before we talk about it.'

A week later, Ghulam Rasool met Yusuf again.

'Chachaji, I discussed this matter with some of my relatives who have more experience of these things than I do. I don't want to sound rude but it would be best for us to terminate this partnership and return the investment you have made. Of course, you are most welcome to visit this shop whenever you like and continue borrowing books as in the past,' said Yusuf.

Saad Ashraf

Ghulam Rasool was deeply perturbed on hearing this since it meant an end to all his plans of being able to provide some extra money to Sara. He collected himself and recalled that as an officer he had handled much worse situations without losing his cool.

'In that case, when can I expect to receive my investment of five thousand rupees and the profit on it?'

'We'll try to refund your investment as soon as possible, but I am not sure whether we can pay any profit on your investment.'

'But your father told me only a week before he passed away that he expected my share of the profit to be about the same as my investment. In fact, he had said that he was just waiting for a final word from the auditors.'

'I am afraid that father was wrong. Maybe he had not been provided authentic information by then. I'll show you their report.'

Yusuf left the counter, went to the back of the shop and returned with some papers. The front page of the auditors' report declared that the accounts of Zaman Book Company showed that it was running a loss of one thousand rupees for the year.

'I will provide you a copy of this report,' said Yusuf, 'according to which if you were to share the loss with us, your investment should be reduced by five hundred rupees but because of our relations we'll refund the whole of your investment.'

'Thank you, but I wouldn't like to impose on your generosity. I would rather you return my investment minus my share of the loss,' said Ghulam Rasool.

Yusuf nodded in agreement.

All the way back home, Ghulam Rasool kept thinking why Zaman, a respected ex-officer of the Indian Posts and Telegraphs department, would make such a blatantly false statement. Maybe Zaman had wanted to bolster his confidence in the business or was given wrong information by his auditors, but the contradiction in what he had been told by Zaman and what his son had said created a lingering suspicion in Ghulam Rasool's mind.

He kept visiting the bookshop as much to borrow books and return the same, as in the hope that his presence would remind

Yusuf to refund his investment. However, as time went by, he found Yusuf becoming unmindful of his presence. He decided to confront Yusuf.

'Yusuf, I've been visiting your shop for several months now, hoping that you would return the money I had invested in your business. Could you let me know when I can expect to receive my investment?' he said in a businesslike manner.

'I have given you my word, Chachaji, that we shall return your money to you as soon as we can. For the moment our business is facing some financial crisis,' Yusuf replied coldly.

Ghulam Rasool could see no sign of such a crisis. In fact, the bookshop had been furnished with additional almirahs for its growing inventory of books and the premises had been recently repainted at substantial cost.

'Yusuf beta, I could have talked to your father more openly than I can to you, but you will kindly do me the favour of delivering my investment to my house within the next fortnight. I won't come begging for my money again.'

Back home he decided to take Sara into confidence despite their strained relations. He swallowed his pride and explained to her how he had come to invest half of his gratuity in the bookshop and the difficulties he was facing in getting his money back. Surprisingly, he found Sara sympathetic to his cause.

'Remember,' she said, 'nobody can swindle a person of his or her hard-earned money. So rest assured, either Yusuf will return your money or he will have to face Allah's wrath. Why don't you go and talk to Ghazi Bhai who is a businessman and has experience of handling such matters. Maybe he can suggest what you should do.'

A month later there was still no sign of Yusuf coming up with the money. Ghulam Rasool realized that he was up against a debtor who had no intention of paying him back. He remembered Sara's advice and went to see Ghazi who ran a provisions store in the Lahore Cantonment. Pakistan had suited Ghazi's business acumen and he had prospered over the years.

Saad Ashraf

His business had expanded and he had brought another store on the Mall. Ghulam Rasool had managed to maintain lukewarm relations with Ghazi though the latter had not forgotten that his brother-in-law had not allotted a shop to him even though he had a rightful claim.

Ghazi listened to his brother-in-law's tale with rapt attention.

'Well, Bhaisahab, I can tell you from my experience that there is no sense in waiting for Yusuf to come up with your money. If he was decent he would have settled his debts according to his commitment. One way of getting your money back is to file a legal suit against him and take him to court. You will spend a lot of time and money in fighting your case but it is doubtful if you will ever recover anything,' said Ghazi.

'Isn't there a faster alternative?'

'Yes, there is. It is called the Pakistan debt recovery system which is much less expensive and produces quick results.'

'What is this system ...?'

'It is simple enough ... we hire a couple of thugs who threaten the party to pay up by a certain date or face the consequences.'

'But that is illegal!'

'What's illegal about recovering one's own hard-earned money that one is being swindled of?'

Ghulam Rasool shrugged his shoulders. He had no answer to Ghazi's logic.

'Bhaisahab,' continued Ghazi, 'you've always been the kind of person who wants to do everything more legally than the law itself. Even when I had left two shops behind in Delhi you wouldn't allot me one in Lahore though that was my right. Well, if you want to be that way in this Allah's protectorate called Pakistan go ahead and file a case in court. It will take a couple of generations before you get anything back.'

Ghulam Rasool was stung by his brother-in-law's remark. Ordinarily, he would have walked out but he realized the predicament he was in. He had yet to be cleared by the government medical board which would entitle him to the lump sum pension amount on which his family's future depended. He could hardly afford to bear a loss of five thousand rupees.

'Ghazi,' he said, 'I leave everything to you to do as you deem fit. I'll pay you the expenses you incur whenever you get my money back.'

'Don't worry about the expenses ... I am glad to be of help. Two wrongs don't make one right. If I don't help you now because you didn't help me in the past it's not going to improve things for either of us.'

A few weeks later, Ghulam Rasool received an urgent summons from his brother-in-law to see him at his store.

'I would have personally come to deliver your money at your house, but business should be settled at the business premises so I called you over. Here's your investment in Zaman Book Company—four and a half thousand rupees. Five hundred went towards the professional charges for recovery. Yusuf decided not to charge the so-called loss of five hundred rupees to your account when he admitted that the auditors' report was a forgery,' said Ghazi, placing an envelope in his brother-in-law's hands.

Ghulam Rasool could recall only a few occasions in his life when he had been happier. He clasped Ghazi's hands in his and kept shaking them for several minutes. There were tears of joy and gratitude in his eyes. He didn't want to go into the sordid details of the Pakistan debt recovery system as applied to Yusuf. He got hold of his cycle and pedalled as fast as he could all the way to his house and broke the news to Sara.

Next day, he went to the post office and brought four and a half thousand rupees worth of the newly floated Pakistan Defence Savings Certificates, which were guaranteed to double themselves every ten years, to provide for the future security for himself, his wife, and his children.

Saad Ashraf

forty-nine

With Noorani Begum's death, Ghulam Rasool's sisters had been left all alone at their home in White Haveli. In their letters to Ghulam Rasool they complained of only one thing—their loneliness and sense of insecurity. Almost everyone known to them had migrated to Pakistan with the exception of the imam's family. They wrote of how Ahmad made it a point to come to their house regularly every Friday after the prayers to enquire about their well-being. The sisters compared their solitary existence in Delhi to two islands which was all that was left of a once beautiful land which had now been submerged by the sea. They urged their brother to find ways and means of resettling them in Pakistan so that they could live among the people they had known.

Ahmad, with whom Ghulam Rasool had remained in touch, also expressed the same feelings. In a letter he wrote in early 1951, Ahmad had said that Delhi seemed to be a city devoid of the people he had known in his lifetime, and for once he felt that blindness was a blessing for if he could see he would surely have died of grief at the absence of so many familiar faces. He wrote about Yasmeen and how she had become more beautiful with age—though he couldn't see her he could imagine her in his mind's eye, he wrote—and how her voice had become huskier and that she still sang old songs with the pathos of the past, sitting under the old peepul tree by the side of the rivulet that flowed near the house. Ghulam Rasool never got down to writing a reply to this letter though he often promised himself that he would do so at the first available opportunity.

One day soon after, he received news from a member of the imam's family living in Lahore that Ahmad had fallen from the stairs of his house, gone into a coma, and after being hospitalized at the Irwin Hospital, Delhi, had passed away that very night. Not believing what he had heard, Ghulam Rasool sent a telegram to Ahmad the next morning enquiring about his welfare. A few days later he received a letter from a cousin of Ahmad in Delhi confirming the circumstances of his death. A grief-stricken Ghulam Rasool remembered Noorani Begum telling him that when one was fifty years old one only received bad news. He recalled the days of his youth that he had shared with Ahmad, and their carefree years at Missionary College. He remembered how Ahmad had initiated him into the revelry of Delhi's red-light area where he had met Yasmeen and how he had stood by her, leaving the comfort of his home in Delhi for the trenches of the First World War. He knew that people like Ahmad no longer came by. When he retired to bed that night he uttered a silent prayer for his dear departed friend. He lay in a state between sleep and consciousness, haunted by memories till the early hours of the morning when sleep overtook him.

When he woke up the next morning, Ghulam Rasool decided to handle one matter on a top priority basis: getting his pension in lump sum with which he could build or buy a house. He had not pursued the paperwork for convening the medical board which would pronounce his fitness for this purpose. After a quick breakfast he made his way on his cycle to the postmaster general's office on the Mall. Since his retirement, Ghulam Rasool had rarely visited his former office. He saw the black Wolseley car which he had used parked in the porch. He climbed up the stairway and made his way to the office of the postmaster general—his one-time deputy, Yakoob.

Saad Ashraf

Ghulam Rasool was told that the postmaster general was busy in a meeting, and was asked to wait in the ante-room. A short while later an orderly appeared to inform him that the meeting had ended and the sahib was free to receive him.

'Sir, to what do we owe the privilege of your visit?' Yakoob said after Ghulam Rasool was comfortably seated.

'Yakoob, I still have to appear before the medical board for the commutation of my pension. I am here to request you to move my papers urgently for that purpose.'

'I am surprised to hear this, sir, because the first thing every government employee does on retirement is to apply for the setting up of a medical board except that tiny minority among us who join the post office rich by inheritance or by marriage. As far as I know you didn't belong to either of these categories unless you acted on some of the suggestions I made to you.'

Ghulam Rasool felt slighted by this comment but kept his cool.

'You're right ... I did not sell any car permits ... if I had, you would have been the first to know because all applications were routed through you,' said Ghulam Rasool. Yakoob nodded while Ghulam Rasool continued, 'I need the lump sum pension money to build or buy a house. Unless that happens I will have no option but to continue living in the house allotted by the rehabilitation department for which I pay a rental of a hundred and fifty rupees every month. These two years since my retirement seem to have flitted away ... if the rest of my life also passes in this manner I might leave my family shelterless.'

Yakoob was moved by the pleadings of his former boss and realized that financial stringency after retirement was taking a toll on this once proud man.

'I promise to do so, in fact, I'll do it right now,' said Yakoob, ringing the bell for his personal assistant who appeared holding a shorthand notebook and pencil in his hand. Yakoob then proceeded to dictate a letter for the health department to set up a board of doctors to medically examine Ghulam Rasool, the former postmaster general, Punjab, and pronounce their decision whether he was likely to live for another five years, based on which he could be given the lump sum payment of his pension.

'Thank you very much, Yakoob, I am personally indebted to you for your prompt action,' said Ghulam Rasool, rising from his chair.

'Don't you worry, sir, I'll use my personal contacts in the health department to make sure that the medical board is set up as soon as possible, and I wish you the best of luck,' said Yakoob, getting up to see Ghulam Rasool off.

A week later Ghulam Rasool received a notice to appear before the medical board in the Punjab secretariat. It said that he would be examined by a panel of five doctors of the Pakistan Medical Service on the appointed date. Yakoob had been true to his word and had pulled the right strings to convene the board quickly. He broke the news to Sara.

'It is the most important thing in my life—the ultimate reward to a government employee for decades of service. With the money I get I'll be able to build or buy a house in which we and our succeeding generations can live forever. A house of one's own is the greatest security that anyone needs in the subcontinent,' Ghulam Rasool said, his voice brimming with pride.

'Sarkar, there is something I don't understand,' said Sara. 'I've been married to you for nearly thirty years and every other year you told me that the most important event of our lives is about to take place. At this time, I am more worried about my unmarried daughters who can't find husbands because they are overeducated. Isn't it more important that we forget about ourselves and start concentrating on settling our children?'

'I can tell you that once we own a house, marriage proposals will start pouring in for our daughters. They do not find husbands because values in this part of the world have changed and money has become the most important thing for people. If we have a house we will have money to show in some form,' said Ghulam Rasool.

Saad Ashraf

'I find it hard to agree with you that money is the most important thing—it may be the most important for you. Since you consider clearing the medical board that important, I'll devote myself to praying for you, just like I have done every time in the past,' said Sara, picking up her prayer mat and getting ready to start her endeavours with Allah on behalf of her husband.

On the morning of the day the medical board was to be convened, Ghulam Rasool got up at five o'clock. He said his prayers, at the end of which he raised his hands skywards to ask Allah for the favour of being cleared by the medical board. He hadn't slept well the night before, thinking of what might happen if the doctors came to the conclusion that he was not likely to live another five years and as a consequence did not qualify to receive his pension in lump sum. He had a light breakfast which Sara had specially prepared for him. She tied an amulet around his right arm and wished him the best of luck.

On arrival at the Punjab secretariat, Ghulam Rasool was ushered into the examination room and asked to change into a gown for the medical examination. He was made to pass urine into a bottle, and his temperature and chest x-ray were taken. Thereafter, one doctor followed another to tap his chest or poke his body. The quiet of the examination room was broken only by the doctors instructing Ghulam Rasool to turn on one side or the other or to breathe in quick succession with his mouth open.

Soon, a short, stockily built middle-aged doctor sporting a French beard made his appearance.

'I am Dr Hafeez,' he said, introducing himself.

He asked Ghulam Rasool a few questions about his health, how long ago he had retired and how he kept himself busy.

'Sir, did anybody ever tell you that you suffer from high blood pressure,' remarked Dr Hafeez.

Ghulam Rasool shook his head. 'No, Doctor. In fact, I haven't been to a doctor more than two or three times in my life.'

The doctor assured him that it was nothing serious and that there were medicines for everything these days. He started talking about government service, and how the increase in the cost of living had eroded the value of the pay and how government service had lost its prestige.

'But, Doctor, you have your private practice during the evenings to supplement your salary. There are countless other retired government employees who don't have such additional means of income. Imagine how hard it is for them to make ends meet,' said Ghulam Rasool.

'I agree with what you say but my income from private practice is quite insignificant. My wife has been nagging me to buy a car and I need ten thousand rupees urgently for that purpose. I am a doctor with some status in society. Every other practitioner of my standing has a car ... surely, I cannot be expected to use public transport to move my family around.'

'I wish I had that kind of money to loan to you but unfortunately I don't.'

'But you would once you get your lump sum pension,' said the doctor, a broad grin on his face.

Ghulam Rasool merely shrugged his shoulders and sat quietly, waiting to do whatever the doctor ordered next. He thought that Hafeez had an odd sense of humour that he combined well with his dexterous hands which he kept busy with the stethoscope on his chest.

When the examination came to an end, an orderly appeared to inform Ghulam Rasool that he would hear directly from his department in about a week's time. Ghulam Rasool took off the gown, changed into his clothes, and stepped out of the Punjab secretariat.

It was early November and the fresh early-winter air had an arrogant nip loaded with the fragrance of flowers which abounded in the grassy plots on both sides of the road. None of the doctors had indicated anything to worry about and Ghulam

Saad Ashraf

Rasool was certain that the board would clear him. All he had to do was wait for a week. With the confidence that hope imbibes in man, Ghulam Rasool walked proudly, brisk and upright, in the direction of his home.

fifty

'They've done me in! They've done me in!' screamed Ghulam Rasool at the top of his voice as he opened the envelope which contained a single piece of paper. It said that in the opinion of the honourable medical board he had not been found fit to receive his pension in lump sum because one of the five doctors had held the opinion that he would not survive for the next five years.

'What's the matter?' enquired Sara, rushing to his side as soon as she heard him scream.

'They've done me in!' was all he could say again. With his hopes and plans for the future all dashed to the ground, it was as if Ghulam Rasool could find nothing else to say.

'At least tell me what has happened,' said Sara.

'They've turned down my request for the commutation of my pension in lump sum. There's nothing left for me to live for. Oh, what crime have I committed to be so punished in my old age!' Ghulam Rasool sat down on the bed, holding his head in his hands.

Sara tried to console her husband. 'Have faith in Allah. All is not lost. After all we have survived thus far on your monthly pension and can continue to do so. So what if we don't have a house of our own. There are millions of people in India and Pakistan who pass away without having one. There's only one thing that your family wants and that is for you to provide them the shadow of your security as a husband and a father.'

Sara's words felt like a balm. It also surprised Ghulam Rasool more than a little. More so given that their relationship over the last few years had been anything but cordial. She had endured him for a long time but was still loyal and sympathetic towards his cause.

'What will happen to you and the children should I pass away. You won't even have a roof over your head,' said Ghulam Rasool.

'Allah takes care of everyone,' answered Sara. 'After all, somebody took care of you when your father died though you were too young to fend for yourself. Who could have said then that you would see fifty years of life and retire with honour as a high government official in a new country? Forget about the lump sum pension and forget about owning a house. It is fools who make houses and it is the wise who live in them. A Hindu barrister made this house for his family's comfort and see who is living in it.'

Ghulam Rasool asked Sara for some privacy. When she came back to the room she found that he had retired to bed though it was only ten in the morning. He had covered himself with a blanket from head to toe with only his nostrils sticking out, and was sound asleep.

Over the next few days, Ghulam Rasool would get up to eat a little, walk around the house, and after a couple of hours he would go back to sleep.

'Sarkar, how long are you going to go on like this—eating and sleeping? Why don't you dress up and go for a walk to the Lawrence Gardens like you used to? It will make you feel better,' Sara said one morning.

'I just don't feel like doing anything at all. There seems to be no reason for me to live any longer.'

'Don't you think your wife and two daughters are sufficient reason for you to want to live?'

Ghulam Rasool sat listless, silent and immersed in deep thought. Sara was deeply concerned and sent word to her brother Ghazi to come and talk to her husband. Ghazi came and spoke to his brother-in-law for several hours in a bid to reach to the root of his problem. Ghulam Rasool opened his heart out to Ghazi, telling him how life had cheated him.

'I wish I knew that you were to appear before a medical board and how important it was for you to clear it. We could have settled the issue with the doctors,' said Ghazi.

'What do you mean?'

'From what you tell me, it seems as if Dr Hafeez was proposing that if you gave him ten thousand rupees he was prepared to forget the disability which became the basis of the medical board's rejection.'

'I don't believe this.'

'You have another chance to appear before a new medical board within six months. I am going to make sure that you are cleared by that board and you get your pension in lump sum— you have worked over three decades for it. In return I request you for only one favour: keep yourself fit and going for the next six months.'

'I can try and keep myself fit but I can't make a promise to keep myself going—that is in the hands of Allah. It seems that I am like a baby who can't take care of himself any more.'

'It's not like that, Bhaisahab. Your experience of life was gathered from pre-partition India whose hallmarks were truth, honour, and integrity. But times have changed. You are unhappy because you've not been able to change with the times—that is all there is to it. Those who cannot change must suffer.'

Over the next few months there wasn't much improvement in Ghulam Rasool's physical condition. He tired easily and became breathless and pale with even the smallest exertion. Dark shadows appeared under his eyes. More ominously, he felt a nagging pain in his left shoulder. He called Dr Nazir, who had a clinic a short distance from Ghulam Rasool's residence, and asked him to make a home visit.

Dr Nazir ran his stethoscope up and down Ghulam Rasool's chest and checked his blood pressure. Then, after a long pause, he came up with the diagnosis.

Saad Ashraf

'You are suffering from angina in which the heart gets insufficient blood. Your blood pressure is high and your heartbeat irregular. You must cut down your weight by eating boiled vegetables. I would also suggest you consult Colonel Mudi of Mayo Hospital—he is the best heart specialist in the country. In the meantime, if the pain in your left shoulder becomes unbearable or you perspire excessively, put this pill under your tongue and lie down and call me regardless of the hour. I live in the apartment on top of my clinic.'

After Dr Nazir had left, Ghulam Rasool called Sara and told her all that the doctor had said to him.

'Don't worry, sarkar, I will start serving you the bland food that Dr Nazir has suggested, though in my opinion you need just the opposite kind of diet. I'll seek divine help to cure you. You know that there is no greater healer than Allah,' said Sara.

Ghulam Rasool nodded in agreement.

Sara got in touch with the imam who looked after the nearby mosque and had him slaughter a black goat and distribute the meat among the poor. She requested him to have special prayers said by the congregations in the mosque for the restoration of Ghulam Rasool's health. But despite the changes in his diet and in spite of Sara's efforts with the divine, Ghulam Rasool's condition only worsened.

Ghulam Rasool decided to go to Mayo Hospital to consult Colonel Mudi, and was able to get Dr Nazir to accompany him. They located Colonel Mudi who agreed to examine him after having an electrocardiogram taken on a machine which had just been imported from England.

After an examination which lasted over an hour, Colonel Mudi and Dr Nazir went into a huddle in the far corner of the room. Ghulam Rasool tried his best to make out what they were saying to one another but, despite straining his ears to their utmost, failed to make out anything meaningful from their whispers. Colonel Mudi concurred with the findings of Dr Nazir. The electrocardiogram substantiated beyond proof that

Ghulam Rasool was indeed suffering from angina. Moreover, his heart was slowly failing. The colonel recommended complete bed rest and wished him luck. The diagnosis greatly perturbed Ghulam Rasool and he remained unusually quiet on the journey back home.

Though Colonel Mudi had advised absolute bed rest for Ghulam Rasool, he found this prescription difficult to follow. He hated lying on the bed whole day long under the doctor's orders. With more time to brood he found the dark shadows of the past engulfing his mind. Sara often peeped into his room and found him in deep thought, twirling his fingers in gestures of regrets.

'Try to cheer yourself up by thinking of the good times you and your family have had together. Remember Rawalpindi, Amritsar, and Simla when the British were here,' she would say.

But all her efforts to boost his spirits ended in failure.

She found him out of bed on one or two occasions and scolded him. 'The doctor has said you shouldn't get out of bed, if you need something why don't you call me.'

'Sara, I would rather be dead than carry on living like this. Bed rest is the biggest torture that can be inflicted on a human being. If I have to go and meet my maker I'd rather go on my feet than lying in bed.'

'Yes, but one has to go in the manner ordained, a person has no choice before Allah's will,' countered Sara.

There was a poignant silence in the room.

'I am sorry I'm not leaving much behind for you and my daughters,' said Ghulam Rasool.

'There you go again, sarkar ... don't talk like this, it's a matter of another fortnight ... you will be on your feet again. That's what Dr Nazir told me privately yesterday.'

'What do Dr Nazir or Colonel Mudi know about the real state of their patients ... deep inside their bodies when illness is consuming them by the hour,' snapped Ghulam Rasool.

That night, he took a sedative which Dr Nazir had prescribed for him. He spent a few hours uncomfortably tossing around in

Saad Ashraf

bed before drifting off to an uneasy sleep in which he had a strange dream. He saw Kiran standing on the mound they frequented on the tract by the river. She stood with open arms and a smile on her face to welcome him. He tried reaching out to her but found that the more he extended his hand the more distant she became until a whirlpool engulfed him in its fold. In the eye of this whirlpool he saw other familiar faces swimming before him. He saw himself as a child on a houseboat in Kashmir, looking intently at the white lotus flowers drifting past him in the lake while two herons dipped from the muggy skies into the cool, crystal-clear water for their favourite fish. It was an endless lake whose white waters lapped the sides of the boat in the eerie silence of a lonesome evening. The houseboat, with him as its lone occupant, was moving slowly in the shadow of green mountains with snow-covered peaks. He saw himself under the street lights of White Haveli, busy poring over his books. He wondered why and for what he was working so hard. He saw himself cycling towards Missionary College in the company of Ahmad who promised to take him to Chawri Bazaar. Suddenly he found himself standing in front of Principal Thompson with his half-moon glasses delicately perched on his nose, raising his hand in a gesture of goodbye. And then he was in Lahore in the company of someone who resembled Sabah, the green-eyed beauty he had met during his first posting in Lahore. Her eyes morose and sad from the sorrow of parting, she stood forlorn, her lips moving silently with a message inaudible to him. He saw his mother, standing at the entrance of White Haveli, beckoning to him, even as Sara tried to hold him back. All this while, from somewhere far off came the strains of an old song that Yasmeen sang so well in her husky voice:

> *I wait for you at these crossroads of life*
> *With my innocent heart wounded by your mellow smile*
> *For the fulfilment of the promise you made long ago*
> *To come and meet me here, in flickering lamplight*
> *consumed by time ...*

The Postmaster {337}

Ghulam Rasool woke up with a start. He looked around him, blinking in the dark, then got up, switched the lights on, and walked over to the almirah at the far corner of the room. He reached out for a locked attaché case which contained his most prized possessions, carried it to his bed and opened it. He found a sheaf of letters which Noorani Begum had written to him while he was posted in various places. He ran his fingers over the letters lovingly, as if trying to conjure up the time it was written. In every scrawl of 'My dearest son' with which she began each letter and 'Your most loving mother' with which she ended, Ghulam Rasool could feel the immense love his mother had for him. Where was she now? Some place where no matter how hard he tried he could never reach. He came across the silver-coloured photo frame which Resham, the maid, had given him years ago when he was leaving Rawalpindi for Amritsar. The silver coating on the frame had worn off and the pictures of Jesus Christ and Resham had faded. He wondered why he had kept the photo frame all these years. He thought he heard Sara's footsteps in the next room, and hurriedly put everything back in the attaché case. By the time he got back into bed after having placed the attaché in the almirah, he was breathless.

Postmaster Ghulam Rasool of the former Indian Posts and Telegraphs Department passed away in his sleep during the early morning hours of 5 January 1952. He was buried the same day late in the afternoon in an old graveyard near the railway station. As per the instructions he had left behind, his grave remained unmarked. The graveyard was bulldozed and sold by the city's development authority to the building mafia in 1963 for the construction of a high-rise apartment building.

That building stands to this day, though in a dilapidated condition. The children from the middle-class families who live in those apartments play their afternoon cricket on a ground which is part of the razed graveyard. They scramble after cricket balls over the remains of many unsung heroes of the Indian subcontinent, one of whom was Postmaster Ghulam Rasool of Delhi.

Saad Ashraf

Sara was provided a special pension by the government on compassionate grounds on an application moved by her brother Ghazi six months after Postmaster Ghulam Rasool had left this world.

She survived her husband by nearly three decades.